The
Puzzle
Women

ALSO BY ANNA ELLORY

The Rabbit Girls

The Puzzle Women

Anna Ellory

LAKE UNION
PUBLISHING

Text copyright © 2020 by Anna Ellory
All rights reserved.

Published by Lake Union Publishing, Seattle

www.apub.com

Amazon, the Amazon logo, and Lake Union Publishing are trademarks of Amazon.com, Inc., or its affiliates.

ISBN-13: 9781542014489
ISBN-10: 1542014484

Cover design by The Brewster Project

Printed in the United States of America

Dedicated to the children lost in time.

Time present and time past
Are both perhaps present in time future,
And time future contained in time past.
If all time is eternally present
All time is unredeemable.

T.S. Eliot 'Burnt Norton'
The Four Quartets

I.

I should like it to snow.

To exist in the hope of newly fallen snow and feel the apple-crunch of it settle under my feet. For it to be both fleeting and everlasting; to be both feather-light and solid. I should like to watch snow explode from the night sky then compose itself to rest, layer upon layer, like the fluttering pages of a book.

Instead, I am swallowed in night. I can't see my body for looking for it. The dark is so porous it is tar, it is suffocation, it is time itself. The absence of sound is viscous in the air around me.

I should like to read. To open the glue-cracked spines and lose myself in the perforated edges of my childhood. I should like to feel the safety of words imprinted on my soul, because to know a book is not to hold it in one's hand, it is to breathe within it.

I should like many things, I think.

Instead, I am imprisoned in waiting.

Until there are footsteps.

I try to calm my heart as it beats in my throat. I dig my nails into my thighs. I want to cover myself, clothe myself, hide from myself.

There is a pause outside the door.

Waiting.

I know what's coming.

My stomach tightens, contracts, and my legs give way. My body holds memory in its muscles. It gives my fear a name.

A scratch of the key in the lock.

And I crawl into the farthest corner.

A sharp slice of light enters as the door is pushed open. I recoil, make myself small, and hide into the dark.

THEN

Friday 6ᵀᴴ January 1989

Epiphanie – Epiphany

He woke with a gentle shake to the shoulder, Mama's morning breath at his ear. Before he could say anything, she placed a warning finger to her lips.

Rune kicked the covers off and saw Lotte sitting at the end of his bed, watchful as a cat. Her thumb was firmly clamped in her mouth. Her Care Bear wellies on the wrong feet, the motif facing inwards rather than out.

Mama's enormous rucksack was leaning against the back of the closed door.

This was it.

A knot of marble settled in his chest as Mama walked to the window and peered through a crack in the curtains.

He was as still as Lotte was silent, both watching Mama. Lotte held out her hand. It was cool and small in his.

Finally Mama turned to them.

'Ready?'

Rune's gaze settled on Moo Bunny, grey, lifeless, propped up among the magazines and sketches that covered the desk in the corner of his room. Moo Bunny was being left behind.

Mama lifted Lotte onto her hip and went back to check the window again. Lotte's hands wound themselves in Mama's loose dark hair as they both looked out into the night.

'Can I go for a pee?' His newly awoken voice was low and made Mama jump.

'Do you have to?'

The stab in his belly told him that yes, he probably did, but he said, 'No.'

Mama put Lotte down and came over to him. They both watched as Lotte wandered over to Rune's desk and he stood, tempted to stop her with his usual yell of *Don't touch my things*. He said nothing as Lotte looked over his drawings. When Mama's arms wrapped him up tight, he was caught off guard. She hugged him and instead of pushing her away, his arms wove around her too. Mama's chest rose with her breath and forced him to breathe. He breathed her in. Her hug was warm-gold and he felt small and safe inside it.

Lotte's voice jumped in: 'Moo Bunny can leave home too?'

Mama shushed her, quickly letting go of Rune. Lotte was cradling Moo Bunny in her arms.

'Look at his little bunchy face,' she said, and whispered to Moo Bunny, 'You are now my best bestest and most favourite.'

Mama whispered to Lotte and he realised that maybe, just maybe . . . this really was it.

She placed her fingers to her lips once more and eased herself out onto the landing. Walking softly in socks, she made no noise.

Rune picked up his school bag and sank under the weight of it, heavy with expectation as he and Lotte waited for Mama.

Last summer, Mama had taken him out of school. Just like that. One day she appeared early, a purple bruise on her neck, her arm busted up, with Lotte's hand held tight in hers, and told him they were leaving.

They had walked in the itchy hot sun to the hostel in the centre of Berlin, in a church hall that smelled of old soup, sweat and damp clothes.

The hostel staff apologised to him for not having anything suitable for eight-year-old boys. Rune had to wash with soap that smelled of old ladies.

For a week, they lived on a small army cot in the corner of a large hall.

Then they went home.

With Mama's arm in a cast and her bruise turned green.

That had been a year ago. Since then, Rune stored away things in his school bag he thought he might need if they ever ended up there again.

He looked around at the room, unseeing, as Mama returned. She picked Lotte up, Lotte's arms wrapping around Mama like a scarf.

Mama then threw her bag over her shoulder and nodded to him to go.

'Will Papa come too,' Lotte whispered, 'or will he meet us wherever we are holiday-going?'

Neither Mama nor Rune answered.

The hallway was as black as silence. It stretched long into the night, until all he could hear was his heart pumping into his ears.

Away and now.

Together.

For the last time?

Maybe.

He paused.

Mama moved past him and he followed her. Placing his feet exactly where Mama placed hers, he followed her through the dark hallway.

NOW

MONDAY 8TH NOVEMBER 1999

RUNE

The walls were blank: no posters, no pictures, not even a photograph. Yet in his head they were alive with his sketches. He imagined the contents of his portfolio covering every white surface including his bed, tucked into the corner of the room. Had his portfolio not been declined, lying abandoned on an old professor's desk at the Berlin Art Institute, he might well have thumbed through some of his prints and placed them against the wall, stood back from them to look at them anew.

Afresh.

He might then have spotted a flaw, a drift where his pencil had gone too far, or not far enough. Picked holes in what he'd done.

But, alas, his work was not around to be dissected and torn apart. Therefore, he folded himself into his childhood desk and placed his larger sketchbook, a recent gift from Lotte, on its surface. It still had the crayon 'L' across the centre of the first page.

From her to him.

With Papa's bluebottle laugh still humming hot in his ears, he pulled out his pencils and Sharpies, turned the page round to landscape format, and imagined how he'd want to paint it. Eventually. When he could.

He knew the spray paint he would use: Molotow. The cap: fat. He imagined how it would land on the glass. Imagining his sketch as a finished piece, sprayed onto the glass enclosure of the tigers at Berlin Zoo. He imagined holding his breath, waiting for the paint to drip.

Imagining.

He started with the pencil. Lines too far here, too short there. Change that, add this. He imagined shaking cans and changing caps with speed and accuracy. His can control wasn't up to much these days, but he'd get better. He needed practice, that's all. He needed the space to practise. He needed many things, but there was no point to his needing.

Instead, he abandoned his pencil for a black Sharpie.

He saw the finished tiger before he'd even started, but when he was drawing on the black stripes, he paused. Realising that instead of the pale ghost in his mind's eye of the former wild cat – emaciated, feeble, broken – this cat was a prisoner.

A queen of the jungle, condemned to life as a domestic pet.

Forced within a shape that did not fit.

He sat back, reassessed, then got out the scarlet Sharpie and changed the stripes on the cat's body to red instead of black; in another time and place he would allow the paint to drip, to ooze and travel down the glass. He took out a Molotow marker, thick and heavy, holding the promise of a future spent spraying his pieces rather than confining and shrinking them to fit the confines of his sketchbook. With the marker he added a blood-red stripe across the tiger's mouth, thick and heavy. He made it drip. Rune kept going until the paint pooled at the base of the page. A tiger tearing at its stripes, gagged by its own torn flesh.

When he had finished, there was an enormous sketch of a tiger. Black stripes turning to red as if they had been ripped off and tagged, counted, like in a prison cell. This tiger was counting with its own stripes. 'Days of Cat-tivity' he called it, writing in small capitals on the back of the page.

He tagged the bottom of the page and set the sketchbook up against the desk. He waited. Wanting to see, to really see what he had created. The half-light was not enough, but it was November and the single bare bulb overhead was all he had.

Adrenaline fizzed and bubbled within him; he lit a cigarette. Opening the window so Papa wouldn't know he'd been smoking in his room, he leaned out, his senses becoming crisp and cold. He tasted burned wood on his tongue as remnants of seasonal fires tinged the air.

He smoked with vacant happiness until his attention snagged on his sketch. From this angle, with the bedroom light ballooning around him, he saw in his mind's eye the piece as it would be sprayed. One day.

A memory sharp as snapped glass pulled him away from the image in his mind – the tiger's gaze. He'd made a mistake. The tiger he had drawn was not counting its days in captivity in the hope of being released, it was tearing itself apart.

He screwed his cigarette out on the brickwork and dropped it into the garden below, then turned back to his sketch. But before he could destroy the picture, he heard a knock at the door.

'Roo? Are you home?' Lotte asked, coming straight in as he closed the sketchbook. 'Papa says I'm tubby,' she said as soon as he looked up.

'What?'

'He says I am tubby and I will get fat if I am not doing good eating and walking faster,' she said in one breath, pinching her stomach to create rolls.

'You're not tubby,' he said seriously, and she wasn't. She still had a child's figure, really; her tummy stuck out at times because she didn't care about how she looked enough to suck it in, as he knew most girls her age did.

'He won't let me wear my yellow tutu any more. He says I'm too big for it.' Tears rolled down her cheeks.

'He's wrong.'

Lotte examined his face for a while and measured his serious claim against that of Papa, which Rune was sure would have been cutting. She let go of her stomach and flattened her T-shirt.

'You're not tubby,' Rune said, 'and if your yellow tutu doesn't fit, we shall just have to buy a bigger size.' He wasn't sure how he'd do that, but he knew he would.

'Do I not need to do better eating and faster walking?' she asked.

'Not unless you want to.'

'Who would *want* to do that?' Lotte laughed, and her laugh made him smile. He lowered his voice conspiratorially.

'Only crazy people,' he said. 'Like Papa.'

'Shhh,' Lotte said. 'He's downstairs.'

'I know.'

She squeezed her cheeks to stop herself from grinning.

'That was not nice,' she said, 'but you always get my best smiles. I love you, my big brother.' And she hugged him tight, pressing her wet face into his T-shirt.

'Will you take me to school tomorrow?' she said, sitting at his desk and flipping through his sketchbook. She screwed her face up at the tiger.

'So long as Papa lets me have some petrol for the car,' he said, knowing that everything that would allow him a glance at the horizon away from home was strictly rationed and measured. A mile to school meant a mile's worth of petrol. No more. Money for clothes was the exact amount of marks, not a pfennig more. He had to beg for 'pocket money', which was doctored when Papa found cigarettes or if he was late to the 'job' Papa had arranged for him.

As a janitor at Lotte's school, Rune cleaned the floors, wiped the blackboards, unclogged the toilets. All without getting paid. Part of the *community action and involvement* his application to the police academy had demanded. He need not have bothered; it was all for show. He would follow in Papa's footsteps or be dragged into them. Community action or not.

The only good thing about the *job* was his access to sketchbooks and pencils. If they'd paid him a wage, he'd have just bought them, but he didn't have that freedom so he took what he needed as part of a wage he believed he was due. One room cleaned equalled one Sharpie; one blackboard, some charcoal.

He didn't want to be a thief.

He sold his sketches to buy cigarettes and to buy paper to draw more, and the more he drew, the more he could sell.

'Art is not a career,' Papa said. 'You only have nine months until you head off to the police academy. Better start acting like you mean it. No son of mine will act like a poof, a layabout – an *artist*. As a police officer you'll be a pillar of the community.' *Like him*, Rune thought, feeling a thick, oily wave of revulsion lap in his stomach.

'I see you drawing again, I'm tying your arm behind your back for a week,' Papa had threatened. Papa's threats were warnings and he heeded them as such. He started washing his hands carefully to remove any stain of ink or charcoal. He took his sketches to the school and kept them in a vacant locker.

He was trying so hard to find a way out. For him and for Lotte, both.

She was looking at another of his sketches, *crown shyness* – a collection of trees as seen from the ground, with the branches and leaves spaced to allow the sun to filter down. Lotte ran her finger along the thick veins of the trees, so closely spaced yet still giving each other room, allowing light through, creating a stunning canopy.

'I like this one,' she said.

He liked that one too, but its scale was too small, too tight.

There was so little hope. He panicked. No space at all. To think. Or breathe. Time was running short.

He'd just turned twenty; at twenty-one he'd have enrolled in the academy and there'd be nothing he could do about it. No escape.

'You have serious on your face,' Lotte said, closing his sketchbook and breaking into his thoughts.

'Do I?'

'Why are you not being happy, Roo?'

He felt as though his feet weren't touching the floor. Although, of course, they were. He forced a smile. 'Sorry, I'm fine.'

'If you take me to school tomorrow, can I wear my tutu?'

'Of course.'

'Night night,' Lotte said and she left, closing the door to his room. He heard her cross the hall to her room, wishing she wouldn't leave him on his own. A pathetic thought and juvenile; he never wanted to be alone, yet more often than not over the past few months he was becoming more so.

Reluctantly he switched off the light and slumped onto his bed, exhausted.

Rune waited until he was sure everyone was in bed and asleep before unfolding the letter he'd received earlier that day. He couldn't read it in the dark, but he unfolded and folded it again, hoping that in the morning it would say something different. He placed it in his pocket, before popping two oxycodone, stolen from Papa's supply after a back injury months ago.

Time zigzagged both ahead and behind. He was lost and alone.

He pulled his knees to his chest, the blanket pooled at his feet. He closed his eyes and saw black, but when he opened them the dark still poured in. He tried to breathe through the viscous black, like breathing underwater. He cupped his hands over his mouth and tried not to panic. Closing his eyes, he felt his breath stream through his fingers. He focused on the in and out until he could feel warm whispers tickling his skin.

He drifted in and out of sleep, but every time he roused he was greeted with a white light of shame. It ate at him.

He had thought the Berlin Art Institute would be his way out. A scholarship. Fees paid. A bursary and a way to earn some actual money. He'd use it to get an apartment that was his and Lotte's, to keep her in school until she turned eighteen, to pay for things she would need, like yellow tutus and badges for her backpack and glittery laces for her shoes and anything else she could ever want. He wanted to be there for her. Always.

He felt sick, syrupy gummy sick. A nausea induced by swallowing his own saliva. The Art Institute had declined his application.

Declined.

He tried not to think of the many words that followed this verdict, printed so neatly on his letter; or the clanging, bashing, grinding pulse of a ticking clock only he could hear.

And he knew he had to do something soon – or he'd be forced to become a policeman. What else could he do? And where would that leave Lotte?

He was suspended in the dark, his heart pinched. It may have been the drugs, but Mama's voice joined his own inside his head. He tried to sleep, to sleep away the longing for her voice, her love. But to sleep was inevitably to wake, and in waking he had to face the double cruelty of her loss. The tiny moment of hope, of her presence . . . and then the truth.

To wake was to lose her all over again.

THEN

FRIDAY 6ᵀᴴ JANUARY 1989

EPIPHANIE – EPIPHANY

He didn't look up as they shuffled along the landing, Mama carrying Lotte in her arms and Rune following a footstep behind.

As he followed her, he *wouldn't* look up.

He wouldn't look up, because just down the hall . . . Just down the hall, in the darkest black, was the door, and behind that door was Papa. And if he looked up, Papa might be in the shadows if he was—

His legs trembled, his foot slipped; he grasped at the handrail as he made his way down the stairs.

Rune hooked his fingers into the corner of Mama's jumper, the fabric softened by age. He held tight. Lotte was hanging over Mama's shoulder; Moo Bunny's dangling ears bounced, gripped in Lotte's small hands.

Mama untangled his fingers from her jumper as they reached the hall and he stood beside the coat rack. His hands were empty and his heart was beating fast enough to make everything around him appear cloudy and edgeless.

They were so close to the door.

A coat was passed to him. Rune held it, clawed his nails into the fabric, and pushed his feet into shoes put in front of him. Unlaced.

Hurry, he wanted her to hurry. He couldn't look away from the top of the stairs, where Papa could appear.

At any second.

It could all change.

Hurry, Mama, he thought. *Hurry. Please.*

The lock clicked.

He looked back, expecting to see *him*. But nothing.

The catch on the door released and he heard . . .

Mama stopped.

Nothing.

Lotte curled her head into Mama's neck. Rune didn't know what to do. He backed up into the wall. It was cold.

Then.

The fresh air from the open door hit him with such promise.

Mama pushed him through.

He tripped down the steps and found his balance by bashing into the gate. Mama was behind him; she pulled him away, grabbed the gate and swung it open. She pointed right and he ran.

Ran without looking back. Ran with all the energy he had. Rune ran fast. But even with the bag, the coats and Lotte in her arms, Mama was right beside him, keeping pace, setting pace.

He was running so fast the wind rushed through his hair, tearing his eyes.

This is how it felt to fly.

NOW

Tuesday 9th November 1999

Schicksalstag – Day of Fate

LOTTE

The house held a warmth-infused sleepiness, as though a spell had been woven into its very foundations; curtains were heavy-eyed, walls dozed upright like sleepy guards on night duty and the sofa rested, open-mouthed, dreaming of stuffing and scatter cushions. Lotte, witnessing the magic of the house in deep slumber, stretched. A shawl of content-ment wrapped around her as she softly made her way to the kitchen.

She put the oven on, gathered utensils, a bowl and two tins, and placed them on the kitchen worktop, then picked out her ingredients.

She would make a chocolate cake for Roo. It would be her best one yet and he would eat it and he would be happy, because who could not be happy with chocolate cake?

Nestling the ingredients in the pocket of her apron, she placed them in a line on the worktop. Carefully arranging them in order, she checked through each item and only when she was sure she had remembered everything was she ready to begin.

Measuring the flour in puffs of white mist, then the cocoa, she licked her lips, tasting dry powder. She sieved the white and brown together; they merged in the bowl as a chocolate fog rose.

A chocolate snowy flour mountain built under her sieve; she watched as it grew, thinking about the moat of melted butter that would be poured like golden sunshine all around it. Imagining a pearl-grey sky with dancing snowflakes, both chocolate and white. She fell silently into a snow dance, feeling as light and soft as a feather skimming across a frozen lake. Imagining snowflakes falling on her upturned face.

The post thudded on the mat by the front door. Lotte jumped, and the last chunks of flour and cocoa did too – over the top of the sieve and into the bowl.

'That was cheeky,' she said, placing the empty sieve in the sink and wiping her hands before going out into the hall. Silence rippled down the stairs like water as the house yawned, waking.

'Morning,' she whispered to the house as she collected the newspaper and a few letters from the mat. The letters had a crinkle-sharp window, which meant they were for Papa. Lotte tucked them to the back; her attention was drawn to a yellow padded envelope. It felt soft and pliable in her hands. Looking at the words stained on the front, she read her name. 'L', with a straight long line down and a sharp pointy one across.

'"L" and "O" and "TT", then the little "e" that sounds like (uh),' she said, and looked again.

Lotte.

No one ever sent her anything.

After her name were the letters she knew to be Rune.

Rune's name came all at once, like a picture. It didn't need to be worked out. It was his name next to hers.

Turning the package over, there were no words to puzzle on the back. She ripped open the envelope and pulled out a battered purple exercise book, just like the ones at school, with a piece of paper wrapped around it.

She looked up the stairs to where Papa slept.

It was still, quiet, unmoving. And yet the upstairs felt somehow heavier, as though the parcel in her hands made the stairs grow and then shrink, like a cat stretching out in the sun.

Back in the kitchen, holding the exercise book and envelope out in front of her, Lotte placed the letter next to her flour bowl. 'Lotte and Rune. Rune and Lotte,' she said. Unfolding the sheet around the exercise book, she saw an entire page of words; they swirled around like fish in a tank. She tried to take each word at a time – Frau Anst had taught her how to do that. One letter at a time, then the word should come together, like adding beads on a string to make a necklace. What actually happened was that some words came together ready-made like a stamp, while others she could puzzle over forever and they still wouldn't work. They called it a learning difficulty, part of her Down's syndrome. It didn't matter; those were words that didn't matter.

But somehow this book, *these* words, did matter. She opened the folded letter cautiously.

Lotte, that word dotted here and there, and *Rune*. She heard a footstep. Her heart stammered wildly.

And then another step; the creak of the stairs.

Footfall startled her into action.

She looked at the letter closely, understanding that as each step came closer, she would have less time to read it.

On the plain white sheet were large swoopy letters, written in black ink and curved like knitted loops.

She read aloud, her voice a whisper:

'*L.O.TT.(uh) and Rune*,' the two names belonging together.

The banister creaked, and as she knew panicking didn't help her read, she struggled to calm her heart. The paper shivered. '*I* . . .' She tried to read the words along the same row but couldn't make her eyes focus. Further down she found *L.O.V.E*, love *AL.WAY.S.* always and *M.A.M.A*.

'Mama!' That sharp pointy word came at her from the page with soft hands and the voice of songs. It was an all-over feeling. It was a new feeling. It was a feeling of holding on so tight, so as not to be left. Of being still, which was far harder than being quiet. Of quiet being the sound that roars on the inside. Of sucking her thumb and listening to words transformed into the cakes of dreams.

It was a memory, a thought, fleeting but real, and she felt it through her entire body. *Mama*.

Papa yawned loudly in the hallway and Lotte, brought back to the letter in her hands, couldn't think of what to do. She didn't want to show it to Papa.

With fumbling fingers, she folded it around the notebook and placed them back into the envelope. She slid the envelope under the other letters on the kitchen worktop, and just as she felt Papa's presence behind her she stepped back to her bowl, picked up a wooden spoon and stirred her freshly sieved flour and cocoa too fast.

Papa flooded through the doorway as a cocoa-flour cloud swirled up from the bowl.

As the fridge door wheezed open and the milk bottles chinked, her thoughts pounded and boomed to the words in the letter. She didn't know what it meant. Why was there a letter to her, and what did it say?

She would ask Roo.

Her heart rattled to the sound of the fridge closing.

The block of butter was to her left. She pulled a knife from the rack.

Papa was behind her, watching. 'Steady,' he said, but she knew to be steady. Knives were sharp.

She measured the butter before placing it into the pan and lighting the stove.

Quickly she made a well in the flour and cracked in two eggs, distracted into forgetting her earlier decision to make a sunshine-moat with the butter first. 'I was going to make a moat,' she said into the mixture. She watched the eggs as they slopped and shifted before settling like sadness, yolk to yolk. She whisked them in the bowl, added the melted butter from the pan on the stove and turned the gas dial to off. The flame went out. As the mixture turned to silk, she saw Papa check the dial, to make sure she had turned it off correctly. She felt Papa watch her for a moment before turning away, and only then could she concentrate on her cake.

The coffee machine whirred to life in a mechanical buzz that set Lotte's teeth on edge. She watched Papa place his coffee glass under the spout and the machine mulched and whined and whirled.

'I know Rune was going to take you to school, but Joann stayed last night and she's offered to take you instead.'

'But Roo was going to take us today, in the car. You said he could have the petrol to get us to school.'

'I know what I said, but Joann's going that way and she offered. It would be very rude not to accept such a kind offer, wouldn't it?'

Lotte folded the mixture onto itself in a figure of eight, over and over, and poured it into the tins, using the long thin spatula to create crested waves.

'I am not rude,' Lotte said, trying not to let the coffee machine noise into her head. She focused on making the cake look exactly right and placed both tins in the warm oven.

'Good girl,' Papa said.

Finally the coffee machine spouted brown-black coffee with a cream-brown foam into the glass, and the whining turned into a buzz-purr. Papa said he was going to have a shower.

Lotte nodded and started running the tap into the sink, where she placed the used utensils. Scooping the leftover mixture from the bowl on her finger, Lotte enjoyed the sticky, chocolatey goo as it slipped over her tongue.

Papa cleared his throat and she turned to see him looking at the letters she had placed on the kitchen side. He lifted one, with the crinkle-window, but his dressing gown sleeve caught on the rest and they fell to the floor.

Turning, she saw Papa pick them up, the yellow envelope exposed on the side. He put down his coffee and looked at her, turning the envelope with her name and Rune's side by side, revealing that it had already been opened.

He looked at Lotte again, but this time she looked at her feet and waited. The coffee machine stopped making its turning-off noise and all Lotte could hear was her breathing as it shook, sheared and shimmered from within her.

Papa clicked open the bin with his slippered foot. He tore the letter in two. Just like that; one piece, then two. Tearing it again and again, until it was in tiny pieces. Then he flicked them into the bin. The pieces landed without a noise, but Lotte's mouth was open and her voice was small. She felt like she was shrinking. She took a step forward.

Papa was bent over the bin, ripping the pages of the notebook. The pages full of words.

Lotte stepped towards him to try and stop the ripping. The words, dribbling their letters, fell silently into the bin. The front and back cover of the exercise book plummeted, and then he was tearing their pages too. Taking one at a time and making two, then four, eight, then more than she could count. She hadn't even opened the exercise book and Papa was turning it into paper snow.

It happened so fast. Her hands were trying to stop his. Moving towards him. Finally using her voice. 'Please. No. Stop.'

Then she looked at his face and a whiplash of thought, sharp and brief, stopped her.

She watched him destroy the words. The words that were to her and Rune. The letter with the up down up down word that she knew was 'Mama'.

As he was tearing, something she thought she had was gone.

The last of the paper landed. The bin lid dropped. Papa picked up his coffee.

'It's for the best, Lotte, I promise,' he said, and his lips moved rapidly, without sound, catching and dropping words before he kissed her gently on the top of her head.

He turned and left the kitchen.

As she heard the boiler churn to life and the shower rinse on, she closed her eyes and tried to blot away the image with the palms of her hands. She pressed hard into her eyes, into the stinging, blinking stars, and opened them. It was her fault. She should have put it somewhere safer. *Stupid Lotte, stupid.*

Papa had torn up the letter. The letter that had made her *feel* Mama.

Lotte swallowed and opened the bin.

She had to rescue the paper from the mess of food and waste at the bottom of the bin. Bin juice. Trying hard not to think, she acted quickly. Plunging her hand down and picking out the envelope first, then piece after piece. She nestled them all into her apron. The bin rubbish hadn't stained them, but they were damp from whatever resided at the bottom. She heard the pit-pat of rain and the usual morning noises coming from upstairs – footfall, radio, toothbrush.

Her fingertips sickeningly touched upon the plump flesh of softened, leaking, rotten cherries. A wave of iron-rust sickness heaved up into her throat. She stood and the lid hushed closed.

Tucking the torn pages, the envelope and the cover of the exercise book up in her apron, she waddled with difficulty out of the room and quietly up the stairs.

RUNE

He awoke in a woolly grogginess wearing yesterday's clothes, which felt square and crunchy against his skin. He lay on his face and tried to move his tongue; it seemed glued to his cheek. Swallowing hard didn't help; he coughed harshly as he heard Lotte's voice in the hallway. The simultaneous noises shattered his nervous system; his entire body was taut and aching.

He felt sorry for himself in the shadowy moment between waking and being awake. In the pillowy present, in which nothing before, nor to come, entered his thoughts, he was weighed down under layers of shame.

His arm was numb and limp from how he'd slept on it at a strange angle; clenching his fist sent a ferocious bite of life up to his elbow. He gingerly lifted his head. His mouth was fuzzed over and his throat dry.

The pity distorted into revulsion as he rolled over to the smell of weak sunshine on dust and his own stale breath. When he opened his eyes, he noticed a triangle of light, filtered through dirty windows, shining hazily into his room. He lifted his numb hand and passed it through the shard of heatless light.

Lotte burst into his room.

'Roo! He. He. He. He. He. Roo . . .' she said, re-jangling all of Rune's recovering senses, and in her greeting a switch flicked on. A mask in which to perform the daily task of living slipped over him, like a cloud across the sun. A performance orchestrated solely for Lotte.

'The bin has stained them and they are torn up and I. I. I. Papa did it,' she added, taking a breath before continuing. 'Papa won't let you take me to school either he says Barbie-woman has to take me I don't like her but Papa says that is not kind I have to go with her and you don't but this came and I don't know why he did it but I opened it to you and to me and I tried I really tried . . .' – her words slurred into each other as she took a breath – 'but look . . .' And she showed him the contents of her apron.

At first he thought it was dirty confetti, and then he thought it was rice and poppy seeds. Only when she lifted her apron higher did he see it was paper.

'Why did he do this?' she asked, crying.

'What is it?'

'I don't know it was to Rune and Lotte. Lotte and Rune. It was from Mama.'

'What?' he asked, stunned into standing. 'It can't be from Mama,' he said.

'But it is. It was,' Lotte corrected, tears falling from her chin. 'Mama sent us something, but, but, but . . .'

'Lotte.' Papa's voice calling. 'Time to get ready.'

'What do we do?' Lotte begged.

Rune shrugged; it hurt to say it again. Over and over. Once was enough at the time and now once was too much. He stretched and then touched Lotte gently on the shoulders. 'It can't be from Mama because Mama is dead,' he said. 'Maybe you read it wrong?'

'I. Did. Not,' she said. 'I tried and I slowed my thoughts down and I did it properly – I swear!'

'Lotte. Now.' Papa's voice was not to be messed with. 'And no tutu,' he added. Lotte squeaked.

'What do we do?' she asked.

'Nothing.' He looked at the shards of mess in her apron. 'Whatever it was, it's gone now,' he said. There was nothing salvageable in the shreds of paper.

'But. But. But,' Lotte stammered. 'It was from Mama.'

And he hated his father in that moment. What harm could it have possibly caused for him to let her have something. Anything. The edges of his vision were dark, but Lotte, at the centre, was yellow and bright; her cheeks were pink and damp.

His stomach clenched, fisted, raw.

Papa knocked on his door. 'Boy!' he called. 'Tell your sister Joann leaves in five minutes and she *will* be ready in time.'

Rune looked at Lotte's snot-smeared, teared-up face.

'Rune!' Papa's voice from behind the door.

'Okay,' Rune called back. They waited until he could hear Papa's footsteps receding.

'Please make it come back,' Lotte begged.

'I can't,' Rune said. His words knotted in his heart, and he looked to the floor to prevent seeing Lotte's disappointed face.

'I'm sorry,' he said, but the room was empty. Lotte had left the door ajar.

LOTTE

Her shoe-box-that-was-her-treasure-box was still under the bed. She tipped the contents of her apron into it and then pulled out a few pieces of the torn paper, filtering them through her hands as she would do with butter and flour to make a sweet pastry for *Apfelstrudel* or, her favourite, *Puddingbrezel*.

With a dry mouth and her stomach gritty, she pulled out the picture of her and Roo taken by one of Papa's 'Barbie-friends' years ago. They were standing side by side, Roo looking straight at the camera; she had been looking slightly away.

She looked at his face. He was no longer the brother who made her laugh, told her stories and held her hand. He tried, but that brother had gone. Nothing in the picture could tell her where he went. She stared at her brother's image then placed it back in the box. Her brother had shrunk into grey sadness.

'I am more than my Down's syndrome.' She repeated the mantra Roo had taught her.

She would take the pieces to school and find a way to get them back. She would do it on her own.

Inde-pen-dent-ly.

She picked up the photo once more and raised it to her lips, as if she could kiss him back; overflowing but empty all at once, she closed her eyes. She could see his face, his mouth curved into a rare smile. She was always able to get the best smiles out of him. But now she could barely find his eyes. He was lost. Maybe the words from Mama would bring Roo back to her too. She brought the picture down to her chest to feel his presence there.

She opened her eyes. Her heart small and wanting.

Slipping the box into her backpack, she pulled Roo's old T-shirt on over her own, so she wouldn't be facing the day alone. She wiggled out of the tutu and admired the yellow-black-yellow combination of her clothes in the mirror. She *buzzed* at her reflection before speeding back down the stairs (not like a bee, whose wings, she knew, beat over two hundred times a second, but like an almost bee, a tribute bee, a LotteBee). Chocolate-steam enveloped her like a hug as she took the cake out and she knew that *this* day, the day that was also today, *she*, LotteBee, inde-pen-dent-ly, would find a way to make the shredded pages whole. She left the cake cooling on the side. Roo could eat it later. The thought made her happy.

Today she would bring Mama back and make it all better.

Somehow.

For Roo.

RUNE

Returning to the bed, he lit a cigarette and opened the letter from the Berlin Art Institute again. The letter invited him to contact the admissions team to discuss his options and collect his submitted portfolio. As it stood, he couldn't attend the university due to a *conflict of interests*, but the wording of the letter was too official to properly understand.

To be able to leave Papa, to create a different life for him and Lotte. To be free to draw, to create, to make Lotte happy and keep her safe. The possibility had felt tangible, but it had been declined.

His head buzzed, skeletal and scraped out. He folded the letter and quickly popped an oxy from his stash in a small hole he'd made in the mattress.

He heard Lotte fly down the stairs and watched through a gap in the curtains as Joann waited by her car. He could smell the enticing chocolate cake Lotte had made for him; he didn't know how to be without her. He wished she were the older sister, and he, being younger, could take safety in looking up to her and be allowed to see the world the way she did.

It seemed a better place.

When he was twelve he had chickenpox, insufferable itching all over, his mouth full of sores, even his eyes blurred and sticky; he'd been miserable. Lotte, only eight, had made such a fuss when Papa tried to make her go to school that he relented and let her stay at home to look after Rune.

She sang him songs and made him sugar-water, which they both pretended was lemonade. She spent hours dotting his chickenpox with soothing calamine and when she'd done them all, she started all over again. At the end of the week, when his pox were less irate, they baked cakes in the empty house; they made wooden puppets and a small theatre out of an old box, where they would put on shows for each other. He had been so relieved the following week when Lotte had come out in spots too, that the whole week could happen again. He wanted life to be like this.

Just the two of them.

No matter what.

He watched Lotte and Joann talking by the car and then Joann looked up to his window. He took a step back.

A few minutes later, Lotte's voice called up the stairs. 'Joann says she can give you a lift too?'

'Hurry up then, boy,' Papa's voice called from the corridor, and he heard him walk down the stairs.

'Coming,' he called, but he waited until he saw Papa start his daily jog to work. When Papa had reached the end of the street, Rune saw him check the straps on his backpack and then his watch before disappearing.

He touched the letter in his pocket cautiously.

He had to do something to get away. Something for Lotte. This had been his only hope. Perhaps he could go to the university and beg. He didn't want to beg. But he would. He would do anything for Lotte, and he knew if the roles were reversed, she would do *everything* for him.

He opened his door and listened at the stairs. He knew Papa had gone, but still. It was better to be sure. His vision was viscous, liquid, plumes and funnels taking him back, pulling him back, to a time before.

A time gone.

A time and place that no longer existed.

THEN

FRIDAY 6ᵀᴴ JANUARY 1989

EPIPHANIE — EPIPHANY

They kept moving. Running from home. Flying away down the hill. Across the park. When they finally slowed, Lotte was pale in the grey-yellow street light. Although she held on tight, she was slipping off Mama's shoulder with every few steps Mama took.

Rune was panting hard, his bag dragging him down. Mama slowed under the lights of the Lutheran cemetery. The headstones jutted from the ground at different angles and early-morning drizzle floated around him, sticking his hair to his neck.

As they walked past the cemetery, he could almost hear the kids at school singing 'Thriller' while attempting to moonwalk along the length of the playground. *It's close to midnight and something evil's lurking in the dark.*

Once the song was in his head, he couldn't stop the words.

It was a sticky song.

He tried to play it fast-forward in his mind, to rush the words through, to speed it up. But like the old record player in the dining room, it wouldn't fast-forward and just kept winding along.

The tarmac shone ink-wet; the road grew bumpy, then he was walking on paving slabs. They wobbled as he stepped on them, the cracks spitting up water. When he looked up, they had reached the bridge.

Mama placed Lotte on the ground and gave her a kiss, before taking her hand and walking on.

Rune held Lotte's other hand. She made little whimpering sounds as she walked, slowly. So slowly that before they had crossed the bridge, with a brown sludge of water far below, Mama had picked her back up. He offered to carry Mama's rucksack as well as his own, but struggled to hold it in his arms.

Lotte flopped back over Mama's shoulder, thumb in mouth and Moo Bunny in her arms. Her hair bobbed to the rhythm of Mama's steps.

As they approached the train station, they saw taxis parked up outside, but all was quiet. He watched Mama as she looked around and he could tell she didn't have a plan.

They had nowhere to go.

The darkness seemed to grip his throat and although he wanted to ask *What now?*, her silence seemed to steal his own voice.

'Where are we?' Lotte asked.

Mama didn't answer but was already heading towards something, a beacon of light – a car? He followed her, watching his step on the cobbles. At the phone box, she stopped. He put both bags down and Mama put Lotte on the rucksack. She sat on it without complaint as Mama rustled in her pocket for change and shut herself in the phone box.

Rune started to sit, but as he lowered himself he could no longer see Mama's face, so he stood and watched as she pulled a tiny slip of paper from her T-shirt. She picked up the receiver and dialled.

'Where are we going?' Lotte asked, her bottom lip wobbling.

'Wherever Mama goes,' he said confidently, not looking away from Mama as she replaced the receiver and tried again. Rune saw her hands shake as she dialled for the second time.

He stood transfixed, trying to know before he was told what might be next for them; after all, this wasn't the first time they had left. He saw Mama glance at him, and after an age she pulled the phone from her ear before lifting it and dialling again.

He pressed the side of his fingernail into his palm to focus on something else.

The door of the phone box opened with a crash and Mama propelled herself out and picked Lotte up, almost toppling over in the process.

'Just call this number,' Mama said to herself, picking up both bags in her spare hand. They were too heavy, and she leaned into their weight. 'I will answer it, day or night,' she said. 'Fucking ridiculous.' Mama was almost sinking under the weight of Lotte and she nodded towards the silent, dark taxis all in a row.

Home. Back. Again.

'I'm sorry,' she said.

Sorry.

It was the word of home. *Sorry.*

He froze, unable to step off the kerb. He didn't want to go home, not again. Not ever. Not to the house where *sorry* came every morning with bruises and burns, where *sorry* followed Mama's wet hand forced into the sugar bowl and then held under the grill until the popping of skin and the sweet-hot-pink smell made him sick all down himself.

Sorry was followed by *more*.

More of the same, and always, always the same sad *sorry*.

Rune rocked on the spot as tears burned his eyes. He pressed his hands to them to stem the flood, but they dripped through his fingers anyway.

'Mama,' Lotte snuffled, her thumb in her mouth, Moo Bunny under her arm.

'One minute,' Mama said.

47

'Mama?' Lotte said again, but clearer this time, free of the thumb.

'Not now, Lotte, please,' Mama said. Then gently to him, 'Everything will be okay. You'll see.'

'It's just . . . I,' he said.

'MA-MA,' Lotte shouted, and he followed Mama's gaze to look at Lotte, sitting on the big rucksack. 'I'VE LOST MY WILLY!'

'Your what?'

'My willy, it's gone,' she said seriously.

'You don't have a willy,' he said.

'I do.'

Mama took in a breath that he thought would never end. She bent down to Lotte's level.

'Lotte, you are a little girl and little girls don't have willies. Only boys have a willy.'

'I had two,' she said, and Rune smiled as Mama looked up at him for help. He shrugged his shoulders, bemused.

'But . . .' Mama started.

'I do. I know I do. I had two, but now I have only one. It's glittery.'

'Your willy is glittery?' Rune laughed.

'And pink,' Lotte wept. 'With Bear Cares on it.'

Mama was silent for a whole minute and then she sat back on her heels and laughed. A sound that shocked him. He was silenced, awed by Mama. Her face softened, and her laugh was loud, as though it came from deep inside her, a forgotten part, and as her laugh rolled on itself, it caught him up too.

'Wellies?' Mama said. 'Lotte, you . . .' But she couldn't get the words out. 'Wellies,' she said again.

'It's not funny,' Lotte said.

'Wellies,' he said, as their laughter eased, but the word caught on Mama's laugh and fed his. Laughter, loud and strong, bounced around them. He wanted to keep hold of the sound, to capture it somehow.

'Look,' Lotte said, and wiggled her toes.

Mama continued to laugh and hugged Lotte close.

'I don't want to go back,' he cried, and his legs wobbled as he stumbled, cold and hard, onto the pavement.

She helped him up and pulled him close.

'We're not going back,' she said, and looked directly at him.

He noticed she hadn't promised.

'But what about my willy?' Lotte bawled.

'First thing we will do is find some . . . shoes,' Mama said, pronouncing the word 'shoes' carefully.

'We're not going back for it?' he asked.

'We're not going back for anything,' she said decisively and walked to the front of the taxi queue.

NOW

TUESDAY 9ᵀᴴ NOVEMBER 1999

SCHICKSALSTAG — DAY OF FATE

LOTTE

Joann's tiny blue car smelled like bubblegum, syrupy and pretend-sweet. Lotte had to put her bag, with the shoebox-that-was-her-treasure-box inside, on the back seat with Roo as she couldn't fold herself small enough to fit everything on her lap. She buckled up as Joann went whizzing off, holding on to her seat with sweaty palms.

Roo said nothing. She knew he was busy in his own head and so she didn't turn around.

At the first set of traffic lights, Joann pulled in and got out with a turquoise purse in her hand. Lotte watched her totter to the roadside café. On her return, she had a cup and three brown paper bags. She handed everything to Lotte before taking the cup back, pulling off the lid and blowing on the coffee.

'There's *Schneckennudeln* for you both,' she said, indicating the bags. Lotte passed one back to Roo, who folded it over and placed it on the floor by his feet.

Lotte could almost taste the coffee and cinnamon pastry as the smells filled the car. The world blurred around her as she nibbled on the *Schneckennudeln*. The raw spice of the cinnamon hardened coarse on her tongue. She closed her eyes.

She was standing on a chair against a kitchen worktop; she was cold and her hands were in a bowl of coarse mashed potato and quark cheese. *Quarkkäulchen*. A word she hadn't heard for years, and as she tried to think, to pry further into the memory, it dissolved in a sprinkle of cinnamon sugar.

Tears pricked at the back of her eyes, and the pastry turned to ash in her mouth. She was remembering. But what?

She looked at the woman beside her and wondered if this was how Mama had been, or what Lotte was supposed to become.

Joann was a puffball blonde, full of curls and baby-pink smiles. Even sitting next to Joann made Lotte feel overgrown, as though she had morphed into twice her normal size. Standing next to each other, Joann was of a similar height to Lotte, but she had such a small frame that Lotte felt like a colossal dinosaur, able to bend its long neck at a moment's notice and bite off the tiny Barbie's head.

She placed the nibbled pastry back in the bag.

She wanted to know Mama, really know her.

She tried to catch Roo's eye, but he was looking out the window. He was all alone where he was. It made her feel empty just watching him. Maybe putting Mama's words back together would bring Roo closer to her; if she remembered Mama too, maybe he would feel less alone.

Joann turned up the volume on the radio and David Bowie's 'Heroes' joined them in the car. When Joann started to sing *I, I can remember. Standing by the wall*, Lotte passed her the paper bag with the pastry inside. Joann put the coffee in the holder between them, and started to eat, leaving Bowie to sing solo: *We can be heroes, just for one day.*

The news came next, and Lotte listened.

The anniversary of the fall of the Berlin Wall was the news; there was a special feature on how East and West had woven back together the divide created by the wall. As the news droned on in a monotone, Joann asked questions about school. Now that food and drink had been consumed, it seemed that Joann wanted to talk.

Lotte ignored her.

Roo ignored her too.

'Ten years on,' the newsreader said, in a tinny, nasal voice, 'the Stasi past is still very much alive.'

Joann started humming 'Heroes' again, not in a gentle hum but in a 'DooDoDoDooodoooo' way.

Lotte looked at the tiny dials and orange backlight of the radio as though staring at it would enable her to hear the music better.

'Known collectively as *The Puzzle Women*, they sit in the Stasi's headquarters and put together the shredded files the Stasi couldn't burn or pulp.'

Lotte turned the dial and the newsreader's voice disappeared as she tuned the frequency instead of the volume.

Joann protested.

When she found the station again, Lotte's heart leaped.

A different voice was talking now – male, slow, deep and loud.

'We are a small team of workers,' he said, 'not all women, I might add. The Stasi left a paper legacy – thousands of sacks of shredded paper were found. It's our job to put them back together, to give people answers to long-ago questions.'

The newsreader asked something, but Joann coughed and Lotte missed it. She slowly turned the other dial and this time the volume increased.

'It's like fitting together a giant puzzle,' the man went on. 'Sixteen thousand sacks full of paper – torn, shredded, you name it, they're all but destroyed.'

'But you can put them back together again?' the newsreader asked as Joann pulled around the corner and Lotte saw her school come into view.

'Yes. On average our workers can reconstruct ten pages each, every single day. That's three hundred pages a day between them. But even as skilled as the workers are, it'll take hundreds of years to reconstruct them all. It's a long—'

'You ready?' Joann interrupted as she swung the car into the no-parking zone outside the school.

Lotte shook her head, still listening.

'And what are in these files the Stasi tried to destroy?'

'Well, it can be anything . . .'

Roo got out and shut the door. He was waiting outside her door when Joann touched Lotte's arm to get her attention.

'Lotte,' she said. 'Time for school.'

Lotte nodded, hoping her silence would make Joann silent too. She listened to the radio.

'These documents shouldn't be lost or left in sacks. They're an important part of our history so they will be reconstructed. They account for individual lives and can help people make sense of their own past,' the man's voice said, his East German accent deepening.

'I know we don't know each other well,' Joann said, 'but I really would like to know you better. Your father and I—'

Lotte reached over and turned the radio up louder so she couldn't hear Joann, who shook her head, hands on the steering wheel, tapping her long nails on the dashboard.

'Serious stuff,' the newscaster said. 'So what do you do for fun, Herr Benedict?'

'Well, I am partial to a puzzle of an evening,' he said, as tinny laughter flooded the car.

'Lotte,' Joann said, turning the radio down just a fraction but enough to be heard, 'your father said I wouldn't have any trouble.'

'That's it from the old Stasi HQ. I'm Ramona Cusk reporting live in Zirndorf, Nuremberg. Back to the studio.'

Deadpan, the nasal newscaster continued, 'And in other news . . .'

Joann turned the volume down until the radio clicked off. 'Have a good day,' she said.

Lotte remained motionless. Stasi HQ. *Nuremberg*.

'You have to get out now,' Joann prompted, leaning over and pulling the door handle so Lotte's door clicked open. Her hair was strangely firm where it nudged Lotte on the chin, as if it were made of hairspray. 'Have a good day,' she said, staring straight ahead, the car's engine purring gently.

Lotte held the paper bag in her hand, and beneath it was Joann's purse. Nuremberg wasn't Berlin, Nuremberg was far away and she would need money to get there. Neither she nor Roo had any money

Lotte quickly tucked the turquoise purse out of sight under the paper bag and got out. It was a bad thing to do and Lotte wasn't bad, but if she could get to Nuremberg, she and Roo could put the letter and notebook back together. Together.

'I am more than my Down's syndrome,' she said.

'What?' Joann looked at her.

'Nothing,' Lotte said, and opened the back door to grab her bag from the seat.

Clutching the purse to her body, Lotte watched the Barbie-woman in the toy-blue car drive away.

'The puzzle women can help us,' she said to Roo when the car was out of sight and they were standing on the pavement.

'What?'

'They can put Mama's letter back together.'

He looked at her. 'Who can?'

'The Stasi people in Nur-em-berg.'

'What? No, Lotte, please. Listen to me. I'll help you with the papers if you like. But it's not safe to go to a place like that.' He lowered his voice. 'Please – I'll explain everything later, but go to school now. I have to do something.'

'Mama was dead for years and years, Roo. But the letter is from her to you and to me from *today*. You can help me. We can do it together.'

'It can't be from Mama,' he said in a tired voice.

Was Roo tired of her?

'Go to school,' he said. 'I promise we'll talk tonight, okay? I'll explain. I have to go now.' And he walked in the wrong direction, as if he was going back home, leaving her alone with the precious shredded words from Mama.

RUNE

He walked back to the house after Joann had dropped them at school and collected his bike and his bag, thinking of the Stasi and of Mama. The official line was that Mama had been 'disappeared' by the Stasi.

But he remembered the truth.

Guilt slid under his skin, wet and cold, amphibian. He tried to hold the image of Mama behind his eyes, but she didn't stay still; there was a smile and then it was gone. Her features glimmered and shimmered in the air, the glow of her eyes flickering in the sky, darkness eating away at the light. And he was angry at her memory for not staying still. For not helping him. For leaving.

He pedalled slowly at first, trying to morph the map on the back of his application letter into the city he knew, and enjoying the dreamlike effects of the oxy he'd taken, he felt slow and conscious of every breath. It was a good feeling.

He'd try and explain it all to Lotte later.

Finally, when he was sure he had found it, 404 Industriebahn Berlin, he locked his bike up outside an enormous red-brick industrial complex. The Berlin Art Institute.

He was unsure of what to do next.

He waited until his stomach started to rumble and a surge of people began to walk into the entrance to the building before taking his own first step over the threshold. Fearful that somehow he was in trouble.

'Professor Obert cannot see you,' the receptionist said, sitting behind a large desk with a great beige phone to her ear, a long earring dangling from her fingers. She thrust his letter back at him with only a cursory glance at it. 'She's busy teaching today. Your application was declined?' He nodded as the receptionist resumed her conversation down the phone.

When the conversation ended, she replaced the phone and her earring and leaned over the desk. 'One hour,' she said. 'Studio 4. You'll catch her leaving class,' and she gave him a wink.

Before he had turned away, the phone rang and she answered it, holding the receiver away from her ear slightly to remove her oversized dangly earring once more. She covered the mouthpiece and spoke after Rune – 'Studio 4' – and pointed with a long finger, tipped with a bright pink nail, to the corridor on his left.

He walked blindly up and down streets, not straying too far from the buildings, not wanting to get lost, until he found a café in Weißensee.

He struggled to keep a nervous tap out of his foot. A few sharp-suited businessmen, revealing only their eyebrows over the top of the day's newspaper, were seated at small tables, while at two larger tables, women with babies chortled, their mingled perfumes wafting over him with every swish of a hand. When they threw back their heads and laughed, a fug of floral fumes, hairspray and unwanted humour seemed to stick to his skin.

The barista was taking her time, perfecting a frothy swirl. She placed it in front of him and met his eyes, her face plain and unsure. 'Latte,' she said.

He shook his head.

'Oh?'

'Black coffee to go,' he said. It came out brisk and blunt and harsh.

She looked at the cup with its perfect milk swirl and back at him. 'No latte?'

'Black coffee to go, how hard is that?' He pressed his fingers into his forehead. He had no other destination so he waited, uncomfortable and under-caffeinated, finding the weight of smells – coffee, cinnamon, pastry, perfume, newspapers – intoxicating. The sounds of grinding, punctuated laughter, the sticky shoes of the barista as she turned, leaving the latte in front of him with a clunk of the saucer.

'Black coffee, yes?' she asked, placing a china mug under the machine.

'To GO!' he yelled. 'Holy fuck,' he added under his breath.

'Did you say latte?' One of the laughing women brushed against his shoulder. The barista looked relieved and nodded, handing over the latte. 'Thanks,' the woman said and, teetering on high heels, wobbled back to her table.

Rune lit a cigarette with tingling fingers. Everything jangled, like a box of loose nuts and bolts. What if it was all over? His application had taken over a year to prepare and submit and now he had one chance to change the professor's mind. He felt ill-equipped to form a complete sentence, let alone create a compelling argument that would persuade them to reconsider his application.

His hoody felt tight around the collar. Sweat pricked his neck and the heat of the café, the smoke, the drugs, and the too-real feeling of being strapped into the back of a moving car careening towards a brick wall made him want to vomit.

Finally a takeaway cardboard cup was handed to him. Black coffee, sleek and strong.

'Milk and sugar behind you,' the barista said, before simpering away to serve a guy dressed in tight gold trousers and a pink boob tube, his heavy beard sequinned with rain.

'Happy Destiny Day!' the guy boomed in a loud, deep voice, gaining glittering looks from the women. 'The Day of Fate,' he added theatrically.

It was the date, he thought. He'd had the same problem last year. It was getting worse year on year. But this year. Ten years, and that must mean something.

A decade.

At least, everyone else seemed to think so. Last year, Rune had spent two days in a drug-infused haze. Unable to bear the wails and calls and memories as they clawed through his skin, he had drowned them out. But this year . . .

He ripped three sugars into his coffee. What was he going to do this year? Until his application was rejected, he had thought he'd be planning for a future. The concept was wobbly, new.

It'll be over in a few days, he tried to reassure himself, stirring the sugar and fitting the plastic lid onto his cup. A few days.

He put a large tip in the cup for the barista – his last marks, a silent sorry for being such a dick – and left the café; sitting on a metal chair outside, he watched the streets hum around him.

He would explain the situation and then, maybe, life could start. He walked back to Studio 4 with purpose and intent, his strides long, his hands warmed by the coffee.

He could do this.

THEN

Friday 6th January 1989

Epiphanie – Epiphany

In the taxi, Mama pulled out sheets of paper. Lots of paper. She had a plan after all.

'Is that Papa's workbook?' he asked, seeing a slim black leather-bound notebook among the papers.

She hid it under the other sheets and looked at him. A meaningful look.

What was happening? What hadn't she told him? He looked out the window, trying to work out what was going to happen next.

The driver talked and talked, with a thick accent. Mama replied with single words until they eventually arrived at a checkpoint.

'Where are we going?' Rune asked.

'We are going to visit my grandmother.' She turned to look at Rune. 'Your great-grandmother. Annika,' she said.

'Who?'

Mama repeated it.

As slow as the car moved, the clock on the dashboard inched forward, drawing out each second, each minute; the tyres rolled on, taking them away from Papa, away from home, but . . . to where?

'Annika. Annika. Aaanni-kaaaa,' Lotte said in a sing-song voice next to him.

'The traffic is heaviest this time of day,' the driver explained. 'Everyone getting back before their overnight visas run out. It's a difficult time right now, with all the reforms.' He looked to Mama to confirm that she understood what he was saying. She nodded absently.

The taxi driver continued, 'No one really knows if it's true, the reforms on travel restrictions, you see, so everyone's behaving like scuttling beetles.' He rubbed at his ear and Rune looked away, disgusted at the watery squelching sound it produced. 'Current reports are saying,' the man went on, looking at his finger before returning it to the ear and rubbing once more, 'that there's no "shoot-to-kill order" for the East German guards if East Germans themselves are trying to flee over the Wall . . .' He droned on, but Rune listened closely. *Shoot? Wall?*

The driver looked at Mama carefully. 'But the ministers have promised the West that if East Germans are trying to flee across the border, they will only receive warning shots. I think it's making people believe that change is happening. That the reforms are true. People are taking more risks. But it's irrelevant to us because no one from the West ever goes East. You have your visas?' he asked, abruptly changing the subject, and Mama answered by holding up the papers. 'Ah, so you *are* staying then?' the driver asked, looking at the papers curiously. From his place in the back, Rune couldn't see what they were.

'We're going across *the Wall?*' he asked, his voice rising high in panic. 'With the communists, the reds' – and he lowered his voice – 'the Russians?'

Mama turned. Her eyes wide, her face pale. Her expression said, *Trust me*; or maybe it said, *Please don't make a scene.* He wasn't sure. He said nothing more, but slumped back in his seat.

As the car crawled slowly towards the checkpoint the driver turned off the radio, plunging them in a thick silence that Rune tried to swallow away. They weren't going home, but was this worse?

'Are you sure about this?' the driver asked, nudging the car forward. 'You know, East Berlin, they aren't to be trusted with their promises for change . . . It's not . . . their track record . . . the kids . . . your *daughter*?' He whispered the last word and nodded to the back seat, where Lotte was looking out of the window, her tongue lolling from between her lips. Rune touched Lotte gently on the arm, motioning to her that her tongue was out. She smiled.

'I love you, my brother,' she said, putting her thumb in her mouth and wiggling the toes of her welly-less foot.

He held Lotte's hand. The driver's words spiralled around in his head. He wanted to understand, but then equally was scared to look ahead. East.

They queued for a long time and as they crawled East, Rune looked for Mama to change her mind and turn the taxi around, because no one from the West ever went East. Even the driver said so.

What was going to happen to them?

NOW

TUESDAY 9TH NOVEMBER 1999

SCHICKSALSTAG – DAY OF FATE

LOTTE

Her fingers were blue with cold as she walked to the bus stop. She kept thinking, *What would Roo do?* She knew he would slow down and think hard, so she did.

She knew that buses took people to places they wanted to go, so she walked to a bus stop and took the bus to the station. Using her thinking head, she decided she was going to be more than what people thought she could be. She was going to find these *puzzle women* and she was going to put Mama's notebook back together again.

And she was going to do this alone.

Once at the bus station, her first stop was to find the toilets. She asked a cleaning lady with a blue tabard and pink gloves, who smiled and took her all the way to the cubicle door. It was a smelly toilet, but after Lotte had had a wee and washed her hands, she looked into the bathroom mirror and repeated the affirmation. 'I am more than my Down's syndrome. I am inde-pen-dent.'

Taking her time at the outgoing terminal of the bus station, she tried navigating the timetables, trying to fix words to times and places, but it was so complicated it made her want to cry. She didn't even know what the word *Zirndorf* looked like. Instead of crying and going home, she thought about the puzzle women; how, maybe, they could bring the pages back for her. She could give them to Roo and Roo could tell her what they meant and she could miss Mama with him.

Lotte took a deep breath before asking a girl with purple hair and rings through her nose, eyebrow and lip to help her. Lotte made sure to speak clearly, and while she was listening she checked her tongue was firmly in her mouth. It was.

Lotte asked the helpful girl to repeat the instructions and she did.

Just like that. The girl told her exactly what she needed to do and even repeated it three times.

Papa was wrong – people were helpful if you asked them nicely and no one was shocked that she was travelling alone. Even though her face revealed to everyone that she was different, no one had made her feel scared or stupid. When she got home, she would tell Papa that he was wrong. The idea tickled a smile onto her lips as she waited in the right line, *Haltestelle 19*, for the correct bus, the 104, to take her on a journey. Alone.

On the bus, grey blurred into green and Lotte felt her head grow light, no longer a weight to be held on her shoulders. She rested her forehead on the glass and watched the sky grow big.

Berlin was drifting away as the bus rumbled towards Nuremberg, towards the puzzle women in Zirndorf, and maybe, just maybe, towards Mama. Because if Mama had written them a letter that said *love* and *always* then she couldn't still be dead, could she? Even though dead was forever?

Hours later, the driver's voice woke her up. The bus had stopped.

She was here.

She felt strange from sleeping in motion and held her rucksack close until she could work out where she was. Wiggling her toes, she carefully waited until everyone had lumbered off the bus before following suit. At the door, she joined the other passengers as they waited for their baggage.

The driver pulled heavy bags from the side compartment of the bus.

'Do you have any luggage?' he asked her.

Lotte shook her head: no. 'I'm looking for the Stasi headquarters,' she said, stuttering slightly as she tried to form the words. 'I heard about it on the radio this morning. The puzzle women?'

'You're ten years too late for the Stasi,' he said, straightening his cap and standing to his full height. He was shorter than Lotte and, standing on the steps of the bus, she could see a bald spot on the top of his head.

Lotte tried to awaken her brain; she felt suddenly sluggish, trying to un-muddle what the driver was saying. Not having planned how she was going to feed her empty stomach, Lotte had eaten nothing since the mouthful of pastry and felt the emptiness travel to her head. She leaned against the bus, feeling cool metal through her coat.

'The Stasi have all but gone now,' he said as he shut the luggage compartment of the bus. She bit her lip hard and the shock of pain cleared the fog.

'I mean,' Lotte said, 'the *former* Stasi headquarters. Where they are working on piecing the torn papers.' Her voice came out wispy, but the driver was looking intently at her now. She tried to mimic the voice that had come from the radio.

'Do you mean the immigration centre? I think the old HQ was turned into a detention centre,' he said, straightening his cap again and consulting a clipboard that had been resting on the steps leading up into the bus.

'No,' Lotte said. Unsure now, she held her bag tighter to her chest. 'I heard on the radio, this morning . . .'

'You're wrong, old man,' came a loud male voice behind Lotte. She whirled around to see a man in a leather jacket coming towards her, cigarette dangling from his lips and black shirt open to the navel.

'This . . . lady,' he said, looking carefully at Lotte as he passed her, 'this lady is right – they're reconstructing Stasi files in Zirndorf. The immigration centre shares the other side of the building.'

'Stern!' the driver said loudly as he recognised the other man. Lotte stepped back as they clapped each other on the shoulder. This man, Stern, wore a dozen necklaces, which jangled against the driver's pristine white shirt buttons.

'Comrade! Long time no see,' the driver said. 'Drink?'

'I'm on duty, but saw you drive by. Thought I'd say hi,' Stern said.

Lotte looked at him, at the open shirt and his visible chest hair, the necklaces and the cigarette dangling off his lip.

'Have you lost the buttons?' she asked. 'From your shirt,' and she pointed. Both Stern and the bus driver laughed.

'That's what Stern would consider fashion,' the driver said.

'I have great taste,' Stern said, rubbing the shirt and losing the dangling cigarette from his lip. 'I like my shirt,' he added to Lotte.

'I like yellow,' she said shyly, 'but I don't wear broken clothes. I use my thinking head when I get dressed.'

The driver hooted like an owl and Stern smiled.

'You want to go to the detention centre?' he asked.

'The Stasi headquarters,' she corrected, and zipped her coat up tight.

'The Stasi headquarters,' Stern and the driver said together.

Lotte wasn't sure why they were speaking together; she thought she might have lost what they were trying to say. People often spoke in the most roundabout ways to say the simplest things. She said nothing, waiting for one of the men to make himself clear.

Stern shrugged. 'My car is over there.' He pointed to the row of taxis parked outside the bus station. It reminded her of ants or small bugs forming a procession and something about that thought dragged at her, an echo of the same thought from another time perhaps. She was grappling with the obscure familiarity when Stern continued, 'I can take you.'

Lotte was quiet for a moment.

'Or,' the bus driver said, 'you can take the U1 – or is it U2? The timetable's posted up on the wall inside. I'm not sure if there's a direct bus that'll take you right there – you might need to go through Fürth, before changing to get to Zirndorf . . .' He left the sentence hanging.

'Please,' she said, stepping forward, her voice high and tight. 'I have money. Please, can you take me?'

RUNE

The smell of paint hit him with force and longing when he returned to the art institute. He walked past studios with pottery wheels, another with racks and racks of printing blocks. He could smell art, in its purest form; it made him crave paper.

The lesson inside Studio 4 was coming to an end; he heard the scrape of chairs and the rumble of talk. As the students filed past him, he waited.

Professor Obert was far younger than Rune had imagined; she wore a faded Mickey Mouse T-shirt and a long plait messily arranged over one shoulder. She was also rather short, so that when Rune introduced himself she had to look up to him, which made him feel self-conscious. He wished there were seats; he'd have preferred to sit.

Professor Obert had kind but exploring eyes. She reminded him of My-lo.

My-lo had started chatting to him when he first joined the graff scene, rattling her cans of spray paint and talking as she worked.

Dots were My-lo's signature. She made huge geometric shapes, straight lines, sharp edges, bold colours, but she made them with dots. It was extraordinary. Rune had watched My-lo meticulously put up piece after piece.

Just before he stopped seeing his friends, stopped painting, stopped clubbing – before he had been forced into the shape Papa had constructed for his future – My-lo had been working on a stunning mosaic near the newly refurbished Reichstag. The dome in her piece reflected not the glorious and symbolic glass of the Reichstag, but the abandoned and wasted Teufelsberg; held together by the forgotten people lost during the Cold War, it was both political and memorial. He suddenly felt the urge to see if she had completed it. What it looked like now. Where she was now, what she was painting.

He missed his old life.

After a few minutes with Professor Obert, Rune knew his dream was over.

'Rune,' she said, looking up from his letter, which he'd thrust at her by way of explanation, 'your portfolio was the best we saw – one of the best we have *ever* seen, in fact. How long have you been working on it?' she asked.

'A while.'

'Here, we've kept it safely for you. I'll show you,' and he followed her. She unlocked a cupboard and pulled out his portfolio. He tried to find some courage; he had to ask, he had to try.

'Can you reconsider?' he said. 'I mean, why was my application declined if the portfolio was good?'

Professor Obert sighed. 'Our school relies heavily on government funding. And it was made clear to us when your application came in that your studies here would . . .' – and she lowered her voice sadly – '. . . affect our upcoming bid on funding. You have a rather influential name – a father who knows many people on the education board.'

Hearing this made him feel absent; his body felt as though it were disintegrating. He didn't know what to say. Papa had known. Papa had stopped it.

Professor Obert continued, 'As I understand it, your father is keen for you to follow him, both in your choice of career and politically too?'

Choice seemed like a laughable word – what choice did he have? What choice had he ever had?

'Have you tried other universities?' Professor Obert continued. 'I'm sure they'd love you, or maybe you could get him to change his mind. Have you shown him your work?'

Rune shook his head; a small snort escaped in protest at the thought. Professor Obert was kind, but she had no idea what she was saying. He had been so careful, and yet—

'I know a professor in Kunstgut if you wanted to try there? I could forward my recommendation, but at the BAI my hands are tied, I'm afraid.'

He took his portfolio and held it under his arm; the large plastic pocket was sharp through his clothes. He hadn't tried other universities. Lotte had friends here, a school here, he couldn't wait until she finished – she was only fifteen. The police force was waiting for him.

It was over.

He thanked her for her time, and she looked sorry to see him leave, but he did, and fast.

He emerged onto the street with nowhere to go.

He gazed at his feet as they walked him through familiar streets smelling of old coins and stale beer. Familiar buildings, large and tall, held him upright. Familiar faces; a woman pushing a pram full of pumpkins in an assortment of sizes; a man staring hungrily at a lump of brown grease-dripping meat turning slowly in the window display of a rotisserie; jaywalkers and the corresponding horns of the surrounding traffic; hairspray and make-up; everyone dressed up. The street one large fancy-dress party.

Everything too loud, too bright.

In animation.

Rune was lost in the familiar, and at the same time thrown into a shatteringly present past.

THEN

Friday 6th January 1989

Epiphanie – Epiphany

At the checkpoint, guards swarmed around the car. Mama turned and told him and Lotte to stay quiet. They did, both of them watchful in their silence. The officers, wearing dark green uniforms, had guns in their belts. Many of the officers touched their guns from time to time looking all too ready to use them. It made him feel afraid. Not of the guns, but of the officers who continued to pat them, expectantly.

Mama was asked to leave the car.

'Stay here. Don't move,' she said and smiled, but her smile was scared. She took all the papers from the small bag and left the rucksack in the car.

An officer held the back of Mama's arm as she was walked through a door. The door closed and Mama was gone.

'What's happening?' Lotte asked, her thumb popping out and her eyes wide.

The taxi driver was nonplussed; he smoked cigarette after cigarette, until Rune felt sick from all the smoke. He didn't dare open the window. He knew bullets could travel through glass, but the glass between him and the officers with their guns made him feel just a little safer.

'How long will Mama be?' he asked.

The driver tapped the clock on the dashboard.

'She'll be back within the hour. Two, tops,' he said.

Rune watched the door until his eyes burned. Every inch of his body was alive with fear. What if she didn't come out? Lotte shuffled over to him and rested her head on his shoulder, looking out of the window too. Waiting for Mama.

Two hours and twenty-two minutes later, even the driver was getting impatient.

After three hours and fifteen minutes, Mama finally emerged.

She looked old. She looked scared, but mostly she looked relieved. She got into the car and the driver started the engine. Mama wound her window down and Rune felt able to do the same.

The driver passed the barrier and they were moving on. Together. She turned and smiled and breathed out a breath that made him cry.

They were across the border, they weren't going back home, and they emerged into East Berlin on a day that was blue-black with cold.

When they had run out of money, a long way still from their destination, the taxi driver stopped the car and left them with a cheery '*Zum Wohl*' before driving off and leaving them to carry all their bags in the rain.

'There's a shelter,' Mama confided after she turned around once and then again, trying to navigate the new road layout. Rune watched the traffic light men wearing funny hats change from red to green. Everything was different here.

'The phone call was to check, to make sure, but now we're here. Let's hope we can find it.'

'What happens if we don't?' he asked.

Mama didn't answer and Rune tried hard not to look at her face.

'Are we looking for your Anorak?' Lotte asked, perched on Mama's back. Rune and Mama took turns carrying the big bag, Lotte holding on like a little monkey.

'What?' Mama asked.

'Anorak?'

'Annika?' Mama smiled. But said nothing further.

When they at last arrived at a large house with a blue door, Mama wheezed and put Lotte down. The three of them standing in a row, Mama rang the bell.

He waited as the rain tinkled on empty milk bottles piled on a crate. He waited as the guttering drip-dripped water onto a wooden tricycle with two wheels. He waited as the rain splashed into an empty can on a lawn of cigarette ends.

And still he waited.

Lotte, having not walked the entire time, climbed the black railings that adjoined the steps. Rune watched her climb, holding on, then leaning back, allowing her hair to flow and swish.

He looked at Mama, her face a blurry picture he couldn't see.

Mama knocked on the door and Lotte hopped down.

The door was blue, but the paint was chipped and peeling away. Under the blue, it had once been white.

'One, two, three . . .' Lotte started to count the milk bottles. When she reached 'eleven, twelve', Mama rang the bell again.

'There are fourteen bottles,' Lotte said, holding his hand. 'Roo, what's the song with the milk bottles?'

He shook his head – 'I don't know' – and focused on the peeling door. The rain poured and he was cold, a cold that came from within and crawled around his body like veins.

He looked at Mama. She was transfixed by the door and banged on it with the side of a fisted hand.

'Yes, you do. It's where the bottles fall,' Lotte said.

But he couldn't understand her because something was happening to Mama. She started to shake while still hammering on the door. 'Please,' she whispered. 'Oh my God, please.'

And then the window to his right lit up and a face peered out from behind lace curtains. He nudged Mama and pointed to the window. A woman smiled and nodded that she was coming to the door.

'Roo?' Lotte asked.

'It's green bottles, not milk bottles,' he said absently. 'Ten *green* bottles.'

'Oh.'

He heard the key in the lock and the door opened. The woman standing there was smaller than he was. She had black hair down to her waist and wore a dark housecoat.

'Hello,' she said, her accent thick and warm, as she opened the door further. 'Do please come in, all of you,' and she smiled as they stepped inside together. She smelled like the garden in summer when the earth gets hot, and the cooking herbs could be tasted on the tongue and . . . *stink out the house.*

He wanted to prise the words, the voice, the thought from his head. He could hear *Papa.* His deep monotone voice. They had left, crossed the Wall, and his body felt as if it had walked for an entire day, yet *his* voice . . . had not left him at all.

He looked down. The woman's feet were in sandals and she had decorated toenails.

'Please.' The woman gestured a little further into the hallway and towards a sea of shoes. 'Welcome to LightHouse. My name is Nanya.' She offered a hand. Rune took it, not meeting her eyes. The touch of her hand was light in his.

She shook Lotte's hand too.

'Are you my Nonna?' Lotte asked.

'No child,' Nanya said gently, taken aback by Lotte, as most people were when they first met her, 'but you'll be safe here,' and she closed the door.

Rune gripped Lotte's hand as they stepped further into the hallway, which smelled of milk and damp leather. A huge staircase was ahead of them, with clothes strewn along the banister like bunting. A door stood ajar to the right, clothes slung over it. Coats hung from pegs on the wall, fixed high and low, like at school.

As Mama's bag landed heavily on the floor, he shrugged his off too. The woman, Nanya, was looking at Mama. Rune followed her gaze to where Mama sat hunched on her knees on the floor, clinging on to the bag.

'Mama?' He took a step towards her, but Nanya put out her arm to hold him back.

'What's wrong?' he asked.

Nanya didn't reply, but bent in front of Mama and gently placed a hand on her shoulder.

Then a noise rushed in at him, as though from a strong wind.

It came from Mama.

She howled, placing her hand on her chest, then folded over herself. She stayed there, kneeling on the floor among all the shoes, which wasn't where she was supposed to be. It took him a while to register what had happened. Was she unwell? Her head rested on her knees as she rocked herself back and forth.

The woman said nothing, her hand on Mama's back.

The strangeness of it pricked his skin like goose pimples. It swelled his mouth, numbed it, now too thick for words and too dry to swallow them. *Mama?* The noise wasn't a cry he recognised, it was something different. There was something very wrong.

Lotte shivered and sobbed next to him. He placed an arm around her and it hung heavily over her shoulders.

'Mama?' she cried and shook his arm off, before launching herself at Mama in a mess of noisy tears.

'I . . .' Mama said, and uncurled to wrap Lotte in her lap. Mama wiped Lotte's eyes and then her own on her sleeve. 'I . . .' she started to say.

'You don't need to say anything. You're safe here,' Nanya said.

'I . . . Oh.' Mama sounded as though she was hiccupping words. 'I didn't, I mean, it was the only way . . .' – and she rocked Lotte in her arms – 'We had nowhere else to go.'

'We could have gone home,' Lotte said, wiping Mama's tears with Moo Bunny's ears.

'Never,' she said, and Rune heard it. Loud and clear.

He launched himself into Mama's lap, squishing Lotte and holding on to Mama tight. Crying with her. They really weren't going back.

'Roo, you are big and heavy and squishing me,' Lotte complained.

He got up, wiping his hands shyly across his wet and snotty face.

'Mama,' Lotte said. 'When is Papa going to get here? Will he bring Home too?'

'No, Lotte, Papa is not coming.' Mama stopped, and the sentence hung in the air.

Would he come for them?

'I want Home,' Lotte said, clambering to her feet. 'I want my Papa.'

NOW

TUESDAY 9TH NOVEMBER 1999

SCHICKSALSTAG – DAY OF FATE

LOTTE

Her mind skipped with excitement as she saw a bunch of denim-clad, hoody-wearing students. Their backpacks created a wall of varying colours as they gathered at the end of the hall at the former Stasi headquarters in Zirndorf, Nuremberg. With a bit of help from the taxi driver, Stern, she had found the entrance and managed to join a group tour.

It had been easy.

A smile crept into the corners of her mouth. It really had been easy. She, Lotte, was being inde-pen-dent, all on her own.

She was handed a bunch of visitor's passes by the boy standing beside her; she kept one and passed the rest along to the girl on her other side and was instantly absorbed in the tour group as a man in front called for quiet.

Lotte looked around as the man began to speak. To the right were offices as far as she could see, and to her left were closed doors and blank walls.

The November breeze ruffled the net curtains in the office closest to her; the painted walls were a faded white, but the edges looked yellow and were crumbling away. A poster of a fuzz of kittens playing with a ball of wool had caught her attention when the loud voice of the man erupted:

'And now we shall show you how these sacks become whole pieces of paper again,' he said, as though about to perform a magic trick. 'The sacks are brought down here, one at a time, to one team. We shall take a peek in here first,' he said, leading them into a room next door that was almost identical, but there were no posters on the wall here and the room was not empty. The swarm of students gathered in the doorway like bees in a hive. Lotte joined them as they all bustled in.

A woman with a round face, small glasses and flat salt-and-pepper hair waited while the students filtered in. 'Continuing tours when we have missing documents?' she said. 'You could try helping us rather than putting us on show,' she added and then left, with a flask in her hand.

'Thank you, Pepin,' Herr Benedict said with false cheeriness as the woman walked away. Then he addressed the students. 'We've been conducting tours in recent months to try and raise awareness and funding. This is important work, after all.

'If you can all line up along the wall, so as not to interfere . . .' He pointed to Lotte. 'Come in, come in,' he said. 'Over this way, that's right – that's right.' Lotte moved further into the room and skirted the entire group, beckoned by Herr Benedict. He was almost double her size and had an enormous belly. Small framed glasses were squeezed onto high, round, flushed cheeks.

White net curtains floated around her and the cool breeze from the window fanned across the nape of her neck. She heard the gentle rhythmic patter of rain on the sill. Without the rumble of noise from the students, this would be a rather peaceful room, Lotte thought.

There was an enormous table in the centre, made up of three smaller ones pressed together. Each desk had a table mat, some sellotape, paper bags and two or three trays, which had smaller inner compartments, not dissimilar to a cutlery tray.

A young woman worked at one end with a mountain of shredded paper between two different table mats.

'No smiles today, Sabine?' Herr Benedict asked the dark-haired woman with the shredded paper. She looked up at him and then at the group. Lotte saw the minute shake of her head before she lowered her gaze.

A man on the other side of the table cleared his throat loudly. He was sitting next to an old lady, her chin resting on her chest; Lotte realised she was asleep. There was an empty table mat in the space, which, Lotte presumed, belonged to the woman, Pepin, who had just left.

'Each worker takes a few handfuls of paper from the sack,' Herr Benedict said, demonstrating with the sack on the floor between the empty desk space and the old woman. 'Then they sort through it – that's what the trays are for. They're looking for type of paper, texture, colour; whether the words are handwritten or typed, pen colour, indentations. You name it, they sort them into similar items, and once the trays are full they start to see if the pieces fit together.' Herr Benedict placed both hands on the table.

'Isolde,' he said at last, looking at the old lady. She breathed audibly, long, slow, deep; sleeping. 'Isolde,' Herr Benedict said again, more loudly this time, and the woman looked up, dazed, and wiped her hand across her mouth, surveying the group watching her. Lotte giggled and waved a hand in greeting as Isolde's wet green eyes found hers among the many.

'Isolde is our oldest worker,' Herr Benedict said. Isolde looked sharply at him. 'Our longest-standing worker,' he swiftly corrected himself.

'Indeed,' Isolde said. Her voice was raspy almost gravelly, exotic to Lotte's ears. She had never really known anyone old, and, fascinated, took a step closer to Isolde, if only to be nearer her voice. 'What is it you want now, Herr Benedict?' Isolde asked. 'Surely there are some cakes that want eating somewhere?' A small gasp punctuated the room. Herr Benedict didn't seem to hear the gasp, or at least he didn't react to it.

'Can you show us how it's done,' he asked. 'Please.'

Isolde, sitting upright, licked her lips. She looked at the empty table mat and equally empty tray in front of her.

'Here you go, Mama,' said the man sitting to Isolde's left, and he passed her his full tray and took her empty one.

'Thank you, Ralf,' Herr Benedict said. 'So, as you can see, Isolde is taking one of the sections, typeface, black ink . . .'

Isolde looked up. 'Do you really have to narrate?' she asked, with an unwavering gaze directed at Herr Benedict, who abruptly fell silent. 'I may be old, but I am perfectly capable.'

Lotte watched closely as Isolde's fingers deftly moved the papers so that they all lay with the words facing up. Isolde's skin looked like moth wings, almost papery. She looked up at her audience.

'These young people seem to have working eyes, and thinking brains too, no doubt. I'm sure they know that with any puzzle you start with . . .' Isolde scanned each and every one of them. Lotte followed her gaze, but none of the students said anything.

'The corners,' Lotte said.

'The corners,' Isolde confirmed, and smiled, looking back at the pieces on the mat in front of her. Lotte leaned in a little, to see exactly what she was doing, and saw three triangular pieces that were clearly corners. 'Then I would look for . . .' Isolde prompted, not looking up.

Lotte didn't wait for a pause from the others. 'The straight bits,' she said. It was the first time in as long as she could remember that she'd been able to answer a question posed to a group not only first, but without the others having the answer.

She thought of the long hours in the 'reading' corner of the classroom in lower school when, unable to participate in the teacher's assigned lesson, she was told as always to sit quietly in the corner and work on a puzzle.

'Then you go from the straight bits into the middle,' Lotte said boldly, watching Isolde's gnarly fingers push paper around the mat.

'Clever girl,' Isolde said, and beckoned Lotte closer to see. 'These pieces have been hand-torn, which is much easier.' She was working and talking at the same time. Her head was low, covered in downy white hair, like fluff. 'When we get the machine-shredded sacks, it's migraine season in here.' She looked at the dark-haired woman on the other side of the table, sifting through paper which had obviously been machine-shredded. 'That's very close, difficult work. For young eyes.' The younger woman smiled into the paper she was arranging.

'Hand-torn documents,' Isolde went on, 'tend to fall into a pattern. Once you have mastered one page, the others in the same pile come easier. That's why we work on one sack at a time. You can find some pattern to the individual doing the ripping.'

'Really?' Lotte asked, holding her bag, with the treasure box tucked away inside, close to her chest. Listening intently.

'Really,' Isolde said. 'You see this piece and this piece?' – she held up two bits of paper – 'they have a similar jagged edge, and voila – a fit.' Lotte took a step forward. She was next to Isolde's shoulder now and the woman smelled of fresh warm bread.

Lotte looked at the paper, but had to blink a few times as black dots travelled across her vision.

'The typewriter that produced this page had a wonky "e",' Isolde said, pointing her finger to a letter that looked like a face with an open mouth.

'A wonky "e",' Lotte repeated. She heard a few mutterings from the students, but she didn't care if they were directed at her.

She was fascinated.

She looked at the triangles of paper and saw a lot of the open-mouth letters that were slightly twisted up, where the other letters lay in a flat line. When Lotte stood up straight again, the room wobbled and she thought she might need to sit down.

She watched as Isolde tried different ways for the pieces in front of her to fit together. After a few minutes and some shuffling, Herr Benedict cleared his throat.

There were two large triangle shapes that made up half a piece of paper between them, but they didn't fit together. It was incomplete. Isolde discarded the other pieces back into the tray.

'When the workers have managed to put something together' – Herr Benedict's voice broke the hypnotic silence that Lotte felt while watching Isolde – 'it gets taped in place, copied and placed here . . .' Herr Benedict walked to the far end of the room, where an enormous shelving unit stood. 'We photocopy all completed sheets,' he continued, as Lotte felt faint. She took a few steps back to lean on the wall.

'The incomplete pieces will stay here, where they can continue to be worked on. We are hoping that very soon technology will help speed up this process . . .' But Herr Benedict's voice wallowed, as though Lotte were submerged in water. She slid down the wall and crumpled on the floor, blinking rapidly to stop the dark spots from multiplying in her vision.

'Are you okay?' Isolde asked and Lotte nodded, because she was. Her head spun, and she felt suddenly light and upturned and sick and hot and cold. She knew what she had to do.

She would put Mama's words back together. It would be as easy as doing a puzzle.

Feet moved and Herr Benedict's voice stopped.

A Mama puzzle, she thought, and faded into darkness.

RUNE

He had nowhere he wanted to go. He didn't want to go home. He pulled his bike out from the rack, put the portfolio in his bag strapped to his bike and plunged into the lengthening November day. He took Tram 12 all the way to Witzleben and then cycled the rest of the way, feeling the wind shrill and snap at his cheeks and fingers.

The wheels on his bike ground into the pavement, then crunched as pavement turned to gravel. As dusk became vulnerable to night, he cycled, faster and faster; the harsh wind bit, causing his eyes and nose to run. And something about the dusk, the scream of wind as it whistled through his ears, held him in a strange sort of limbo. Not in the past, nor in the present, but in a space where nightmare and reality overlap.

Seeing Papa's unending influence over the city had caught him off guard; he wondered if there was anywhere he was safe or any way to get out from under his grasp. The police department, the education board, the many dinners and black-tie events he had attended over the years with a variety of politicians and influencers who were knitting Germany together again. Papa had influence everywhere he went. Rune supposed, as Professor Obert had said, it was his name, his grandfather too – a judge in the federal court of justice. Großvater lived in Karlsruhe and Rune and Lotte rarely saw him; when he did come to the house, only once or twice a year, Großvater was a man who frightened Rune more than Papa did. It was in the eyes, a calculated coldness, a stillness that made Rune feel like prey to this wrinkled old man whose hunter's eyes bored into him.

There was nowhere left for Rune to turn. It was his fate to join them, another Schäffer to rule the city.

He reached Teufelsberg, sweating, out of breath, enjoying the racing of his heart. The listening tower had been built by the Stasi; it had been abandoned when the Communist regime fell, gutted by thieves in search of copper, inhabited by junkies and hippies and then left to rot.

He had come here years ago with My-lo and the other graff artists to start spraying and tagging, but it was more for practice and experiment than actual images, because although it had huge scope for art, no one would ever see it.

He locked up his bike and climbed the staircase; the night-black and crawling cold made him shiver. As he climbed the flights of stairs he disappeared into the dark and the stink of urine.

Most of the building was covered in white plastic sheeting that had come loose and whacked and flapped around the metal interior. The noise was deafening; it roared in his ears. The wind, fresh and cold, swirled around him, sprinkling him with the glitter of fallen rain held fast on the sheeting.

He found the many changes Teufelsberg had undergone through its history an odd comfort. Despite the past scarring the land, it kept reinventing itself, growing and changing with the times. He rolled a cigarette and listened to the thwack-whack of the plastic as it hit the frame. There were parties everywhere;

fireworks lit up the sky, turning the rain into liquid gold before fading back into darkness once more.

It reminded him of the strobe lights in the clubs where days and nights blurred in the fog of steaming, dancing bodies. He'd been pressed in on all sides, held and withheld, present in the single moment, immune to the passing of time. Submerged in the purls of smoke, the thick wet air, and the single beats as they pounded and bounced around the club, he became one with the dance floor. Feeling only the pulse of his feet, his breath, his heart.

He missed his life, the narrative of his choosing. He was alive, but he was far from living. He took his hat from his pocket and pulled it low over his head, then riffled through his bag and seated himself on an old hoody. With the sketchbook in one hand and a Molotow marker in the other, Rune looked into the blank page until he felt himself part of it.

Invisible.

The marker scratched across the page over and over, until the page was no longer blank, but black. Either way, his mind was furiously at work and he couldn't calm himself through drawing. He discarded the sketchbook and opened his portfolio, kindly returned by Professor Obert.

He examined every print and every sketch until the layers of night peeled back, revealing the moon as through an open hole in the sky. He reread the rejection letter; the words felt like bullet holes, fossilised wounds – a constellation of stars, and just as unreachable.

He stood at the edge and one by one threw his pictures out into the rain.

Feeling small and terrified, he could recall as though it were yesterday waiting at the bottom of the stairs.

Alone.

Waiting for Mama. Remembering the smell of her neck as she carried him up to bed, snuggling him into her body, holding him tight and safe as she soothed him with her voice, her words.

He would fall asleep holding on to her, as though he could keep her safe with his small hands. His fingers screwed up, achingly tight, to cling to the fabric of her. But waking in the night, she was gone from his bed and he unravelled.

LOTTE

'Fräulein.' A gentle shake to the shoulder roused Lotte, disorientated and foggy. 'Fräulein, wake up.'

'Papa?' Lotte said dopily and then, feeling silly, blushed. The students were filtering out of the room with shuffling feet and muted voices. She could hear Herr Benedict saying, 'Let's give her some room, shall we? Okay? Now, down the hall are the shredded film reels, photograph negatives and audio tapes . . .'

'Here.' A warm hand helped Lotte into a sitting position and a tiny glass of water was placed in front of her.

'I'm sorry,' Lotte said, as a cold sweat pricked her skin like needles.

'Oh, there will be none of that, thank you.' It was Pepin, the woman who had been cross. Her face was nice now as she squatted in front of Lotte. 'Now, tell me, Fräulein – do you have a carer or a friend with you?'

Lotte shook her head. 'I'm inde-pen-dent,' she said with a shy smile.

'That's fantastic,' Pepin smiled. 'Do you have a name?'

Lotte gave it.

'So, Lotte, what have you eaten today?'

Lotte looked from one worried woman to another. The young woman who'd been sorting the shredded paper was perched on a chair close by. Isolde and her son were at their desks, not working, but watching her.

'Ummm,' Lotte said, and tears formed in her eyes. She suddenly wanted to tell everything to these women with their kind faces and gentle words.

Instead, she cried.

'Sabine, how about we get this girl something to eat,' Pepin said, and the woman disappeared in a whirl.

'Right, do you think you can sit up on a chair?' Pepin asked. 'You'll get cold down there.'

Lotte nodded and did as she was told.

'Young girls these days,' Isolde tutted, and Lotte noticed she was working again, moving paper, adjusting, sorting. 'All trying to be too thin . . .'

'Papa said I was tubby,' Lotte said without thinking.

'You tell your papa from me,' Isolde said, 'he's wrong.'

Lotte smiled. 'That's what Roo said too.' She drank the lukewarm water pressed into her hands and took a small bite out of the biscuit that had been passed to her. She couldn't find the words to explain herself, so she focused on trying to stop her stomach from whooshing.

After a few minutes of fuss, Sabine went back to her desk. Pepin stayed close by, asking where she was from, which school she attended. Lotte gave small generic answers and after a while her attention rested on Isolde as she worked. Pepin stood.

'Do you think you'll be ready to rejoin your group now?' she asked kindly, taking the glass from Lotte's hand.

Without waiting for an answer, Pepin helped Lotte to her feet and passed her bag to her.

'It was lovely to meet you, Lotte,' Pepin said, leading her out and into the corridor. The students were now bundled by the lift. Lotte panicked as Pepin turned away.

She heard Herr Benedict's voice: 'So that concludes our tour.'

'Um,' Lotte said quietly, and Pepin turned around. 'Where are the toilets?' she asked.

Pepin pointed. 'Around the corner, second door on the right.'

'Thank you,' Lotte said, and walked away, leaving the group behind.

She locked herself in the cubicle furthest away from the door. Her mind sparked, excited; she was doing something. The bathroom floor was cold. She took off her yellow coat, folded it and seated herself, cross-legged, on the floor; she pulled off her Doc Martens too, when they dug into her thighs.

She opened her treasure box. Inside it were hundreds of pieces of paper. She carefully filtered them through the pads of her fingertips. *The puzzle women have millions of pieces*, she tried to reassure herself, *and if they can do it, so can I.*

'Corners first,' she said quietly to herself, and started searching for all the corner pieces, putting them in the lid of the box. She used a pencil to separate the box lid – one half for corners and the other for sides.

It took a long time.

As she was filtering through the box of shredded paper for side pieces, she heard the tumble of feet and voices diminishing outside the bathroom. Her head ached terribly and her tongue felt like sandpaper as she rubbed it across her dry lips.

She had just stood up to jiggle her feet when the bathroom door opened. The light flicked off and the door closed.

Lotte froze.

In the thick blanket of darkness, she felt her heart shudder. She couldn't move. She listened, but there was nothing.

Finally she took a long, deep breath and put her hands out in front of her. She touched the cubicle door, but was aware of all the pieces of paper at her feet and, unsure of what to do, nudged forward with her toes. She found the latch with her fingertips and eased it open, still listening for any sound at all.

She padded her way to the door and opened it a sliver. Night had poured into the corridor and painted it black. She listened through the door and then dragged her fingers across the tiled walls, looking for a light switch.

When she found it, the bathroom erupted into a clean, dazzling white. Her eyes slowly adjusted to the explosion of light and she tiptoed out. As soon as the door closed behind her, though, the corridor was once again black. Keeping close to the left-hand wall, she walked around the corner, feeling rough wallpaper turn into coarse paint, and finally saw the light of the lifts, still bright and illuminating the door of the puzzle women's office.

She tried the door and it opened. Although the lights were off inside, street light filtered through the big windows. There was no one around now. She stepped in, feeling bold, her heart pounding pebbles in her chest; she found the table lamps by the window and switched on one, then the other.

A yellow glow ballooned into the room and Lotte seated herself at the empty space at the large desk. Pepin's spot, to the left, was immaculate, but the others had all left something in progress, unfinished, on their mats, their trays still full.

Lotte found an empty tray in the middle of the desk and a spare mat. She copied how Pepin's desk was set up, finding the additional things she thought she would need. When her space looked like Pepin's, Lotte cautiously went back to the bathroom to collect her box.

The papers from the 'side' compartment overflowed, and Lotte noticed that although all the words were written in black, there were a few where the ink was less dense – a grey-black, rather than a thick inky black.

She found another tray and separated these pieces too. There was also unlined paper. This must be the letter that the notebook had been wrapped in. She looked carefully at the fragments. What she wanted was to bring the name Mama out from the dark, and in this enormous puzzle that was what she would do.

The box looked full of filling pieces, but, as Isolde had shown her, there was some pattern to it, and she would work it out.

She worked for hours, not stopping other than to stretch her arms and wriggle her toes. By the time her head drooped and she fell asleep, Lotte had put together an entire page.

NOW

WEDNESDAY 10ᵀᴴ NOVEMBER 1999

RUNE

He rolled a cigarette as the sun started hatching into a new day. Cracks and shards of light pushed through the night sky. He watched the sky lighten, knowing he needed to move, but unable to. The wind dropped and the streets were silent, aside from the claws and wings and snapping of small animals, beginning or ending their day. As the people rested, the city-dwelling animals emerged.

He thought of Lotte. Would she be worried he hadn't been home? That thought alone made him get up. He'd promised to explain about the Stasi, he thought, about Mama. The cold clawed into his bones and a sense of unease lapped in his stomach as he pushed off on his bike and started cycling slowly through the sleepy streets in the full tide of anxiety, back home. If he could creep in before Papa woke, maybe his absence wouldn't be noticed and maybe Lotte had forgotten his promise.

The house was silent when he pushed open the door. He tiptoed up the stairs.

Papa was in Rune's bed, his collar open, his hair sticking up on his head, an empty tumbler in his hands. The bottle by his feet.

Rune tried to back away, but Papa's slumped body woke as though magnetised to the movement of Rune's retreat. He rose up from the bed, glaring at Rune, then blinking in confusion at his surroundings.

Rune knew better than to speak first. He waited.

'Ten years,' Papa slurred. 'I have raised you on my own for ten years, *boy*.' He tipped the bottle and filled the glass, almost to the rim. 'And this—' he said, dropping the bottle to the floor, where it rolled under the bed. 'This,' he shouted, 'is how you repay me? Taking your sister out to who knows where all night? What were you thinking?'

'What?' he asked, but wished he hadn't, for Papa stood, wobbled and glared at him.

'Where is Lotte?' Papa asked, punctuating each word.

Rune turned as if to leave his room and venture into Lotte's. 'Don't act the fool, *boy*. Your sister has that role. Tell me now and I may think about forgiving your callous disregard for the rules in this house.'

'I don't understand. Lotte went to school.'

'Did she now. So why, when I called the school, did they say she hadn't been there all day?'

'What?' Something heavy sank in his stomach. 'She's missing?' Rune asked, shocked.

'Very clever.' Papa laughed and spittle ran down his chin. 'You two are as thick as thieves. So tell me, *big brother*, where is my little girl?'

He said nothing, but recalled Lotte's face with the apron of shredded paper. Why hadn't he listened to what she was saying?

'I have the whole force out there looking for you both. If you are here, then where is she?' Papa's distress came through in his voice; Rune felt sorry for him. 'Where is she?' he begged, drunken tears pouring down his face. 'Please.'

'I don't know,' he said.

The tumbler in Papa's hand whistled past his ear and smashed into the door at his back.

'Tell me!' Papa yelled.

Rune kept his silence as tiny shards of glass spiked across the back of his neck. He kept his silence and waited for Papa's fury to flame. It was in the waiting that his body loosened and slithered. Waiting for Papa to strike because Papa's every syllable lived in his hands. As Papa's fingers curled, they made the smallest of small sounds, but as he approached, the sight of his fisted hands roared and pulsed deafeningly.

The power of the pain yet to be inflicted was stronger than the remembered pain of the past.

Tense was everything because pain only existed in the present.

THEN

He woke up feeling empty, hollowed out and instantly weary. He had slept on a mattress on the floor with Mama and Lotte. It was their first morning at LightHouse. Lotte was tucked into Mama, while Rune leaned back against the wall, breathing evenly. Watching. As the morning grew brighter Lotte joined him, eyes still puffy from the 'I want my Papa' scene the night before, which had left Mama shaking and Rune angry. Thankfully, Lotte was silent now and, thumb in mouth, held Moo Bunny tightly.

The other women were gossiping, a loud mass of chatter that pressed into his ears, until all he heard was their noise, their busy, moving, doing, talking noise. They dressed themselves and their kids, laughing when bottoms bumped into each other, throwing a T-shirt: 'Just your colour, Suzi', 'Pass us the talc', 'Where's my Petra's bottle?'

Clothes floated through the air, then scattered around naked feet. The morning light flickered as the women moved in front of and then away from the small window.

Everyone was buzzing and flapping around, yet Mama didn't move, just stared into space.

Lotte crawled to the top of the mattress and started smoothing Mama's hair. She placed Moo Bunny in Mama's arms, but Mama wouldn't cuddle him. Moo Bunny was just there.

'What's wrong with Mama?' Lotte asked, scared. He didn't know what to do. His tummy was flying and falling all at the same time, and he wanted to run, but to where and to whom?

'Is that the new one?' a hat-hair-woman asked, nodding towards them.

'Yes,' a younger woman said, with a baby sucking on her booby. 'Came over the Wall, you know.' The women oohed and aahed.

'Watch your back, girls,' one said, 'we've caught a Wessi spy here, I'll bet.'

'Be nice, Ida. She's just like us,' another said. One of her eyes was cloudy blue and didn't look towards him; the other was bright and straight and sad. He looked into her one lonely eye and it made him want to cry. He returned his gaze to his feet.

'Sure, women from the West have it bad, eh? Who knew!'

'They have wankers there too,' the cloudy-eyed one added.

'She'll make it,' booby-woman said, and stroked Mama's shoulder. The baby kept sucking and her booby stretched as she bent over; the baby looked back, mouth full, and placed a hand on his mama's chest.

'It's all right,' booby-woman said to Lotte. 'Mama just needs a bit of time to settle, what with all of us noisy mares,' and she smiled, revealing bright white teeth in a neat line, almost like an advert for toothpaste, if it wasn't for three of her bottom teeth, jagged and chipped. 'Takes a bit of time to adjust,' she said, sitting back on her mattress again – the baby, settled, looked up at her as she patted its bottom – and she added, 'Nanya will come up and see you in a minute, I'm sure. We'll give you some space for a while so you can settle in.'

The women poured out of the room, taking their children and their noise with them.

Rune was left with Mama and Lotte. The stuffed-up smell of clotted air pressed tight on his chest. Mama's eyes were open, but they didn't see him. He sat back against the wall once more, and waited. Eventually the distant sounds of children faded below the sharper sounds of a single woman making her journey up the three flights of stairs towards them. Nanya came in.

She held a white cup in her hand, steam twizzling from it.

'Can I get you two some breakfast?' she asked, placing the cup on the floor in front of Mama. 'We have some Heinz baked beans? I don't know what you kids like – you're the first to come to us from the West.'

'Beans make you fluff,' Lotte said.

Nanya laughed and seated herself next to Rune at the end of the mattress. She had a freshness about her that the other women here hadn't. While they were all crumpled and off-smelling, yet sweet and hot too, Nanya smelled like mints and clean sheets. 'Something else then?' she asked.

'My bestest favourite breakfast is scrabbled eggs,' Lotte admitted quietly.

'On toast?'

Lotte nodded, looking up.

'I think we can manage that. What about you?'

But the tightness in his chest had made its way to his throat; he said nothing. He just watched Mama breathe. In and out.

'What's Rune's favourite breakfast?' Nanya asked Lotte.

'Oh, he likes the Nesquik cereal, but they are not Snap, Crackle and Pop, they are chocolate and breakfast at the same time. I like Nesquik cereal best too' – she twirled a bit of Mama's hair in her fingers – 'but not as much as scrabbled eggs.'

'What did you say?' Nanya asked. 'Can you say it again for me, a little slower?'

Lotte did.

'Oh, we won't find cereal like that here, I'm afraid. We have baked beans because one of our odd-job helpers has a son from the West, but I could do oatmeal for Rune?'

Rune found his voice. 'I don't want anything,' he said.

'No problem. Would you like to help me?' Nanya asked Lotte. 'We may even find a bit of carrot in the garden for your bunny.'

Lotte stood; her legs were bare and thin, her nightie covering to her knees. 'Can I crack the eggs?'

'And you can whisk them. You sure you don't want to join us?' Nanya asked Rune.

He shook his head.

They left the room, hand in hand, and a distant but constant buzz of voices from the house below swarmed around him.

Lotte returned a long time later with a handful of rough-cut toast, flattened by a layer of butter. She gave him a slice, and as he ate he watched her offer some to Mama, before nibbling the rest.

Lotte plucked Moo Bunny from Mama's arms and snuggled him, sucking her thumb.

Rune would have liked Moo Bunny in his arms. Like all the times, back home, when Papa shouted downstairs, Moo Bunny would cover Rune's ears with his long ones so he couldn't hear Mama's cries, and they would wait together for Mama to come back to him.

A little girl bounded into the room, her hair tied in neat plaits. She slowed as she walked over to the mattress by the window. She picked up a small rag before walking back, her eyes fixed on him and Lotte the entire time.

He watched her watching him, and wanted to shout that it was rude to stare.

Something had broken Mama and no one was fixing her.

The cup beside Mama was full of now-cold tea and he wanted to throw it at the small girl with her plaits, who had a mama who could tie them for her. He wanted to throw the cup so that it hit her and made her cry.

'Wanna come and play?' she asked in a small voice.

'Me?' Lotte asked.

'Yu-huh.'

'Can I?' Lotte asked.

Rune wanted to stop the tears burning at the back of his eyes, but more than that, he wanted the red-hot whiteness to hurt the little girl with a working-mama to go away.

'YES!' he almost yelled.

Lotte paused and Rune looked at her dirty, tiny feet.

'Roo?'

He looked up and swallowed hard. Trying to find a smile, he said, 'I'll watch Mama,' as though she needed tending and watching her would make everything all right somehow. As if she were a snowdrop emerged too early into a harsh winter. If he blew his warm breath on her tiny petals, would she survive? Would he?

On second thoughts, he suddenly did not want to be alone. Alone with Mama, solely responsible for her survival.

'Wait,' he said as they pattered away. He stood on shaky legs, took one last look at Mama. She rolled away from him and curled up, facing the wall.

It was the most she had done since he had crept onto the mattress to sleep last night. They had been shown around and Lotte's wails were muted by the wails of so many of the other children. They had been fed, but he was disorientated by the workings of LightHouse, so when they were shown to a free mattress, on a floor with three taken ones, and two bunk beds squished into the corners of the room, Rune had crawled onto theirs, like a raft in a storm. He closed his eyes and, relieved at finally being still, went straight to sleep.

Rune looked at Mama. Maybe the further he got, the better she would get. He followed Lotte out of the room.

As he walked down into the belly of the house, where doors led to a lounge, another bedroom and a brighter, louder playroom, the smell seemed to stick to him. Not warm, but suffocating. He was touched by the heat that came from everyone else, pressed close to each other and to him. Lotte skipped off with the little girl. He watched them blend in with the others. It was like being in the middle of a playground, but worse. Young children yelling, babies crying, older kids shouting, and the mamas – the mamas smoking or swearing or crying or laughing, and many doing it all at the same time.

He wanted to cover his ears. He wanted to cover his eyes, so that not to hear or see would make it not real.

They were in a house full of mamas, but his was broken.

II.

All I have is the flicker of my face in the window, a candle flame of existence that serves only to make the darkness darker.

I watch the flame gasping at air, burning low, burning itself out, dreadful and yet beautiful. It shocks me back to a memory I am unable to recall, yet can physically remember.

A flame can burn. A flame can melt. A flame.

'Your children are dead.'

And the flame touches my skin, not hot at the beginning, not a heat at all, just a sensation on my skin, becoming a deepening heat; flowering sharp, then spitting tangles of thorns. Angry. Unmanageable.

I cry out.

The flame drops away from my arm.

'Your children are dead.'

Salt is rubbed into the red weeping sore exposed by the flicker of fire.

I do not cry out.

The smell of my burning skin makes me sick. I vomit, burning inside and out.

'Your children are dead because of you.'

He sets the matches down.

I do not cry out as he rapes me.

Only when he leaves do I cry, silent, smouldering tears, because I do not know what is true. This long midnight road may never lead me back to dawn, yet, in truth, there is only dawn if he says there is dawn, there is only day when he says there is day, there are only children when he tells me there are.

I am as fleeting as the flame.

NOW

WEDNESDAY 10TH NOVEMBER 1999

LOTTE

A nudge to the shoulder woke her up. Lotte jumped and the woman behind her jumped too.

'Oh,' the woman said. She was the same young woman Lotte had met the day before, the one who was piecing together the shredded paper. She had large green eyes and dark, almost black hair that fell below her shoulders.

'You're a puzzle woman?' Lotte said, looking up and orientating quickly.

'Yes,' the woman said. Curiosity and cautiousness, both, lowered the decibel of her voice. 'But who are you?'

'I was here for the tour with the fat man, and the old woman puzzled together a page with a wonky "e".'

'Pardon?'

Lotte slowed herself down, thought about what she was saying and tried again. It was amazing how fast words seemed to want to jump out of her mouth; they rushed to her lips and then – blump – all out in one go. She apologised and tried again, slowly, carefully giving one word at a time.

'You're the one who fainted?' the woman asked.

Lotte nodded.

'What are you doing here? If Pepin saw you' – the woman looked around cautiously – 'she'd have a fit!'

'It's not what you think,' Lotte said, sounding like the television, her mouth clogged with sleep. She felt groggy. The woman stared at her with interest and Lotte swallowed, took a long breath and then felt able to go on. 'I came to find how to put this together.' Lotte motioned to the table and the trays of Mama's words.

The woman was looking over Lotte's shoulder at the papers.

'Mama sent a letter and a notebook, but it got torn.'

The woman looked shocked at the pile. 'I'll say,' she said.

'It was an accident,' Lotte added firmly, untruthfully, quickly. 'I didn't know how to get it back, but look . . .' And Lotte sat back so that the woman had a clear view of the table. Lotte had reconstructed one piece of paper – one fully formed piece – and two small fragments, both at the top and bottom of other pages.

The woman carefully picked up the formed page and held it to the light. Tape stuck out of the page at all angles, but Lotte watched the woman's eyes flash as she read.

'Did I do it right?'

The woman didn't answer, but collected the other fragments.

'May I?' she asked.

Lotte nodded.

'You've read this?' the woman asked.

Lotte shook her head. 'I wanted it to be whole first,' she said. 'You know, complete.'

The woman looked at Lotte, and the piles of paper. She pulled her chair closer, so close they were almost touching. 'Maybe I can help?' the woman asked.

'Really?' Lotte was astonished.

'I'm Sabine,' she said, and offered Lotte a cool hand to shake, but Lotte hugged her instead, tipping her chair on to two legs in the process. Sabine allowed herself to be hugged and patted Lotte's back gently. A subtle perfume of lavender held Lotte's senses as Sabine gently untangled herself from the knot of Lotte's arms.

'Thank you,' she said.

'Don't thank me yet,' Sabine said, 'I can only help until nine, when Pepin comes in. I'm not sure what she will say about all of this – there's been some issues in our little hub recently and everyone's a bit on edge . . .'

Lotte looked to the window; it wasn't yet light outside. 'What time is it?' she asked as Sabine pulled one of the trays close.

'Just after seven,' Sabine said quietly. 'I'm in early this week.'

'Why?'

Sabine looked at her thoughtfully. Lotte turned away and blushed from the intensity of her gaze; she thought she was being examined.

'We have less than two hours,' Sabine said eventually. 'Would you like to show me what your system is?'

Lotte did, showing Sabine the corners and the sides, the piece of paper that had no background lines, and the still enormous pile of centre pieces in her treasure box. While Lotte was talking and pointing out what she'd done so far, she was also watching Sabine carefully. Lotte was curious – why was Sabine here so early and why was she letting her stay and even helping her? And why hadn't she asked about her parents or a carer, like everyone else did when they met her for the first time?

The fact that she was going to help made Lotte swallow her questions and they worked together, Sabine pointing out different ways to know which pieces may fit together.

As they bent their heads to the work, Lotte realised that in such close quarters her breath must be foul, her teeth uncleaned, and her tongue sticky from lack of water. She excused herself to freshen up in the toilet, splashing water on her face and swilling her mouth. She chewed a peppermint before returning with her purple-glitter-laced shoes, her yellow coat and her bag with its dozens of bright badges, which she had left in the toilet cubicle the night before.

The sun was a bright orange ball in the sky when she returned, casting a yellow light into the room.

'Yellow is my favourite colour,' she said, admiring the glow of yellows.

Sabine had completed a page.

'Wow, you work fast,' Lotte said, seeing another page coming together.

'You have a good system,' Sabine said, and as Lotte sat down Sabine passed the completed sheet to her. 'Did you say your mama wrote this?' Sabine asked.

'I don't know.'

Sabine offered her the page. 'I'll give you some space.'

And before Lotte could say anything, Sabine left the room.

Lotte looked at the two completed sheets of paper. Her teeth started chattering. The writing was a mess of black lines and marks. *The*, she began. No. *This* Then *is*. Whole and fast, *This is*. She kept on staring hard; focusing on the letters, they wobbled and wiggled. *This is how it*. Lotte closed her eyes and opened them fast, hoping to catch the letters momentarily still, unaware, off guard, so that they might be frozen just long enough for her to read them.

On.c.e Once . . . fast. fast Ti.me . . . Liet.zen.see.

She tried to sound out the letters as Frau Anst had taught her to do. But as soon as her eyes focused on one word, a block, a single letter, it smudged, wriggled away into the next and became lost in a sea of looping swirls and squiggles.

The letters wouldn't keep still, but still she kept trying. *It was l.o.v.e love at f.i.rst . . .*

When Sabine returned, Lotte was in tears. She'd never been away from home for a whole night before and she wanted to go back now. It was all too hard.

She pressed her palms deep into her eyes. *Stupid Lotte, stupid.*

Sabine said nothing but passed Lotte a small handkerchief from her pocket, her kindness diffusing Lotte's longing for home.

'I won't pry, but I didn't want to leave you alone for too long.'

'It's not that,' Lotte said gratefully, wiping her eyes with the handkerchief. 'I can't read it. The words. Not just because I don't want to . . .' She wanted Sabine to understand.

Lotte handed the pages to Sabine. 'Please,' she said, 'can you read them to me?'

As Sabine's face registered what she was being asked, she started to shake her head. She looked at the first page. 'Maybe it's better if someone else . . .'

'No. You. Please—' She thought of Papa shredding the pages and the empty feeling of watching Roo walk away from her yesterday. 'Please,' she repeated.

Sabine took a deep breath before reading . . .

This is how it started:

Once upon a time a young man and a young woman met.

They are both jogging around Lietzensee; the summer sun is glinting off the lake. The trees are green, the sky is blue. You can picture it. It's a cliché.

His story: A beautiful woman ran straight past me, her dazzling smile momentarily blinded me, I stumbled into her and we fell.

It was love at first sight.

Her story: I was running around the Lietzensee lake, focused on pushing myself. I was coming up to another runner and was about to run past him when he stopped abruptly. I stumbled into him and we both fell. I helped him up. I even offered him my arm back to the U-Bahn — he couldn't hobble alone, and my injuries were only minor scrapes to the palms. I left him at Sophie-Charlotte-Platz. I didn't think of him again.

His story: I couldn't train for a week, I had to rest, but I limped back to the Lietzensee every day in the hope of seeing her again.

Her story: I trained as I always had. I saw him one day lazing on a bench, his injured foot stretched out over the path. So I had to go around him, or stop.

I jogged on the spot.

Their story: 'I'm out of action,' he complained, sweating slightly in the haze of the sun.

'That's a terrible pick-up line,' she said.

He blushed. She laughed at his embarrassment and stood still.

'You know I blame you for this,' he said. 'I'm going to miss the most important event of my life because of your beautiful smile. Perhaps,' he added, 'I will miss the most important event of my life for the chance of another.'

She looked at him closely, saying nothing. Offering nothing.

'Can I buy you a drink?' he said. Standing, a pained expression flashed across his face. She felt guilty; she was back to training, but their fall had incapacitated him. He did look forlorn.

This is how it started – in the Biergarten at Lietzensee, sipping Pilsner on a beautiful summer's day.

This is how it ends:

'Do you take her as your wife?'

'Yes.'

'To love, to hold, in sickness, in health?'

'Yes, yes, yes, yes.'

'And you?'

. . .

'I do.'

Lotte couldn't say anything. She looked at the pages, how neatly the writing covered the lines. How some words had been crossed through, but not many. Was this how Mama and Papa had met?

Lotte was about to ask one of the dozen questions buzzing around her head when the door opened and the main lights were switched on. Both Sabine and Lotte jumped.

Pepin, her salt-and-pepper hair tied up in a severe bun and a long knitted purple scarf hanging down past her knees, walked a few paces into the room, nodding her head and carrying a large bag, before she looked up and saw them.

Pepin looked from Sabine to Lotte to the papers on the desk and back again.

'Morning,' Sabine said.

'What's going on in here then?' Pepin asked.

RUNE

He waited until he heard Papa's drunken snores vibrate from his room down the hall before he moved. Fast. His breathing felt laboured; he rolled his tongue across the back of his teeth. Checking. His nose was clotted with blood, but didn't feel broken; his cheek swelled into his vision and pulsed painfully. But that was it. There were no other bruises. Nothing broken.

Relief started as a drip, then flooded his body as he stood up, both arms stretching, whole, unscathed. He tiptoed out of his room, trying to avoid standing on broken glass, and into Lotte's. He needed to make sure Papa's claim that she was missing wasn't just a trick.

Her bed was made, the curtains drawn. She hadn't been home.

Dragging his hands through his hair, a light rain of the shattered glass tumbler tinkled onto the floor. Where was she?

He didn't know what to do.

He felt time stagnate in the gloom. A pitch-black, fidgeting, humming darkness moved within him. What if Lotte had been taken? What if she was hurt? Lost? What if she was dead?

Returning to his room, he packed his bag. He couldn't stay still, he needed to do something, but what? He smoked his last joint out of the window, staring up at the sky for answers. The weed soothed the pain in his cheek and calmed his thoughts so they were cohesive, rather than scattered across the floor like the shattered tumbler.

He thought about the car journey to school yesterday. He couldn't remember any of it; it had zoomed past, like the scenery. And his thoughts about the day did too, its texture porous and full of loops and swirls.

Lotte had said *Stasi* and *Puzzle Women*, hadn't she? He recalled the image of Joann's car pulling away and Lotte holding a shoebox outside the school gates. His mind had been on the letter in his pocket. On other things. Not on Lotte.

He shrank within himself; his thoughts thick and slow, his brain numb. He closed the window.

Nuremberg! These puzzle women were in Nuremberg – she'd wanted to fix the letter she thought was from Mama. He couldn't think of anywhere else she would go. The fragments of his memory solidified – that was what she wanted. That was what she'd been telling him, but he was too distracted to listen. She'd wanted him to go with her. He recalled her face when she'd asked him to bring the shredded letter back . . . how she had needed his help and he had turned away.

Lotte had asked him for help, and he had refused. His skin felt too tight, constricting him. The mention of the Stasi had triggered an almost vortex effect. Associations he'd been trying to avoid had dragged him back. His thoughts had shuddered and stopped. There were no trials for what the Stasi had done to its subjects, but there was still the people's justice. A newspaper had recently reported names and addresses of previous Stasi personnel and tensions were high because it had all been buried. No justice. No closure. And Lotte wanted to dive into the midst of all that? What did the letter say that she thought came from Mama?

He heard Papa's rumble as he snored on from his own room. Rune pulled out the last of the oxycodone from his mattress and his cigarettes, and tucked everything into his bag before carefully making his way down the stairs. He slipped his coat on and dipped his hand into the pocket of Papa's jacket where it lay discarded at the foot of the stairs. He pulled out his father's wallet and pocketed over a hundred marks and his credit card.

Pausing at the door, he thought of the morning he had left with Lotte and Mama all those years ago. Mama had run out of the door.

Maybe the easiest way to leave was to take it at a run.

At the U-Bahn, he paid for a ticket to Nuremberg. He saw the navy uniforms of police officers and sank lower in his seat as the train pulled slowly out of the station. It felt illicit to be on a train. It had been a long time since he'd been free to do so. Not since some of Papa's officers had found him spraying graffiti at the back of a building and hurled him into the police station. After that, everything had changed. Rune had put away his spray cans and started to do everything Papa told him to do, including applying for the police academy. All because Papa had found a 'special' boarding school for Lotte in Hamburg.

He had been blackmailed.

Behave or you'll never see Lotte again.

Almost everyone who passed by his seat stole a second glance at his face. He pressed his cheek against the cold window. Hope seemed to control his body temperature and it plummeted in the agony of unexpressed, unfinished thoughts:

Was Lotte—?

Where had she—?

Had someone—?

What if he was wrong and she wasn't in Nuremberg at all? What if she was lost? What if, what if, what if?

An ice-cold sweat dripped down his back. He tried to close his eyes, but couldn't. He was travelling with a white-churning intensity of fear, urgency and sorrow. With his nails biting into his palms, his teeth grinding together and his tongue turning to ash in the furnace of his mouth, he wanted to be heading towards Lotte – but, perhaps inevitably, the past was ahead of him too.

THEN

JANUARY 1989

Mama spent the first three days at LightHouse on the mattress, getting up only to use the bathroom.

On the morning of the third day, Nanya led him and Lotte outside with the instruction not to come in again until teatime. Although unhappy at first to be wrenched away from Mama, Rune knew that if she was going to come back, they had only Nanya to rely upon to do it.

He and Lotte soon got involved in games with the others and played all afternoon in the bright sun to the sound of birds twittering and children laughing.

When they struggled back up the many flights of stairs, a guilty ache of a smile on his cheeks, he and Lotte found Mama dressed in a blue smock, her hair washed, a cup of tea in her hand half-drunk, and Nanya by her side, looking proud.

He had never been so happy to see Mama smile. It cracked at the edges and she was crying, but she was back. Later that same day, as Lotte slept on Mama's lap, he asked her tentatively, worried she would retreat into the shell she had just emerged from, 'What did Nanya say to get you back?'

Mama put her arm around him and pulled him into a hug. Lotte's sleepy face was on Mama's chest, mouth open, her breath sweet and milky.

'She said we were safe.' Mama looked fully at Rune. 'Do you know, the Wall was put up the year I was born. My papa always said I was born at a time when people thought freedom was something found using the feet, not the mind. My papa believed in the power of thought.' He looked up into her face. She rarely talked of her papa; Rune tried to form an image of him, but it was old and wrinkled and vague.

Mama continued. 'One night in August 1961, while everyone was sleeping, barbed wire was being stretched across our city, separating families and dividing us forever. Berlin was now two cities. The Wall – a strong and solid symbol of man's right to protect his "freedoms" – ran through the middle. Now we are on one side and Papa on the other. The Wall protects us now, as well as a big blue door, over twenty women, and Nanya herself. We are safe and we are free.'

And although slowly at first, Mama did more and more, until after just one week she was part of the gaggle of women that all answered to the name *Mama*.

Three weeks after they had arrived at LightHouse, it was a new day and their first day at school. He, Lotte and Mama were up early, yet the chaos of LightHouse never seemed to rest. Children were screaming, mamas smoking and laughing.

The radio was always on, spouting speeches from a man called Honecker. Rune tuned in to the radio as Honecker preached that the Wall would still exist in fifty, even a hundred years' time.

It is necessary to protect our republic from robbers, not to mention those who would like to disturb the stability and peace of Europe. The protection of borders is the sovereign right of every state, and thus also of the DDR.

He listened, and yet despite desperately wanting the solace that Mama seemed to get from these words, none came for him. He was now in the East and everything was different.

The steam of newly baked bread made up for the crashing and bashing and yelling that happened all around him, all of the time. The noise hadn't faded, but he had started to tune it out, taking himself deeper inside his head, away from the sound.

Lotte buttered the hard, dense dark bread – so different from home – but Rune didn't think it was bad, especially when they ate it warm for breakfast. He filled the sandwiches and Mama cut and put them in boxes with the rest of their lunch, ready for the day.

'It's a new day,' Mama said, putting sandwiches in a box for herself too.

'It's cold,' Lotte complained, her feet bare on the concrete floor.

'That's just because it's early. It'll turn out good,' Mama said, glancing out of the window. All Rune could see were the bricks of next-door's wall.

'Are you nervous?' Rune asked Mama as she was sweeping the crumbs from the table into her hand.

'A bit,' she said, but a smile lit up her face.

As they shuffled around the house, jostling for space, Mama collected all their new things. Their 'property of the state' things. They were warm, they smelled clean, they fitted him when he put them on, but they were all the same. Even though Lotte had a blue pinafore and a green one, the overwhelming colour of their new clothes was army surplus, bland, camouflage. *Universal* clothing.

Mama couldn't have been happier when she slipped on her new clothes, tied her hair back in a scarf. 'Isn't this great?' she said, over and over. Rune had dressed too, but he wasn't sure it was so great.

He felt he was missing something. The move East had made Mama come alive, but Rune felt lost and alone. Mama was becoming a person he didn't know.

Rune didn't want to miss things from home, but sharing a mattress on the floor with Mama and Lotte made him wish for his own bed and his own room with its own door. Hearing some of the other kids call him 'Wessi' and make fun of his accent made him wish for the dead arm and the physical fights with the bullies at his own school. At LightHouse he couldn't speak to defend himself because every word proved he was indeed a 'Wessi'.

'Come on,' said Mama, looking at her watch, 'let's get out of here for a bit.'

'Where? It's still early.'

'Lotte, put your coat on. Rune, can you help her with the buttons? Both of you . . . shoes.' She pointed to the sea of them, black, smart, clean, all in a line. He picked up a pair for Lotte and a pair that were his size. 'I'll be right back,' Mama said.

When she returned, she had a bag on her back.

'Are we going home?' Lotte asked excitedly.

'No.' Mama's voice dropped, flat. She opened the door without a word, and they all went out into the fresh morning air.

The sky was pale; clouds moved, long and thin like swallow wings. Swallows: birds that migrate, move from one place to another. Would that be what they did now, the three of them? Always in motion?

They walked together, Lotte nearest the garden fences, Rune in the middle, then Mama closest to the road. The same arrangement as when they'd been making sandwiches, standing at the side in the kitchen.

The roads were quiet – only a few bikes, and people walking home after night shifts. Their footsteps echoed. Mama turned many times to look behind; she was watchful, her face at first concerned, then relieved.

'It's like your own personal security,' she said.

But when Rune looked back, he saw no one.

When they rounded a corner, there was a park. Swings, slides, a merry-go-round. Rune stood and listened to the quiet. The birds waking up, the rustle of a tree, Lotte's feet, Mama opening a bag.

'Happy?' Mama asked, throwing a blanket on the hard, cold grass.

Tears pinched unexpectedly at his eyes. He nodded.

'Join me,' she said, laying out their breakfast. Warm rolls, butter, cold sausage and some pathetically thin slices of almost white cheese.

Rune swallowed down his tears. Mama was happy – he'd never known her happier. In fact, he didn't recognise her, and this was half of the problem: where had *his* mama gone? He chewed over what Mama said about how safe they were, but Mama was changing every day and every day she was moving further away from the Mama he knew.

They had been at LightHouse for three weeks – longer than they had ever been away before – and Mama talked and laughed and played with them. She had lost the jumpy nervousness that had her flitting between things and never actually doing anything; lost the stoop in her shoulders and the frown between her brows. She stopped chewing her lips and they grew larger, bolder, brighter; they even smiled widely, regularly, genuinely.

All three of them spent a lot of time with Nanya, in a cupboard that had been fondly named 'cubby' and functioned as an office. She told him a lot about 'the state' and what they, as a family of three, were going to do. Lotte would start kindergarten, he would start school, and Mama would work in a factory down the road where a lot of the other mamas sorted letters, and when she was done Mama would meet them at the gates and they would walk home together. There were youth groups they could join; leisure time could be spent in all manner of ways. Rune could become a Pioneer, take music classes, practise sports, *you name it*, Nanya said.

Mama spoke of work, listening intently as the other women talked about sifting through letters, straightening them out on a conveyor belt. Rune thought it sounded dull, but Mama seemed more and more excited. She spent many days at offices, signing forms and completing papers. It was as though she had converted and her new religion was socialism, and she wasn't alone in this belief either.

The other mamas were all broken in some way; if you looked hard enough you could see the cracks, as if their pieces didn't quite fit together. Rune tried to keep away from the other mamas, scared that his was morphing into one of them, so he would join Lotte and her games with the others, using her innocent popularity to get him involved too. They spent their days playing, Rune trying to understand what was expected of him in this new world. Mama spoke to them every evening and he was absorbed, not in what she was saying but in an energy she now possessed, an energy he had never known.

Rune and Mama ate in silence, watching Lotte on the swing. A man dressed in grey was sitting on a bench reading a newspaper, periodically glancing over at them.

When Lotte joined them for breakfast Mama was drinking coffee, and because of the pure smell of the morning – coffee, bread, cool air, blue sky – he pulled out his notebook. Fresh clean pages, ready for a fresh clean start.

Laying his sketchbook on the blanket, he heard the birds argue in the trees and imagined daisies opening in the sun. He hadn't drawn anything since they'd left home.

Sweeping a pencil across the page in a thick line, he created Mama's heart-shaped face, her hair tucked up in a bun. The wind picked up and his pencil undid her hair, allowing it to blow around her face. Her eyes were bright and bold. He drew their shape, added a hint of brown, and her eyes smiled. He smoothed out the wrinkles and worked on the lips. Added a tint of pink, but he could not make it look right. It wasn't good enough. He was about to turn the page—

'Wow,' said Mama, 'that's amazing.'

Lotte looked at the picture too. 'It's Mama!'

Rune closed his book without saying anything. As Mama packed away the picnic breakfast, he couldn't move. He didn't know what was going to happen. At school, in the West, they had learned about the East – the way people brainwashed you, told lies. Was he going to have no thoughts of his own in his head after he'd been to one of their schools?

'It's a big day for everyone today,' Mama said, sitting next to him. Lotte, on the other side, rested her small hand on his knee.

'I don't know what it'll be like,' he said, soft as the breeze.

'We won't know until we try, all of us. We all have to do today on our own. Lotte's first day at kindergarten! None of us knows what we're doing. I haven't worked since I had you and look at you, almost ten!' Mama said. She took a breath. 'Tell you what . . .' she said, picking up his pencil case. She had a black permanent marker in her hand, and proceeded to draw a heart on her palm, as small as a thumbprint, on the squishy bit just under the thumb. She blew on the ink and then pulled Lotte's hand towards her, drawing an identical heart on her palm too.

'That tickled,' Lotte said, looking at her palm and blowing it, like Mama had done.

'You?' Mama asked Rune.

He held out his hand and she drew yet another heart.

'If you are scared, if you miss me, if you're unsure, if you feel lonely, ANYTHING,' Mama said, pulling Lotte onto her lap for a hug and squeezing Rune's shoulder, 'you press the heart.'

Lotte did so. Jabbing it, as you would a button on a TV remote.

'I feel that in my heart too. We're linked, us three. I can feel you, even if we're apart. I'm never far away.'

The knot was still tight in his stomach when Mama stood up.

'Ready to go?' she asked.

'Ready.'

NOW

WEDNESDAY 10TH NOVEMBER 1999

LOTTE

In stunned silence, the page of puzzle words in her hand, Lotte looked up at the tall, straight, sharp-angled woman in the doorway.

Sabine explained to Pepin what was happening before Lotte could open her mouth. As Pepin put her bags down at her desk and took out her flask, she listened as Sabine spoke. Explaining that Lotte was here to do her own work and not get in the way, Sabine told Pepin she wanted to continue helping Lotte before the work day started.

Sabine's words were full of assurance, her voice beckoning trust; Lotte focused on her and not on Pepin's sceptical look.

'Has Herr Benedict signed off on this?' Pepin asked, nodding to Lotte.

'It was his idea. Supporting the community, rising talent, opportunities for those who may not have the same access as others. You know what he's like.'

Pepin snorted in agreement. 'What are you putting together?' she asked Lotte.

Lotte held up the paper. 'A . . . um, I don't know. A story? Mama's, I think.'

Pepin poked her finger around the loose pile of torn paper. 'You have a hell of a mess here.'

'I did two pages already,' Lotte said. 'I don't want to be under the way,' she added, aware that Pepin might say no. She'd have to go home and everything would be normal again. But then Roo wouldn't ever be happy, and Papa had shredded the words from Mama. She felt something catch in her tummy.

'You're the girl who fainted yesterday?' Pepin asked, looking at her closely, but she was gentle; there was a softness behind her stern gaze and clipped words. 'Where are you actually from?'

Lotte took a deep breath and went with as much of the truth as she thought she could get away with. She focused on making her words clear. Pepin didn't ask her to repeat anything. She told Pepin she was from Berlin; that she had been sent Mama's notebook, but it had been ripped apart and she'd come to Zirndorf when she heard about the puzzle women on the radio.

'I don't know what happened to my mama,' Lotte said calmly, recalling how she'd got there and the echo of the past where memories should live, but didn't. 'Roo says she's dead, but dead people don't send letters. This is all I have.' Lotte gestured to the paper.

Pepin took a considered breath and looked carefully at Lotte. 'Does your father know you're here?' she asked.

'Yes,' Lotte said, the lie escaping her lips before she could swallow it down. It was a bad thing to lie, but she didn't correct herself.

'I'll make myself a coffee and then we shall see what the others think before you can stay. I don't know, Herr Benedict changing all the rules on a whim . . .' She trailed off as she left the office.

Lotte turned to Sabine. 'What happens when Herr Benedict comes in?'

'Herr Benedict is on leave for the next two days,' Sabine said thoughtfully. 'Do you have a visitor's badge from yesterday?'

Lotte fished into her pocket and produced the card, bent at the edges, and put it on.

'It'll look better if the others see it. Isolde and Ralf, you met them yesterday? I don't know if they will be happy with you here. The work we do is . . . delicate,' Sabine said, searching for her choice of word. 'I think Pepin will help.'

'Why?'

'She . . .' Sabine started, and then checked herself. 'She understands what it's like to lose a mama,' she said slowly. 'She lost hers twice.'

'How can you lose someone twice?' Lotte asked, but Sabine didn't answer.

'I can help you at lunch and after work,' Sabine said instead.

'I think,' Lotte said, suddenly struck by how nice Sabine was being and she didn't look much older than Roo, 'you could be my big sister.'

'Do you have any brothers or sisters?'

'Yes,' Lotte said. 'My brother, Roo.'

'Does he have Down's syndrome too?'

'No, but he does have sadness,' Lotte said. 'I think that you are being my very best friend,' she said as Sabine sifted through the slips of paper. 'Only best friends do such nice things for each other.'

Sabine's smile was wide and genuine and surprised all at once; it made Lotte want to hug her.

'Best friends,' she repeated. 'Best friends understand each other.'

'They do.'

Sabine quietly picked up another handful of Lotte's pieces of paper. 'Does Roo know about the notebook?'

Lotte nodded and fished the envelope out of her bag. 'It's to Lotte and Rune and if I can make it whole, Roo and I can read it together and maybe . . .' But she wasn't sure what maybe led to.

'Will you read the rest to me?'

Sabine carefully picked up the two whole pages and read from the closely written words.

Nanya gave me this exercise book and a pencil and told me that this was my therapy.

The old exercise book reminded me of school, of my father's study, of his gentle worn hand on my head. Of erasers and chalk and the squeak of leather shoes as the soles rolled over cracked floorboards.

Therapy? I was repulsed by the idea. Just the word: therapy.

'Isn't therapy a two-way thing?' I asked.

'No,' Nanya said. 'Therapy is a conversation within yourself.'

'What if I don't have the answers to the questions that my unbound traumatised mind composes?' I was being petulant. Nanya drew me close.

'I shall tell you a secret,' she said, leaning forward to whisper in my ear.

The proximity to her made me feel whole, loved, new.

'The best therapists don't say anything anyway. They let you find the answers all on your own. So, here – the cheapest and best therapy one person can offer another.' And she thrust the exercise book at me. I clasped it to my chest.

I hugged her, and within the hug Nanya relieved me of the pressure of trying to hold myself together; she gave me respite from the unending job of keeping myself whole.

'You may have lived in the dark, suffered from it, but you are the brightest of lights.'

She sounded like a shaman so I laughed because her words cut close to the seams.

'Treat your words kindly, offer them light, because the light will turn your tears into art.'

'That's very poetic,' I said cautiously, but she laughed.

'One last thing,' she added as I rose to my feet. 'All the women here understand that we have to work together, with each other and not against. But we are living in difficult times and there is pressure from the state to work against each other. If you choose to use your book, make sure you don't leave it unattended.' It was a note of warning, but also a kindness. I tried to decide if her warning meant the women couldn't be trusted or if there was just one woman I should watch out for. Were the Stasi inside LightHouse too?

And chewing on her words, I left the cubby and found my children sleeping together on our mattress.

As I settle down with them, I see many of the women pull out the same dog-eared old exercise books. Some write, some draw, and it gives me courage. Regardless, I start hesitantly, as if I were being watched. My pencil pauses, holding back, in anticipation.

In fear.

I cannot recall the last time I had the freedom to write anything, let alone my own, unfiltered, unchecked thoughts. The freedom to do so is an exhilaration of opportunity, and yet what can I say? Unable for years to form my own thoughts – and now there are pages, lined, blank pages, ready, expectant, for just that. My thoughts and a pencil, alive between my fingers.

Dear Diary . . .

And I laugh – I'm fifteen again and mourning over the loss of a boy, whose name evades me now, as he asks a girl smaller and prettier than me out on a date . . . This is the power of my trapped, imprisoned voice, my words? But I suppose I have to start somewhere. I'm trying to be nice to myself, which is not something that comes easily.

'Oh, dear Diary, my heart is broken,' I wrote once, a lifetime ago. I smile. This is a good feeling: a free thought.

I try.

But the first thing I encounter is the memory of my fifteen-year-old 'broken' heart, and I want to shame her into silence. For that boy did not break my heart. My heart was not broken then. Even now, after it has been torn, shredded and pulped, I do not think my heart can break. I think of a 'break' and the break I think of has nothing to do with my heart.

My fifteen-year-old self had no idea what was to come.

My smile dies. My cheeks burn.

Heartbreak is loving a man who will take my child, my tiny baby boy, and wrap twine around his neck; heart-break is the man who will throw that twine over the pipe in the garage and . . .

Maybe, after all, heartbreak is something that cannot be laughed at.

I am telling myself this story. The me that I am in the future, a future self; and in doing so I am writing her alive, I am writing her safe. I am willing her an existence past this present. I believe myself into being. Into being more than this.

Pepin returned, her flask steaming, and poured black coffee into a little mug. She pulled out a chair and took her place beside Lotte. She grabbed a new tray and placed a handful of Mama's notebook pieces onto her mat.

'I'll only help until the others come in,' she said seriously. 'Then it's back to our actual job, Sabine.'

'Yes, Pepin,' Sabine said, as Lotte's head swam with the words. This book of words had been sent to her and Rune, but how and why? Twine? And the neck of a *baby*? Was this Mama?

And who was Nanya?

When Isolde arrived in the office, Pepin took her to one side and spoke quietly about Lotte being present during the day. Isolde took her seat and watched Lotte with interest.

'Where's the man?' Lotte whispered to Sabine and nodded to the empty space.

'I think he had a meeting this morning. He'll be back at lunch.'

Lotte kept her head down, doing exactly what Sabine had suggested she do – she worked on her pages, thinking of the words written by Mama that Sabine had read, and what they could possibly mean.

As the day wore on there was only silence around the table, a silence that felt cautious and not comfortable, as though everyone was watching the others as well as their paper puzzles.

Pepin spent a long time searching through the office filing cabinets and Sabine explained that a few documents had gone missing in recent weeks and Pepin was anxious about it.

'The thing is, it's hard to trust anyone again after what the Stasi did to us all, but we were a bit like a family. Once the files started to go missing' – Sabine lowered her voice so that Lotte couldn't quite hear what she said next – 'things changed.'

'Why would there be missing files?' Lotte asked.

'I'm sure it's just the old Stasi officials reminding us that they're watching. It puts everyone on edge. Pepin thinks someone in this building is siphoning the files out,' and she smiled.

'What do you think?' Lotte wanted to know.

'I think it's very difficult to keep track of millions of pieces of paper,' Sabine said honestly, then she looked back to the paper in front of her. 'It's annoying that they're trying to impede our work though. It's not like all the files will come together overnight anyway, so why do it? Senseless sabotage.'

Lotte wondered, as her fingers sifted scraps of paper, why the Stasi would want the files now? What did they contain that was so important?

She remembered Roo's advice: 'It's not safe for you to go there.' And wondered if he meant her specifically – not safe for her, or just not safe at all.

As she tied herself in knots, thinking and puzzling and pushing her memory as far as it would go to try and find Mama, to try and link her to the pages she had been read, the day wound on.

Everyone stopped for lunch as Ralf entered. He was about Papa's age, Lotte thought, but tall and skinny like Roo; he had big whiskers on his cheeks and small squished-up eyes. Lotte watched as he passed an open letter to Isolde, who drew in a sharp breath. As Ralf shifted from foot to foot, he watched Isolde read. When she looked up, Ralf turned on his heel and left the room at speed, upending his chair in the process. Isolde stood, but didn't follow him.

'What's happening?' Lotte asked Sabine.

'I don't know,' Sabine said.

'It's the verdict,' Isolde said quietly. 'It's not good.'

'Are you okay?' Lotte heard Sabine ask as she went out into the hallway and joined Ralf.

'A hundred marks!! A hundred marks!!' Ralf was yelling. 'That's it! Years in and out of that . . . that place and they give me a hundred marks per night, but only on nights I can prove I was there. After all I've been through to try and get some justice, not just for me but for Winola . . .' Ralf's voice trailed off as Isolde left the room and ushered him down the corridor. Sabine closed the door, ending Lotte's eavesdropping too.

Lotte wondered if Sabine had remembered her promise to help her through lunch, but guessed that Ralf was more important. Left alone in the room, she continued to work with her pieces.

RUNE

He found the Nuremberg offices with difficulty. He had to take two buses and ask for directions more than once. When finally the building loomed, large and bland, he moved towards it fast. He prayed with every step that she was inside, and safe; he couldn't think what might have happened to her if she wasn't. Thoughts, metallic and sharp, scudded across his mind.

When he opened the door, a young woman of about his age bustled out, dropping her lighter by his feet. As he handed it to her, she began to thank him; her face was blotchy as if she'd been crying. She stared at him as she took the lighter.

'God, you're a sight,' she said.

He touched his cheek self-consciously. 'Yeah, sorry,' he said, and held the door for another woman, who took the first one by the arm and walked away with her.

The receptionist took an instant dislike to him and nothing he did could change her view. He tried to smile, but the pain in his cheek must have made him look as if he were grimacing instead. She held a poker face that no amount of pleading could win over.

She was not going to let him in. Under any circumstances. There were no lost children here and he was not allowed to search the building without permission.

When she threatened to phone the police, he left. Tearing his hands through his hair, he wasn't sure what to do next. The women he had met on the way in were huddled together, one smoking in a frenetic fog and trying not to blow the smoke directly at the other; she looked like she was flapping at flies.

'I'm so sorry, Pepin. It's just what's happening with Ralf, it brings it all back, you know. I'll be fine in a bit. You go back in.'

'Sure, but—'

'Sorry,' he said to her. 'I just – I'm looking for my sister. I think she came here yesterday. She's fifteen, wearing a yellow coat and yellow Doc Martens . . .' He tailed off; he should have brought a picture with him. 'She has Down's syndrome,' he added, though he hated to do that, marking Lotte out in such a way.

'Are you Roo?' the smoking woman asked.

'Yes – well, Rune, actually,' he said, and offered his hand.

'Sabine,' she said, taking it. 'Lotte managed to stay here overnight. We're helping her with your mother's notebook.'

She was safe. He daren't exhale his relief; he was worried that if he did he would completely deflate, as though the worry itself was the only thing keeping him upright, keeping him going.

'I'll take you to her if you like. She's talked about you a lot. I'm Pepin.' Rune shook her hand too.

Pepin muttered soft words to Sabine, before leaving her outside and escorting Rune in.

At the door, a short brown-haired man wearing a dark jacket stepped up to Pepin. 'Got nothing better to do?' he spat. 'Trying to bring back the past won't change anything. We know you. We know you. We know you,' he chanted.

161

Rune pushed him aside and moved quickly with Pepin through to reception.

'What was that about?' Rune asked as he completed the form and was given a visitor pass by the receptionist, who snorted at him dismissively. He managed a full smile at her disgruntled face before Pepin took him up in the lift.

'Thank you for moving that man away,' Pepin said gently as the lift ground its way up. 'They're harmless, but they do put me on edge.'

'What was he talking about?'

'Stasi sympathiser – may well have been an old official. They used to follow us home. Mainly it's just nuisance things like you just witnessed, or prank phone calls; we used to get deliveries of things we hadn't ordered. It's just petty-level sabotage but . . .' – and she shivered – 'I don't like it.'

As the lift opened, Pepin showed him into a large empty office. Lotte's coat was draped over the back of a chair and her bag was on the floor, but she wasn't there.

'She was just here,' Pepin said. 'Maybe she's gone to lunch with the others. Wait here a minute,' and she disappeared.

Rune touched the fragments of paper in a box on the table by Lotte's coat, but, unable to keep still, he ventured out of the room, agitated. Worried. His momentary peace at being in the right place had been disturbed by the man in the doorway. The knowledge that the Stasi officials were still around to this day was unnerving.

His lack of proximity to Lotte made him feel sick. He needed to know she was okay. That she was safe. He left the office and walked softly down the corridor, peering into other rooms, hoping for signs of his sister.

The door to a small windowless office was open and he heard a tinny recording, punctuated by breaks as though it had been repeatedly stopped and then started again. Rune slowed to listen. A nondescript male voice was speaking:

'You have been here for more than forty-eight hours. If we keep you here any longer, we'll have no choice but to—'

Rune watched from the doorway as the archivist, a man wearing beige trousers with white Nikes and a white shirt, rewound the tape in a giant cassette player and played the section again, scribbling notes as the recording played on.

'Your children will be put into state care – all of them . . .' The voice had turned to steel, uttering sharp, biting words.

As the fuzzy recording continued, all he could hear was a woman crying – soft sad sobs and sniffs.

'Is that what you want?' the voice barked. The change of tone made Rune step back in case the archivist should see him.

It was when he turned his back to the recording that he heard the woman speak.

'Please, let me sleep – just a bit of sleep. Please.' Her voice was low, her accent pronounced; she sounded exhausted, as though putting those words together took extreme effort. 'Please, just some sleep.'

The tape played on.

'Answer the questions asked of you and we will consider your request. Who supplied you with the contraband material?'

There was a long pause where Rune could hear sobbing once more. A lump formed in his throat. He didn't want to hear any more.

'I . . . I . . .'

He heard the woman mumbling, then the interrogator: 'Speak clearly!'

An arm on his shoulder made him jump. 'There you are.' It was Pepin.

'Please.' The woman's voice again from the tape. 'Please. I need to sleep.'

He followed Pepin willingly, walking away from the sobbing woman. He knew this place was a bad idea. The past tugged at him. He felt the exhaustion of the woman's voice filter down the corridor and deep into his bones, a weary ache. He needed to find Lotte and they needed to leave.

Now.

THEN

MAY 1989

The sun shone down on the playground at the end of another day at school. Rune fell behind as Lotte kicked up the grass with shrieks of delight. It was the *International Day of Struggle and Celebration of the Workers*; everyone was heading out to join the march for peace and socialism. Nanya had told them that last year's march took four and a half hours. Rune suspected that workers would rather have a day of rest than a march after work.

Socialism, it seemed, was something that had to be seen from the outside. It didn't seem to matter what you thought, as long as you did what you were told. In his mind, East and West were very similar. Follow the rules, or else.

Each side just had different rules.

'How was your day?' Mama asked as he and Lotte approached the school gates. He saw two men in grey suits, one carrying a newspaper and the other a briefcase. They glanced in his direction. He tried to ignore them. It wasn't easy.

Two girls joined Lotte and they started walking ahead, leading the way. A couple of the boys from his class waved goodbye and walked off in the other direction.

Mama threaded her arm through his. 'Tell me,' she said.

Rune looked at her. She looked pale and exhausted and he moved in to hug her.

'Good,' he said. 'What about you?'

'Well,' she started. 'It's factory work,' she smiled, 'but I love it just the same. Anyway . . .' she prompted him, ruffling his hair.

'Mama!' he complained, smoothing it down again.

Lotte had now joined forces with yet another little girl and all four of them were walking arm in arm, trying to match their steps. He could hear their giggles.

'Lotte seems to have had a good day,' Mama said. 'The other kids . . .' she prompted, 'are being nice?'

'Yeah, it's not like at LightHouse,' he said, then hurried to correct himself. 'I mean the kids are nice at school.' He looked at Mama. 'Nicer. Well, they think I'm cool.' He blushed and changed the subject slightly. 'You know some kids have never been to a McDonald's and haven't watched a thing, not even *ALF*! Can you imagine!' he laughed.

Mama laughed too and hummed the theme tune of the TV show they all watched together. As Mama finished humming, Rune felt a dip in his stomach. He missed home.

'I'm very pleased you like school,' Mama said. 'Can I ask you something?'

He nodded.

'Do you really hate LightHouse?'

Rune didn't answer.

'I mean, I know it's noisy and busy and everyone's always under your feet . . .'

'And we still share a mattress on the floor,' Rune added quietly.

'Yes, that too. But is it really that bad?'

He couldn't look at her because she would see he was about to lie.

'No,' he said clearly. 'It's better than home.' And although he wanted this to be true, when he thought of home it was full of longing – for clean cotton sheets that smelled of the sun; for fresh

168

green air; for a door that closed; for space he could think in . . . All of this combined made him feel like a traitor. However much he hated it, it was better than home; it was better, but it was worse too.

They were close to LightHouse now and Rune's footsteps became heavy, slower. Any minute now and he would encounter the onslaught of noise as they collected placards and joined the district march.

A few of the mamas had disappeared over the past few weeks and not returned home. When Nanya had enquired about them she was told they had returned to their husbands, but Nanya was suspicious. After each 'disappearance' the volume of noise would increase as each of the remaining mamas tried to unpick why she had gone. Was it the Stasi? Or had they in fact gone 'home'? No amount of discussion led to a firm answer.

Rune was sure it had something to do with the men in grey that followed them all. He checked behind him and sure enough, he saw the legs of a man dip into an alcove, almost out of sight. He was too scared to ask Mama if these men had anything to do with the disappeared women.

Too scared to make it real by talking about it.

The blessing of sleeping together on the mattress was that he could hold Mama's hand all night. If anyone tried to take her, they'd have to take him too.

Lotte was waving to the girls as they crossed the road. She waited for Mama and Rune to catch up.

A man was banging on the door of LightHouse and shouting. They were at a distance, far enough away that Rune couldn't hear what he was saying.

'Papa?' Lotte said. Then started running.

Mama stopped.

'Papa,' Lotte called.

Vaguely he heard Mama whisper Papa's name, and that was enough. He set off at full speed. He wasn't sure if he was running after Lotte or towards Papa. Either way, he was running.

His bag bounced on his back; his jumper, tied around his waist, flapped like wings.

As he drew closer, he realised the man was not Papa. He felt relief and disappointment, both, and slowed down to a stop.

Lotte had reached the bottom step. 'Papa?' she asked.

The man turned to look at Lotte. Rune saw Lotte's face register that this was not in fact Papa and he walked quickly to stand beside her.

'You're not my papa,' she said indignantly.

'Nope,' the man said. 'Can you let me in, little girl?'

'Nope,' Lotte said, mimicking the man's tone, then she looked at Rune – 'I thought he was Papa' – and started to cry. Rune looked around and saw Mama approach.

Mama walked cautiously up the steps, even though, up close, the man was evidently shorter than Papa. Lotte threw herself into Mama's arms and sobbed into her neck, 'I miss my papa. I want my papa.' Mama's face was white, her lips thin and her eyes wide.

Rune looked at the man who could have been Papa and tears pricked his eyes too.

Nanya opened the door and he, Mama and Lotte slipped through.

The man shouldered the door and followed closely behind them. 'I'm here to collect Elke Stein. Elke Yolande Stein.' The man's voice was gruff. It echoed in the silent house.

LightHouse had never been silent before.

Looking around, Rune saw the women. All the women. None of the children, aside from a few babes in arms. They stood arm to arm in the doorway of the living room, the hallway leading to the kitchen, and all the way up the tall flights of stairs.

'I'm afraid Elke doesn't want to be collected,' Nanya said in her cool, calm way.

'Of course she does. Elke!' he called. 'You here?' he yelled up the stairs, ignoring all the women looking down on him. 'It's time to come home.'

Mama put Lotte down and stood next to Rune; all three of them backed up to Nanya's cubby.

'What's he doing?' Lotte whispered to Rune.

'He's come to take someone away,' Rune said.

'Why?'

'Shhh,' he said, watching the man. A dozen women were blocking his path into the living room.

'*This* is her home,' Nanya said to the man.

The man, unable to get anywhere in the house for the sea of women, rounded on Nanya instead. 'What do you know about it?'

Nanya took a deep breath. Rune noticed the women watching her, taking notice.

'I know it's 4 p.m. on a Wednesday,' Nanya said. 'I know you should probably be at work. I know that even if you work in a distillery the alcohol on your breath is not permitted, and I know that if this *scene* . . .' – she gave dramatic emphasis to this word – 'should find somewhat unsympathetic ears . . .' Nanya had his attention and she continued, gently taking him by the elbow to lead him out of the house. 'It's one thing to have a wife leave you . . . but to be beating up your own mother? Can't imagine that would look too good for you . . .'

'Who are you, eh – the people's police?' he asked, but his voice wavered.

'It wouldn't look good in your file, though,' Nanya continued. 'Life's much harder if you're written up as having *questionable morals*.'

The man scratched a rough hand over his stubbly chin. The action reminded Rune of watching Papa in front of the bathroom mirror, before he foamed up his brush to shave.

The women were all silent. Waiting. The babies stared, wide-eyed.

'I know you're here, Elke,' the man called over Nanya's head. 'I'll be back.' And he left, slamming the door as he went.

Nanya went to lock the door. Once the chain had slid across and clunked into place, an enormous caterwaul of noise erupted, like a Mexican wave. The women whooped and laughed; the babies screamed at the sudden change of tempo; and the patter of children's feet grew into a rumble as they cascaded down the stairs.

A small voice shouted above the din: 'Has he gone? Has my husband gone?'

Nanya found the woman called Elke and put an arm around her shoulders. She must have been close to sixty years old. Her bright white hair stuck up in tufts so that she looked like a bleached rag doll.

'It wasn't your husband,' Nanya said gently.

'My son?' Elke shivered and stumbled slightly. 'I'm so sorry.' She looked around as Nanya gently steered her past Mama, Lotte and Rune and into the cubby.

Later, after the march, Rune's head was still spinning at the number of people he'd seen, his ears full of talk and speeches on a podium, the shrill hum from the speakers vibrating in his ears. He twisted a synthetic red carnation between his fingers; it was the symbol of the workers, Nanya had said. It didn't really look like a carnation, but frayed fabric glued into a plastic green stem. Like everything else, it felt badly made and worn out, even though he'd received it only that day. He passed it to a toddler, who was eyeing up the snacks Mama had laid out for them.

He and Lotte dug into the chunks of bread, cheese and ham at one of the kitchen tables, Lotte resting her sore feet on his legs.

'Why do they call that man her son?' Lotte asked.

It took Rune a while to recall what she was talking about, and then he remembered – it was the man who came for Elke.

'Because he is,' Mama said, standing elbow to elbow with booby-woman, preparing a meal together.

'Like Roo is *your* son?' Lotte asked.

'That's right.'

Rune could see Lotte consider this as she rolled the heavy black bread into small doughy balls before popping them into her mouth.

'No,' Lotte said. 'That was just a big *man*.' She said the word in disgust, which made Rune smile.

'I'll be a man when I grow up,' Rune said to Lotte.

'But not like *that*?' Lotte argued.

He let her words sink in and they started turning and turning until they whirled around his head like a propeller. Would he turn out to be a man like that – a man like Papa? Was the future mapped out already? Boys grow to be like their fathers, no? Elke's son evidently had.

The thought made his stomach contract.

Later, on the mattress, Lotte leaned close to him and whispered, 'Can you stay being a boy?'

He looked at her askance.

'That man, earlier, the "son". I want you to stay good and be nine and be a boy.' She wiped her nose on her sleeve and cuddled Moo Bunny under her arm. 'Will you promise?'

Rune listened to the knotted words, confused, but nodded.

'Promise – you won't ever be a . . .' she stuttered. 'A man,' she said.

'I promise not to be a man like *that*,' he said as solemnly as he could muster. Lotte put her thumb in her mouth and curled into a ball on the mattress.

'Maybe you could be a man like Papa instead?' she offered.

Rune said nothing.

There was nothing to say.

NOW

WEDNESDAY 10ᵀᴴ NOVEMBER 1999

LOTTE

Isolde collected the completed pages from all the desks in the office to photocopy.

'Go along to lunch with the others,' she told Lotte. 'I can copy yours too, if you like?'

'Oh no, that's okay – I don't need them copied.'

'They're easier to read once they've taken a turn through the copier,' Isolde said. 'The tape becomes invisible and it makes the words join up better. It's easier on the eye, I promise.' Isolde's breath was coffee-bitter and lipstick-sweet at the same time. 'You're very brave,' she said.

'I am inde-pen-dent,' Lotte said emphatically. She had one piece missing from the ninth page she had completed that morning, four of which Pepin and Sabine had helped with. 'Can I bring this one in too?' she asked.

'I'll be in there for a bit, third door on the right, when you're ready,' and Isolde left Lotte in the empty office as the door hushed closed.

When the final piece came into place and Lotte had taped it together, she took it with her other completed sheets into the photocopy room.

'Wow,' Isolde said when Lotte handed over her sheets, 'you work fast.'

'People say I'm *high-functioning*,' Lotte said happily, repeating the words Frau Anst had spoken many times to her. '*High-functioning* is a good thing for me, I think, but maybe other people just have low ex-pedi-tions.'

Isolde laughed. 'I didn't think I could find it in myself to laugh today,' she said, but tears formed in her eyes.

Lotte was unsure of what to say. 'I'm the only one with Down's syndrome at my school, so maybe people don't really know what I can do. Everyone is different, after all.'

'They are indeed,' Isolde said, 'but I have a feeling that you, Lottechen, are very special.' Her skin was soft and cool – like silk, Lotte thought, as Isolde touched her gently on the cheek.

'Is Ralf going to be okay?' Lotte asked.

'Yes,' she said. 'I think so.'

'What work are you doing?' Lotte asked, watching the copier spit out completed pages of the morning's work.

'I've been working on a surveillance case,' Isolde said, stuffing her tissue into her sleeve. 'One family – normal East Berliners, suspected of negative attitudes towards the state. Their entire life was infiltrated. I mean, as simple as a child picking a flower from the ground is documented and reported upon. How the mother hugged her children. It's as if it were code for something more sinister, and yet it couldn't be any more normal. It's dull work at times.'

'Why did they watch people like that?'

'That's just what happened. No one trusted each other, and the Stasi were everywhere. Eyes and ears. Nothing you said was safe and no one you talked to was to be trusted. Even within families, and they had a way of getting to the weakest part of you and playing with that to get what they wanted. In the case above, they went after the children.'

178

'That's bad,' said Lotte. 'How can you help each other when you cannot do trusting? Bees all have to work together as a col-on-y to survive.'

Isolde nodded. 'Exactly. Most Ossies – that's East German people,' she added, checking Lotte's confused face, 'felt very alone and very scared.'

'Always?'

'Yes.'

'When I feel alone or scared, I think of Roo. I trust Roo very very much.'

Isolde smiled warmly.

'What else?' Lotte asked, watching the machine churning out its paper.

'Even after the fall of the Wall, the Stasi kept working until January 1990 – I've been dealing with the case of a Stasi informant who was disappeared. If the Stasi couldn't rely upon someone to keep quiet, then they would make them.'

'How?'

'Hohenschönhausen, or many other prisons like it. I've been working on the pages for months now.'

'But informers are bad people, telling lies about other people and people they are supposed to love. They should be in jail.'

'The Stasi destroyed so many lives, Lottechen. The informers were informed upon too. They can't lock everybody up, can they?'

Lotte watched Isolde change the paper. How many people were bad, she wondered? Everyone? But not Roo and maybe not the puzzle women either. But then Sabine said that files and pages had gone missing *inside this building*. Was missing the same as stealing?

'What happens after you finish the pages?' she asked.

'We send the copies upstairs, where they get added to a file if the item relates to someone who's already on record, and if not they start a new one.'

'Who are the files about?' Lotte asked. 'Was it just the criminals?'

'Heavens, child. The Stasi had files on just about everyone.' Isolde smiled, and added thoughtfully, 'As many files as bees in a hive.'

'Really?'

'Probably more.'

Lotte thought about that. All the files were people and all the people were talking about each other or being talked about and all the words were being typed up and then all the files were shredded and now all the paper was being put back together. It sounded like such a waste of time. Why couldn't people just be nice, she thought, as Isolde removed her sheets from the copier tray. 'It's all yours,' she said, and Lotte lifted the lid of the copier, where she found a single sheet of paper still on the glass plate. Holding her own pages tight, she followed Isolde back to the office.

'You left this behind,' she said, holding up the page.

Isolde frowned, cracking the pale skin on her forehead. 'Thank you,' she said. 'Just leave it on the desk.'

'Isolde, can you read this to me?' Lotte said, thrusting her own reconstructed pages at Isolde with a confidence she didn't feel. 'Please.'

Isolde lifted the sheets, took a measured look at Lotte, then said: 'Sure.' She sat down and carefully held the paper up to the light.

'Would you like to sit . . .?' She offered the empty chair. Lotte did, and shuffled closer to Isolde, feeling her breath tickle her cheek as she spoke.

Isolde's voice was whispery thin:

In honour of the woman who left.

When life changes, the mind becomes free of its cage, the tongue acting like a key, unlocking, opening, permitting the sky to become a blank page on which to write, to fly.

I have found freedom at LightHouse, I have friends. A concept that feels alien to me.

But now I can see the cage, the key is to speak it. To hear it spoken aloud, and at LightHouse there are so many recently escaped. We have become free as a group. Not just 'I' alone, but 'We'.

When life changes, the mind that was once so lonely, so unsure, finds company. Listens. Finds heat from the blackened summer streets of a shared past. Shared with other women, who laugh at what happened, laugh at how life offered them a hand that fisted. Laugh at each other and all the new things they've started to do. And in that laughter, through the tears and the words, there is something shared. Something softened, melted away. For this is not all my fault. It cannot be – when so many others are here too.

When life changes, I can see how violence cuts the fruit, splitting, splicing, open, but it does not spoil. For in the wreckage there are others. And at LightHouse there is noise. Consuming, overwhelming noise that drowns out the thoughts that aren't my own, the seeds that he planted, making his thoughts mine. They cannot come to the fore, because in this mass of female noise, womanly heat and power, there is no room for him. None. At LightHouse, he has gone.

When life changes, I remember to write light into the room and poppies into the field, because with women who all share the same name, we are flowers upturned to the shabby sun, burying our secrets in the earth.

Here we are all called Mama.

'There's a small note at the bottom,' Isolde continued.

It took me almost a week to write that out, but I keep thinking when I was back there, when I was trapped in a marriage, I had no concept of what leaving would look like. What living would look like.

Life can change in a day; every day there is a choice and life, free, may look like chaos to an outsider. But to me, living free looks like love.

Isolde looked up as Sabine walked into the office.

'Look who I've found,' she said as Roo stepped out from behind her and into the room.

'Roo!' Lotte said, jumping up and running over to him. He held her so tightly she was sure she would be as flat as a pancake when he let her go. He said some lovely words – he missed her, he was so worried about her, he was so sorry for not listening.

He was the best big brother ever. Eventually she let him go and stared at his swollen eye, his bruised cheek. 'But, oh, what did happen to your face?' she asked.

'A door,' he said, glancing at the others in the room.

'This is the puzzle women and Ralf.' Lotte pointed each of them out to Rune.

Pepin smiled at Roo. 'Your face looks bad – do you want some ice?'

'It's okay,' Lotte said before Roo could say anything else. She left Roo's side and went back to her seat next to Isolde. Roo stood in the doorway, looking big and tall and lost. 'Our house is bad sometimes. It wakes up and moves things around so Roo is always tripping and bashing himself.'

Isolde nodded and looked at Rune.

'The house doesn't ever do that to me. I think it's because I talk to it nicely,' Lotte added, reassuring Isolde. 'I believe in magic, but Roo doesn't.' She turned back to Rune. 'Mama wrote about a place called LightHouse – do you know where that is? I think we were with her,' she added, her voice trailing off as she looked at the page Isolde had read.

RUNE

'I'm sorry, Lotte,' he said, not wanting to interrupt her. He didn't want to explain why in front of all these people, 'but it's time to go home.' He tried to say it quietly but everyone was listening. For something to do, he picked up her coat from the chair and wrapped his hands in it.

She held on to the old lady's hand. 'No,' she said. 'I'm not done yet.' And she stood to show him her tray. 'We have to know what Mama wrote to say to us, Roo, we do.'

He watched her silently for a while and waited.

'I can do this inde-pen-dent-ly and I am not going home until it is done,' and she was very clear. There was nothing he could do, he knew, when she'd set her heart on something. She was staying.

When he said nothing, she seated herself in her chair with her back to him. He watched her head bend to the task of shuffling through the torn scraps of paper. He watched her concentrate on piecing together the fragments, and understood it was much more than a simple puzzle to her.

There was no way he could take her away from this, but . . . He felt suspended in the doorway, unable to sit next to her, unable to be part of the process, because he knew how it ended.

The voice on that recording was a doorway to the past and with it the certainty that he was responsible for Mama's death. The official line was that the Stasi had 'disappeared her' but he'd been there, and it wouldn't have happened without him. Rune had made her death inevitable, even if he hadn't killed her himself.

How was he ever to explain *that* to Lotte?

He didn't want to see Lotte's face when she ran out of the notebook entries. When the reality of death and the beginning of grief began for her. And the questions that began with 'how?' started.

If Lotte too knew what he had done, would she be able to understand? He wasn't asking for forgiveness – he could never forgive himself. But for Lotte to look at him differently, that would destroy him.

'Sit with me, Roo,' Lotte said, and pulled over a chair. With no choice, he folded her coat back over her chair and seated himself alongside her. At least he was next to her and she was safe. She shuffled closer so they were touching. 'These pieces,' she said, offering him a small envelope with white paper inside them, confetti strips of paper, 'these pieces are different from Mama's writings. Do you want to fix these?'

'Where did they come from?' he asked as Lotte showed him half a page taped together.

'Mama, silly,' Lotte said. 'It came in the post to Lotte and Rune. Rune and Lotte.'

'How did it end up like this?' he asked, filtering some of the fragments in his fingers and listening to Lotte, the way he should have done the first time.

'I was Stupid-Lotte and I forgot my thinking head. I didn't hide it well and Papa tore it all up.'

'Are you sure it was from Mama?' he asked.

'Yes,' she said, and he watched Lotte show him what to do. He tried to keep his eyes down, worried that the other women were looking at him. But after ten minutes he caught a glimpse of Lotte working: she made it look easy, piecing the strips together, matching torn edge to torn edge.

Pages that were from Mama. It was impossible, and yet . . .

After an hour, he had four corner pieces and a few sides; after two hours, he wondered if there was an easier way. He had made almost no progress. The pieces wouldn't go together. The writing torn up was impossible to match together to form words.

'Can you show me again?' he said. 'I can't do this very well.' Maybe because Lotte was looking at edges and not at the truncated words, she found this easier.

She moved closer and smiled. 'I like having you here with me,' she said. 'I like helping you too,' and she righted some of his pieces and gave him four distinct sides before going back to her own space.

He kept trying and trying and, as time ticked by, he found the constant scratch of sellotape and piles of pages accumulating next to Lotte infuriating. All he had was a whole sentence, which could have come anywhere in the page:

I have had to clear out some items that belonged to

That was it.

'You are making cross breathing,' Lotte said to him as he leaned back into his chair in frustration, a fine sweat prickling at the nape of his neck.

'And you are extremely good at this,' he said. 'I don't think I can do it at all.'

'It's okay, you do *everything* better than good,' and she smiled and leaned in front of him to make some changes to his strips of paper. When she leaned back, he could see two more sentences. He didn't want to feel shocked by her ability; he was astonished and completely in awe of her. If it wasn't for her, he'd have given up hours ago. But in less than a minute she had made a sentence *and* an entire paragraph:

> *I have been away for some time and so LightHouse has closed.*

> *If you want to come and collect the other items you would be welcome. The telephone number is above so we can arrange a day that suits. I think of you both often. I have included your mama's notebook for now – I hope it finds you both well.*

He didn't need to find the name at the bottom of the letter, but once he had started looking for it, he placed the two halves together.

> *Nanya.*

He hadn't thought of her in a long time. Her cool hands, how she held him without touch, how her silences allowed him to think, to find his own truth before she offered him hers. The only woman who knew Mama, beyond the weight of that one name.

Nanya.

Lotte stood and shuffled her pages over to Isolde. They started whispering in the corner of the room. Was it worth it, he wondered, was it worth knowing the truth for the pain that would follow? He would give anything to forget and yet Lotte was doing everything to remember.

'Can I borrow you for a minute?' Pepin called to him, and Rune was grateful for the interruption, both to his thoughts and the impossible reconstruction.

'Sure,' he said. 'I don't think this task suits me very well.'

'She's a natural,' Pepin said, nodding her head at Lotte, who was absorbed in Isolde's words as she read from the pages once more. Rune wanted to plug his ears so he wouldn't hear, wouldn't have to go through the loss again and again. He didn't want to hear what Mama had written; living through it once was enough.

'Would you like a coffee?' Pepin said. 'I've just put the pot on.'

Suddenly aware of tears forming in his eyes at the simple kindness offered to him, he cleared his throat and followed Pepin out.

The staffroom was empty, but a similar size to the office. A long table with chairs either side went down the middle of the room.

'I'll get some ice for your eye,' Pepin said, taking down a mug.

'No, I'm fine,' he started, but she pulled out a tray of ice cubes from the freezer and wrapped them in a small blue cloth.

'It'll help the swelling and get the bruising out. It looks bad.' Pepin's hand covered his as she directed the ice over his cheek. It smarted as the chill penetrated his skin, then started to numb, which felt better.

'It wasn't a door, was it?' she asked with her back to him, pouring black coffee into white mugs.

He shook his head as she offered him milk and sugar. He added two spoons of sugar and stirred slowly. He couldn't articulate that Papa had hit him; it was better that Pepin think he got into a fight with a friend or something. She allowed him time to answer, but he remained silent.

Eventually Pepin spoke. 'Lotte is very good at this,' she said. 'Give her another day and she'll have completed the whole notebook. If she was a bit older, Herr Benedict would be jumping up and down trying to hire her.'

Rune smiled.

'My mama had Down's syndrome,' Pepin said, blurting out the words. 'She found it a great comfort when she could achieve things, when something came easily.'

Rune looked more closely at Pepin, at her salt-and-pepper hair, her stern face. He realised that she held herself like he did. Completely locked away from others. The recognition of this stunned him slightly.

'I have never told people about my mama,' Pepin continued steadily. 'She's dead now and I wish I had, so I could talk about her more.'

'When did she die?'

'Only recently,' Pepin said, sipping her coffee. Rune followed suit, giving her time.

'I'm sorry about your mama.'

'I'm sorry about yours.'

'Lotte's here looking for memories, to understand what happened, but in all honesty – all I want to do is forget.'

Pepin placed her cup down.

'I mean, forget what happened, not Mama of course, but . . .' He held the ice away from his cheek, but realised he might cry in front of Pepin, with her kindness and the shape of her loss that looked a little bit like his own. He placed the ice back on his face.

'Can I ask you something?' Pepin said. 'You don't have to give me an answer now, but I want you to know it's an option. From the pages Lotte has reconstructed, it looks like your mother lived in the DDR for a time. We may have files for her. Would you like me to look?' She paused, but the look on his face must have given away his horror. 'I mean, for the future, Lotte may want to know more than the notebook can offer her. The Stasi were notorious note-takers. There may not be much, but it might offer her some comfort.'

He imagined Lotte taking comfort from the men who had followed them, from the men who had taught him at school, from the great socialist nation. If she could get more information, more hard cold 'facts', from them than from him, then surely he was failing her.

But the very idea of talking to her about what happened made him feel cold. He lifted the ice pack from his cheek and placed it on the table. The cloth fell open and he pushed the small cubes of ice around with his finger.

'You don't have to give me an answer, we may not even have the files, but I wanted your permission to check. I didn't think it's my place to offer this to Lotte. You were older and probably . . .'

'Remember?' he said slowly. 'I do, but I don't know what to say, how to tell her. She knows Mama is dead, but what happened, I . . . I don't know.'

'That's okay. I understand.' And she did, Rune thought, she really did; this woman had had a mama who might well have been just as sensitive and gentle and loving as Lotte. He felt a mild surge of jealousy.

'What was your mama like?' he asked, changing the subject.

Pepin smiled and it changed her face; her eyes brightened and grew wet as she spoke. 'She was extraordinary,' she said. 'A bit like Lotte – she loved colours too. We collected colourful things every day. We lived together inside a rainbow. They were my happiest memories.'

'It must have been difficult too,' Rune suggested gently.

'I was taken away from her when I was little,' Pepin said briskly, her face guarded and closed again. 'I was raised in a foster home until I was twelve. I ran away and found Mama. I was with her every day after that. We were inseparable. I don't know what it would have been like to have had a young childhood with her, but she was the most wonderful mama. Honestly.'

'I find it hard when people think Lotte can do nothing. It frustrates her but it drives me crazy. I've always said she's more than the Down's syndrome and she proves it every day.'

'And your father? Does he agree with you?'

The ensuing silence was punctuated by voices from the office next door. Rune thought long and hard, about Papa, about Mama, and mostly about how he was going to protect Lotte from Papa. Because *the house* was only hurting *him*, but when he was at the academy it would surely come for Lotte, and without Rune to get in the way . . . He couldn't think about her getting hurt.

When Mama was alive, when they lived with Papa, he would hear her telling the same lies, the same stories about how she'd got hurt. And now it was him, lying to Lotte – living with lies.

But Mama had left, all those years ago, and in doing so she had shown him there was another way.

Maybe there was still another way.

'How long would it take to see if there were files on Mama?' he asked.

THEN

July 1989

'What's wrong?' he asked Mama. She had interrupted his home-work, laying a hand on his shoulder while he coloured in his peri-odic table. He was on the bed, his textbook perched on bent knees, his back against the wall. One of the toddlers had crawled over him and was rubbing toothless gums on the strap of his bag, leaving a long stream of saliva from chin to Lotte's *Soldier Heinz* book.

Mama waved a key and put a finger to her lips, which seemed like a crazy thing to do, because although the light was dimmed, the noise of bedtime hassles flooded in from every room. Their mattress was on the top floor and the heat of the day, the heat of the house and the restlessness of its inhabitants bled remorselessly into the atmosphere. Some of the mamas were talking about dem-onstrations at Alexanderplatz in protest of vote-rigging and how many police had been deployed to break it up. Rune felt as though he were breathing inside a box.

Mama pointed to Lotte, fast asleep on her tummy, Moo Bunny in the crook of her arm and hair across her face. She nodded to the doorway.

'Want to come and see our new house with me?' she asked.

'What?' He plucked the toddler from his bag and placed his book carefully inside.

Mama nodded excitedly and handed him a key. 'You won't need that,' she said, pointing to the bag. She lifted the toddler up before it was able to crawl over Lotte and wake her, and perched it on her hip.

'I've asked Nanya to watch Lotte,' Mama said, looking around for a mama to hand the toddler to. She finally passed it to a woman on the mattress closest to the door, who was feeding a bottle to a tiny baby and dozing as she did so. The toddler crept into the crook of its mother's arm and plucked the bottle from the baby to suckle on itself.

A caterwaul of noise erupted.

Lotte snored on.

'Come on, just you and me,' Mama said.

Rune didn't want excitement to bubble, because he knew that as soon as it did, something would burst it and everything would be worse afterwards. The opportunity to be with Mama, all on his own, was luxury enough. She could be taking him to see a patch of grass and he would grasp at it. His legs felt as though they were made of water as he stumbled down the staircases after Mama.

She held his hand as they opened the big blue door. It wasn't yet dark and they followed the sunset. The sky was raw and pink, tinting the windows and dusting the concrete buildings in firelight.

Mama was talking, her voice bouncing: 'a flat, furnished, two bedrooms, around the corner, garden . . .' Her words were a stream of excitement; she was smiling, Rune noted, and he tried to keep up with her as they crossed the street and turned right. She was excited and every word was catching Rune in a web of anticipation.

He had nothing to relate her words to, not here in the East anyway. He visualised what the new home would look like, but the images were from home, from the West, and he had discovered nothing in the East was what he imagined it to be. He kept a careful smile on his face and observed Mama.

The idea of his own space, his alone, made the blood beat loudly in his ears. A space that was just for him and Mama and Lotte, a place where they could get a radio, maybe? And he would be able to hear it because the only noise in their house would come from them.

The pavements echoed their footsteps as they rounded another corner. The buildings on this street all looked the same as each other, but Mama pointed one out.

'Ours,' she said, and suddenly it stood out.

Ours.

The first *something* that could be claimed, could be owned, could be theirs. He walked faster, eager to see, to really see if this was real and true and 'ours'.

'Ground floor,' Mama continued. 'We even have a small garden.' She took the key and placed it in the lock. It clunked heavily as she turned it and pushed open the door. The flat looked shadowy, foreign, lived-in, and smelled of someone else. Mama slid her hand along the wall and felt for a light switch; it clicked on, washing the room in a yellow warmth.

'Who else lives here?' he asked, seeing a coat hanging on the rack and furniture in the darkened living room at the end of the corridor.

'No one – well, not any more. We'll need to clean it up a bit,' she said. 'They told me the previous tenant left in a hurry. The good news is that we can move in as soon as we're ready.'

'Move in here?' Rune walked around the living area, taking in the shocking sight. The flat looked as though it had been trashed – beige chairs upturned, beige and orange cushions scattered with their innards bleeding out white foam. The brown table lay on its side, a huge gash through the centre of it. Orange lamps had overturned. A brown and orange rug had been rolled back.

His new friends, Aaron and Inga, twins he'd first met when he joined the Pioneers and had sat with in every class thereafter, told stories about people who were 'disappeared'. This mess looked like the images they'd painted for him of the people who vanished in the middle of the night. Mama always seemed quite happy when she thought these men were following her, and he couldn't tell if she was doing it to try to put him at ease, or whether she genuinely thought it was a good thing.

Rune stepped carefully, following Mama into the small kitchen. Some of the doors were hanging off the cupboards and there were packets of food and tins visible inside.

Mama breathed deeply and placed her hands on the worktop. 'What do you think?' she asked.

This was everything he had wanted, but it felt like it belonged to someone else. A second-hand homeliness; second-hand fear.

He wanted to know how she'd got it, what had happened to the person who'd lived here last, for them to be able to take it as it was.

'Does it have . . . bedrooms?' he asked instead.

Mama smiled and led him out through the living area and towards another small white door. There were two doors to his right and one to the left.

'One for you,' she said, opening the door to a small room with a single bed.

The mattress had been upturned and leaned against the frame at an angle. There was a small set of drawers with a shade-less lamp on top, and beige curtains hung limply on rails that had come away from the wall. Through the curtains, he saw outside. Stepping closer to the window, he could see a patch of grass, a small paved area and a raised flower bed. It was a garden surrounded on every side by a tall, sun-bleached grey fence.

Mama stood at his shoulder. 'Come on,' she said, and took his hand. 'There's more.'

The bigger bedroom opposite had a wardrobe and a double bed. 'For Lotte and me,' Mama said. This bedroom was in similar disarray.

The bathroom was small and basic and brown; a bare bulb hung from the ceiling and grey toilet paper was threaded on a string. *Neues Deutschland* lay stacked on the floor. It was the only room in the flat that didn't look as though it had been upended.

'A bathroom, just for us,' she said, as if this was the pinnacle of luxury.

There was a small door at the end of the corridor; Mama had to search to find the key and struggled to open the door out onto the garden. The end-of-day heat held the aroma of the other occupants cooking dinner. It was a comforting smell. Fresh, nourishing. Rune breathed in the scent of herbs and roasting meats and tears welled in his eyes.

Mama spun around, her blue smock rigid around her legs. 'It's ours,' she said. 'Look,' and she fingered some of the foliage flowering in the patch of dirt. 'We have carrots, onions, potatoes . . . I think.' She gazed intently into the pattern of large green leaves. 'I don't actually know,' she admitted, 'but we'll eat it anyway,' she said and wrapped him into a heat-hot hug. 'And you're not to worry. I want to tell you something that you are never to tell your sister, can you do that?'

He nodded.

'The Stasi, the government here, they protect us. They will always protect us.'

'I don't understand.'

'You remember I took Papa's workbook when we crossed? That's what allows us to stay and to have a house and a job. So you mustn't worry – the people who follow us are doing so to keep us safe. You'll see. I promise it'll be okay.'

That's all he kept thinking as Mama took them back inside and locked the back door – the key seemed sticky in the lock and the door had expanded in the frame, so Mama had to push hard to close it. *It'll be okay.* He didn't understand how something of Papa's could protect them here – and how could Mama be working for the government when the government made people disappear?

She locked the front door and they walked the long way back to LightHouse. The sky turned into a bruise of purples and blues and the silence stretched between them until he could almost hear it. It was strange to be going back to LightHouse, knowing it would soon be over, for another page to begin, for another start.

It'll be okay, he thought as the full force of LightHouse hit him on their return and Mama was lost in a sea of other mamas.

It'll be okay, he thought as he lay next to Lotte on the mattress and with practised breaths tried to extinguish the fire-flames of noise as they popped and burst and surged around him.

He touched Lotte's dirty foot and closed his eyes.

It'll be okay.

NOW

WEDNESDAY 10ᵀᴴ NOVEMBER 1999

LOTTE

'I don't understand,' Lotte said to Isolde, sitting next to her with a newly formed sheet that spoke of a LightHouse and changes and cages. Something dragged at her memory, but nothing stuck; somehow her memory was filtering out the stuff she wanted to know. 'I don't even know if it's from Mama. She's dead,' she told Isolde. 'If it came from the past, how did it arrive only now?'

'LightHouse sounds like a women's shelter,' Isolde said, touching Lotte's hand with her own cool one.

Lotte said nothing for a long time. 'Was I there too? Or did she leave me behind? Or is she there now? If she is, that means she is un-dead. Could Mama be un-dead?' And she bit down on her tongue hard and covered her mouth with her hand as Isolde tried to hush her. 'I didn't want those words to leak out,' she said.

Isolde took her hand from her face and held it gently in her own. Lotte looked down at the pages. When Lotte noticed Pepin take Roo out of the room, she nudged at them again. 'There's more,' she said, and Isolde picked up the next sheet.

'Are you sure?'

Lotte nodded. 'Please.'

'Maybe later,' Isolde said.

'But . . . I have to know NOW,' Lotte said, sounding like a small child, picking the page up and trying to press it into Isolde's hand. 'Please.'

'Time ticks slowly as you get older; its meaning changes. Your urgency is understandable, but be gentle to yourself, Lottechen.' Isolde pulled Lotte into a hug and Lotte sagged into her warmth and strength.

'I lost my daughter a long time ago,' Isolde said into the top of Lotte's head. 'And I remember every single moment of that time. Sometimes not remembering is a blessing, child,' and she tapped Lotte gently on the hand again.

'When will you find her?' Lotte asked, thinking perhaps she could be found, like the posters on street lamps of dogs or cats that shout LOST and then FOUND.

'I've started to think some of the files relate to her. It's hard to tell and I don't want to hope,' Isolde said in a whisper.

Ralf returned to the room. He seemed calmer and his face bore little visual resemblance to the man who'd been shouting earlier. Lotte wondered what had happened to him. At his appearance Isolde changed tack, as though she had never uttered the last sentence. 'Winola was killed by the Stasi; they took her life away.'

'But *she* took her life,' Ralf said, and seated himself next to Isolde. He touched her hand with his before resuming work. 'It was a suicide, Mama; we shouldn't affix blame. Winola chose to do what she did.'

'Because her life was unliveable – *they* made it unliveable,' Isolde said, and Lotte saw her hands shaking. She pulled a tiny tissue from her sleeve and dried her eyes.

Ralf touched her gently on the arm. 'I know, and they should pay for what they did to her – to all of us,' he said. 'But who knows what would have happened if she'd held out? It was two months, that's all, two months. She should have held out. If she had just held on—'

Lotte watched Isolde's hand find Ralf's hand and they held on tight.

Suicide. The finality of the word thrummed through her. Suicide was the same as dead. It was the same as gone. Was it the same as lost? Was Mama lost as well as dead? As well as gone? Tears pricked at her eyes and she touched Isolde gently on the other hand. Isolde was looking for her daughter in shredded paper, just like Lotte was looking for her mama.

'We are just the same,' Lotte said. 'You and I are both trying to find someone in tiny bits of paper.'

Isolde laughed. Ralf cleared his throat and continued working.

'I'll read the next one,' she said eventually, as Ralf's presence faded into the background once more, 'but then I'm getting back to work.'

Lotte didn't say anything as Isolde picked up the page to read.

When I was pregnant with Lotte, I tried to leave again.

'Me!' Lotte exclaimed, relieved that they had been together. Even though they weren't any more, knowing she was part of something Mama had written felt nice.

'Wait, I think it starts here,' Isolde said, shifting the pages around.

When Rune was three months old I left home with him in my arms. I walked to the police station.

The first few months had been rocky. He called Rune 'it'. 'It' needs feeding. 'It' needs changing. I should have heeded it as a sign – you have to create an 'it' where a person was before so you can harm the 'it' – the thing. I had become an 'it' a long time ago. But now Rune was becoming one too.

'I see it in the job, you know,' he said smoothly. I waited in a knowing pause. This was the blow. 'I can understand it. Why a man kills his child when his wife leaves.' He bounced Rune in his arms, who started to cry.

'Are you leaving?' he asked.

'No.'

But my answer was not heard. In a flash, he was out the back door and into the garage. My baby in his arms. When I chased after him, he was searching in his toolbox.

I wanted to ask what he was doing, but it was best not to know. He came out with rope – thick twine. He wrapped it around Rune's neck. Rune was screaming-red and crying.

'Are you leaving me?' he asked.

'No.'

'Are you leaving me?'

'No.'

'Because you can leave. You can leave and "it" will hang here like a piece of meat at the butcher's. Are you leaving me?'

I didn't know how to get close without causing him to let Rune drop. To let my baby hang. He threw the rope over the frame of the garage ceiling. The end fluttered into his waiting palm. He pulled.

A scream came out of me that shocked Rune into silence.

He stopped winding. He stopped talking.

I waited.

He waited.

'Are you leaving me?' he asked, his face laughing, jesting, as if this performance were a joke.

I looked only at Rune strung up, waiting to see if his mama would save him. Powerless to the whims and tantrums of the entitled, the privileged. My knees kissed the hard ground. I looked up at him, at the power of him, and I knew that from this moment everything had changed.

Shattered.

'No,' I said. 'I will never leave you.'

And yet, less than twenty-four hours later I was at the police station.

'I want to report a crime,' I said. 'My husband tried to kill the baby.'

The officers looked at the chubby, pink-cheeked boy in my arms and smiled.

'He failed,' I added.

'We can see that.'

'I want to divorce him.'

'Okay.'

They were kind enough to take my name, my address. They were kind enough to make me a coffee. They were kind enough to show me into an interview room. They were kind enough to take me seriously.

They were kind enough to call my husband.

They were kind. And I think about the kindness they offered me as I was returned home.

Home. A place where I was beaten and made to watch as Rune screamed for me as I screamed in pain. He blocked me from touching my baby. That was my punishment. Absence. Him, and a shut door preventing me from being able to touch my baby boy.

Isolde stopped reading and the air became fractured with the words that she had just read out loud.

'Papa?' Lotte asked, breaking the silence. 'Does she mean Papa?' Trying. Trying to remember what she had forgotten. Thinking of Papa. Her papa. Could he, would he, have hurt Mama, hurt Roo? Her instinct was – no.

But then she recalled his face as he ripped the notebook.

'These are not nice stories,' Lotte said, and she took her pages back to her place at the table. 'I don't want Roo to know, it's sad sad sad. Maybe he has the sadness now because of the bad that happened,' she said quietly to herself, wanting to cry for all the hurt in the world but knowing there weren't enough tears.

Later, back at her desk next to Sabine, Lotte worked on more pages. She looked up at Sabine, whose face was calm, composed, as she flattened tiny strips of machine-shredded paper.

'Can you read this one?' she asked, flattening out yet another page.

Isolde and Ralf were working on pages together, taking up most of their table. Pepin looked up and nodded that Sabine could. Lotte was pleased. Since Roo had arrived, things had been better, but the things in the notebook, the words written by Mama, were awful and made Lotte feel scared, but she wouldn't stop. She needed to know and there was so little time. The day was dark and night was coming. She was sure no one would let her stay in the offices again, and what about Roo? Would he make her go home? He was pushing the paper around in a tray; she knew his mind was somewhere else.

She didn't want to ask what was going to happen next, so she worked on with a fury she had never known before.

When I was pregnant with Lotte I tried leaving again.

Sabine whispered, holding a sheet of paper in her hand and moving closer to Lotte's ear. Lotte listened. Listening was easier than thinking.

> *This time I packed a bag and walked with Rune all the way to a friend's house (she had a child the same age). I was at her house for three days. I had a hot bath and hot food and someone I could talk to.*

> *Until—*

> *He, and some of his friends, came and 'collected' my friend. My friend with her small child torn from her arms. Just for helping me. My friend threatened with prison, for some drug-related crime she hadn't committed. Just for helping me.*

> *He watched my face. He liked to see the defeat. He made me walk all the way home.*

> *With Rune holding my hand tight, my swollen feet, my sore hips. Lotte was born the following week.*

> *My friend was reunited with her child with a clear message – Do not help this woman – and she never opened her door to me again.*

> *The final time, Lotte was four. She was just starting to talk and be understood; she was just becoming herself. When she was a baby, I would push the buggy down*

the street and strangers would look in to say something nice, then give a start or jump back before apologising. Sympathising. That hurt.

At four years old, Down's syndrome was no longer defining her to everyone we met; they would speak to her, rather than me. The apologetic looks reduced and people saw a happy, smiley and very funny little girl.

'That's me,' Lotte said, and tears tried to burst out of her. 'Mama thought I was happy and funny!'

'We do too,' Isolde said, looking up from her tray. Pepin nodded also and Lotte was filled with an odd sense of warmth, of light, of fitting in just like a puzzle piece, exactly right. She never wanted to leave.

RUNE

He listened to Sabine's voice read in a whisper, words that were from Mama. He heard Lotte's excitement. He heard the love the women had for his sister, but the words in the notebook were useless.

These pages and Mama's voice within them were just delaying the inevitable. These women would go back to their jobs, their homes, their lives, and where would he be? Trying to help Lotte with a grief that even he couldn't comprehend. Lotte didn't know it yet, but forgetting is the greatest freedom a person can have.

He stood and grabbed his jacket.

'I'm going out for some air,' he said to the door, by way of explanation and not having to look Lotte in the eyes. 'I'll be right back.'

Outside, his senses were crisp and cold; his cheek stung in the air, a sting that grabbed at his eyes and penetrated deep into his teeth. Pain. He understood pain. He walked around the building to where he had met Sabine only hours earlier and lit up.

He enjoyed the heat of the cigarette as the smoke slowly filled his lungs, finally letting it filter out of his nose. He wanted to plead with Mama: *Why?* Why was this happening now? If only for a few minutes Mama would come back, would help him, would just be beside him. Would just be. But on every occasion he had begged and pleaded for her presence, he found the lack of it only reinforced his awareness that silence separated them and would do so forever.

He popped the lid of the pot of oxycodone and took two.

A car buzzed past with the beats of 'Café Del Mar' playing. It had been the sound of the summer a few years back, and it was as dreamy and direct as when he first heard it. Expansive and endless. Only a year ago, he had led a completely different life. He missed it.

'Rune-boy,' My-lo had said as she spotted him in the old trans-former station that had been turned into a nightclub, the strobe lights changing colours across her face, like a rainbow through glass. Her face spoke her joy as he joined her and she introduced him to the others. 'Come with me,' she said eventually when he'd nodded a *hello* to her friends.

She dragged him by the hand and they retreated into an alcove, their backs to the rest of the club. It was the most intimate feeling in the world. Sharing this confined space with My-lo. He cherished it and was scared by it equally, yet he stood tangled up in her breath, their arms touching.

She undid a tiny plastic bag of white powder and dipped in her pinky finger to scoop up the coke in her long fingernail. She offered it up to Rune, who pressed one nostril firmly and sniffed in deep. My-lo offered a second hit.

The pieces of his mind were running like the wheels of a clock moving too slowly. Backwards.

My-lo had turned to watch the sea of dancing as it swelled around them. Her hair fell onto her neck in damp curls. Rune was mesmerised by her pulse, which thrummed under her skin, and the drip of sweat that traced lightly down her neck, heading for the dip in her collarbone.

Furtive thoughts brought him back to the present, back to himself; thoughts that made him aware of his legs as though they existed as a separate part of his body; thoughts out of his control. Her body was lightly touching his; she turned and looked up at him and smiled before offering him a smaller bag.

'Want to bump up?'

He rubbed the MDMA into his gums and swilled the taste away with her bottle of bitter lemon. When he turned to thank her, My-lo kissed him on the cheek. It was gentle, sweet, a peck of a kiss, but her lips burned into his skin. He tried to speak, to catch My-lo's eye, but before Rune could fashion words in his mouth that weren't tainted with the bitterness of the drugs or the drink, My-lo was swallowed up in the crowd as the very first notes to Paul van Dyk's 'For an Angel' filtered through. The crowd heard it as soon as he did.

The excited ripples grew louder as the track gained prominence over the current beat.

He sank deep into a long velvet seat, raised to overlook the dance floor. My-lo had managed to get hold of some great stuff and he was not the only one enjoying its highs. Beautifully lost to himself, Rune smiled as he watched My-lo's glorious face.

Aware of Three Drives' 'Greece 2000' now playing, Rune felt inspired suddenly to move, to dance.

'Wanna dance with me?' My-lo asked as she plucked the cigarette from his mouth and took a long drag. She played her fingers down the bare skin on his inner arm, and the shock of nerves spiked from her touch all the way up into his neck. He stood unsteadily as

My-lo bounced back onto the dance floor and he followed, feeling the echo of her touch like iron filings; she was everywhere, magnetised to his heart, spiky, charged, itchy.

He followed her into the centre of the floor until there was only dance. All was dance, and he surrendered himself into it.

Willingly.

He didn't want to tell her this was his last night out. He didn't want to tell her everything was over. His life was over – again, just when it had started.

Papa had found his weakness; he knew what to push, and how. He wouldn't see My-lo again; he would do what Papa wanted. Always. Because Papa could hurt Lotte, could thwart Lotte's life in ways no one else could. He had to protect Lotte in every way he could, even if that meant doing what Papa wanted.

He wanted happiness for Lotte, and he would sacrifice his own for her.

My-lo deserved to live without police harassment. Her work was more important and Papa's influence could stop her, could imprison her. There was no way Rune wanted to live life knowing he had caused My-lo any pain at all. She was his best and only friend.

He held My-lo that night, their last night, and she moved closer, fractionally, marginally, but the proximity set his whole body humming. She leaned further in. Impossible as it was to pull away from the breath that touched his lips, from the eyes that seemed to hold his heart . . . and yet he did.

He had no choice. Papa had, once again, destroyed something more precious than words.

When he reluctantly returned to the office, his face felt numb and he floated back to his seat, only to realise everyone else was standing and packing away.

'Where are you staying tonight?' Sabine was asking him.

'Er . . .' His voice felt slurred, slurried; he hadn't thought about what they were going to do. He was supposed to be in charge, looking after Lotte, yet all his focus had been elsewhere. 'I have money, maybe a hostel or something?' He gazed at Lotte.

'I'm not finished though.' She pointed to the tray. 'I want to keep working.'

'Tomorrow,' Pepin said, her head emerging from one of the long cupboards that formed the back wall of the office. 'You can come back tomorrow. Both of you,' she added.

'Thank you,' Lotte burst out. Her happiness felt too bright to witness; he wanted shelter from her joy, just for a moment, a patch of shade from her sun.

'You can both stay with me tonight?' Sabine said quietly, making her offer into a question.

'No, it's fine,' Rune started, but Lotte jumped in.

'Yes, please!' Lotte said, and hugged Sabine tight. It seemed settled and all Rune had to do was wash with the tide.

'There'll be sunshine tomorrow, Lottechen,' Isolde was saying, 'if you are returning.' And she kissed Lotte on both cheeks and brushed Rune's arm as her small frame shuffled past.

'Night, Pepin,' Sabine called, buttoning up her coat, but Pepin was distracted and just waved a hand to acknowledge that she had heard. Rune wondered if Pepin was looking for Mama's files. If so, what would they say? What secrets had the puzzle women revealed already? He was starting to think it was all a terrible idea.

Lotte threaded her fingers through his, her face wide, smiling, satisfied.

'Home with my best-bestest friend, Sabine,' she announced. 'It'll be my first sleepover.' And he tried to smile for her.

He failed.

THEN

July 1989

'Can you come with me?' Comrade Dietrich asked him, just as Rune was about to step into the school auditorium. The Pioneers were practising for the forthcoming fortieth anniversary of East German communism.

Rune wasn't sure exactly what they were planning – something to do with Gorbachev – but he and his new friends donned their blue neck scarves and caps. He was in the Pioneers, which meant he could stay late at school to practise with them. It meant he could stand as one with the other kids. It meant he belonged.

He had a *borrowed* neck scarf for Lotte in his bag and he wondered if Comrade Dietrich knew he had taken it. All the teachers and most of the older kids dismissed or ignored Lotte and she was desperate to belong. It made Rune feel small, seeing her rejected. He had taken a scarf for her. Was he going to be in trouble?

Comrade Dietrich was a small greying teacher with a sharp nose; he walked with his nose raised to try and be larger than his students, but this only accentuated his beak-like appearance.

'Comrade Ackermann wants to see you.' Comrade Dietrich patted him on the back.

'Now?' Rune asked, closing the door to the hall and turning to face Comrade Dietrich. He heard the piano strike up.

'You don't keep Comrade Ackermann waiting. It's an honour and a privilege he took time to come to our school at all. I suggest you flatten your hair, straighten your tie and hotfoot it to the Principal's office.'

Rune did as he was told. Hearing his friends sing to the piano: '*Flying higher and higher and high-er. Our emblem the Soviet star.*' Sitting when invited by the large man who took up most of the room; the song was silenced with the closing of the door.

'I hear great things about you, Comrade Schäffer, many, many great things,' Comrade Ackermann said. 'And over the course of our meetings I happen to agree with the evaluations of others who know you.'

Rune kept silent. Watching. Comrade Ackermann took off the tiny glasses squeezed onto his round face, the arms of which left indents along his cheeks as he squeezed the bridge of his nose. 'Your sister, on the other hand, has very little to contribute . . .'

Rune panicked. 'Where's Lotte?' he asked.

Comrade Ackermann flicked the question away without answering. 'My interest is in you. Your sister is of no consequence to me or the party. You, on the other hand, are the future of socialism. You have plenty to offer. Your mother is a wise woman, is she not?'

Rune nodded.

'Choosing socialism for her children over the commercial and hostile West. Very wise. I wonder what she will think of her son, whom teachers call . . .' – here he lifted a piece of paper in front of him and read from it – 'hard-working, with a positive attitude towards the DDR.'

'I think she would be proud,' Rune said. 'She wants me to be happy here.'

'And are you?'

He knew the correct answer was yes, so he nodded his head.

'Excellent. Well, the ministry for state security is offering to make you even happier. You can join your comrades and become an *Inoffizieller Mitarbeiter*,' he said with gusto. 'You will have many privileges, joining as an unofficial employee at such a young age. But your teachers and I see great potential in you, Rune.'

'But,' he started, 'I'm only nine. I don't know anything.'

'The correct answer,' Comrade Ackermann boomed, 'is *thank you, Comrade*.'

Rune repeated as he was told.

'Good,' Comrade Ackermann said. 'Please read this.' Comrade Ackermann slipped a page across the desk and stood; walking round, he placed his heavy fountain pen in Rune's hand. He also placed his weighty hand on Rune's shoulder.

'Once you have signed, I shall be the person you report to. I shall come to school once a week. You are to be the eyes and ears of the ministry. I will need to trust you to be my eyes and ears too. Here.' He tapped on the page.

Rune skimmed it over; it was already completed with his name. All he had to do was sign. He unscrewed the fountain pen.

What choice was there? He realised, as he signed and passed the pen back to Comrade Ackermann, that no one ever asked him what he thought, they just told him what to do. Always. It was probably for the best because he wasn't sure *what* he thought any more.

'Congratulations, Comrade. I look forward to working with you,' Comrade Ackermann said, shaking his hand vigorously. In it was a fünf-mark note. 'Your primary task will be to ensure the party principles are kept within your home and the homes that you go into. I think it's a great achievement when a son can correct any Western influences latent in another family member. Do you understand what I'm saying?' Comrade Ackermann asked.

Rune nodded, but was unsure.

'It's for the best you don't speak of this to anyone,' Comrade Ackermann continued. 'Adults tend to overthink things and we don't want your mother to worry unnecessarily, now do we?' Suddenly Rune had become part of a 'we'; he belonged to Comrade Ackermann, to the party, in ways in which he didn't want to belong.

He didn't want to understand, but it became clear as Comrade Ackermann continued talking in convoluted jargon that Rune was to be the eyes and ears of the party. He had no choice. He'd already signed.

He recalled a time, not too long ago, at home in the West, when Papa would take him outside, to tinker with their bikes or under the ruse of playing football, and ask him, *What did you and your mother do today? Where did you go? Who did you meet? What did she wear?* The list of questions was always the same.

He realised at that moment that, just as Papa had done in the past, Comrade Ackermann could make Rune say whatever he wanted him to say. The feeling was shapeless and encompassed him. He had no choice.

Rune pocketed the money and left the office.

He didn't want to go back to the Pioneers, which he loved. Everything seemed to keep changing, just when he was feeling more settled. He pulled off his tie and cap and went to find Lotte. What did Comrade Ackermann mean about Lotte? Was she safe? The fact that Comrade Ackermann had mentioned Lotte at all made him quicken his step.

He knew where she would be.

NOW

WEDNESDAY 10ᵀᴴ NOVEMBER 1999

LOTTE

Sabine opened the door to her apartment. She lived above a deli, where the smell of steak sandwiches and grilled cheese had awoken Lotte, in the cold, to the heat of her hunger.

The apartment was small and the living room was dominated by a sofa: faded pinky-red and dotted with rich green and blue cushions. There was a small television set in the corner and heavy pink curtains over the only window. As Lotte moved further into the room, she could see the walls were covered in childish sketches and prints, dripping a rainbow watercolour. Those above the radiator had dried out and were flaking off. Lotte saw, in the rugs randomly aligned on the floor, a mess of dogs asleep. New, unexpected sleeping dogs littered the floor in varying shades of yellow.

'Yellow is my favourite colour,' Lotte said to the rug-dogs as she watched them breathe.

'Can I sleep on the sofa?' she asked, dropping her bag and taking off her hoody. She'd sleep safe next to the yellow rug-dogs.

'Sure,' Sabine said. 'But there's a bedroom down the hall. My daughter's room,' she added, almost reluctantly.

'You didn't say you had a daughter?' Lotte asked. Sabine didn't look any older than Roo.

Sabine nodded. 'We share custody, her father and I. She's with him this week.' Sabine's voice was raw and Lotte didn't want to say anything, but Sabine continued, 'I really admire you, Lotte. I had Clio when I was fifteen years old and everyone told me all the things I'd never be able to do. Always negative. No one ever gave me a chance. You have to deal with that every day, whereas as Clio and I have grown older, it's been better.'

'I just have to prove I can do things, that's all. Some things are harder, but as long as people give me a chance, I can show them I am Lotte first. Down's syndrome is just one of the things that makes me – me! One of the pieces of the Lotte-puzzle.'

'More than the Down's syndrome,' Roo echoed, taking off his jacket and placing his bag on the sofa. 'She's my hero,' he said with pride to Sabine, then he gave Lotte a grin that made her giggle.

'Please, make yourselves at home, both of you.'

The house had a lived-in happiness; it was also playful. Lotte shimmied her hand along the top of the sofa and it rippled. Sabine's house was young and energetic, like a puppy. Lotte smiled, thinking this was exactly the right house for Sabine to live in. It suited her. Lotte wondered what her daughter was like.

'I love your house,' she said.

'Thanks. My room is this one, closest to us, and Clio's is down the hall. You can sleep in Clio's bed or on the sofa,' she said. Roo placed his big bag on the sofa.

'The bathroom is to the right,' Sabine said, 'if you want to freshen up, and I'll cook us something.' She walked into the open-plan kitchen and filled the kettle. 'I bought pasta earlier . . .' – she placed a brown paper bag on the counter – 'with Luise's fresh pesto and *challah*,' she said to Lotte. 'Will that be okay?'

'Thanks,' Roo said, and took off into the bathroom. 'I'll take a shower before we eat.'

Lotte, hearing his voice, felt so sad. Nothing was making Roo happy; she wondered if anything ever could. When Lotte heard the water running for the bath and the familiar sound of a boiler firing up, she felt more at home, and seated herself at the breakfast bar, on a nice wooden stool that had been painted purple. The kettle was boiling and Sabine was making tea.

Lotte stared at the *challah*, its plaited shape golden and sprinkled with sesame seeds.

'Herbal?' Sabine asked, and Lotte nodded absent-mindedly.

She remembered beating eggs, watching frothing yeast foam in a jug and four hands in a bowl. She remembered the sticky puffy dough as she was shown how to plait. Four hands and three strands of dough. The hollow tap on its bottom, the breaking crisp crunch. She'd never baked bread with Papa. So were the hands of her memory hers and Mama's?

'Sabine.' Lotte started thinking of the last entry from Mama. The only one that mentioned Lotte. 'Can you read more of the pages for me tonight?' She lifted her bag and took them out; the shreds were still in their box back in the puzzle women's office, but she didn't want to be parted with the completed ones. 'I just don't understand them, and maybe when I know more I can fix the bits in my head that won't work.'

Sabine moved around the kitchen, rattling pots and pans and preparing pasta. Lotte had at least five unread, newly completed sheets. She was proud to have done so many in just one day.

'If I can build them back to pages, then maybe I can build my memory in the same way?' Lotte said, pleased, happy that she had a plan. 'If I have all the pieces, then I can put it all together. Clever. Clever-together,' and she laughed. 'Words are funny. Funny.

Honey. Buzz,' and she pointed to her T-shirt to show Sabine what she meant. 'Yellow. Black. Yellow.'

Sabine smiled.

'LotteBee,' Lotte said.

'We can eat and then we can talk. Put the telly on if you like?'

Sabine looked tired too. As Lotte looked around the house she saw that, other than the pictures on the wall, there were no toys or anything that would make her think a child lived here.

'How old is your daughter?' Lotte asked.

'Seven,' Sabine said.

'You must miss her when she's not here.'

'Unbearably,' Sabine said, turning away.

Lotte said nothing further and placed each sheet out on the table, happy they were whole. She could see the fractured lines through the pages, but photocopied, as Isolde had instructed, they looked almost as good as new. She didn't look too closely at the words, just marvelled at their ability to be formed anew and at how much Sabine had helped her. Sabine yawned loudly, then apologised.

'Why do you go to work so early?' Lotte asked. 'You must always be tired.' Sabine clanged a pot down onto the stove, sizzling water over the side of the pan and causing the gas flames to spit high.

'It's my work,' Sabine began, sounding as if she would continue, but then said nothing more. The boiler stopped its whirring and the flat became small and very, very quiet. Lotte allowed it to seep in through her skin. Sitting within the confines of the silence, Lotte watched Sabine finish cooking, draining the pasta into the sink. The smell brought Lotte's stomach to her throat with a starch hunger. A hunger tasting of boiled, salted pasta water.

Roo came out of the bathroom. His hair was damp and his cheek looked worse, pink and raw and open. His eye was swelled-up closed. 'Do you have a plaster or a tissue of any kind?' he asked.

Sabine fashioned him a pad of kitchen roll and Roo pressed it to his cheek. It looked painful.

'Do you need any help?' Roo asked.

'No, but thanks. You just have a seat – it's almost ready.'

Roo settled himself on the sofa.

'What happened today with Ralf?' Lotte enquired. 'The com-pos-tation?'

'Compensation?' Sabine asked, swishing the green pesto through the creamy pasta then filling three bowls and placing forks down next to them. Lotte gathered the papers back into one pile.

'I wanted to ask Isolde,' Lotte continued, 'but sometimes I am not good at knowing when to ask questions that come from my head. But as you are my best-bestest friend maybe you know, because I do not want to be hurting Isolde by using the wrong words.' Her voice stacked the words up like bricks and they tumbled out of her mouth as Sabine dragged her bowl and fork towards her. Lotte, realising Sabine was on the verge of tears, watched her twirl pasta onto her fork and lift it up to her mouth, dragging more strands of pasta up with it. But then she stopped; fork, pasta and all, went crashing back into the bowl.

'I'm sorry,' Sabine said, pushing the other bowl towards Lotte. 'But, please, just eat.'

Lotte realised that maybe it was not okay to ask Sabine about Ralf either, that maybe there were too many things she couldn't understand. She turned to the sofa to beckon Roo to help her, as he always did, but his head was slumped back, his arm resting over his backpack. Roo was asleep.

'Can we save Roo's for later?' Lotte asked. The smell of the pasta invaded her every sense; she could taste the pesto as though it were viscous in the air. She ate with relish.

'Your brother seems to have had a tough day.'

Lotte nodded, pasta in her mouth.

'Have you heard of Torgau?' Sabine asked Lotte, once most of the pasta had been eaten.

'No, is that a place?'

'Yes. Torgau is why Ralf was upset today . . .' Sabine shook her head sadly, before sitting back down and taking another mouthful. 'Ralf heard today that he wouldn't get the compensation he'd been promised.' Once she'd chewed and chewed and swallowed, Lotte swallowed too, salivating over the glossy food.

'Torgau was a reform school for children. I think it began as an institution for children with special—' Sabine stopped.

'Needs? Children like me?'

'Well – no. I mean. Yes, children with additional needs. Not like you, but I think—'

'Children like me were sent away from home.'

Sabine nodded sadly.

'Papa says that's what happens now, that special schools take us if we can't be inde-pen-dent. But I am inde-pen-dent so I can stay with Roo. Ralf doesn't have Down's syndrome, so why was he sent away?'

'Isolde and her husband were critical of the socialist regime. When Ralf and his sister were ten, they were imprisoned for six months. A lot of the children were asked to give testimonies a few years ago, for compensation and justice for what happened to them.'

'Why?'

'Torgau was the Stasi's way to try to get parents to conform. Most parents would do anything to be with their children.' There

230

was a weighty pause, and Lotte couldn't help but ask, 'Would you do anything to be with Clio?'

'Yes,' Sabine said, her voice guarded. 'I have to be without my child every other week in order to see her at all. People call that fairness. Compromise.'

'What do you call it?' Lotte asked.

'Torture,' Sabine said.

'Did Isolde do everything to get Ralf back?' Lotte asked when the bowls were empty and Sabine's eyes were less glazed.

Sabine nodded. 'But it was unjust and horrific abuse they encountered there. The problem is, no one wants to go back and find out what happened; everyone just wants to move on. But that means children like Ralf feel even more neglected. By the unified Germany as well as the old Eastern Bloc.'

'Could Isolde have stopped it?' Lotte asked.

'They tried, but Ralf and his sister were regularly in and out of Torgau. Just pawns in a larger, more dangerous game.'

'How awful,' Lotte said, aware of how little she knew about the things that had happened around her. The places where people had been disappeared, that Isolde had mentioned – she couldn't recall the names – and now this place, for children, for Isolde's children. Was this place why his sister, Winola, died by suicide? Lotte thought that perhaps those questions were not ones she should ask.

Lotte realised she knew so very little and tried to think hard about something she did know, something relevant, but she was tired. She listened to Roo's deep breaths, his sleepy snores, and felt comforted.

Sabine was sipping her herbal tea when Lotte spoke again.

'Did your parents send you to Torgau?' she asked. Sabine blew on the tea and looked carefully over the rim.

'Why do you ask?'

'I was just thinking because the sacks contain information, maybe that's why you go in early. Maybe you're looking for something?'

Sabine put her cup down. 'I can't tell you what we find in the sacks. It's Stasi documentation, but it's also confidential.' She took a deep breath.

Lotte didn't say anything and Sabine carried on slowly.

'I go in early on the weeks I don't have Clio, so I can leave early and pick her up from school when I do have her.' Sabine's shoulders slumped and she sighed heavily. 'I grew up in a children's home.' Her smile was half-hearted and it hurt Lotte to see it. 'I met Clio's father as soon as I left, at fifteen. I had Clio less than a year later.' She picked up her tea and looked at Lotte. 'Now I just sift through millions of fragments of paper, earning enough money so I can continue to have half of her life.'

'I'm sorry,' Lotte said. 'I hated being away from Roo, even for just a day. It must be the worstest thing ever.'

'Enough about me,' Sabine said, so gravely she reminded Lotte of Roo, and returned her cup to the table with a jolt. 'I wanted to know why you can't read. Is it part of your . . .' She trailed off. 'Down's syndrome?' she asked.

'No, I think a lot of Down's people can read and write fine, I'm just a bit slow at it. I find it very hard.' Lotte looked down into the cup below her. Untouched. 'I find a lot of things very hard,' she admitted quietly.

'Do you have a blanket so Roo doesn't feel the cool-cold while he sleeps?' Lotte asked, returning from the bathroom wearing Sabine's spare pyjamas, which were too long and flapped around her feet, but were super-soft and lavender-smelling. Once still-sleeping Roo had been covered up and they both had another cup of tea in their hands, Sabine seated herself at the end of the sofa, her feet tucked under her, holding a photocopied page into the light.

'Is that one of Mama's pages?' Lotte asked.

'Yes, it's part of the pages you put together today. You make it look easy, by the way,' Sabine said, placing the page down as Lotte sat down next to her. 'It took me a week to complete my first page when I started. How many pages did you make up today?'

Lotte tried to suppress a smile. It wasn't a question that needed an answer. Sabine knew what Lotte had done and was gazing at her in awe, as if impressed. Lotte had never had anyone look at her like that before. It felt good. 'Will you read it?' she asked.

'I will,' Sabine said, lifting Mama's papers.

'You are my best friend, Sabine,' she said. 'Thank you.'

'No problem,' Sabine said, and took a deep breath. 'I'm happy to help you.' She turned the page into the light and started to read:

I had no plan to write this. I suppose my only plan was to be free. Maybe this is my freedom, locking the past safely within these pages. Damn Nanya for being right. Therapy sucks.

I tuck myself into the sleep-warm bodies of my babies and thank every star that I am alive to breathe them in, because it is in these tiny moments I am free.

And yet:

Vergangenheitsbewältigung means coming to grips with the past. The past, with grip, is coming back: mean.

I took a chance with my life and theirs, and went to a hostel. I applied for supported housing. The man who was 'helping' us worked for a charity that was unable to find us housing immediately. We stayed in a hostel on the other side of the city. We lasted one week.

When we returned home, his bumped-up ego-driven story later relayed in joyful sadistic detail how just the power of his name had made the man at the charity stutter and inevitably stopped us from getting help. There was no help available to me or my children. Our names identified us. He wasn't going to let us go.

I tucked the children into bed and did my best to acclimatise myself to the thought of the death that awaited me. Time was bleeding out and I was helpless, hopeless. Waiting, just waiting. I didn't know what would happen.

When nothing happened for a week, I couldn't manage the fear. It scuttled under my skin, gnawed at my fingers and scurried around in my head.

Recalling the time I used my arms as a shield. A shield and a sword. To keep them from their father's promises, their father's threats, should I ever leave.

And I had left.

'Why would he kill them?' Lotte asked as Sabine placed the page down. 'Does she mean us? Rune and Lotte? Lotte and Rune?'

'I don't know,' Sabine said darkly, glancing over at Roo. He was hugging his bag close to his chest again, but his mouth was open and he was snoring.

Sabine read on:

Two weeks went past after our return from the hostel. He hadn't raised a hand, hadn't raised his voice. There had been no response at all.

A tiny shard of hope glinted menacingly — maybe things had changed.

Two weeks . . .

Then one normal day, I dropped Rune to school and Lotte to her physio appointment. I was on my way home, just for an hour, before collecting Lotte. I never made it. At the end of the road I was bundled into a van and a bag was thrown over my head.

It feels ugly when you're powerless and the only thing you have is your voice, and what emerges makes you ashamed of yourself. Begging. I begged. I just wanted to be with my children, I wanted to go home, to keep my children safe, to keep myself safe. Battle fatigue silenced me as we drove. I had no idea what was happening.

When the doors opened, I was almost lifted out. In front of a building, nondescript, not anywhere I had been before. There were gates all around me. I tried to see the way back, the way out. But roughly, two hands grabbed the bare skin of my arms and I was walked into the building; the door creaked and shut. Once my eyes adjusted to the half-light, a long corridor stretched ahead of me. My shoes clacked on the plastic floor and my skirt rustled and rubbed against my legs.

I was placed on a chair in front of a narrow desk with two identical police officers, in uniform, behind it. And I knew my husband was somewhere, out of sight, puppeteering the whole event. I couldn't decide if this was a good or a bad thing. I looked around for him. Asked to speak to him.

The officers said nothing.

Fear ballooned inside me. It pressed everything to the edges of my body, so I couldn't see without flitting, jumping, bouncing from one thing to the next. I didn't look, kept my eyes staring ahead. My ears were swimming, wet without water. I was drowning in air, listening but not hearing, trying to pave my way out of this, but not engaging my brain, not thinking, just reacting. Thinking pushed aside by the power of my fear.

'Why am I here?' I asked.

'We ask the questions,' the officer said from behind the desk, and silence knotted my throat. I waited until he finally opened a file on his desk and spent a long time flicking through the pages. He didn't ask me one question.

The thought of holding my children, of being together, my purpose fulfilled. It kept me going as I waited, hoping that if I did whatever they asked I would get to collect them. See them again.

They told me to get undressed. I paused. Looked. Checked.

'We can always lock you in a cell until tomorrow. Maybe the overnight stay will change your mind.'

I thought of Rune, of Lotte, of what they would think if I wasn't there.

They used the word 'routine'. The officer said it with a relish that made me shiver. Revolted, I passed all my clothes to the female officer who was called upon for the occasion – to supervise? To hold my clothes? I didn't know.

Without clothes, and under the gaze of three officers, my skin no longer felt like my own; while fear was expanding inside of me, my skin had shrunk. It felt wobbly; fluid. It was no longer attached. My body no longer attached to it.

'Do you want me to stop?' Sabine asked. She was scanning the pages. 'It's not nice and it goes into detail here,' Sabine's voice continued. But Lotte couldn't listen, she couldn't understand.

'Why did Mama have to do that? And is her husband Papa? Why would he do that to her? What—' But she stopped and saw Sabine's confused expression. Lotte's words a jumble in her mouth as her mind whirled.

'I want to know,' she said, but the words meant nothing. Sabine placed her hand on Lotte's, took a deep shuddery breath and continued.

My body betrayed me. I followed the officer as she walked me up the long corridor. I was placed in a new room, with a large chair, stirrups. A man with a tray of stainless-steel tools.

'Do we need to get reinforcements?' I was asked when I refused, not verbally but physically. I couldn't command my body to move. Reinforcements?

This is what we are doing to you, so behave or more of us will do it to you. That was the message loud and clear. We will all witness your exposure, your fear, your shame.

I was strapped in. Held down. I tried to find a place in me to hide – it took a while, it was surprisingly hard to do, but then the pain came as the man inserted cold steel items, and the pain took me into the smallest part of myself.

And it took me back to him, who ran himself through me, calling names to my pain.

As soon as my body was free of violation, I wet both myself and the man's hand; the urine splashed on the floor.

I turned my head, away from where I was, from them. I turned away from myself.

Then I heard his voice.

His voice.

The man I had loved, the man I married, the man I was attached to for the rest of my life. We shared children. His voice stung my eyes, along with the smell of my incontinence. Was he here to save me? To hurt me further?

I was in the unknown.

His voice told me to hold still. I did. The steel instruments clattered into a waiting stainless-steel tray. 'Test results will be around a week,' the man said, and stood. I turned away so I couldn't see his face.

Test?

'Thank you,' he commanded, and everyone in the room left. Leaving me with my husband.

'Test?' I asked.

'How do you think it feels for a man to know his wife is a whore?'

I didn't answer. I was being punished for leaving.

'You. Will. Never. Leave. Me. Again. Ever,' he said.

Sabine's voice, large and strong, broke into Lotte's thoughts, which had drifted as light as a wisp. She was trying so hard to understand, but everything was jumbled up.

'Whatisawhore? Wherewereheyputtingtheinstruments? Why was Mama so scared?'

'It sounds like a Stasi abduction.'

'But it couldn't have been,' Lotte said, looking at Sabine's flushed face. 'Because my papa was not the Stasi.'

'I don't know then,' Sabine said. 'I'm sorry, Lotte.'

'I want to understand,' Lotte said. 'I am inde-pen-dent.' But the last words she spoke didn't make sense. Is this what inde-pen-dent meant? Roo would never have read this to her. He was so tired he was sleeping, but he should have been awake, he should have known too. Or maybe he already knew?

Papa tore everything away. *He tore it away because it says he did bad, bad things*, Lotte thought, and Roo knows the bad things he did? Her mind confused itself and halted, stalled, stuck.

'I'm so sorry, Lotte. Your mama—' Sabine's voice wavered. 'She experienced so much.'

Lotte's thoughts were far away.

'I need to do more of the pages . . . I have to find out what happened. Mama is dead and . . .' Although she tried, she had no energy to stand, she had no energy to keep awake. She felt world-hurt and untethered as she drifted off into uneasy sleep, curled into the corner of Sabine's old sofa, her hand resting on Roo's foot.

III.

The water is cold.

My first thought: How cold it is. My hands are tied. My feet scrabble against the cool floor, I kick out, buck and pull and rip myself as far away as I can from his face. From his joy. From him.

A cloth is put in my mouth. It is wet.

A warm hand presses my forehead back. I rise up onto my tiptoes, my feet grasping for purchase. My body a bridge.

Water is poured over my face.

It burns. I panic. Water goes up my nose. In my mouth.

My head is on fire, my nose and my whole face are swollen, filling with water, water to drown me. Water pouring. My ears ring and lights flash in my eyes. Water pouring over me. Into me. Inside me. Drowning.

I can't breathe.

I am drowning. I am going to die.

He lets go of my head and I am upright, coughing, vomiting; water. I breathe in blades of ice, my face a fire of pain. He pats my face dry with a towel, scratched from use.

He asks me a question.

I cannot see him. I pull and pull, trying to free my hands from their ties. I am aware the pulling should hurt my wrists, but I feel nothing.

'Please,' I beg. 'Please.'

His hand touches my forehead, forcing my head back, the cloth forced in my mouth. I scream, I fight. Every muscle in my body pulls away from him, from death. I fight with all of my strength.

The water is cold as he drowns me, again.

NOW

THURSDAY 11TH NOVEMBER 1999

MARTINSFEUER – ST MARTIN'S DAY

RUNE

He woke with a head that ached, an empty stomach and a heart so heavy he could have cried. On opening his eyes, he heard Lotte's voice, her laughter; he smelled toast and the day began. Refusing to think of Papa or the trouble that awaited them both, he ate his toast, apologised for falling asleep so early the night before, and then walked with Lotte and Sabine to the office to start another day.

Fatigue, irritation and boredom slowed his fingers as he shuffled the pieces of paper around in the tray left abandoned from yesterday. Nothing had changed overnight. He spent the morning watching Lotte and finding some numbers within all the letters on the shreds that Lotte had given him. He could arrange the fragments one way, then another, then back again. He didn't know what he was doing. When Pepin came into the office late morning with a steaming coffee and motioned for him to join her, he was relieved.

'I found files,' she said. 'Do you want to see them? There's a few more that are in progress, so I'll find those and come back.'

Rune nodded as something huge and heavy and slow and far away began to press on his heart; it lurched and, unsure of what to do, he stood and his heart hammered as if he were sprinting.

'These are mainly related to you. Your mother's are the ones that are in progress.'

'What does that mean?'

'The stacks of files were kept within the same bags the Stasi used when they were destroying evidence. I think your files, your mother's at any rate, are in the sacks we're currently working on.'

'I've been here most of the evening and very early today to try and get them ready for you. I haven't got everything, but if you're happy I'll leave you here and keep going in my break.' She jotted down a number from the top of the file.

He followed her, aware that by doing so, he was making a decision. To accept her help and to read files that were about him. Pepin led him into a small room with a single table and chair, facing an old blackboard that was grey from overuse.

The room was almost completely taken up with stacked files and Rune placed his feet carefully, not wanting to disturb the thickness of the air around him. The atmosphere was heavy with expectation and Rune's headache magnified under the pressure.

'These are yours,' Pepin said, resting her small hand on the stack of blue and grey files on top of the table. She left time for her words to melt before continuing. 'I've put them in order so if you start at the top, those are the oldest ones, and the ones underneath, the newest.'

Rune looked at the files.

'I'll leave you. I'll be back in the office if you need anything.'

'Thank you,' he said.

He took a deep breath and thought of Lotte, then picked up the folder on top of the pile. The oldest.

Reg No. 889641/52

Operation: 'Schäferhund'

He opened it and read the first sheet:

Observation of active staff operative.

Surname: First name

SCHÄFFER, Rune

~~SCHÄFFER, Lotte~~

~~SCHÄFFER, Remy~~

His heart beating in his throat, he turned pages and read.

Surveillance of subject 889641/2 began at 07.43.

889641/2 was observed leaving the facility named 'LightHouse' with his mother and sister. They walked along Thälmannstraße. The person to be observed held his sister's hand. The subject looked frequently to his mother.

As he read, he was not aware of any pain. He skimmed the pages as memory snagged at his chest. He looked at the words. The pages and pages of surveillance astonished him.

08.02 The subject ate small amounts of food prepared and laid out on the blanket and then took out a folder of paper and proceeded to use a pencil to mark a page.

He read and read, turning page after page. A holy terror gripped him. He could not stop reading; the truth, which had been recorded brutally, factually, lay in these files.

Rune turned the pages, moving through the months and changing seasons.

Code name 'Schaf'

Declaration taken by Comrade Ackermann 'Operation Handler'

I, Rune SCHÄFFER, freely commit myself to work unofficially for the state security. I want enemies to be rendered harmless and for people on the wrong path to be helped.

The words bled into each other and the page pulsated in his hands like a beating heart. At the bottom of the page was his young signature.

He was an informer, a member of the Stasi, and all the things he'd said in Comrade Ackermann's office – the people he'd denounced, the stories he'd told – it all came flooding back on a wave of nausea.

And have you witnessed any crimes against the state at home?

As a member of the Pioneers, it is your job to seek out those who would take the wrong path towards capitalism.

He was dismayed; he remembered the questioning, remembered the drone of his own voice. He couldn't recall his own words. His past fell into place with alarming intensity; the edges of his vision became opaque, viscous.

Not only had he been an informer, but he was also a suspect, a person who was surveyed to the same extent as those who were harbouring secrets against the state. He had not been special, not someone the state trusted.

What had it all been for?

And something else, something that felt worse as he turned page after page. Within these lines of type, he had been a child. Nine years old. But between Papa and Comrade Ackermann, he hadn't had a childhood at all.

He had been part of the Stasi – an informer. A traitor. He discarded the file in the stack; he didn't want anyone to know, and yet here it was, black on white. He opened the last file. The word INCOMPLETE stamped on the front:

> Surveillance of subject 889641/2 beginning Friday 10th November 1989.

The date. *That* date.

> 08.30 Subject leaves place of residence with mother and sister. Subject walks on ahead as mother and sister delayed by looking at a patch of grass emerging from a fence panel.

> 08.45 Subject joins mother and sister and all three walk to the school gates. Subject remains in school.

> 13.45 Nothing to report.

15.00 Subject collected from school gates by mother. No sign of sister. Subject leaves mother at school gates and goes to the park, where he looks around and leaves. Surveillance falters and resumes due to volume of persons on street. Subject difficult to follow on foot.

15.15 Surveillance continues outside address.

15.40 Subject leaves home at a run.

———

Surveillance stays on the house after subject cannot be followed due to chaos on streets as people flock to the Wall.

Contents of further report have been filed under SCHÄFFER, Remy.

Remy, SCHÄFFER – current status: ~~DISAPPEARED.~~

A whole section of his brain stirred to life, hot, low, and laden with pain. The rest of the page was fully blacked through. Rune turned over; the final pages were thicker, whiter, cleaner. The first read, simply:

Reg No. 889641/54

Remy SCHÄFFER was taken from residence on Winzer by ambulance to hospital, despite many delays due to mass migration to the West, subject under-went emergency surgery. Surgery declared a success. Surveillance discontinued once subject conscious by request of Comrade Ackermann.

End Report.

Officer – HIN X/21

He could feel the surge of tension through his entire body.

The final page held a description of Mama underneath the title MISSING from December 1989 and a sketch of her that he himself had drawn. It was a childish drawing with the proportions off, but it was Mama.

He had never seen the poster before, but his picture had formed the basis of it.

It had been a long time since he had seen her face, but doing so made him feel empty, for reasons he wasn't able to articulate. Things returned, even if you'd rather they didn't. He closed the file and stood up. He needed to get out of here.

Missing was not dead. *Conscious* was not dead. *Successful surgery* was not dead.

The room wobbled, the colours lost. He remembered the flat, he remembered the ambulance; he knew they didn't put the sirens on.

He knew she was dead.

Didn't he?

Turning to the door, he bumped into the table, toppling the pile, sending them to the floor.

The room quivered as weak sunshine fractured his vision. The truth plucked at a part of his memory grown numb from inattention. Incomplete, said the file, but his memory was not.

The world turned into patterned fragments. Broken images spliced with guilt. He couldn't see or think straight. Just two words filled his head – both holding a gravitational force, pulling every other thought into its field. *Conscious. Missing.*

Then there was a pair of hands beside him. Lifting the files with him, arranging them. It was Sabine.

'You need some help?' she asked, peering at the file in her hand. 'I wanted to have a quick chat about some of the things I read to Lotte last night. I don't know if now is a good time?'

'I'm sorry,' Rune said softly, and turned away. 'I'm sorry.' He tried to take the file, not wanting her to see the truth contained within its pages.

'What are you doing?' she asked.

'They're mine,' he said. 'My files.' His hands fell to his side.

'*I, Rune Schäffer.* That's you?' she asked, flicking open the cover and reading his name.

He nodded, his face blazing, his eyes burning with the heat radiating from his cheeks.

He was powerless to stop her reading on. His declaration.

'You were a spy? An informant?' Sabine spat, snapping the file shut, slapping it down on the desk. He stood as still as she did. 'What are you doing here?' she asked.

He couldn't find the words, any words. *I'm dying*, he thought.

'Do you know what you did, by informing, by telling on innocent people?' she said, her voice a hiss.

'I . . . I . . . Please,' he begged.

'You destroyed lives.' He looked into her eyes, which had glazed over a little; she wasn't aiming her words at him, just in his direction. This wasn't about him. It was about her.

'People like you destroyed my life and no one has ever given a flying fuck about it.'

'I'm sorry.'

'What are you doing here?' she asked. 'Sending your sister as a what? A decoy? Distracting us with this *notebook* from your mother while you steal files?'

Rune looked at her, shocked. 'No,' he said, finding his voice at last. He took a deep breath.

'Do you know what the Stasi did to kids with Down's syndrome? Kids just like your sister?'

He shook his head.

'You make me sick,' she said. 'Do you even think about what you've done?'

She glared at him and his face burned with shame, pure shame. He wanted it to end.

'Can I get these destroyed?' he asked, holding the file. 'Can I take them with me now?' Thinking of the sizeable bonfire this amount of paper would make.

'What?' she asked, and he realised he'd said something stupid. Her face was cold and small and watchful, so different from the face he'd seen that morning over toast while she and Lotte laughed and joked together. 'You want to shirk your responsibility? The government protects scum like you, when it's the victims it should be looking after. Come with me,' she said. 'Now.'

As she turned away, he placed the last file – the one with the picture of Mama – into his jacket and zipped it up. It was the only picture they had. A tiny flicker of fear burned within him as he followed Sabine down the corridor.

LOTTE

Sabine burst into the office in a fog of words that seemed to bounce around the room. Roo was behind her and Sabine looked cross.

'I found *him* in the reading room trying to destroy the files.'

Pepin stood up. Lotte didn't understand. 'Destroy?'

Roo's face was white and his bad eye looked purple-red and sore. He didn't say anything, but he looked terrible.

Pepin started to speak, but Sabine continued.

'We're told we should respect the privacy of the people whose privacy has already been grossly exploited by the Stasi. We can't trust people like *you*!' she spat at Roo. She pulled out her chair, but remained standing.

Lotte stared at her. Sabine was dressed formally in black, but with a lime-green top under her suit. She flicked her dark hair from her shoulder. 'I'm just saying these documents we uncover, they should be protected from the likes of him, exploiting his sister, sending us all on a wild goose chase with a notebook that—'

'Sabine!' Pepin said, a warning note in her voice.

'He,' Sabine said, pointing at Roo, 'is an informer. A Stasi. A . . . a—' But she stopped. Lotte thought she was going to hit

Roo. Instead she continued, her voice making Lotte's head hurt. *Roo, a spy?*

'That's enough, Sabine,' Pepin said.

'The people in these pages are probably still alive. We owe it to them to try and maintain some *professionalism* . . . I thought you of all people would understand, Pepin.'

Sabine sat in her seat with a flourish. Lotte couldn't understand why Roo was destroying files. What was going on? She looked at him, but he didn't look back.

Ralf spoke. 'Sabine is right, Pepin. There are people out there waiting for answers. If we'd have known, we wouldn't have let you in here. We already have problems with files going missing,' Ralf said to Roo, 'and you come here to deceive us. To torture us further?'

'Lotte's doing her own work,' Pepin said. 'She has nothing to do with the files; they've been going missing for weeks. She only arrived yesterday.'

Pepin moved to Lotte's desk and lifted the copied sheet of paper that Lotte had returned from the copier yesterday.

'This isn't yours,' Pepin said, her face furrowed and frowned.

Before Lotte had a chance to speak, everyone started to exchange words loudly over the large table. Lotte rested back into the chair and checked her tongue was in her mouth. What had happened to Sabine's face? Why was she so mad at Roo? Who was *exploiting*? And why was her name involved? She thought of the notebook pages from yesterday – had Mama been ashamed of her when people said they were sorry she had a child with Down's syndrome?

Lotte looked at Roo – was he ashamed of her too? Was he a bad-man like Papa was in the pages? Or as Sabine had said – a Stasi, a spy? Lotte watched him take in the commotion in the room, and then he met her eyes, touched her on the arm.

'Time to go,' he said.

Lotte swayed as he bent to pick up her backpack.

'Come on.'

'But,' Lotte started, and the room rested back into uneasy silence. 'No. I won't go with you. I won't go with anyone.' His hand dropped from her arm. She turned to Pepin. 'Please, I just—' she implored Sabine and then Pepin. 'I don't remember her, Pepin. I don't. I don't understand any of it.' Lotte held her breath and watched Pepin's face and then continued, 'Please, she's in there, I know it.' She pointed to the stack of discarded paper. 'I've learned so much and done so much already. Please, with your help, I'd know more about her, and maybe there would be something about me too.'

Roo was there, but silent. She was doing this alone.

'How would you feel if you were searching for someone?' Lotte's words jumbled onto themselves as she turned to talk to Sabine. She had to repeat the last line for Sabine to understand her.

Sabine nodded and looked around at the others. 'I didn't mean to speak badly of you. I'm sorry, Lotte. I just find these things very difficult.' She went to hug Lotte, but the hug looked more like a small soft prison. Lotte crossed her arms instead.

She looked to Roo, her Roo, and he kept saying nothing. Not one thing.

'Perhaps they should go home?' Isolde said, her body hunched over. 'Lottechen, you can do it all yourself now. You're very good. You don't need our help any more.'

'No,' Lotte said. 'No. I cannot go home till it's done. It cannot all be forgotten. I will not let it.' She looked at Roo and the image of him swam as tears grew. 'You did not need to do bad things,' she said.

Pepin spoke: 'They can work in Herr Benedict's office. That way we can help, but they can't access the archives.' She turned to Roo. 'And nothing gets destroyed,' she added clearly.

Roo tried to say something, but he just opened and closed his mouth; his words were missing.

'If you must,' Sabine said stiffly. She wiped her eyes on her sleeve.

Lotte watched as Isolde nodded. Ralf looked at Sabine, who said quietly, 'Pushover,' before pushing a pile of shredded paper towards her.

'Come on,' Pepin said, and she lifted Lotte's table mat. Lotte carried her trays and backpack and followed.

'I have to go somewhere,' Roo said to her inside Herr Benedict's office, which was woolly-cool, both stuffy and cold. Lotte was confused.

'What?'

'Will you stay here, with Isolde or Pepin? I promise I'll come back for you.'

He didn't wait for her to answer, just walked away. She watched him speak with Pepin in the doorway; it was a short conversation during which Pepin looked confused, then happy. She touched Roo on the arm and then went back into the office. Lotte was left all alone.

She felt punished and pushed away.

She covered her ears and whispered *RooRooRooRoo* to try and make the scared go away and make Roo come back, but not the Roo that had been bad, not the *informer*, but the one she knew – from before.

Maybe Sabine had been wrong, and in that thought she found some comfort.

RUNE

What if she was alive? The question circled around and around in his head. He knew Lotte wouldn't leave the puzzle women now; there was little point in trying to make her, and where could they go? To go home would inevitably mean to be separated.

She was safe with Pepin or Isolde; they would look after her.

He told Pepin where he was going, desperate to know if his memory was wrong, if Mama had survived . . .

He called a taxi from reception and handed back his visitor pass. He knew where he wanted to go – a place he had never been able to forget, a place he had never thought he would ever return to. He was heading back to Berlin on the train without Lotte. But he was going to try and find Mama.

Hours later, hands thrust deep in his pockets, Rune's focus was on moving forward.

Memories were leapfrogging over each other as he paced the shrunken familiarity of the roads, and all too soon LightHouse loomed, tall and towering, standing alone on a road that had been all but demolished. Developer's signs had been strategically placed on every street corner and fences erected to keep people out. New housing, the signs showed, was coming soon on the greyed-out streets of his past.

LightHouse looked empty and quiet. It was the quiet that ran a skeletal hand of fear up his back. He stopped at the bottom of the steps.

For a moment he was desperate to turn away, to forget.

But no more.

He didn't want to recall the last time he was here. The last time he was here he could taste the bitter-iron roughness of blood on his tongue.

He could hear one word within him as though his entire body was made up of it and echoed it back to him with every beat of his heart.

Mama.

And he could remember that feeling, the stomach-dropping bowel-loosening skin-tightening eyes-widening feeling; the absurdity of something happening that shouldn't. The something that should never happen, happening right in front of him.

He chewed down on his inner cheek, as he had done then. His tongue grazed perforated skin, bringing the iron taste of blood back into his mouth and into a red haze.

He climbed one step and then another, until he was in front of the door. He leaned on the rail, the same rail Lotte had swung from on the very first day they arrived.

Please don't be in, a small voice in Rune's head whispered as he knocked. Each memory brought back events behind this door like skimming stones, each hurtling past before it dropped, sank, stopped. His breath was coming thick, fast, a torture to wait, to want, to know . . . and yet maybe, just maybe . . .

His violent heart. Its beat.

His breath. Its ferocity.

His shame. His guilt. His fault.

Mama.

THEN

He held a new fünf-mark note, one of many he was regularly gifted from Comrade Ackermann, who advised him to slip the money into Mama's purse to see how good it made him feel. He held the taste of the words he had spoken to earn it; it lay bitter on his tongue.

Pro-Western sentiments. Contraband materials. Antisocial behaviour and cavorting with East German dissidents.

He had no idea what most of these things meant, but he was getting quick at anticipating Comrade Ackermann's pauses and filling them with words that made no sense to him. Quite satisfactorily on most occasions.

Yet still Comrade Ackermann was never satisfied for long.

He had squeezed Rune's shoulder, slipped the money into his hand and asked, 'What about your mother? It must be hard for her to adapt to our ways? Especially when she spends time with "those women".'

Rune felt a sharp stinging pain weave across his forehead. Not Mama, surely, not Mama. He knew of some friends in the Pioneers who had denounced their parents to the party, but not him. Not him.

He held Lotte's hand tight as they walked from the park to the corner shop on the quest for sweets. He could put the rest of the coins in Mama's purse, but trying to slip in paper money was far harder – she'd notice and he didn't want her to know, he just wanted to help, in small ways, to make what he was doing better somehow. Comrade Ackermann was right – it made him feel good.

Rune hadn't ventured into the corner shop before, and as soon as he walked in he wanted to leave. The shop was small. Lights blinked at the back and it smelled of onions and cardboard.

The shelves were full of packets, faded through age or the sun, or both. The tins were dusty and had labels Rune had never seen before. Rice, noodles, fish in tins, beans, pulses, toilet paper, soap. A whole aisle had pickled cucumbers, which Nanya said were the 'Jewel of the East'. He had yet to be convinced.

Rune came to the end of the aisle and saw Lotte, just tall enough to look over the counter. She was talking to the shop-keeper, whose hat was pulled so low over his head that it covered his eyebrows. Rune joined Lotte at the counter; he could sense her frustration and had the instinct that this was about to end very badly and very soon.

The man talked directly to Rune, ignoring Lotte's question, uttering a deep guttural noise of disgust. 'Kids like that should be locked up, the lot of them.'

'Do you *have* sweets here?' Lotte asked innocently, still looking around.

'Does it look like it?' he answered gruffly, picking up his paper. 'Go on now, you lot cause nothing but trouble.'

Rune looked carefully around and saw a card in a stack just by the counter. The card had a bike on it. The same kind of bike that everyone had.

Perhaps Comrade Ackermann would be able to get him a bike. It was something he missed so much, pedalling and racing around. He thought of Papa.

'How much is a stamp?' Rune asked, taking a card from the rack. The man's face was blank. 'I want to post something,' he said tentatively, looking at Lotte, whose attention had been caught by a glass cabinet of cigarette packets, assorted matchboxes and lighters.

The man opened a folder and gave him the stamp. Rune quickly paid for both the stamp and the card and they walked out.

'That's not sweets,' Lotte wailed, looking at the card. 'That's a picture of a bike.'

In the street, the afternoon sun was high and hot; they quietly walked back to the park.

The voice of the shopkeeper, combined with Comrade Ackermann, made him worry; he knew Lotte was different, but to him she was special. His friends all complained about their little brothers and sisters, but his was funny and kind – yes, she made almost everything difficult, but she made him smile. Maybe he was soppy.

'Want to see what I thought we could do?' Rune asked, pushing his thoughts aside and putting the card down on the bench with the stamp resting carefully on top.

Lotte shook her head. 'I want LightHouse and Mama and our house with our things and my toys and the shop with the sweets and the things I like and and and . . .'

'And Papa?' Rune added.

'YES! And I want Papa most,' Lotte cried.

'Here.' He rummaged in his bag and pulled out the drawing paper he had received for Christmas. He sighed deeply. So long ago.

'Do you want to use my special paper?' Carefully he ripped out a sheet of paper for Lotte and while she rummaged happily through the pens and pastels, colours and charcoal, he dived into the pencil case for the tiny stub of a 4B pencil.

'Who are we drawing to?' Lotte asked.

'Papa,' Rune said quietly, unsure as he said it that it was a good idea, but settled on the impulse. Would joining the socialist party make his father proud? 'We can send him a picture so that he knows we love him and miss him.'

'Okay,' Lotte said. She pulled out her crayon roll from her own backpack and set about laying the paper flat on the cosmonaut book from her bag. She drew Papa a picture of a huge yellow house on a hill, with large pink flowers and a purple-blue sky.

Rune leaned on one of his school books and wrote 'Papa' at the top of the card. But nothing would come to him. He watched the empty park fill with other children, and still his paper remained white, because even though he missed home and Papa, he also didn't. He was caught up between wanting and not wanting. Missing and yet fearing. Sad and yet relieved. It was such a mosaic of feelings that, for the first time, he found he had nothing to draw.

When Lotte handed him her finished paper, he passed her the card.

'Do you want to sign your name?' he asked her.

'Oh yes,' she said, and scattered crayon blocks everywhere in her haste. She used the red crayon and, across the entire side of the card, she concentrated her efforts, tongue out.

'L: down and across. Look. I did it,' and she smiled. 'Come on, let's post it now, then Papa will get it and know we love him.'

Lotte was happy; that's what he had wanted. Rune wrote Papa's name and their old address on the front of the envelope, sealed it shut and licked the stamp. He placed it carefully in the corner and they went back to the shop to post it.

The man looked the envelope over, front and back, as if trying to find fault.

'You'll be wanting your address here,' he said, pointing to the back of the envelope. 'Or it won't get sent.'

Lotte shifted her weight from one foot to another and pulled hard on his sleeve.

'Do you have a toilet here?' he asked.

'No,' the man said, and pointed to the envelope. 'The address,' he prompted.

Rune scribbled their new address under the glare of the shopkeeper and handed the envelope back to him. He watched the man put the envelope into a big sack behind the counter.

Outside, on a quick-march skip-run back home and the toilet, Lotte said, 'I hope Papa likes my picture.'

'I'm sure he will love it,' he said.

NOW

THURSDAY 11TH NOVEMBER 1999

MARTINSFEUER – ST MARTIN'S DAY

LOTTE

Later, when Lotte's head felt strangely fluid and she was focusing so hard on pieces of paper that pages were coming together fast, Isolde poked her head in through the door.

'Any more?' she asked, and pulled up a small fold-out chair to sit next to Lotte. 'It'll be time to go soon, so I thought I would check in on you.' She leafed through the pages.

'Will you read them?' Lotte asked.

Isolde closed the door, gave Lotte a wink and nodded.

After he had finished with me in that clinical cell, my husband spoke words that do not belong here, in my book, written by my hand.

His words do not belong anywhere. He deserves to have no voice.

My ordeal that day was far from over. He had orchestrated the entire thing and he contained my cold lifeless body until it was no longer mine. I retreated so far into myself I could not answer to my name.

I was lost.

All I could think about was 'Why?' but the why came with an answer – I had left him and this was my punishment – correction – his discipline; disabling; disgust.

When he was done, he gave me my clothes, helped me into them. My mind was whitewashed, soiled. I couldn't button up my blouse. Whatever he aimed for, he had succeeded. The incredible lengths he had gone to, to prove his point. To realise his power over me. My lack of power over myself.

He gripped my arm tight as we walked away from that place. To anyone watching we looked like a young couple in love, arm in arm onto the street, ready to collect our children together.

'The Stasi Zersetzung technique is really rather good,' he laughed. 'Between you and me, I think we could learn a lot about psychological torture from them.'

'I was an experiment?'

'Only a small one. Very effective though.'

I vomited all over myself, unable to keep it in; expunged. Instead of allowing me home, he took me to the school, to Lotte's physio, and created a new image of himself: as a victim, a caring husband to a mentally unstable, poorly managing wife. How I had disturbed him from work, how I had removed him from his important day, and 'Look at her,' he told the physio. He told Rune's teacher too. 'Look at her.'

They did.

I did not look back at them to see what they saw of the 'her' that was me.

Only when both children were ready was I permitted to go home. Rune and Lotte walked ahead, each holding their papa's hand. I followed behind, covered in my dry-ing vomit. Unable to look up and see in my children's faces what they thought of me.

Questions formed on Lotte's tongue, but before she could voice them, Sabine opened the door. It slammed into Isolde's chair, knocking Lotte's question away with it.

'Time to go,' she said.

'Good luck, Lottechen, and thank you,' Isolde said, kissing Lotte on both cheeks before standing to leave. 'You have brought sunshine into my world today.'

'But— No. I—'

Lotte's heart sank as Isolde kissed both her cheeks and left the room. 'Go?' Lotte asked Sabine. 'But I haven't finished.' She looked at the pile still to complete. It was disappointingly big.

'That's okay. Would you like to come home with me again tonight?' Sabine asked. 'You don't have to. I know I wasn't very kind to Rune earlier and I'm sorry if my behaviour frightened you, or . . .' She swallowed. 'But I would like you to come back with me, if you would like to. If not, you can stay with Pepin tonight. Rune said he'd be back tomorrow.'

Something in Lotte's head snapped on. 'Tomorrow?' she asked.

'Yes. Pepin said he's trying to find someone called Nanya. Something about your mama.'

Nanya was one of the names in Mama's pages. Nanya was a friend.

'Do you need to tell your father where you are? I don't know if he would maybe worry. Perhaps Rune already has, but perhaps you should check?'

Lotte carefully dialled her home, saying each number out loud as she pressed down. Sabine watched her. She breathed a message to Papa, covering her mouth and the receiver with her hand. *Hi Papa, it's me. Lotte. I am going home with Sabine. I am fine and you are fine.*

'He says it's fine.' She turned to Sabine before putting the receiver down. Lying was bad, but going home without finishing the notebook was worse.

RUNE

At the small window beside the great blue door of LightHouse, a face peered out then disappeared.

He was sinking into a remembered helplessness. Nanya's face appeared from behind the half-opened door. She looked smaller than ever, and despite a smattering of white slicked through her black hair she looked almost *exactly the same*. She looked at him, confused. 'I'm sorry,' she said. 'We're closed . . .' and started to shut the door, but then stopped when she saw he was alone.

She paused, enticing him into a speech that would be ineffectual, as Rune, mouth open, could not find words to explain how he had come to be standing on the doorstep of his childhood.

'Nanya,' he said, her name furred on his tongue. 'I don't know if you remember me. You helped me and Mama, a long time ago.'

The door opened wider, revealing Nanya in a white and turquoise top with silver trim, bangles twinkling on her wrists. She smiled cautiously. 'I did?'

'I wanted to talk to you—'

'Rune?' she asked, astonished, as he nodded.

He checked he'd zipped his feelings up tight before continuing.

'I wanted to talk to you about Mama.'

A tangled silence followed; it curled around Rune's throat like a snake, but Nanya searched for something in his face that prevented him from having to speak. She didn't speak either and, standing on the doorstep, he wondered if she would turn him away.

'Rune?'

He nodded.

She looked at him until he felt cold, scared. Was this Nanya? The Nanya who welcomed everyone? She stared long into his eyes; he tried not to blink, but the intensity of her gaze made him shudder.

Finally Nanya looked away. 'I don't want any trouble,' she said. 'I suppose you're here about the notebook, but you should know I don't want to go over the past any more. I wrote that in the letter to you both.'

'I – well, I don't want to cause trouble either,' Rune said. 'It's just . . . Mama.'

Nanya nodded her head slowly. 'I understand. Why don't you come in?' she offered eventually, but warily. She peered over his shoulder and down onto the street before saying a little too abruptly, 'It's been a long time since I had visitors.' She opened the door wider to admit him and said, louder still, 'I rattle around in here all alone since we closed.'

He said nothing, but stared around him, astonished. There were no shoes littering the hallway. No clothes hanging on the pegs, bar a garment that obviously belonged to Nanya, a deep sapphire scarf draped over it.

It was silent.

Absolutely silent. The hallway seemed to vibrate in the peace, as though the cacophony of noise it used to bear was still held tight within its walls.

Nanya closed and locked the door, then peered out of the side window.

'What brings you here, Rune?' Nanya asked. 'It's just, I don't really see anyone any more. I've only been back a few years and they're still watching me, I know it. Things haven't changed much.'

But they had. Nanya didn't have an open smile for him any more. Her eyes darted and she wore suspicion on her lips, her face tight.

'I—' Rune started, but then found his words had nowhere to go, so he continued staring wildly around the hall. 'Why are you closed?' he asked, instead of answering her.

'New housing. New regulations. New world, Rune. I'm supposed to move to a small house a few streets away. Nice park nearby, but I can't seem to part with this place. I haven't really run it for years, but still it's mine to empty. Nobody needs it now but me. Drink?' Nanya added, and pointed him down the hall and into the kitchen.

The kitchen, where once there had been row upon row of tables of all shapes and sizes heaped together with barely any space to turn, now had just one small round table near the window. The room looked enormous.

Nanya filled the kettle, then looked at him. 'You're old enough now to want a proper drink.' And she pulled out a bottle of vodka from under the sink and offered it to him.

'Thanks,' he said.

'The refuges all have to conform to health and safety standards and so a place like this would never pass. There's only one family per room allowed now.' She poured two large glasses of vodka and seated herself opposite him.

Neither of them spoke for a while. He watched Nanya sip her drink.

'Are you keeping well?' Nanya asked eventually.

He shrugged. He felt like an idiot. 'Yes,' he said, but couldn't manage any more than that.

'And Lotte?'

Rune couldn't look up. Nanya stood and opened a yellow pack of *Russisch Brot*; he watched her arrange the large biscuit letters on a plate, which she brought to the table.

'I need to talk to you, about when we lived here,' he said, trying to work out how he could possibly admit to what he had done.

'You were the first family I had that came across the Wall at that time. It just wasn't heard of. Your mama went through a lot to get here,' Nanya said.

Rune nodded, recalling the taxi, the guards and a long, slow walk to LightHouse.

Nanya looked at him closely, as though expecting him to say something. But he was thinking of the heat of the summer-stealing sun as the colour wheel of autumn memory turned to grey. Then stopped.

'I think of your mama all the time,' Nanya said, sinking behind the table. She took off her glasses and rubbed her eyes wearily. 'I've spent years trying to find out what happened to her.'

Rune wrung his hands, fighting a losing battle over his breathing.

'What do you mean?' he asked, swallowing hard.

Nanya nodded as though she expected him to ask that very question. 'Five years I spent in Siberia, Rune. Five years for seeking out the truth – for trying to understand what happened to your mama. Five years . . .'

'I don't understand, Nanya – after the Wall fell, you were in Siberia?'

Nanya nodded. 'Siberia made Hohenschönhausen look like a playground. The Stasi . . .' she said softly, seriously. Rune gulped his vodka too fast; he felt it burn all the way down his throat. She must have known it was him all along, he thought. 'The Stasi sent me to Hohenschönhausen when you lived around the corner, you remember?'

He nodded.

'Then after what happened with your mama, the authorities sent me to Moscow, then a longer stay in Siberia.'

He wanted to say 'sorry', sorry for it all. But words seemed ineffectual. Useless. Unsuitable. He allowed Nanya to continue uninterrupted.

'Hohenschönhausen, first. Siberia, later. Interrogated, jailed, sleep-deprived. What did any of it matter when I didn't matter? My life meant nothing. All they wanted was to cover it up,' Nanya continued. 'Even years later, they're still trying to cover their tracks. They follow me and steal my post, even to this day. They don't want me asking questions, that's the truth.'

'I don't understand.' He leaned forward, closing the gap between him and Nanya. 'I was there on the day Mama died and I saw . . . but I found a poster that said Mama was missing. *They* said she was missing.' He took the file out of his bag, opened it to the poster, and handed the file to Nanya. 'Is she alive?' he asked, trying to stop himself from reaching out to her, to make her speak to him.

She looked closely at the picture. 'It's just right, you know – not pretty, not constructed, but so real. You had a gift.' And Nanya looked at him and smiled fully, looking more like the Nanya he remembered.

'Faces,' Nanya said. 'It was all about faces, expressions – like a palm reader, you could just see the essence of a person from their face and actually sketch it too. Can you remember drawing me in my cubby once? I still have that picture.'

Rune remembered drawing portraits all the time. He loved creating faces from the stroke and shade of a pencil and at LightHouse he'd not been short of different expressions to capture. Mama's face too. All the many fractions of expressions. He wished he could draw her again with the new skills he'd accumulated over the years.

The wish to draw was alive and busy under his skin. It was a good feeling. He allowed it to live there and hoped it might stick around long enough for him to put pencil to paper again. He missed the light-feeling of ink sinking into paper, of his mind resting, flowing, creating.

'I am old now, Rune. Very old,' Nanya said, closing the file. 'And finally, it seems life is covering me with a blanket of forgetfulness in my old age.'

She looked to the window behind Rune's head, then got up and stared into the darkening street.

'I honestly don't know, that's the truth,' she told the wall behind his shoulder, and then shook her head and spoke louder. 'I'm just an old woman raving about a friend she once lost.' She turned around to look at the poster on the table. 'Where did you get this?'

'The notebook you sent to us got shredded, so Lotte's at the archives, piecing it together.'

'Shredded?' Nanya asked.

'Papa tore it up. I went after Lotte and there were some files on us from when we lived here.' He stopped talking, finding he couldn't go on. He didn't want to expose the truth, so he asked instead, 'Where did you get the notebook?'

. She withdrew a key from a chain around her neck. 'The flat,' Nanya said, as though *the flat* itself was a difficult thing to say. 'There were things left after Elke died. Things of your mama's.'

He felt pinned down, exposed; it was his childhood self that had brought him here, unable to deny the possibility that she might be alive.

'I boxed them up. After . . .' Nanya said. 'We still used the flat on Winzer for other women. Elke lived in it last – do you remember Elke?' Her voice was splintered and after each sentence she was struggling for breath, as though the words were a sprint.

'She stayed away? From her son and her husband?' He recalled the scene with her son – Elke, her white hair sitting atop her head and wide, misdirected eyes.

'She stayed away until the day she died.'

'I'm sorry.'

'Just a few weeks ago,' Nanya said, answering a question he hadn't asked. 'There was no one to clear the flat. It's taken me a long time to clear everything that accumulated both here and in the flat too.' And she seemed frail, scared, jittery, not looking at Rune, but again at the window.

'I petitioned the consulate, I reported your mama missing to the Red Cross, I went to the police every day. I did everything I could, Rune. I loved her very much. I tried and tried. But they sent me to Moscow, and then on to Siberia.' She stopped talking and examined the bottom of her glass. 'I always thought she was alive. I just couldn't believe the other options.'

He became defenceless, without skin. Nanya carried on talking, unaware of his skinlessness. The past whispering here, whispering there: *FlatHouse. Missing. Lotte. Mama.* Forming words in the shape of breath, becoming a weightless sound sent in the air to dissipate and die.

THEN

AUGUST 1989

Mama had worked hard on the flat, but Lotte behaved like a baby, crying and unpacking and hiding both herself and their things. Mama was angry. Lotte screamed the whole way there; Mama carried her in the end. It was horrible. Rune put Mama's bag on the now upright table and noticed a small television set perched on a stool. He looked it over, but didn't turn it on in case it didn't work. He didn't want to hope, because hope always led to disappointment.

Lotte and Mama came into the room, both in tears. Lotte howled and kicked, her hair plastered to her head with sweat. Mama sobbed gently, her face as red as Lotte's. Rune took his bag to his room.

He listened as Mama showed Lotte the house.

'This is our bathroom,' Mama said.

'Where are the smelly babies and the nest-towels and the stinky nappies?'

'This is our bedroom,' Mama said.

'But there is a door!' Lotte exclaimed. 'And the curtains look like orang-u-tangies. Where is Roo?'

'Roo will sleep in here,' Mama said, poking her head in.

'On his own?'

'Yes.'

Lotte started crying again.

Rune shut the door.

He lay on the bed, freshly made with grey-white sheets and a grey-black blanket, with one of the burst cushions from the living room fixed up as a pillow.

He fell asleep in the blanket of calm, swaddled in peace.

He woke to Mama calling, 'LOTTE!' and bashing around. She opened his door and it slammed into the wall. The unsaid on her face was a frozen fog of fear. It fizzed in him as he slipped on his shoes.

'LightHouse,' Mama said. 'She'll have gone back to LightHouse.' Her voice was more worried than cross.

He held Mama's hand as they walk-ran the sun-baked streets and turned the corner to LightHouse.

When Nanya opened the door, her smile was confused. 'Well, that was quick,' she laughed, and Rune knew that Lotte wasn't there and Mama knew it too.

'Lotte,' is all Mama said.

'I'll check the park,' he said.

Mama held him back.

'If she's not there I'll come straight here,' he said and reluctantly she let him go.

He ran to the park. He ran to the corner shop. He ran to find Lotte, and in every footstep he hated her for turning what was supposed to be the best day into the worst.

He was sweating, thirsty, scared and dirty when he returned to LightHouse without Lotte. There were mass protests happening and the streets around LightHouse were quiet. Many of the mamas had gone, to protest for freedom of movement.

Freedom of movement. It was a strange concept. There was no freedom of that kind that he knew of; every time they moved, something else caught them. Trapped.

A mama he didn't know answered the door and welcomed him in. She took him by the hand and spoke to him as though he were a baby. 'Mama and Nanya have gone out to look for her with some of the other mamas. Don't you worry. Aunty Tanja will make you a drink and clean you up, ready for when they get home.' He allowed her to lead him into the kitchen and took the mildew-smelling flannel from her.

'This isn't my home,' he said, giving it back and taking the glass of water on offer.

The mama said nothing more as they waited and the hubbub of LightHouse grew around him, like a rainforest; its oppression and heat came from the floor and penetrated him at every angle.

'I'll wait for Mama in the garden,' he said as a mama dropped an enormous saucepan into the sink and the babies started wailing.

'Do you want me to stay with you?' she asked.

Rune just walked away.

His vision was jumping with each beat of his heart. He was so mad with Lotte for doing this, but what if neither she nor Mama returned? What if *he* became the forgotten one? The lost one?

He sat under the oak tree in the corner of the garden. The heat from the sun was yolky under the cloud of leaves. Fear whipped at his skin as he waited.

Finally, as massive clouds rolled overhead, he heard Nanya's voice calling his name.

Make them find me, he thought, but stood almost instantly, his resolve wilting like the weather.

'Rune?' It was Mama's voice, and she sounded worried.

'Roo?' And Lotte too.

'We found her,' Mama said, coming out into the garden and walking down the steps.

He didn't know what to say. Lotte had been crying, her face was red, but she was whole, unharmed.

'What were you thinking, Lotte?' Mama said after Nanya had delivered cold drinks from the kitchen.

'I do not like FlatHouse,' Lotte said. 'I want to live at LightHouse.'

Mama held her tight. 'It doesn't matter where we live as long as we're together.'

'At LightHouse?' Lotte asked.

'No,' he said.

'No,' Mama said. 'In our own home. Together.'

'But. But,' Lotte stuttered. 'What if the *mans* come, and we do not have all the mamas to stop them or Nanya to make them go? We need all the mamas to be the big wall to make the *mans* go away,' she wailed.

Mama opened her mouth to speak, but Lotte continued, 'At school, Jutte said that the *mans* came for her papa and took him away. And . . . and Tasha said both her mama and papa were taken by *mans* and she lives with her aunty Hannele who is NOT her mama or her papa. And . . . and Rebekka was taken by the *mans* in a bakery van for a long holiday without going anywhere.'

'It'll just be you and me and Roo,' Mama said, but Rune wondered just how Mama had got the apartment in the middle of a housing crisis and why she didn't have the same fears of the Stasi as others did.

The next day, Nanya, with her toolbox, fitted a lock at the top of the front door. Too high for Rune to reach, unless he stood on a chair. Too high for Lotte to reach at all.

'To keep the mans out,' Lotte explained to Moo Bunny as they watched Nanya. But as Mama slid the lock, Rune thought it was probably to keep Lotte in.

Later that day, Rune was drawing at the table, spreading his pens across the full space with the old television showing *Aktuelle Kamera*, the state news, in black and white. Mama and Lotte were baking a fruit cake in the kitchen, talking about getting a lady-hen to lay eggs. Lotte was clucking and making Moo Bunny sit on the eggs as though he was hatching them and Mama's tinkling laugh lit him up inside.

They were home.

NOW

THURSDAY 11TH NOVEMBER 1999

MARTINSFEUER – ST MARTIN'S DAY

LOTTE

'When does your Clio come home?' Lotte asked as Sabine was clearing away the evening meal.

'Saturday,' she said.

'That's still a long time,' Lotte said, after working the days of the week through in her head. *Thursday. Friday. Saturday.*

'It is. She'll be at the lantern festival tonight.'

Lotte waited for Sabine to say more, but when she didn't Lotte tried hard to use her thinking head to understand what might be going on inside her, but she was feeling very tired and very sad and Roo was not here. *Inde-pen-dence is very difficult when you feel alone*, Lotte thought.

'Would you like to sleep in Clio's bed tonight?' Sabine said, holding a pillow and a blanket in her hands.

'Oh no – I'll sleep on the sofa. I do not want to be getting under the way.'

'You aren't,' Sabine said. She was dressed in joggers and a small T-shirt. 'Shall I make cocoa before bed?' she asked, but Lotte yawned widely and giggled.

'Tired seems to come at you from all ways and then when it's inside you have to sleep.'

'Indeed. I am sorry about Rune,' Sabine said. 'The Stasi caused so much damage. If we can put the pages together, maybe a few more families would be reunited. Maybe there is more the past can offer us than the present and seeing what he was doing with the files, I – I don't know, maybe there is something wild inside of me waiting to emerge.'

Lotte listened hard. 'I think that you have been through tror-mat-ik times and that when Clio is home-here then you are feeling better. Babies come out of their mama's bodies and I think if they are apart the bodies miss each other.'

Sabine stopped what she was doing, her hands poised in mid-air. 'I agree,' she said.

'When you are doing missing with all of your body your heart can be wild because it is sad,' Lotte continued. 'Roo will under-stand, because he knows more than me.'

'I don't think that could possibly be true,' Sabine said. Her gaze was gentle.

'I have always missed Mama in my body, my head just didn't know it. Maybe your body is speaking loudly to you and your head just has to listen. My body is tired so my head has to sleep.'

Lotte placed herself happily on the sofa and admired the yellow sleeping dog-rugs again.

'I think you are one of the smartest and kindest people I know,' Sabine said, bringing cocoa to Lotte.

'It's a good thing I am your best-friend then,' Lotte said.

'My very best.'

'Sabine,' she asked, 'will you tell me a story?'

Lotte pulled her blanket up under her chin and Sabine seated herself at her feet.

In the darkening light, Sabine told a story about an owl, who was stolen from its nest when it was very small and lived in a large tree full of birds. The tree was noisy and many of the other birds were sad and lost too.

Finally, when the owl's wings were fully grown, she was able to fly away from the giant tree. She was looking for her nest again, looking for a place she belonged. On her journey she met another bird, who looked and sounded just like an owl. It was only after they had built a nest together that the owl discovered her mate was a fake, not another owl at all. But the owl already had an egg and then a small owlet. She didn't want the owlet to be taken from the nest like she had been, so she stayed and stayed and learned how to love.

But one day the fake-owl flew away, taking the baby owlet with him. The mama owl was very scared. When the fake-owl had a car accident, the little owlet got badly hurt. She was in hospital for a long time and the mama owl was allowed to see her again. The mama owl refused to let the baby owl go. Older, uglier birds made lots of big decisions for the mama owl and her little owlet that she didn't like. She fought long and hard to keep the owlet; she almost lost everything, but in the end she didn't lose the owlet.

Now the owlet has two nests where she is loved, but the mama owl misses her love, which only returns when the owlet is by her side.

'Your story is sad,' Lotte said when Sabine had finished.

'Maybe that is because I am sad.'

'Do all stories tell only of ourselves?'

'No,' Sabine said. 'I just wanted to share something of myself with you. You have shared so much with me.'

'I like having you as my friend. My owl friend.'

'You to-wooo,' Sabine said.

'Did you make a joke?' Lotte asked sleepily.

'I tried.'

Lotte thought really hard; she heard Sabine get up and walk back into the kitchen, then she grasped at the word as it flew into her head.

'You're a hoot!'

Lotte could hear Sabine's laugh roll around the flat; the posters on the wall shimmered in its power. Lotte felt good, really sunflower-yellow good, and she fell asleep listening to the warming glow of Sabine's laugh.

RUNE

Nanya cleared her throat and he looked up from the file that had Mama's picture in it and the words of hope that were just that. Hope, unfulfilled hope. The first inklings of panic rumbled like the rolling of distant thunder. What was he going to do now?

'I haven't eaten dinner yet. Would you like to join me?' Her eyes were focused on him, her gaze warm.

'That would be nice,' he said. 'Can I pop out for a bit of fresh air first?'

Outside, the night opened him up in a violent twist, a crack, back into the present. He walked in the darkened streets of his childhood, resting on a bench in the local park where vodka bottles, syringes and cigarette ends littered the grass. He smoked, watching the ash creep up his cigarette and melt off.

Nanya was cooking for him. She'd thought about him and Lotte; she'd tried to find out what happened to Mama. He had to tell her the truth; he didn't deserve her kindness. He'd taken advantage of it time and time again.

Pockets of families started a St Martin's Day procession; it passed through the park, brought alive by the warmth of children's voices, singing. They grew around him in number as lanterns, lit and bobbing, welled towards him on the bench. He stood, attempting to leave, but as the song picked up, more and more families emerged from their houses to a chorus of song:

> *I go with my bright little lantern*
> *My lantern is glowing for me.*

Rune tried to keep away from the sea of tiny bobbing lights, but was swallowed up in the wave and found the golden drop of song on his lips:

> *In heaven, the stars are shining*
> *On earth shines my lantern for me.*

A woman pushing a sleeping child in a buggy offered him a small handmade paper lantern with a tiny tea light in it. He declined, but because he couldn't push past her and she kept offering it to him, he finally, on the road leading back to LightHouse, accepted. He would give Lotte the lantern and tell her about the times they had made their own and joined in the procession as children.

As Nanya let him back in, he blew out the tea light and placed the lantern by his bag. She offered him a bowl of vegetables and rice noodles, which were fresh, zingy and hot.

'How is Lotte doing now?' Nanya said, breaking the clotted air that held them.

'She's good,' he said.

'I had such a soft spot for that girl. And your father?' Nanya pointed at his eye.

Rune nodded. 'He got a promotion – *President of the Federal Police*. He's been worse since.'

'I'm sorry.'

'Nanya, I have to tell you something. It's about when we were here. It's about what I did, and—'

'It was a long time ago now, Rune – try not to dwell on the past. I believed your mama was alive all these years and it got me into no end of trouble.'

He took her advice and grew quiet.

'When I was in Hohenschönhausen, do you remember? – all those years ago,' Nanya said, 'I was put in an isolation cell where you couldn't stand up straight. They would pump them with water. Imagine, standing hunched over in the dark and feeling water rushing in, ever rising, and not knowing when or whether it would stop.' Nanya stopped. 'I kept looking for her for all these years, even when I was in Siberia, because when I was locked away for those long days in Hohenschönhausen, she was here, she kept LightHouse running, and she came to get me when I was able to leave. I couldn't live with the thought of her there, forgotten, and no one looking for her.'

'But, Nanya,' Rune said, standing, 'it was my fault you were in there. I did it. They forced me to say things I didn't understand, to inform on everyone I knew. I told lies about you. I caused you pain and I hurt you, after all you did for me and for Mama.' His shame was too big for tears. He wanted to peel off his skin entirely; he was raw and he prickled with revulsion at himself.

'You informed on me?' Nanya said. Her voice held a soft solidity, then a disbelief. 'You informed on me?' A sudden tone of panic.

He didn't want to see her face.

'I am so sorry,' he said, sitting and staring into his bowl of noodles.

He waited for her to speak, to shout, to tell him to leave. She said nothing. For hours, or minutes or seconds, with time a non-linear entity that seemed to move in abstract form. He remained seated, eyes down. The only thing he saw were his noodles getting cold in the bowl in front of him. Finally, Nanya got up from the table and returned with a pillow and a blanket.

'You can sleep on the sofa,' she said, her voice whispering into the darkness of Rune's heart. 'We can talk in the morning, if you would like to stay?'

He nodded and she excused herself to bed, looking older and sadder than he had ever seen her. It was all his fault. All of it.

But he had nowhere else to go. He didn't stay because he wanted to stay. He stayed because he had to be somewhere; he could not be nowhere. He hoped at LightHouse he would find Mama – that she was alive, that his memory was wrong. If he went back to Lotte, what would she say when she knew all he had done? Where would they go when the notebook was finished? Papa could take Lotte away from him; Lotte might even want to go.

He washed his and Nanya's bowls before moving onto the sofa. Unable to be still with his thoughts, nor alone. His body and mind felt both weary and agitated. He took two oxy, some painkillers to kill his pain, if pain was able to be killed in such a way – then two more when it didn't help. The need for some respite from his own thoughts crept through his hair and nibbled away at him.

The enormous house was eerily quiet.

With his nails biting into the palms of his hands, his teeth grinding and his tongue ashes in the furnace of his mouth, Rune cried.

He didn't stop. He had hoped that coming here and speaking to Nanya would offer him a different ending, where something else had happened that he'd somehow missed or forgotten. But he was wrong to hope. The past seemed always to be present and he was about to lose everything.

IV.

Time seems to pass both forward and back.

I am here, yet I am not; I take myself back to be with my children, in order to keep moving forward. The thinking part of my life has been over for so long, it's hard to form a thought, an illicit thought, one that is purely my own.

I have forgotten how.

My thoughts, like my wrists, are bolted, chained, tethered.

My greatest fear circles around; it catches me, it tears my breath from my lungs.

I am running, leaving.

Don't look back.

Our freedom stretches like the horizon, an untouchable, unreachable destination.

I focus on the children. On their needs. Their presence by my side should calm me, but I know if I fail they will be ripped from me. That I will have to live without them and they without me. That no matter how I stretch out my arms, or use my entire voice or my body to propel me towards them, my babies will be taken from me and I from them.

This fear is untouchable, and yet I have lived it every day since I gave birth, consumed by its presence.

Don't look back.

I am surrounded by the sound of my breath, poised, waiting, to feel his breath join mine, his fingers outstretched to clasp my arm, my neck, my children. I feel flat, white, thin. Like paper, but transparent. How will I be able to hold on to them when I am no longer substance? They will slip through my arms as if I were made of smoke. I will fade and they will be left alone.

Don't look back.
But how can anything other than my breath move forward?

NOW

FRIDAY 12TH NOVEMBER 1999

LOTTE

She dreamed of a cool hand resting smooth and gentle upon her warm pink cheek. A hand brave and well and strong, and its essence soaked into her; she was drawing in the hand, the touch colouring her. She dreamed the essence, a rainbow drop, of the person who set their hand on her cheek. She dreamed that person had a name. She dreamed the hand belonged to Mama, who was nothing more than a hand pressed to her cheek.

When she awoke, she didn't want to open her eyes, wanting to keep the cool hand, the touch, but . . . she could hear someone bashing around. Bleary and confused, she finally peeked. Her head hammered and her mouth was so dry she was unable to move her tongue.

'Morning,' Sabine said.

Lotte got up and stumbled; she felt horribly tired. She looked around for Roo.

'Is Roo back?' she asked.

Sabine shook her head. 'But I have made more of your mama's pages this morning,' she added, pointing to three closely written pages on the kitchen side. 'I think they fit with the one you brought back with you last night.'

Lotte felt shame that she had to have other people tell her about Mama. What it meant. Mama was being defined by those who read her notebook and she felt powerless to stop everyone knowing so much more than she did. Before she did. The feeling she couldn't articulate was jumping around inside her head. She didn't understand. She was finding out about Mama from the outside, yet nothing was coming from within. She had been read the notebook and still she couldn't remember.

'I am grumpy,' Lotte said.

Sabine nodded. '*Pfannkuchen* might help?'

The smell of giant puff-pancakes seemed to melt some of the grumpy away from her shoulders. Lotte nodded.

'I am going to fill mine with fruit. Would you like the same?'

Lotte nodded.

'And while you wash up, I can go down and get you some more of Luise's cocoa. Chocolate always helps the morning grumps, I find.'

'I like making chocolate cake for breakfast, or other cakes. I like baking,' Lotte said slowly.

'Baking is the best.'

'The smell,' they said together, and laughed. Lotte felt lighter; she had never had a friend before and it was a very lovely feeling.

'Go and have a shower,' Sabine said. 'There's no rush.'

Lotte sighed and walked away. 'There's some fresh clothes on the toilet seat for you,' Sabine called as Lotte shut the bathroom door.

Lotte washed with pink foamy soap in the sink and put on the clothes that did not have her name labelled on them.

Lotte took a long time to think over Sabine's story about the owls and about Ralf and the children's home. How Isolde was the reason why Ralf was taken away and why Winola had been lost. How Ralf couldn't forget and had hoped for money for what was done. Lotte tried to make the thoughts slow down, but she was scared they would swim over her and drown her. She thought of her notebook, of Roo and of Mama.

'I don't remember my mama,' Lotte said, blurting out the words as Sabine sprinkled cinnamon sugar on their *Pfannkuchen* and offered Lotte a cup of cocoa. 'All I know is that she's dead,' she said slowly. 'I think my papa did really bad things, hurt Mama, and Mama . . .' But what she was about to say melted away. 'Papa ripped up Mama's words,' she continued, 'but I don't know why, and Roo left yesterday and I don't know why.'

Sabine paused before putting the plates down.

'I want to know things that make sense. All I feel is tired and more unhappy. Can knowing more things make you feel worse?'

A long weighty silence stretched over them and Lotte felt so deeply sad she wasn't sure what to do with herself. She picked up her cocoa and drank the delicious, rich, creamy chocolate. Its deliciousness make her feel worse somehow. She set it back down.

Sabine was sipping a cup of tea that smelled of mint; Lotte ground her teeth together to try and distract herself. Something tickled at the corners of her memory, then scratched and stung like nettles.

'I was in that children's home, Torgau, like Ralf,' Sabine said. 'We never met. I've never told him.'

'Why?'

'It's always been a huge part of Ralf's narrative. I didn't want to take any of that away from him,' she said. 'And also, when you say things aloud, they feel more real. If it exists only inside me, then maybe it's not true.'

'Like Papa may have hurt Mama, but if I don't read the note-book I will never really know and then I will not feel all crumpled up and con-fuzzed.'

'Exactly.'

'Do you want to tell me about that place?' Lotte asked, spiking some blueberries with her fork.

'Torgau was a terrible place. Many children with Down's syn-drome were there too. They were so trusting and it made me sick to see what was done. Everyone suffered, but children like you more than most.' Sabine's face changed and she looked younger suddenly. 'Another girl – like you,' Sabine continued, 'she told one of the guards our plans to escape, just because the guard asked. Fucked us right over, she did.' Sabine swallowed hard and Lotte saw she was crying.

'I'm sorry about your mama,' Sabine said, as quietly as a con-fession. 'I understand some of what she went through. The guards in Torgau – there was a lot of abuse. If it wasn't you, it soon would be, if you know what I mean?'

Lotte didn't know what she meant, but she did want to cry. She felt hot tears prick in her eyes and her cheeks flush, because Sabine was hurting on the inside and those hurts are much harder to heal. She swallowed and, sitting up straight, took a long deep breath.

She thought of Mama's words . . . how she heard them through Sabine or Isolde. She couldn't do any of this alone, and therefore she was having to share everything about Mama when all she wanted was to *know* her. Really know her.

Perhaps she never would.

They ate the pancakes in silence and Lotte finished her cocoa. She enjoyed the puff of pancake and the bright pop of fruit. She ate with relish. Having placed her plate in the sink, Lotte turned, and before she could work out what was happening, Sabine picked up a page and started to read:

This is how it starts.

New words, new stories. Lotte couldn't find space to hold anything else; she felt completely full of things she didn't understand. Yet she listened as Sabine started to read.

I was chained to the life of wife.

'Oh my God, is it moving? The growth — it's fucking moving?'

'The growth is our child!' I corrected him.

'Do something, cover it up, it looks like a fucking alien crawling around in there . . . fuck!'

I laughed at his frightened face.

And he slapped me.

A sting. A flash. A growing red welt. The shape of a man's hand grew red on my skin. My husband's hand.

I covered up.

This is how it starts.

Funny how I had his name, I was his wife, we lived in his house, spent his money, I was growing his child. I never thought I would look back and see the person I was in that moment — the moment when everything ended. The moment when he first hit me.

And now I look back and write her – the me that I once was – I write her fresh and new, seeing her through eyes that are free. I know she should have got up, covered her stretching skin and walked out of the door. She should have kept on walking and never ever looked back. The me that is writing this now doesn't pity the me I was then; she stayed, she was in shock, she needed time to think. The question 'Why?' formed an endless cycle. And the chains grew tighter, slithered around her until she was incapable of movement at all.

This is how it ends.

She was wary; the next time he slapped her face she didn't feel shock, she had expected it. The baby that had been the bump was now attached to her breast. She had lived in the waiting for the next slap, and the relief when it came was instant. She knew after the first time it would happen again; she just didn't know when. And in the instant it arrived, the fear evaporated with its sharp hot sting. The waiting was finally over.

The she that is me writes this and wonders; this kind of thing doesn't happen to smart, educated, empowered women. So what does that make me? Because it did happen. It happened to me.

This is how it ends.

Removed from my own story, my own life. I watch as the me I thought I knew is killed. Destroyed. I watch as her body turns into his, for his amusement, his ridicule, his disgust, his pleasure; his object to torment and erase.

There was not a 'me' left in my body.

This is how it starts.

When the burns scab, the flesh bruises and the semen is wiped from my thighs, I remove myself from my body, I can no longer see the me that I am. I crawl away from the shame, that he has made me into a thing, he has dehumanised me and he has done it in front of my children.

My rapist was not a shadow, a crook, a stranger. He was not a person who stalked or scared or insulted me on the street.

My rapist was the man lying in my bed at night, choosing when to attack, choosing his advantage. It was in waiting that I knew what would come to me – and there was nothing to stop it.

I fought back, time after time, but time after time I was overpowered. Until there was no fight left.

My rapist owned my body, disabled my mind.

My rapist was no stranger.

Each rape was a fight that I could not and did not win. Each rape was a defeat and in each defeat the language

315

I could use to speak this truth became shamed on my tongue.

Screams or silence – it didn't matter what I did because every part of me was limp, raped, numb.

My rapist was the father of my children. I watched him play with them, fix bikes, kick balls, read stories.

My rapist was my husband. A man my children called 'Papa', the man I said I loved.

But finally, this is how it ends.

On a blanket on the floor, a pillow under me, an hour of silence, of peace, unbroken; a small tub of vegetable oil, two fingers and finally a way to find my body again, to love and be loved and orgasm unhurried; again and again through love, joining my mind and my body together with me; finally. And sated, satisfied, whole, I laugh and I raise my middle finger, my slimy, sticky, beautiful, glistening finger, and I say: 'Fuck you, who knew nothing of me, of the power of me, of the restlessness of me. Fuck you, who took pain where pleasure hid. Fuck you, who harmed and hurt and laughed and turned me into nothing. Fuck you, because look who's fucking me now!'

'Fuck,' Sabine said, and stepped forward to Lotte, still holding the page. 'Fuck.'

'That's a bad word,' Lotte said.

Lotte's mind was swirling with things she did not and could not understand. *Mama wrote bad words. The F word is a bad word and Sabine keeps saying it.*

'I wish you would stop,' Lotte said, and tried to pinpoint what had happened in the words Sabine had read. There was so much, and it hurt. All the confusing words came at Lotte in words filled with pain. Mama had been hurt by Papa. *Raped* was a word she knew from Frau Anst's class on relationships. Rape was making love without the love. Without saying 'yes'. And Papa did that to Mama?

'And I thought I had problems,' Sabine said, and although the words were harsh, Sabine touched Lotte's hand gently. 'Men are fucking wankers, Lotte. Just remember that. Your own father included,' she said, and sighed. 'I'm sorry, but your mama . . .' – and Lotte watched Sabine read the letter again, as though there was something to treasure within it – 'Your mama is a fucking hero,' and Sabine put down the page and started to sob. Thick, fat, wracking breaths wheezed out of her; she doubled over and Lotte was not sure what to do.

She watched as a noise, a big, horrible, scary noise, came out of Sabine. Lotte looked around; she didn't know what to do. Roo would know what to do. Where was Roo?

But there was just her, and there was Sabine, who had read one of Mama's pages and was contorted in a pain that must have come from the inside.

Lotte stood up and fetched the toilet roll. She passed the whole thing to Sabine, who unravelled it gratefully.

'Can you not tell anyone about this?' Sabine asked when she had gained control over the thing that was hurting her – could it be a memory? Lotte wondered if a memory could cause pain like that.

'I won't say anything,' she said, and touched Sabine on the arm. Sabine wiped the last of the mascara away and blew her nose. 'All I have done is cry these past two days,' she said, and tried to laugh, but it was false and short.

'Can I hug you?' Lotte asked. 'I think you need a hug more than anyone.'

Tears welled in Sabine's eyes again and she nodded, a minute movement, but as Lotte wrapped her arms around Sabine's tiny frame, Sabine hugged her back, her arms strong.

'Thank you,' Sabine whispered, and broke away from the hug.

Lotte fell into a deep silence, watching the words on the page whizz and scoot around as Sabine washed her face in the bathroom. She came out pristine, as though nothing had happened.

'You coming?' Sabine asked her. 'We've got work to do,' she added, but she smiled at Lotte when she said it.

Lotte placed the bad-word letter and all its confusing meanings into her bag. Slowly, and with an enormous amount of effort, she followed Sabine.

RUNE

He had woken early and drawn the curtains. He and Lotte were under the same sore-looking sky; he wondered whether, if Lotte looked up, she would think the same. The blush of pink, becoming a raw-red, held his focus and he tried just to exist in the now, but it seemed impossible. Everything seemed impossible. He wondered what the point was to his suffering, the point of him living. The effects of last night's double dose of oxy made his skin feel too tight and his eyes dry; he wanted more, he wanted anything that could take him away from his life. Anything at all.

He folded and refolded the blanket and paced the room hundreds of times. Back and forth, back and forth. He was awaiting Nanya's judgement; she would tell him to go to hell, tell him he had ruined her life, tell him what scum he was. Tell him he was just like his father. He wanted to allow her that right – the right to tell him. He tried to prepare himself to face it; he wasn't a coward, he wouldn't run away from the truth.

He would hear all that Nanya wanted to say and then he would leave. He would collect Lotte from the puzzle women and then what? And then what? And then . . . what? There was nothing after that.

He'd come all this way in the hope that Nanya knew something about Mama. That Mama was alive. Nanya knew no more than he did, and she had held her hope ablaze for years, whereas he had found no reason to hope, not even for a moment.

Finally, he heard footsteps. Morning light, bright and white, landed with a freshness on Nanya's skin. As she walked into the living room she looked at him, her face tired and worn out, but kind. It was a face from his past.

He wanted to sketch her. In biro, or a sharp pencil. Clear, clean lines to show her wise, considered face. He put the thought away as she spoke.

'There are so many memories left in this place,' Nanya said, looking around the room, then abruptly changed the subject. 'I'm sorry I was rude to you yesterday. It took a lot of courage for you to tell me what you did.'

'No – I'm grateful you let me stay, but I don't deserve anything more from you. I took enough. I wanted to apologise again and leave.'

'Please,' Nanya said, 'come, and I'll make some breakfast.'

He followed Nanya into the kitchen, noticing for the first time that she had a significant limp and that her left leg dragged. He felt protective; he wanted to look after her.

'Can I help?' he asked. Nanya directed him to the bread and gave him the knife while she put the coffee on.

'You did what you had to do,' Nanya said, once breakfast was arranged on the table. 'You were a child, Rune.' Nanya wrung out a cloth over the sink and kept wringing it out, bringing forth her words with every twist.

'I ruined your life.'

'If it wasn't your information that had me sent to Hohenschönhausen, then it would have been someone else's. It's what happened during the Stasi's domination. I was lucky they didn't take me sooner.'

'But still . . .'

'You don't have to forgive yourself, but you can hear my forgiveness and accept it. It wasn't your fault,' she said again. 'I'm sorry I caused more trouble sending the notebook; it's the last thing I wanted to do. I thought it would bring you some peace. There was so much hope in it, so much of her in it.' Nanya's sad smile squeezed at his heart. 'I think of her every day. I didn't want who she was to be forgotten by the only people she loved.'

'I didn't forget,' Rune said. 'I tried, I wanted to, but I could never forget. But all I remember is how I failed her,' he said. 'How I kept failing her and now, how I keep failing Lotte too.'

'That's nonsense. You never failed anyone,' Nanya said. 'I've never met a more devoted brother' – she paused – 'and son. You give yourself a hard time, Rune,' she said. 'Have some faith in yourself.'

Rune said nothing. Nanya's words replayed and the word *faith* made him look out of the window to the sky, as though faith resided up above him, inaccessible and elusive.

'You're nothing like him, Rune,' Nanya said.

'Who?'

Nanya gave him a withered, knowing look, which said *cut the bullshit*. So he did.

'I worry, I worry every day that somehow I'll change, that it'll be – that I'll be . . .' He sighed.

Nanya stroked his arm. 'It's *because* you're worried that *proves* you are nothing like him.' Her words were gentle, but Rune had the distinct feeling he was being told off. 'It's hard to take risks. It's hard to love. But Rune . . .' – she caught his eye again – 'have more faith in yourself. You are *nothing* like him.'

'Uh—' Rune stammered, but Nanya continued.

'It's our choices that define us, not our past, and every day you choose to not be him. That counts,' she added, before turning away.

'But I don't know how to keep Lotte safe. How to get away from him.'

'You can always come here,' she said slowly. 'I still have the house for a few months yet, and if it works out, then we can go from there.'

They drank coffee and ate toast in silence, Rune ruminating on her words. Did she mean it? But how could they? Papa would find out, and Lotte would be sent away to school and – the *ands* chased themselves around his head like marching ants.

Nanya understood, better than anyone ever had, the combination of fears he seemed to carry, always, somewhere near his heart. And she was offering to carry them with him.

'There were more things left at FlatHouse,' Nanya said after breakfast. Her voice was breathless and the words thrown at him in panic. 'I put them together in a box in case you or Lotte ever wanted them. Would you like to see?'

His breath caught in his throat, but he nodded that, yes, he would.

Nanya returned moments later with a box, and he stood up. Trying to feel ready.

He found a few textbooks, some drawings and many old purple exercise books with names on the cover. None of which belonged to Mama. He discarded them all. He found his old sketchbook and a book about drawing portraits.

322

He flicked through his drawings. Pictures of the many faces from LightHouse.

He turned the page.

Mama's face was there, drawn and withdrawn on one page and shiny pink-cheeked on the next.

'This is Mama,' Rune said, turning the page for Nanya to see. 'You used this one for the poster.'

She nodded.

From the bottom of the box he pulled out a piece of black-and-white cow print fabric, a small grey bunny attached.

'Moo Bunny?'

He looked at Moo Bunny. His grey body thin with age, his nose rubbed down with love.

'It's all my fault,' he said.

THEN

September 1989

'It wasn't my fault,' he told Mama when she came home that night, tired and worn out from queuing all day for food. She had only a small bag of items. The queues were long and only battle-worn women or children managed to get what they wanted. When Mama heard what the shop had in stock she would be at the end of a queue, and six hours later there would be nothing left. She found this waste of time deeply frustrating.

'What wasn't your fault?' she said, placing her bag on the kitchen side and filling the kettle. Her face was full of crossness, as though a vacuum had sucked at it from the inside.

'Are you okay?' he asked, changing the subject.

'Hmmm?' she said, distracted, as the kettle sizzled on the stove. 'Where's Lotte?'

'Her room,' he said, nodding down the hall.

He watched her lean back against the sink and fold her arms. 'What do I need to know?'

'It wasn't my fault,' he said slowly.

'We've established that, but what wasn't your fault?'

His heart dribbled in his chest and he knew, right then, that what he had done would change something that he couldn't change back.

'Can you fix it?' Mama asked, taking the kettle off the hob.

A balloon was in his chest, growing and growing. Mama looked at him.

'Have you tried to fix it?'

The prick of her words caused the air inside him to whoosh out and his tears fell. Mama put the kettle down and placed an arm around him.

'Let's try together, shall we?'

She led him down the hall into Lotte's room. He clenched and unclenched his hands.

'Mama!' Lotte wailed. 'Mama. Moo Bunny is all dead and gone and broken and unstuffed and deaded and torn and fluffy where he used to be soft and perfect and rubbed perfect and smelly-perfect and talking and listening and being all Moo.'

'Slow down,' Mama said.

But she didn't. Her words tripped and fell and jumped and bounced and hic'd out of her as she told Mama everything.

'Poor poor poor poor Moo Bunny he is being alive no more, Mama. It is worse than dying. It is death.'

He was watching from the door as Lotte started to yell at him.

Mama yelled for Lotte to calm down.

'I don't know how,' Lotte wailed.

Mama put Lotte on her lap and smoothed her hair, like she did when she was a baby.

'Please explain,' Mama said to him. But he found that words tore through him, just as the scissors had torn easily through Moo's chest, like cutting through paper. It had felt easy and the slice of the scissors made a satisfying crunch-rip, a sound that made him want to cut further.

He had operated on Moo Bunny on the dining room table to prove that Moo Bunny could not, as Lotte had claimed, speak to her because he was made only of fluff, not words. Voiceless.

He was not magic.

There was no such thing as magic.

Lotte's mouth was open and screaming without words. The point he had been trying to make slip-slid off his face and puddled in his belly.

Placing his scissors down on the table, he had watched Lotte sob and steal Moo Bunny away from him. He felt the word 'sorry' on his tongue, but it was sour and dry and brittle.

The look on Lotte's face stretched his skin apart.

He sat on his hands. The hands that had sliced through his own childhood toy. The best one. The one they both loved the most. The only one that came from home.

'Let's try and fix it,' Mama said.

'I am dying,' Lotte cried, throwing herself back on the bed. Mama looked at him, and he felt guilt slither in his mouth.

'I am doing dying,' Lotte said, digging her hands into her tummy. 'It's in my tummy. A dying death.'

'No,' Mama said. 'You are not dying. This feeling in you is huge.'

'It's bigger than big. It's. It's. Ig-nor-amus.'

'Do you mean enormous?' Mama asked, and he and Mama exchanged a look that made him feel a little lighter.

'You are feeling anger,' Mama said. 'And grief.'

'Grief? I don't know grief.'

'It feels like grief for Moo to have been hurt so badly.'

'Grief is Moo Bunny being deaded?'

'Yes.'

'Is it grief that it was Roo what did it?' And she looked at him standing in the doorway and the feeling of shame, or hurt, of doing something infinitely wrong settled deep within him. It was no longer a new sensation, but was the same every time he walked into Comrade Ackermann's office to talk about his responsibility to protect the socialist state. He felt terrible after each session; it made him ill. The same emotion as when he now watched Lotte's red bunched-up face wail her pain. Pain that he had inflicted.

'Yes, and hurt,' Mama said, looking at him.

'I am hurted. I am hurted so bad,' Lotte said, buried now in Mama's hug, the very place Rune wanted to be too. Mama started humming to Lotte.

'I am sad,' Lotte said.

'Can I help fix Moo Bunny?' Mama asked. 'Where is he?'

'I do not want to show what Roo did-do,' Lotte said. 'He took the magic away.'

It was a lot later and darkness had fallen like a wall when Mama came out of the bedroom without Lotte, holding a pillowcase.

He knew what was inside.

Mama joined him and placed the bunny-shaped lump on the table.

'Right then, my little surgeon,' she said. 'How are you planning on making this right?'

When morning light dripped bright through his curtains, he heard Lotte wake up.

'I love you, my mama,' she said, but it was quickly followed by, 'Moo Bunny is gone.'

He padded into her room, Moo Bunny on his arm.

'I'm sorry,' he said, his voice hoarse and broken with sleep.

'It's Moo Bunny!' Lotte squealed, and plucked him from Rune's arms.

'Why is Moo Bunny wearing a dress?' she asked.

And he was – it was a white dress with big black spots like a cow and it had a pocket at the front. Mama had helped him sew and shape it last night. He had wanted to tell her about Comrade Ackermann, but couldn't seem to find words to do so. Time blinked and the moment vanished.

He had stitched Moo Bunny back together.

Inside the pocket was a piece of paper.

Lotte opened it and asked Mama to read it to her.

'It says *Sorry*,' Mama said, looking at him.

'But Moo Bunny doesn't have to be sorry,' Lotte said, looking under the dress.

'*I'm* sorry,' Rune said, sitting on the edge of the bed.

'But the hurt is all stitched up now.' Lotte showed him Moo's stitched chest. 'Look,' and she pointed.

'Moo Bunny has a scar,' Mama said.

'A scar?'

'Yes.'

He watched Lotte run her finger down the scar. 'It's bumpy,' she said.

'Scars bridge up the hurt,' Mama said.

'That's clever,' Lotte said. 'Mama?' she asked as Mama lay back onto the bed, yawning.

'Yes?'

'I know there is still magic.'

'That's good,' Mama said.

'All the magic in the world is in you,' said Lotte, and she was right.

NOW

FRIDAY 12TH NOVEMBER 1999

LOTTE

Sabine walked towards the office. Lotte, following, held Mama's notebook in single sheets tucked in an envelope. She touched the envelope full of words that changed everything. Hungry for something she couldn't remember the taste of, she had heard Mama's words, but instead of finding the Mama of the past, of memory, of truth, she was faced with paper and letters and words that ached. Mama was not who Lotte wanted her to be and, worse, Lotte hadn't remembered her. And even more worse than all of that was Papa being a big boom of bad in all Mama's pages.

And the absolute worst thing was that Roo wasn't there.

Thinking of Papa and going home caused fear to curl up in her chest, purr into her bones and hiss. A spitting, spine-tingling fear that had no name. She wanted so much to remember, but Mama was a mirror of absence – the depth of her loss was just reflective, it didn't mean anything to Lotte, despite her wanting it to.

There was a heaviness in her step, and a strange dreamy weariness coated her, as though it was the early hours of the morning and she had been up all night. She had stepped out into the real world again, but real life seemed to have no importance since being confined with the pages of the past.

Her thoughts plunged in volume; they dug, dredged. Dissected. Dotted. Still she came up empty. She didn't know anything any more. She just followed Sabine, whose hand held hers firmly.

Once she opened the office door, Lotte's thinking fell short and flat at her feet.

Isolde and Pepin were seated head to head, working on what Lotte recognised immediately as Mama's notebook. Ralf was rustling copied paper, passing sheets from pile to pile.

'Surprise,' Pepin said, standing up. 'We've been in working early for you.'

'We wanted to make sure you went home with something whole,' Isolde said. 'You deserve the truth you have been searching for, Lottechen.'

Lotte was stunned.

'Come. Sit,' Pepin said, pulling out a chair. 'We haven't done it all. Isolde has something exciting for you too – but she'll explain later.' Lotte looked at Isolde, who smiled warmly.

'There is still a bit left to do,' Pepin said, 'but we think we've completed one long and coherent piece for you.'

Lotte did as she was told, sitting next to Pepin, who started to read:

Lotte crashed into the room and I spilled cold coffee over my hands. The stability I had enjoyed here has dissolved overnight.

'Mama, Roo says . . .' Lotte started, hair across her face and her cheeks pink from sleep; dishevelled, more a baby when awoken from sleep than at any other time. She's growing up so fast.

The innocence of her wrapped around me and swelled in the room like a sunrise: expansive, hopeful. Her pyjama bottoms scrunched up on one side, hair in a tangle, Moo Bunny under her arm, the cold morning light at her back, but standing in front of me was the warmth of my child fresh from sleep.

A light within light.

Awoken from bliss, to the world . . . and into a world that has changed. I placed the cup down and moulded her soft sleepy body into my arms; and, in holding her, my arms came into being, as though woken from a dream. This is what they were made for, to hold her lithe body as she curled into them, the weightiness of her head on my chest.

My children were made within my body and my body seems to know its purpose when they are near. I wake up to her light – bright, ripe and pure – and breathe myself alive.

'Shall I help you get ready for school?' I said, because what else is there to say, or to do? Routine, normality, it's all we know. Keep going, even when everything stops.

School.

Out on the streets, the roads were quiet as we walked. Together. Lotte's hand in mine and Rune just ahead. I kept looking back. No one was there. The peace I had felt knowing I was being watched had gone and an unease at what was going to happen started like a seasickness, wave after wave, growing stronger.

'What are you doing today, Mama?' Rune asked.

I had no idea. There had been a plan, but now . . . Now, I didn't know what I was going to do today or tomorrow or any other day. Because by the end of the day Rune and Lotte would know and I would have to do something.

The tears caught the back of my throat, thick and hot. I swallowed them and said, 'I'll meet you at the gates.'

'Sure,' he said, and walked off at a brisk pace, the dry blustery day rustling the trees along with our feet tapping on the road, the swell of the air, the cold stinging my lips and cheeks.

Lotte bent down so abruptly that I almost tripped over her. 'What's wrong?'

'So tiny, what are they called?' she asked, tenderly stroking a crop of blue flowers that sprouted between the pavement and a fence.

'Um, I'm not sure.'

'And blue.'

Rune had walked ahead. 'Come on,' he called back.

'One minute,' I said to him.

'Wait,' she said, placing her book bag down. She carefully picked off the heads of the blue flowers. Like tiny little buds, they nestled into her palm. 'Will you give them to Nanya?' Lotte asked. 'Make sure she puts them in water,' she insisted.

'I will,' I said as we started walking, rounding the corner as the school came into sight, and with it, Rune, waiting for us at the gates.

'She needs to put water in a bowl, then the blue buds will sit on top of the water and float around for her all day.'

'Like a lily pad?'

'No. That's for frogs, Mama, and these' – and she arranged each one delicately in my open palm – 'are for Nanya.'

I kissed her on the head; buttery soft.

'I'll be sure to tell her. Have a great day . . .' But she was off. I watched her wobble up to Rune and they walked through the gates together and out of sight.

In that moment, I wanted to follow after them, to kiss them both again, to tell them I loved them, but I couldn't.

I wanted to hold them both in my arms, to feel their heaviness, their love, their bodies pressed against mine. A rope burn of pain pulled through my stomach.

I walked away with a handful of tiny blue flowers, weeds most like. I didn't go to Nanya, because to say it out loud would make it true. I went home.

I put the flower heads in a small bowl of water and as I sit here now, I watch them bob around. Susceptible to everything. These tiny flowers, tender and so vulnerable that I ache for their grace. Floating, calm, serene on top of water that will inevitably drown them.

Moo Bunny, left behind, watches me as I write. I wonder what my children will be told if I am gone from their lives? What will they think, what will they remember?

I think of a way I can be preserved for them and with my sewing scissors I start to untangle the stitches Rune put into Moo's chest—

Herr Benedict's booming voice from the corridor stopped Pepin.

'I am afraid you are quite mistaken,' he was saying. 'There is, without doubt, some error.'

Isolde let out a small squeak and pulled out the pages she and Ralf had been working on into the space between them. Isolde nudged Ralf and both Lotte and Pepin looked over to them.

'It's got to be,' Ralf said. The tangle of words and excitement spangled in the room. Ralf pointed his finger to the page and whispered to Isolde, who shook her head in disbelief.

'Winola?' she whispered.

Lotte could hear nothing further. All she could make out was Herr Benedict's voice.

'Searching the premises is absolutely fine, but I can assure you . . .' The door opened and the vast presence of Herr Benedict came into the room.

'As you can see,' he said to a person behind him, 'you have been . . .'

Herr Benedict looked directly at Lotte, and from behind his shoulder came a uniform, blue and smart, with gold insignia. It stood away and apart from the man who was wearing it.

But there was no doubt. That man was Papa.

Herr Benedict stood, mouth open, just inside the doorway.

'I . . . I . . . I . . .' Herr Benedict spluttered. 'How did—? When—? Pepin?'

Pepin stood with Lotte's pages in her hands. 'Yes, Herr Benedict?'

'There is a *child* in the office.'

'Yes, Herr Benedict. Actually . . .' – and she placed a hand on Lotte's shoulder – 'A young woman, I would say, is more accurate.'

Herr Benedict spluttered, turning red in the face. 'Why is . . .' – he took a shuddery breath, as though trying to control himself – '. . . she . . .' he said, pointing to Lotte, 'here?'

Papa pressed a hand on Herr Benedict's arm. 'I'll deal with this,' he said, and entered the room. He took off his hat and placed it on the desk where Sabine usually worked.

'Lotte? Oh, my Lotte,' Papa said. 'I am so glad you are safe,' and he walked straight to Lotte and sank onto his knees. He looked older somehow, ragged, and she felt tenderly towards him in that moment, their usual proportions changed.

'You could have been anywhere, hurt, lost . . . I'm so glad I found you before anything terrible could happen.'

'Nothing terrible happened, Papa, and I called you to tell you where I was,' Lotte said, confused.

'I traced the number as soon as you called. I cannot lose you again,' he said, standing and speaking more to Pepin and Herr Benedict than to Lotte herself.

'You haven't lost me once,' Lotte said indignantly. 'I am working. I am doing work to make the pages that you tore whole again. I am inde-pen-dent,' she said, and smiled a little, because she had been. 'I am a puzzle woman,' Lotte said. 'I can do it all by myself.'

'And she is very, very good at it,' Isolde said softly.

'She is a young disabled girl. She is mentally retarded and you have taken advantage of her soft nature. Shame on you,' Papa said to Herr Benedict, ignoring Isolde. 'Shame on you all.' He tried to catch Lotte's hand.

Disabled? Retarded? Soft? That didn't sound like her, when he reported it in that way. Maybe Papa's words were what everyone else could see but she could not, just like when she looked in the mirror. Her reflection didn't belong to the person she was on the inside. It was the public part of her, her face; it made people think they knew her before she even spoke.

'I am more than my Down's syndrome,' she whispered, but when no one said anything, Lotte felt fatteningly hollow, as though a balloon were expanding in her chest.

'Mama sent me these words even though she is dead, and I didn't find out how she could do that,' Lotte said eventually, speaking the most pressing question on her tongue.

'Let's forget it ever happened, shall we,' he whispered, but it wasn't a question. 'You're safe. That's all that matters. Thank you all so much for taking good care of my daughter,' Papa said in a professional boom, his tone now sickly sweet. The sudden change in him scared her.

He spoke to the table where Isolde, Ralf, Sabine and Pepin were watching. 'I am sure the powers that be will financially reimburse you for the hours spent helping my little girl in her games.' Papa held Lotte's hand tightly. 'I shall be taking her out from under your feet now.'

But that was not what Lotte wanted. Papa smelled clean, of soap and bubbles, but under the minty-fresh smell was smoke.

The confusing mix made her think . . .

And she remembered – wearing pink Tiffy gloves, gloves so pink that flapping them made her think of wings, Tiffy's wings from *Sesame Street*. She was blowing washing-up bubbles into the air, kissing Mama's hand that was puffed up, red, sore. How Mama had pain inside. How the cleaning stopped as Papa snuck in like smoke.

'Papa?'

He turned and stopped pulling her hand.

'Did you hurt Mama when I was little? Did she run away from you?' His face shifted and Lotte felt uneasy.

'Where did you get such an idea?' he asked, looking closely at her and then at the faces looking up at him.

'From her notebook. She wrote about a place called LightHouse and about being hurt, about being free, and . . .' – Lotte thought back to the last page – 'she wrote about me.'

'Would you mind giving us some privacy?' he asked, not very kindly, in the general direction of Herr Benedict at the door. Pepin, red-faced, continued to stand and face him, but Sabine stayed where she was, a clutch of papers pressed to her chest.

'All of you,' he said briskly, and there was a rustle as Ralf and Herr Benedict left the room. Sabine, Pepin and Isolde lingered.

Lotte picked out the page from the top of the pile. 'After you tore them, I wanted to know. To get them back, because I thought they would help me remember her.' She sounded foolish and stupid, even to her own ears. 'I wanted to show Roo, because Roo is always knowing everything.'

Papa pulled the sheet of paper away from Lotte's hands.

'Who did this?' he asked, his eyes doing something fluttery and anxious.

'My friends,' Lotte said, the words loose in her mouth, wobbly, wet.

'I see.' He gathered a bunch of papers, a variety of newly formed taped pages and their copies, and rolled them like a newspaper to swat a fly or a bee. 'Lotte, your mother is dead. This is nonsense. You cannot do such things on your own. I'll have to employ a carer for you if you do such a thing again, or' – and his voice softened – 'you can go away to a special school.' The threat was there, sugared up. Lotte shivered.

'No, please, Papa. I want to stay at home. I want to be close to Roo.'

'And where is this wonderful brother?' Papa asked. Lotte looked to the door as if he might just appear and things would suddenly get better – just by his presence.

'Excuse me,' Pepin said, and Lotte was relieved to see Papa turn his gaze to her. It gave Lotte a moment to think. She plucked a page, almost complete, from Pepin's work space and rolled it in her hand. It was hers, but Papa was going to take her away from it all.

'Lotte is a very independent young woman,' Pepin said. 'She hasn't run away. You knew she was here. She called you. She has been responsible and—'

'Who asked you?' Papa said. 'What do you know about my daughter? She has Down's syndrome. She should be at home where I can care for her properly.' And with that he swept the letters and pieces of paper from Pepin's work space into the big sack of shredded paper that Sabine had been working on. 'Unfortunately, my disabled child has been sneaking into official buildings and destroying archives.' He swept across Isolde and Ralf's desk too. Sabine stood, still holding handfuls of pages to her chest. She said nothing, but her eyes were wide, watchful.

'She has been poorly controlled. Experiencing hormonal imbalances. Suffering from anger issues. Confused,' Papa said, as though telling a story, creating a story – telling lies. Lies about her. She felt a deep echoing sickness; she was powerless to stop him.

'Please,' Lotte said, 'that's not true. That's not me. I haven't done anything wrong, or bad. I—' But weariness, heavy and cumbersome, echoed inside her. 'Why won't you tell me what happened to Mama?'

344

she asked. Her voice sounded strained, as if it had to push past something round and heavy. Papa had a look in his eyes she had never seen before. Lotte took a step away from him, to get her pages, her link to Mama. It wasn't over, but she was afraid.

'Excuse me,' Pepin said, 'Lotte has done no such thing. She hasn't destroyed any of our files. And I know that people with Down's syndrome can be responsible and caring and compassionate.' Pepin took steps towards Lotte, and held her hands; she looked at Lotte kindly. 'My mama had Down's syndrome,' she said. 'She was the best mama in the world to me. Don't believe what he says, Lotte. You can be independent and live a big life.'

'Very touching,' Papa said smartly. 'Are you done?' Papa raised the rolled-up pages, Mama's words, and banged them down on the desk. 'Enough!' he said, his voice too big, too loud. His face was now angry-purple; he was getting bigger and bigger.

'They are mine,' Lotte said. 'They are not yours. They are mine.'

Papa was expanding into the entire office and she felt small and scared.

'Hide!' Lotte said suddenly. Remembering. 'Mama told me to hide!' And she saw a carpet, green and fuzzy, flat, worn. She remembered words bashing around, hurting, hitting, and Mama had told her to hide. 'What did you do to my mama?' Lotte asked quietly.

'No more!' he yelled at Lotte, in a way she had never seen before. He yelled the words *No more* at her like he yelled at Roo at home. He didn't look like Papa any more, she thought.

Lotte tried to take the pages from Papa, but he held on to them.

'It's from Mama,' she said. 'Please.'

Papa composed himself, rubbed down his uniform and took out a lighter from his pocket. At the flicker of flame, Pepin said, 'Stop, or I'll call the police.'

'The police are already here,' Papa laughed, and Lotte watched the pattern of his face as he smiled. She heard a hiss of gas and a flick of flame and, stunned, Lotte watched Papa hold the roll of papers, her papers, the pages stuck together with tape, all the tiny pieces she had worked on – all of them – over the flame.

They caught quickly.

'No!' she said, and rushed towards Papa. He held Lotte too close to the flame; it was so close to her ear she could feel the heat. She tried to pull away; she couldn't understand what was happening. She saw Isolde's face, as she seemed to understand. Papa flapped the flames some more and tiny pieces of ash fell over Lotte's arm.

Grey snowflakes.

'Setting fires. Completely out of control. Say goodbye to your *friends*, Lotte.' He dropped the flaming pages into the bag of shredded paper that Sabine had been working on. Flames sparkled and spat and a sliver of paper floated up out of the bag, burning, white, yellow, red.

It fell black.

Lotte stood motionless, tears rolling down her cheeks. Her pages were completely aflame and Papa stood in front of them, blocking her way back to Pepin and Isolde, like a guard.

'I remembered,' she started, and she had remembered all on her own. It should have meant something. It was what she wanted all along – it was what all this was for. But in the moment, with the flames chewing at the pages, and Isolde and Pepin's horrified faces, it meant nothing. The pages that she and Sabine and Pepin had put together were burning, belching, flaming, and Mama was still gone. 'I remembered all on my own,' she said again.

Papa wasn't listening. He retrieved his peaked hat and placed it heavily on his head.

'It's all over,' Papa said, and grabbed her around the waist. 'I advise you to put that out,' Papa said to Herr Benedict in the hall. 'My daughter has got a little out of hand. My office will deal with the damages.' He passed Herr Benedict a card from his top pocket and frogmarched Lotte out of the office; hip to hip with Papa, she was forced down the stairs and before Lotte heard the fire alarm going off they were out of the double doors and onto the street.

'No talking now,' he said, and touched her arm kindly. He was Papa again – he had changed back; how could he be both? Papa who set fire to all she had left of Mama and then said soothingly, 'Time for home now, Lotte.'

She said nothing.

'It's over,' Papa repeated, and opened the door of the car for her to get in.

Her head was spinning. She had so many feelings bashing into each other, she felt like a tree when it loses its leaves in autumn and bleeds for each one. She was pricked by thousands of tiny wounds, wounds that left her, a single tree, cold, open, and in enormous pain. A pain that smelled of burned paper.

The words had been cremated. It was all gone. Again. But this time it was different.

'Now, Lotte,' Papa said. 'Get in the car.' And he grabbed her arm.

'No. I won't.' She tried to pull away. 'I won't go with you. I am inde-pen-dent. I am more than my Down—'

She saw a golden spark of light, and heard a crack; it wasn't until a mist grew between her and the rest of the world that she felt the pain. In her head. There was something wrong with her head, but she had no way to say this. In the back of her mind she heard a small scream, faraway voices; she heard her name being called, but it was vague, background noise. The pain in her head held all her focus.

'Very clumsy,' Papa was saying. 'Hitting your own head on the car like that. Carefully now, Lotte. In you get.'

Her vision was black, even though her eyes were open. She felt a seat belt strap her in and the burr of an engine, but she was alone and it was all dark. Dark was easy, she thought, it was everywhere, but light was much harder to find.

347

RUNE

He stood feeling like he was sinking in deep water, Moo Bunny in his hands. He'd forgotten what he'd done to Moo Bunny.

'It was a long time ago,' Nanya reassured him.

And yet he was here. How could Moo Bunny survive when Mama couldn't? He placed Moo carefully in his bag, knowing that Lotte would love it, even if she couldn't remember him.

He would have to talk to Lotte and bring her to see Nanya, then get a job. There were a lot of things to consider, but Nanya's offer of support and shelter gave him an alternative to the nothingness that was eating him up.

When Nanya went to answer the phone, he opened the file, to see Mama's picture again.

'It's for you,' Nanya said. 'A woman named Pepi?'

'Pepin?'

Lotte. He raced into the cubby and lifted the receiver. Nanya followed him and stood in the doorway.

'Pepin?'

Rune heard a lot of background noise on the other end of the phone, then Pepin's clear voice.

'There has been a fire,' Pepin said. 'It's very noisy. Can you hear me okay?'

'Yes, a fire? Is Lotte okay?' The world shrunk to just the phone in his hand and the voice coming from the other end of it. He pressed his ear harder into the plastic and it crackled.

'I thought we might have missed you. You said you were coming back.'

'No, I'm still here with Nanya. I'm leaving shortly. Is Lotte okay?'

'Your father arrived early this morning. He was here just as the office opened. They left hours ago. We had to stop the fire and the police are here too. It's a mess. The damage . . .'

'Is Lotte okay?'

'She didn't want to leave with him. He forced her to go. He was taking her home.'

He didn't know what to say; the noise at the end of the phone growing.

'Rune, I thought you should be there when she gets home. Sabine thinks she saw Lotte hurt as she got into the car. We are all very worried. Please, I have to go, but let me give you my number – will you call me when you're both safe?'

Rune nodded, but couldn't think of numbers or calls or anything other than getting to Lotte. He passed the phone to Nanya and heard her talk for a few moments, then the scratch of a pencil as Nanya wrote down a number and replaced the receiver.

'What can I do?'

Before Nanya could say anything, Rune answered his own question.

'I need to go to Lotte. She's in trouble,' he said.

'You can come back,' Nanya said. 'You know that, right?'

He nodded and she gave him a hug. At almost twice her height her face was buried in his chest, but she had a warmth about her that made him feel small.

'I'm so sorry, Rune,' she said. 'Really I am.' Nanya broke away from the hug and looked up at him.

'Will you call me too when you know that Lotte's safe, please?' She added her own number to the one she had written down from Pepin and gave it to him.

He set off from LightHouse, the bag with Moo Bunny on his back, the lantern in his hand and Nanya behind him. All the way.

Bone-weary and exhausted, he watched the daylight collapse under heavy clouds. He followed the street lights, bringing light to the dark of his thoughts – how Papa would never let them go; how Papa would find them wherever they were; how they would never be free of him. He'd intended on getting to Lotte quickly, but his travel was impeded by a delayed train, so he had to get a bus instead, and once he had made it to the bus stop close to home, he ran. Home. To Lotte. His footsteps pulsing to the beat of *Please. Let her be okay. Please.*

THEN

TUESDAY 10TH OCTOBER 1989

RUNE'S BIRTHDAY

He was awake. Waiting. For the day to begin and for all eyes to be focused on him.

He didn't want Mama to look too closely, for surely she would see that he held secrets on his lips? That he had signed something he shouldn't, and that each week he ventured into Comrade Ackermann's office with heavy steps and an even more corrupt heart. He was performing for his country. He was no longer a separate being. He was *one* of many, a *we*, no longer an *I. A comrade.* And in becoming collective, he was telling things to Comrade Ackermann that he wasn't sure were true, things that were none of his business. Telling things about Nanya, about the women at LightHouse, the women Mama worked with in the factory; the stories they told, the things they got up to that they probably shouldn't.

Mama was rewarded with a promotion at work. He was given stockings once, silk stockings for Mama, but mostly he was given money, which he slipped into Mama's purse. Hiding the guilt. Mama began working in the opening of letters instead of the sorting of envelopes. She spent the days sitting instead of standing; she came home with a smile.

Nanya disappeared, just for a few days, but when she returned, haggard, jumpy and broken, he knew it was his fault.

Mama would know too if she looked closely. But he had been keeping busy, and she was busy; they were trying hard not to look at each other. But today all eyes would be on him and he swore to himself, as he woke up on his tenth birthday, that he would not talk to Comrade Ackermann any more. He would find a way to get out of it before he ended up saying something he'd never be able to forgive himself for.

Lotte came into his room with Moo Bunny wearing a chef's hat made of paper. She had a similar one on her own head.

'It's cake-fast,' she said. 'We made cakes for your birthday. Happy Birthday!'

Mama was behind her and he smiled and got up, nervous for the day ahead.

Wrapped up in old newspapers was his present.

A bike.

'A bike?' he said, tearing the paper off. He was so shocked to even get a present that he couldn't stop saying, 'A bike.'

'It needs new tyres and I think the chain is loose, but we can work it out. I'm sorry it's not like your old one . . . it's not perfect,' Mama corrected herself.

'Oh but, Mama, it is!' he said. 'A bike! Can I go and ride it now?'

'After breakfast.'

'Cake-fast,' Lotte said cheerily. She was bouncing in her chair with a present wrapped up in newspaper with blue balloons drawn on it. 'I have a present for you too,' she said, thrusting the small package at him.

The present was a notepad of thin plain paper and a small book on how to draw portraits.

'Thank you,' he said to Lotte.

'Mama chose it,' Lotte said. 'I wanted to get you a . . .' She looked across at Mama.

'Lotte wanted to get you a cigarette lighter,' Mama said, smiling and shaking her head.

'It was so shiny!'

After cake-fast, Rune rushed to get dressed and then he was off.

Out of the house.

Down the street.

The autumn flavour of the air in his mouth, through his hair, lapping at his face as he pedalled.

Free.

Mama and Nanya picked him up from school.

'Happy Birthday,' said Nanya, presenting him with a gift.

'Milka?' he asked, smiling.

'Chocolate,' Lotte said, her eyes greedy, and her fingers reached out to touch it.

He felt guilty, as if he'd eaten the chocolate already. He thanked Nanya again and placed the chocolate in his bag, away from Lotte. He pushed his new bike, with his friends either side. Everyone coming back for a party tea.

'My friends are not coming around,' Lotte said to Nanya, 'because it's not my birthday.'

'No?' Nanya asked. 'I must have got you a present by mistake.'

'You did?'

'Well . . .' Nanya looked at Mama and Mama smiled.

'You got me a present even though it is not my birthday?' Lotte asked. 'I can have it, can't I, Mama?'

'Yes,' Mama said.

'Can I eat it now?' Lotte asked. Rune looked back; it was a small bar, no bigger than her hand.

'Chocolate is being happy,' she said.

Lotte was full of bubbles and bounce so Rune pushed on, moving forward, listening to the talk of his friends, Aaron and Inga, beside him – he wondered half-heartedly if they too had private conversations with Comrade Ackermann that played on their minds all week. He listened to them chat and he could also hear the talk of Mama and Nanya and Lotte behind.

He was getting used to the idea of spying, collating information to dutifully pass on to Comrade Ackermann. He pushed on, not wanting to hear any more.

His resolve strengthened. He wouldn't say anything further, not ever again – he would start making things up. He'd lie if he had to. He was ten now, and things had to change. Every day so far this month there had been protests and arrests. Rune knew, from listening carefully, that demonstrations and petitions for freedom of movement to cross into the West were happening all over the DDR; it was the fortieth anniversary of communism and the people believed Gorbachev would help them. Rune believed it too. Things were changing.

Rune wanted to open his chocolate, like Lotte, but he felt a guilt weigh him down, and he doubted the chocolate would taste sweet, melted in a mouth so treacherous.

Regardless, it was the best birthday ever.

His bike was fast and although he would need to pump up the tyres and fix the chain and learn how to change the rust into paint again, he couldn't have been happier.

Aaron, Inga and he were all working on the bike. Mama had let him wheel it through the house so it could be admired by his friends in their back garden.

Some of the LightHouse mamas came around with their children and gave him cards and kisses. One of Lotte's friends gave him a handful of leaves she had picked on the way over. Their reds and bronzes, golds and browns filled him with warmth.

'Thank you,' he said.

'Open your cards now,' Mama said.

Aaron and Inga were stuffing cake into their mouths and he gave each card a cursory glance, wanting to get to the food himself. Mama had saved their sugar for a whole month to be able to make the lemonade. He wanted to be with his friends and his bike.

The last card he opened had a cowboy on it, swinging a lasso rope. The lasso was made from real twine and looked exactly like rope. It was a card unlike all the others.

> *Dear Son*
> *HAPPY BIRTHDAY*
> *One year closer to being a man!*
> *Say hello to your mother and Lotte for me.*
> *Love*
> *Papa*

'Papa?' he whispered, unaware that the hubbub of noise around him had stopped, watching him read the card.

Mama was by his shoulder.

Mama held the card in her hand.

Mama read it and passed it to Nanya as she searched through the rest of the cards and envelopes he had discarded. Scattering his bunch of leaves on the floor as she did so.

He saw her face.

The party was over.

The evening of his birthday grew long and dark. Rune watched a robin perch on the rusty handle of his bike. Everyone bar Nanya had left. Nanya was talking to Mama in the kitchen. He heard Mama's repetitive *How? But how?*

Nanya would hold it together for them again. But what had he done to Nanya? He was stuck inside himself and being him was a tight place to be.

It was his fault.

It was his fault that Mama was scared.

He heard Mama's voice. 'But how? How? How?' she kept asking.

He was tired of getting everything wrong.

He curled up on his bed and took out his new sketchbook and the book on portraits. He sharpened his pencil all over the bed and swept the shavings to the floor. He followed the tiny writing in the portrait book and started to sketch, to be absorbed in drawing, to create something that took him away from what was happening just outside his door. The scent of the newly sharpened pencil and the feel of its soft wooden body in his fingers, along with a new book to tell him how to do what he was doing, but how to do it better – these were all good things and enjoying these, he didn't have to think.

He used the templates he found in the portrait book to draw Mama, the old Mama, the worn-down broken Mama of several months ago: her thin hair dragged back off her face, her eyes darting and deep in her head. Big bruises that echoed on her cheek and her jaw. Thin lips . . . He kept going, adding more and more detail. Shadowing the shape of a man in the background.

He turned to a fresh page and drew the Mama he had seen this morning. Fresh and bright, her lips smiling, her face happy and clear. He found some coloured crayons in his case and shaded her cheeks pink, her lips red, her eyes brown.

Both of these pictures were his mama.

One with Papa and the other without.

He flicked back and forth. How could one person be so changed? Yet the same.

Was Rune now the shadow that would bring the old Mama back?

Was it all his fault?

Lotte crept into his room, Moo Bunny hanging by his ear from her mouth. She had cupcakes and two cups balanced on a plate.

'It is still birthday-day,' she muffled through Moo's ear. 'Happy Birthday,' she said, presenting the plate towards him, spilling the lemonade as she did so, so that it slopped over the cakes.

She was utterly, utterly oblivious.

NOW

FRIDAY 12TH NOVEMBER 1999

LOTTE

She roused when Papa opened the car door. They were home.

Papa carried her in. The house was as cold and unyielding as stone, just as it had been when she left. Papa's face was a complicated knot and Lotte couldn't see straight. Her head in agony, she couldn't hold it or touch it; the pain was just there, throbbing, tearing. Papa stood her on her feet, where she swayed horribly, the living room carpet lurching underfoot.

'You have caused me a lot of trouble,' he said seriously. 'I'm sorry for the notebook, but I am your father and I do know what is best for you. You've had a hard couple of days. Rest and watch some TV, okay? I'll be back later. There's something I have to do.'

Lotte said nothing.

He disappeared from the room and she stumbled into the sofa. She heard him lock the door behind him. Where was he going? Why? She needed someone to hold her head up. What was happening?

RooRooRoo, she called. But he didn't answer her either.

She was all alone.

'I know,' she whispered to the room, clutching a cushion to her chest. Her tongue was too big and getting in the way of her words, but she spoke them to the empty room anyway. 'I know that my mama had a soft voice. She made dream cakes and I could always lick the spoon.' Her voice floated up and out of her. It made twinkle-lights around the room; her voice that spoke of Mama was full of magic. 'She wore tinsel in her hair at Christmas; she would read stories and tell me stories she made up; she laughed a laugh that tinkled. She had wild hair like mine and it stuck up; she wore it in a band. She had long fingers that were always warm.' She trailed off. There was a pain in her head, but a bigger one in her chest.

The pain stopped Lotte's voice and started talking instead. Pain screamed, it shouted, it whispered, until finally pain became numb and mute and was gone.

RUNE

He stood at the front door of the house he had lived in for most of his life. It was an unremarkable house amid a street of unremarkable houses. There were no lights on in the house that he could see. He checked the street, both ways. No one was around. He wondered if he'd got there first.

He had the key in his hand, but could not manage to fit it into the lock. His hands were shaking so badly they seemed to have come alive, tingling and rebelling. He dropped the key and searched with his fingertips in the damp grass to retrieve it, leaving the lantern-gift on the mat.

Once inside, he closed the door with his elbow and the latch banged loudly.

'Lotte?' he called.

He stood frozen by the door, looking at the stairs. The stairs he had crept down so many times to leave the house and go clubbing or graffitiing at night. The stairs he had snuck down with Mama and Lotte the day they left. The stairs Papa had made him sleep on when he had wet the bed for the third time in one night. The stairs from where he watched Papa hurt Mama night after night when he was too small to understand what was happening.

'Lotte?' he called quietly.

He shook off the past and made it into the living room, where the lack of light drained the room of colour. Lotte was on the sofa, her skin bleached in the dusk.

She was crumpled, like a piece of paper strewn carelessly into the corner. He touched her cheek; she was cold. He tried to lift her head, but then panicked. What if he hurt her more?

'Lotte?' he said, touching his hand to her head. There was a deep cut; it sagged slightly and felt spongy. Dried blood was matted in her hair.

'Roo?' Her voice was tiny. 'Roo, ouch.'

He called for an ambulance.

While he waited for them to arrive, he wrapped Lotte in the blanket from the sofa. The pain he felt as he listened to her ragged breathing was indescribable.

He didn't touch her. He was scared to.

He had left her.

Watching her, he knew that Lotte had seen harsh, unspeakable things when she was little; it was a blessing she didn't remember them.

It was his punishment to witness this now. Because he had left her then.

He held her hand and prayed for the ambulance to arrive faster.

'I won't leave you, Lotte,' he said. 'I won't leave you again.'

He seated himself next to her and rested her head gently in his lap. And waited.

He wondered where Papa was; where Joann was; why Lotte was all alone.

She murmured under her breath *RooRooRooRoo*. And he grasped her hand. In her fist was a tube of rolled-up paper. He took it from her and tucked it safely in his pocket.

'It's okay, Lotte, I'm here. Roo's here. You're going to be okay. It'll all be okay.'

He rocked her body gently in his lap and began to hum the song closest to him: *In heaven the stars are shining, on earth shines my lantern for me.* To soothe her; to soothe himself. The humming made him feel calmer, made him feel closer to Mama.

When the ambulance arrived, he was cast aside. They moved Lotte, strapped her to a number of machines and then onto a stretcher before lifting her into the ambulance.

'Are you coming?' a paramedic asked.

Rune climbed in and pulled his bag onto his lap. The paper lantern lay crushed on the doormat; he watched it recede through the window as the ambulance sped off. As the journey to hospital flashed by, Rune was asked questions about Lotte, her name, age, medical issues, medical history. He told them everything.

As they wheeled her blanketed body into the hospital, a paramedic held his arm out to stop Rune following.

'She's in the right place now. The doctors will help her.'

His bag slipped from his shoulder and gaped open. Moo Bunny.

'Wait. Please,' he said as the paramedic followed Lotte behind a door marked *No Entry*. 'Can you give her this?'

He pulled Moo Bunny out of his bag, still in its cow-print dress, and passed it to the paramedic, who nodded and walked away, leaving Rune alone. Once his hands had stopped shaking, he unrolled the note he had taken from Lotte and saw fracture lines through it, tiny grey veins; the page was covered in tape.

I cannot tell if I am plagued by my guilty conscience or I am plagued by a ghost. Or a practical joke has gone awry. I feel somehow hysterical, as though any one of those things could have occurred. That maybe what I knew was not; and what I am is over; what I thought was freedom has been denied. I am not making sense to myself.

Rune received a birthday card. It was from him – love Papa. It even had a rope on the front of it, a lasso. Is it a threat? He knows where we live? How? How?

Does he know how I bought us our freedom by writing down everything he talked about in his job – dates, times, names, locations, anything and everything that the East Germans could make use of? I even snuck his black book from the inner pocket of his uniform before we left. The names of former spies in the East living under protection in the West – he knew their names, so I knew them too. Absolutely everything I could think of. This was my way out, but how many people did I harm to achieve that?

My marriage was over and life had just begun. But it was a life I did not know, where I am a traitor to my country.

The page was ripped at the bottom.

There had been a price to their freedom; it had been too much. He turned the page over and read:

Dear Lotte,
Let me start again.
I should like to tell you so much, about so many things. Things I had wished to know, before knowing them.

368

But,

you keep interrupting me!

You stand at my shoulder asking what I am writing.

I say I am writing love. You giggle and tell me you cannot write love – what a silly mama I am! – love is only something you feel.

I had forgotten that to write was to breathe in love and no matter where we've been, I always had love beside me. Because my love is in you.

My love for you, Lotte, is placing a petal at your feet, singly, slowly, perfectly. Fragile and precious. Affixing your path with the soft new petal that I plucked from me.

Love is the petal, it is the pluck, it is the blood I shed for its singular loss, and it is the imperfect wilting rose, trying to get it right, piling petals, a bouquet of love at your feet. As much love as I can before winter arrives.

A mother's love is never perfect, but it is plentiful, dedicated and true. I may not be able to write love, but Lotte, love isn't something you feel, it's something you do.

His limbs jumped and juddered with a crawling anxiety. It was Mama's handwriting, it was Mama's words. But he hadn't expected Mama's voice. Mama's deep, calmly poetic voice. She had come back into his head. Her voice and her smell. Fully formed and coating him, all over, inside and out.

He had no news about Lotte. No one would tell him anything. As he waited on a plastic chair, his entire body wired, electric, he found Mama's voice in the letter. It soothed him and she was beside him. They waited for news of Lotte, together.

His eyes felt heavy. His limbs soft. Waiting.

The hospital had been slowly waking up when a nurse took him to the Family Room and told him a Dr Metze would find him there. A cleaner buffing the squeaky hospital floor had paused his rumbling machine as they passed and the quiet nurse had taken him up three floors in the lift, past a Rainbow Room, a Chaplaincy and an Advocate Service, until they reached the Family Room. The nurse pushed the door open for Rune and switched the door sign from vacant to occupied. By the time Rune had turned to thank her, she had silently slipped away.

He seated himself on the low sofa and framed both hands in his lap, linking his fingers in inverted prayer before enclosing them in his palm.

He folded his arms, crossed and uncrossed his legs, sitting taller and then slouching. No one would tell him anything as he waited in the emergency department, just that Lotte was in surgery and they would update him when they had something to update him with. The nurse had offered him this room – was this where they would tell him that Lotte was dead?

He couldn't find his balance, sitting, standing or walking; in bodily exertion, he was still waiting. Moving didn't speed up time nor did it offer him any comfort, yet he couldn't keep still.

The space around him was similar to a schoolroom. There was a car-track carpet on the floor; a blackboard that took up an entire wall; a pool table; books and toys in boxes and on shelves.

A pile of paper covered the table, along with some wax crayons, wrappings torn, snapped or scribbled to the quick. Orange squash in a plastic cup teetered at the edge of the table. A doll's house leaned on its hinges into a play-garage, with a bucket of cars beside it.

The high-back red chair had a new smell that reminded him of a teacher's chair. There was a sofa, three bean bags, a dozen cushions and a stack of tiny school chairs. He counted five of them.

The room was trying too hard.

It had a two-dimensional effect that warped his vision, softening it into a stream of pastels and greys, like a smeared watercolour.

Finally he heard voices.

A door shutting.

Footsteps growing louder. He stood as the door swung open.

'Herr Schäffer?' a man asked as he entered the room with a mug balanced on a thin green file. He didn't look like a doctor. He just looked like a guy in his late thirties, albeit a rather large one – his presence filled the room as he entered. But no white coat, no stethoscope. From his exhausted eyes and the way he moved as if this place was his home, Rune presumed it was Dr Metze. 'Apologies for the delay,' he said, shutting the door, and Rune returned to the sofa opposite him. The doctor placed his mug onto the heap of paper, scattering Crayolas. The red chair crunched against the wall as he lowered himself onto it. He offered Rune his hand.

'Nice to meet you. I'm Dr Ueli Metze.' His outstretched hand encased Rune's like warm dough. 'I am the doctor in charge of your sister's care. Most people call me Dr Ueli.'

Dr Ueli relaxed into the chair, legs splayed and arms behind his head. Lotte's file rested on the edge of the table.

Rune didn't know what to say or where to begin. *Do . . .? Has . . .? What . . .?* The start of questions, but nothing to join them to. The silence curdled in the air; he cleared his dry throat, twice.

Dr Ueli leaned forward and lowered his voice. 'Let's start from the beginning,' he said. Lines ran along his face in all the right places and his teeth shone white; his eyes were flecked red and swollen. 'Lotte is stable, but we had to operate. She had a fracture to the skull, and her heart stopped during surgery. She's stable now, but she won't be out of the worst of it for a while.'

'Heart?'

'It seems your sister had an underlying heart condition. We repaired it without a problem during the surgery. It's a relatively common problem for people born with trisomy 21, normally fixed during early childhood, but it seems that Lotte's was missed, so thankfully she was in theatre at the time so we could repair it without causing any long-term damage.'

Rune had forgotten to breathe and in trying to catch his breath felt as if he were panting. 'She's going to be okay?'

'The skull fracture was the tricky bit, but she's all patched up. Your father is by her side. She's in intensive care now but should be moved down onto a paediatric ward in the next few days.'

'Can I see her?'

Dr Ueli took a long slow breath and interlocked his fingers.

'I can't allow that, I'm sorry. I wanted you to know she was okay before I explained what will happen next. Your father has accused you of causing the fracture. There are police officers outside the room. Your father says you've been finding the demands of caring for your sister increasingly difficult—'

'What? I would never, ever . . .' He had felt such relief at knowing Lotte was alive that he couldn't find thoughts to work out what Dr Ueli was saying.

'You did the right thing in calling the ambulance. Any later and she might not have survived. Because of that I wanted you to have a few minutes before I let the officers in. I'm sorry,' he said.

'I would never hurt Lotte.' Rune tried to order his thoughts. 'I would never.'

Dr Ueli stood.

'Please,' Rune begged, 'when Lotte wakes up, can you tell her I love her, please? That I love her and I'll never leave her—' Dr Ueli was at the door and time was moving too fast. As he said it, he realised he *would* leave her. He had no choice. The police officers were going to take him from her. Papa was taking him from Lotte. Papa knew he would never hurt Lotte and yet he was accusing him of exactly that. 'Please, I didn't do anything to her. I wouldn't.' He tried to stem the tears with the palms of his hands. 'Please just tell her I love her. Please.'

'I will,' Dr Ueli said, and opened the door to three officers, who came at him like bullets, their reasonable tones speaking horrible words.

He didn't resist. His body deflated. He had nothing left. What if Lotte woke up and Papa told her that Rune had hurt her – would Lotte know it wasn't him?

The officers cuffed him and walked him roughly out of the hospital.

He was pliable, compliant and checked into the station. And then he was in a cell, in the dark.

Love isn't something you feel, it's something you do.

Mama's words to Lotte; and now he was separated from Lotte and powerless to *do* anything at all.

He dug his fingernail into the palm of his hand, just under the thumb, and scratched a small heart into it. A heart as small as a thumbprint, and he thought only of Lotte and of Mama and of *that* day ten years ago.

THEN

FRIDAY 10TH NOVEMBER 1989

It was all the school was talking about. 'Our Wall', 'Our Wall has fallen', Rune heard over and over again. He couldn't find a way to put it into his world.

How?

How could it have fallen?

The teachers maintained that many Wessies would flock over to enjoy the benefits of socialism, but most of the kids said their parents were going to take them to see the West.

Rune kept his head down to try and just get through the day, but that was harder than usual. He asked Comrade Dietrich where he could find Comrade Ackermann, how he could contact Comrade Ackermann, but Comrade Dietrich seemed distracted and didn't answer.

He was a 'Wessi' and *everyone* wanted to talk to him about Levi jeans, McDonald's, Milka bars; about shops and . . . cinema, music, television . . . It just wouldn't stop.

What he tried hard not to think about was that Papa was in the West and if 'our' Wall was down and people could cross, would he come for them?

Would Mama go back?

Would everything go back?

He asked every teacher he could find and all his friends how to find Comrade Ackermann, because he needed to know that he could help keep Mama safe. But Comrade Ackermann was nowhere to be found.

At the end of the day he looked around for Lotte. He wanted to get home and shut the world out. He couldn't see her, but Mama was tucked in the corner of the playground.

He crossed the playground, checking for Papa. Was he here already?

He needed to pack his bag, just in case they were going to move away again. Somewhere new. He hadn't done it since LightHouse, but now it was necessary.

Would he be able to take his bike?

The Wall had fallen and Mama hadn't told him. Was she going to do anything? Would she tell them before she made a plan this time, or just wake them up in the middle of the night again?

She looked just as she had that morning. Dark under her eyes and she'd been chewing her lips. They look thin and red.

He hugged her tight, catching her off guard.

'You okay?' she asked.

'Yes,' he said.

'Where's Lotte?' Mama asked.

He looked around at all the faces spinning by – none of them Lotte. Her class normally finished before his.

Mama walked over to Comrade Dietrich at the door.

'Where's Lotte?' Mama asked.

Rune checked Lotte's classroom and the hallway. Comrade Dietrich was complaining loudly to Mama about Lotte. 'Lack of commitment to her education. Flighty. A fidget. Difficult. Immature.' He was an idiot. Mama knew it. He knew it. Importantly, Lotte knew it too; Lotte had taken to calling him Comrade-Beak, which made him laugh.

'Lotte's gone,' Comrade-Beak said.

'When?' Mama asked.

He stuttered and stammered and gave no answer.

'She'll be at the park or LightHouse,' Rune said wearily. 'I'll meet you at home.' And he went off to find her.

Leaving Mama behind with Comrade-Beak pulling on her elbow.

He wanted one more chance. To see Mama. To hug her. It was the last time. The last time and it came too soon.

Lotte wasn't at the park. There were people standing in small groups everywhere, talking animatedly about the Wall. All he could hear was talk; it was like waking up at LightHouse, but this time, on the streets, the thing they were talking about was something that was going to change his life. Again.

Lotte wasn't at LightHouse. Nanya wasn't at LightHouse either. Someone had burned something on the stove and he carried the bitter smell of boiled-dry pan with him as he walked back. The thick smell prowled his nose and mouth and settled on the back of his tongue, pawing at his throat.

He didn't run. He took his time. He didn't leave a message for Nanya. He walked slowly around the corner. If Lotte wasn't at the park and Lotte wasn't at LightHouse, she would be at home. He was sure.

His steps dragged. He was anticipating Mama's fearful look and a night of waiting, or of running.

When he opened the door, he found Lotte at home.

Mama was home too and, between them both, was Papa.

NOW

Sunday 14th November 1999

Volkstrauertag – National Day of Mourning

LOTTE

She was dreaming, floating in black, empty light. The skin of her dreams became thin and she heard a voice. It was a voice she knew, but she couldn't place it. The voice made her think of Mama, but it wasn't Mama – that she was sure of.

'Keep watch, Sabine,' the voice said. 'You can't let him see us here. God forbid what he could do—' The voice kept talking; it wriggled around in her head. *Safety. Social Services. Complaint. Privilege. Guardianship. Abuse. Brother. Evidence.* The words wiggled like worms, then slithered away, leaving just the voice. She listened and found, in its rhythms, a soothing music. A hum that reminded her of bees.

'*Dear Lotte . . .*' the voice said. And it kept repeating the words that followed over and over again.

> *Dear Lotte,*
> *A spiderweb trapezes across the corner of the ceiling*
> *as you sleep. In the dark it is not there. It needs light*

to bring it into existence. New light, bright light,
or a hard frost to kiss its design. Ice to cement it;
to make it whole when it was just lace; interlaced,
single lines. Ice would make it solid. Beautiful. The
web itself caught in time.

The spider creates line after line after line.
It weaves in the dark. It is art in the light.

My heart curls, shrivels, stitching itself small. I
cling to the image with some gentleness; an infinite
shard of hope that draws me out. To breathe in fro-
zen time. To always be present, so that I can exist in
your future.

It's to me, Lotte thought, but she couldn't find words, her head hurt, her voice lost, but Mama was writing her love.

Roo? Where was Roo? She tried to ask, but beeps started beeping and footsteps rocked the floor and then things went dark and wobbly and out.

When she woke again it was to another voice, a gentle voice, a sad voice. Lotte knew this voice was the voice of a friend.

Dear Lotte,
Again I start where I should end. Unable to complete
something, to bring the circle to a close. Instead I
open it up further for you. I would crack the sky
open for you.

I would share every drop of my ocean with
you. But instead, let us sit together and allow time
to curl in on itself, to loop and coax it into giving

us moments that are elongated, held, precious and
expanding. Moments that live without time.

Let us sit while I braid my name into your hair,
write my stories into the air, weaving my words into
your heart. Let us taste sea on our tongues and feel
sand between our toes. Let us watch the sky together.
Let me hear your thoughts on life, on love. Let me
protect you, let me strengthen you. Let us fight the
world off together.

Each moment becomes a wish of expanding,
unending time, and for the briefest of moments,
everlasting.

Lotte heard the voice begin to cry. It was a sad low sob and she
wanted to put out her hand and touch it, but she couldn't feel her
hands and she couldn't move. She listened once more as a soggy
voice, full of emotion that Lotte couldn't understand, spoke:

Dear Lotte,
I write my love in the blue of the sky. It is vast and
deep and, although it looks blue, every colour is held
within it. I write my love to you in blue, so all you
need is light.

When she woke again, Papa was holding her hand, rubbing his big
thumb over the same spot, making her skin raw and alive and hot.
He was a giant, tall and large, and his body put Lotte's into the
shade. She was swallowed by his shadow and she wanted to move
away, far away.

'Get better, Lotte,' Papa's voice said. His voice low and drippy
like a cave. 'Time to get better, Lotte.'

Another voice joined Papa's in the cave. The second voice was deep and boomy, like a really good drumbeat. It drummed lots of words that made Lotte feel sleepy. It was a good voice. The good voice was talking to Papa in the cave and Papa was saying untrue words, bad words, words that made no sense at all.

Trying to understand what was happening was too complicated and when she felt her body become heavy she fell into a deep and uneasy sleep, wanting to stop Papa from saying the lies and wanting to hide away from him too.

She knew her head was hit by the car. She felt Papa's hand on the back of her neck before the door sparked pain in her head. Papa's hands were big and bad and she wanted to say this to the kind boomy-voice, but Papa's was all over it, all over the room, jumping and butting and lying.

Lotte wanted to move her hand away before Papa's thumb rubbed a well of fire into her palm, before his hands could break her again.

Roo, she thought. *RooRooRooRooRooRoo*

The wild wind of his name made her safe in the storm.

Somehow.

RooRooRooRoo

RUNE

He dabbled in the shallows of sleep, hearing the rain murmur against the windowsill outside his cell. The dark was porous, thick and dense. He tried to breathe more lightly, to inhale less of his confinement.

He had been held for two nights so far. He had fought, claimed innocence, told his story, but the words had all left him with an ache in his chest.

'Please,' he begged. 'Please can you tell me how she is? Is Lotte okay? Is she doing okay?'

Not one officer answered his pleas. Unable to fight his way out of the cell or his own skin, all he could do was beg.

Left alone, he felt ravaged by the silence. An eerie, untouched quiet. He imagined being buried by an avalanche and lying under the snow not knowing up from down, desperate to dig his way out – but which way would lead him out?

He was helpless and in his helplessness he knew that all good things are fragile and so easily lost. Mama and Lotte. And now he had lost the sky and fresh air and freedom. He lay thinking, losing himself in the darkness. Not fighting, just waiting for someone to show him which way was up.

Without a pencil and without paper, all he had were his thoughts, and they were dark enough to suck out all feeling. He was motivated into forgetting, because nothing good happened to anyone from journeying back.

Journeying in his thoughts back to *then*: to a time when he had Mama and Lotte.

To a time when he thought everything was bad.

To a time when he didn't know that everything was going to get worse.

THEN

FRIDAY 10TH NOVEMBER 1989

He stood silently in the doorway. Mama, he saw, was sitting straight-backed, eyes wide, at the table in the living room. Lotte was sitting beside her, her small hand in Mama's. Moo Bunny was seated on the table and Lotte was making Moo's feet wobble over the edge. Papa was standing between them, his hand resting on Mama's shoulder. Rune looked at the hand, but didn't look up to see the rest of the man attached to it. He didn't need to. He knew it was Papa by the look on Mama's face.

The hand was Papa's.

Rune shut the door behind him and joined them. He walked in, knowing that everything had gone wrong.

'Rune,' Papa said, catching him by the shoulder as he attempted to sit with Mama. 'My son.'

Papa gushed a flood of words at him. Rune shook the words off like rainwater. Papa's arm became tight around him, coiled, hard, unyielding. He tried to break out of it.

He tried.

To get away from Papa.

To get to Mama.

Papa was strong.

Rune was not.

He looked at Mama, his mama, unable to help him, as he, always, was unable to help her. Unable to get to her. He was stuck, next to Papa, looking at Mama – desperate to get close to her.

What will happen next? he thought. Mama's eyes were almost empty – where was she? *Please*, he thought. *Please, Mama.*

He was selfish. Stupid. Scared.

The grip of Papa's arm loosened around Rune, but he still couldn't move. Frozen. Waiting. Watching Mama's face as horror and terror merged into one expression. Mama was as frightened as he was.

He heard the cold snap of a buckle. The leather popped as Papa pulled his belt through each of his trouser loops. He didn't turn to look; he heard the pop. Pop. Pop. Papa held him. His hand had a metal smell, just like the burned-out pan.

'Do you remember?' Papa asked Mama, his voice low, and his words streamed, like bugs, from his lips. 'What I promised to do?' The words dripped and crawled and dropped all over Rune, through his hair and over his skin. 'You left me. You left *me*.' The words crawling. Creeping.

Wee leaked out.

He didn't notice.

He looked at Mama.

Only at Mama, as the belt was tied around his neck.

He put his hands up to it, felt the leather.

His neck.

The belt.

Skin-leather-skin.

Mama.Mama.Mama.

Mama stood, knocking over the chair she had been sitting on. He heard it crash to the floor. He saw Lotte jump up, Moo Bunny clenched in her tiny hands.

The belt was tight. Tighter. Tight. He scratched at his skin. Clawing at himself to try and release the pressure of the belt on his neck.

He heard Mama's voice. He tried to speak. Nothing. Tears welled in his eyes.

He heard banging and wondered if Mama had taken Lotte and left.

Left him. Alone with Papa. If she had run, again, but left him behind. He couldn't see, his vision a grey-misty-blank, then clear and white-bright. In his blindness he couldn't see Mama.

He was tearing, pulling at the belt, needing to run after her. *Wait, please, wait for me*, he thought.

Finally, he saw the shadow of Mama and he blink-blinked and pulled the belt loose.

Papa still had hold of it, but he could breathe again.

Mama came back into focus with a knife in her hand.

The only sharp knife they had.

It had a black handle, he knew this, but all he saw was the sharp steel blade.

Papa laughed and Rune was sick; thick-treacle-sticky sick. Sick from the laughter or the belt, or the fact that Mama held a knife in her hand as she came towards him, he didn't know.

Papa pulled the belt tight again, and Rune gagged.

'Enough,' Mama said. Her voice didn't quiver. 'Let him go!' She yelled, shouted, strength and surety in her voice.

Strong. She was strong. So strong.

'What are you going to do with that?' Papa asked.

'It's over,' Mama said. 'Go away. Leave me alone.'

'I'm not here for you. I'm here for them.'

Rune saw Mama's face. Mama's expression.

He wished he'd looked away, that he couldn't see her face. He didn't want to see her face when she realised it was the end.

'You left me,' Papa continued, speaking like he was saying a prayer, his voice low and slow. 'You. Left. Me,' he said. 'Now it's time for you to say goodbye to your children. You are a mama no more. First Rune, then Lotte. You will watch as I—'

The grip tightened and Rune struggled to stay with the world upturned, righted, then turned again. He focused on Mama as she looked at him. She looked at him. Not at Papa, but at him.

'Sorry,' she said.

Sorry. Sorry. Sorry.

A stupid word with no meaning.

'Sorry,' she said, then the grip on the belt loosened, dripped and fell away from his neck. His legs felt weak. He dropped to the ground with the belt coiled around his fingers.

'Run,' Mama said. 'Rune, RUN!' she yelled at him. Screamed the word. 'RUN!'

He stood, wobbled and held his hand out for Lotte. *Come on*, he wanted to say. *Lotte, come on.* But Lotte was wearing a mask of sheer terror and, like sunshine glancing steel, her face reflected painfully back at him and the look made him recoil.

Papa stepped in between Rune and Lotte, closing the distance towards Mama.

Lotte stepped back.

Away.

Rune turned.

Away.

Wobbled to the door and pulled it open.

He didn't think this at the time, but later, as the word circled back and through and around his mind, he wondered if he knew. If he knew that at the exact moment Mama said *sorry* to him, she had also been slicing the knife into her arm. A long line, from elbow to wrist. Deep. Bleeding.

Rune left.

He left Mama behind.

He left Lotte behind.

He ran.

He ran and ran and ran and ran and ran and ran.

He ran until he had no breath left. His eyes streaming.

He ran himself lost amid the cheering, the chanting, the vast sea of legs and all the people talking and laughing and moving, catching the same word said over and over: West.

He should have run back. To Mama. For Lotte. He should have run to Nanya, to LightHouse. Or the police. Or ANYONE.

He was scared, scared, scared, scared.

He should have run to anyone at all.

If he had, everything would have been different.

If only

he

had—

NOW

MONDAY 15TH NOVEMBER 1999

RUNE

He couldn't get the cold out of his bones as he walked away from the police station, with no knowledge as to why he had been released and no news on Lotte. Without looking back, he clattered down the steps and on to the pavement, where fat drops of rain hit the ground and splashed into tiny crowns.

In the shadow of November light, he stopped abruptly. Nanya was sitting on a bench opposite the station and beside her, holding a bright umbrella over both their heads, was Pepin.

They stood when they saw him. He was unsure of what to do but slowly walked towards them. Nanya hugged him tight and her hug travelled around him, lighting him up from the inside.

Pepin took Rune's bag from his shoulder. 'We thought you could use a lift,' she said.

'You're here for *me*?'

Nanya held his hand. 'I should have been there for you all along. I'm sorry, Rune.'

They walked towards an old red car afflicted by large patches of eczema-like rust. Sabine was in the back seat with a small girl, the image of her, at her side. The girl's hair was pulled into a tight ponytail and she was holding on to a stuffed owl almost as tightly as she held Sabine's hand.

'I'm Rune,' he said, seating himself next to her.

'I'm Clio,' the little girl said, and as she smiled up at him, he saw a large patch of skin across her jaw and neck that looked bunched up and webbed. It took a while for him to draw his gaze away, and as he did so he realised that the skin had been badly burned long ago.

'We're taking you to see Mama's friend Lotte now,' Clio said brightly. 'Only we've been waiting ages for you.'

'Clio,' Sabine said, then turned to Rune. 'I mean, she's right, we have, but you know – we're all here for Lotte, really.'

'Thanks,' Rune said, appreciating her honesty, however harshly it was delivered.

As Pepin drove, she and Nanya took it in turns to update him on what had happened.

'Lotte is out of intensive care and on the paediatric ward,' Nanya said.

He was dizzy with relief that she was alive.

'We all made statements that your father came to the offices and that Lotte was forced to leave,' Pepin added. 'We didn't know where you or Lotte lived so we contacted Nanya,' she continued. 'Nanya invited us to stay. We've been visiting Lotte at the hospital.'

'You're staying at LightHouse?'

'Yes,' said Pepin. 'The office is in a mess and so we've had to take leave.'

'It's a real weekend retreat,' mumbled Sabine, her sarcasm making Rune smile.

'Aunty Nanya is the best cook. We are making *Kartoffelpuffer* and *Apfelmus* tonight,' Clio added.

'I loved that as a child,' Rune said, remembering him and Lotte mashing the apples and shredding the pancakes. 'You're lucky,' he said to Clio. He watched her absent-mindedly smooth down the feathers of her toy owl. She reminded him painfully of Lotte when she was small too. He wondered how this tiny little girl could have come to be so horribly burned. He looked over at Sabine, who was focusing on the road outside; soon he was doing so too. The journey to the hospital was slow, stunted by traffic.

'Where are Isolde and Ralf?' Rune asked.

'They wouldn't fit in the car, and,' Sabine said, 'there was a slight issue at the offices.'

'Isolde was very upset after your father set fire to the bag of pages she was working on. She and Ralf thought they were Winola's files,' Pepin said gravely. 'It's obviously affected them both.'

'On the other hand, we found out what had happened to the missing files,' Sabine said.

Rune didn't care about files, or words. All he wanted was to get to Lotte. 'What happened?' he asked, uninterested.

'Isolde,' Sabine said.

'She thought they were related to Winola,' Pepin said. 'She was taking them home, trying to bring back her daughter's last days from the Stasi's surveillance material.'

'It's sad, really, but she could have told us,' Sabine said to Pepin. 'Would have saved us all these weeks of worrying.'

Pepin nodded, and then caught his eye in the mirror. 'The fire caused a huge mess, and in the tidying up we found your mother's file,' she said. 'Well, most of it. You just need to be with Lotte now. There'll be plenty of time to explain later.'

'Mama's file? What does it say?' he asked.

'It's all at LightHouse. We're working through it,' Pepin said.

'There's nothing that says what happened,' Nanya added. 'We are looking, though; we're all trying.'

But it was a useless task, he knew. Mama had killed herself to save them, and he would make sure that Lotte knew how much she had loved them and what she had done to try and protect them.

The files would be for Lotte, for the future, if she wanted them.

He thanked them all for helping him as Pepin pulled up outside the hospital. Nanya told him which ward Lotte was on and how to find her room.

'Come back to LightHouse later. You have the number?' she asked. 'Just call and we'll come and pick you up.'

Dr Ueli came to greet him at the entrance to the ward. He walked him to Lotte's room, pointing out the nurses' station, which was empty at the moment; her room lay at the far end of a darkened corridor. He tapped at the door, then pushed it open. A sweet, cool aroma wafted over him, not the invading hospital smell he had been expecting. Something between lavender and toothpaste, held within a musty scent of sleep. Dr Ueli pushed the door open further and allowed Rune to walk in ahead of him.

'Just shout if you need anything,' Dr Ueli said. 'She's sedated at the minute, just trying to rest the body as much as possible. She'll be okay, she's responding well to treatment.'

Rune's eyes adjusted to the dusk-webbed room and the tiny figure on the bed, curled up in a ball.

'I'm glad things are sorted with the police,' Dr Ueli said.

'Well, not exactly,' Rune confessed, having no idea what was happening now he'd been released. 'I'd never hurt her though, honestly. Not ever.' He was desperate for someone to believe him.

Dr Ueli nodded and gave him a weighty look, which made Rune think he was questioning Lotte's safety in leaving him alone with her.

'I'll be back later,' Dr Ueli said eventually, and Rune heard the door hush behind him.

'Lotte?' he asked, her name thin as air. He was unsure if the sleeping figure could be his sister at all. But she turned and he saw her face, her bruised and wrapped-up face.

Her eyes were shiny, teary, and the tissue-thin skin underneath was bruised purple-black, as though her skull was sucking them back in. Her lips were deeply cracked and her hair was loose, short, stuck around her face, pale as bone. She looked at him, looked deep within him, a look that was thick and weak; she looked and then closed her eyes. She wasn't awake, but 'sedated', as Dr Ueli said.

Her body spoke for her. The fragility of it held down by a thin yellow blanket.

He pulled a chair up to the head of the bed. She looked so frail. 'Lotte,' he said, and took her hand. It was cool and clammy.

He closed his eyes, holding her hand like a fallen petal in his own, and searched for something to say, his tongue on a cliff edge; to speak would be to drop off into the void. The void of the unnamed.

'Lotte, it's me, it's Rune.' He looked around him, self-consciously; his words were wrong, misshapen and clunky. Repulsed by himself, he tried again.

'It's Roo, Lotte.' And it was. Just as his sister had turned into a tiny delicate thing perched between being and not, of seeing and not, of hearing and not, he too had returned to a small boy, holding tight to a hand, trying to make someone *be*, just be, to exist in the world as he did, so he wouldn't be all alone.

Lotte reminded him of Mama. So concretely of Mama that he pulled his hand away. Watching Lotte sleep was like looking back in time. Holding on to Mama's hand those first days at LightHouse.

Dr Ueli walked through the door a few hours later as Rune was watching Lotte's heart beat across a screen. He watched it until he forgot that he himself was in possession of a heart, that his also beat on within his chest, but privately, while Lotte's was recorded and assessed, examined and noted as evidence of a broken body. A broken heart?

Rune listened to Dr Ueli, fatigue making him focus hard on some words and lose others as the doctor's sentences became more and more oblique, explaining each line on the monitor and talking about the effects of the heart surgery, about Lotte's heart, her blood results, electrolytes. He could have been speaking in Greek for all Rune understood of it, but still he nodded, holding Lotte's hand in both of his, in prayer. Holding on to her.

Maybe touch was the only language she could hear.

He had an overwhelming urge to close his eyes and hope that tomorrow would bring with it some clarity.

'When will she wake up?' he asked.

'In the morning. Go on home and I will call you if there's any news. Put your number on her chart here.' Rune did. 'Get some rest,' Dr Ueli added, and left.

And in the slumber of the hospital, the regular breaths of Lotte's sleeping form, Rune lay his head on Lotte's bed. He didn't know what he was doing any more; he was being washed up by the tide, unable to stop. Not even trying. Dr Ueli had told him to go home.

Home. As if there was such a place. He was next to Lotte; it was all the *home* he had.

'I'm so sorry, Lotte. So sorry,' he said. He was failing. Just like he always had. And with that thought, he fell into a dreamless sleep.

When he woke, feeling shabby and ruffled, the sun was dipping and the dank day was at the mercy of dusk. He watched the clouds part and Teufelsberg came into view, three round clouds up on the hill. He could see them from Lotte's room.

Instinctively, he pulled a paper napkin from above the sink and a thin biro from the clipboard at the bottom of the bed, and before he realised what he was doing, he started sketching. He sketched and his mind stretched; he let go of a breath he hadn't known he'd been holding. As he sketched, his memory offered him Mama's face, every single detail, as though she were right in front of him. When he had completed it, he smiled until his cheeks hurt; he looked at what he had drawn and laughed. After the laugh he cried silently, selfishly, safely.

Something had been lifted.

He saw Moo Bunny in the corner of the blanket, tucked away. Rune picked him up; his cow-print dress had fallen over his head, revealing the big deep cut that had been stitched together under his belly.

'Do you remember when I cut him up?' Rune asked, his voice cautious into the sleeping air. 'You said you would never forgive me. But you did,' he added. 'Magic,' he said sadly. Rune's fingers found a small hole where the stitching had come apart. There was something inside Moo Bunny.

Wordlessly, his fingers delved inside the cut he had made and sewn shut, so long ago. His fingers touched paper.

'Did we stuff Moo Bunny with paper,' he asked, 'when his stuffing came out?' But he knew they hadn't. He had just sewn Moo Bunny back up in terrible, uneven stitches. He pulled out a small, folded sheet of paper. His head felt so hot, he was sure it was going to explode.

It was his fault that Papa had gone to FlatHouse. It was his fault that Mama was dead. It was his fault that Lotte had got hurt.

He should never have left her.

He couldn't understand what he was seeing. What he was reading.

'It's from Mama,' he said out loud.

There was a buzz in his head that kept getting louder and louder. 'It's from Mama,' he said again.

Dear Rune and Lotte,

I am capturing these words in ash from the blaze I have made of our lives. If you are reading this then I am lost.

Please know that I love you.

Please know that I fought back, for a life, for a free life. For a life with you both.

If I could give you a different life I would do so – I would have given you a papa who would allow you to have a mama too. The life I have tried to make for us is over.

I have failed and time has started to leak, a muffled, suffocating tick, pulped into nothingness. Time lost. The second hand has soured, dripping its ticks, and I am panicking there may be no more. If only I could go back and erase and erase and make something better for you. There is so much I need to tell you both, but the bitter truth of it is that time is up.

But you, my children, will live on to soar and live a life without regret.

You carry me in your hearts, because I made them with my own.

Hold me close forever as I hold you: in every beat.

Mama

Unable to breathe, chest tight, eyes stinging.

Flames spat, grew blue at the tips. White and blue and cold. Rising from his chest into his throat. A stinging pain screamed across his forehead. The periphery around him was white, erased. Scrubbed. Rubbed. Bleached.

There was just him. He couldn't feel the weight of the page in his hands, nor could he see Lotte in bed before him. He heard once again the pink-pop like pork of Mama's skin as it was held under the grill; and him sitting, helpless. Knowing and watching. But that was in the past. Gone. Over. The knife and the blood and the green carpet that turned into tar. The files at the Stasi HQ. The report, the *Missing* poster. The reference to the Wall falling, *that awful day* and surgery and *Alive?*

Reluctantly, he folded the precious letter back and tucked it safely into Moo Bunny, and Moo Bunny back under the blanket. He left Lotte sleeping, her body weeping even in sleep. Pain was salient now, visible, outside. No longer within. He promised her sleeping, shuddering body that he would never leave her again.

V.

I am coming unstitched, as though somehow I am peeling open, stitch by stitch. I want to stall the process, but the more I pull on the thread, the looser it becomes. I'm afraid I am going to fall apart.

I am going to fall and part.

The minutes are razor sharp. I bite my cheek to taste the iron-rust metal as it spirals over my tongue.

I imagine the seed; silent. The growth of madness; invisible.

I fear I am lost to myself. Only a collapsible skin that sags and puddles and leaves me open. Only a primal naked longing to be free from my flesh, my blood, my bone; every nerve and muscle trapped. Only confusion as to how I can keep being, how I can keep living, when the water, air, earth and sun are gone from my life.

My children.

Gone.

Time does not heal all wounds.

All wounds do not heal.

NOW

TUESDAY 16TH NOVEMBER 1999

LOTTE

When she awoke, she felt a hand on hers and she smelled lavender. The *Dear Lotte* voice had gone and was replaced with a voice she thought she knew.

'Hi, sleepyhead,' the soft voice said. As she opened her sticky eyes, she saw not just one person but several. Lotte was surrounded by people. She couldn't move her head, but she saw Sabine right away, beside her bed. Pepin was at the foot of the bed and a little girl stood by the window. There were people in pink uniforms around her too, scary-talking words Lotte didn't understand.

'Roo?' she said, her tongue so thick it didn't fit into her mouth at all. She tried to move, but flashes of pain shot through her body and stopped her thoughts.

'Rune is coming,' Pepin said.

Lotte tried to look at her but she still couldn't move her head; she closed her eyes and started to cry.

'Rune is coming,' Pepin repeated. 'He's on his way.'

'My head,' Lotte said. 'My head is ouch.'

'I'll bet,' said Sabine. 'Rune found you.'

'I want Roo,' Lotte said again. 'Where is my big brother, Roo?'

'Stay awake, Lotte, he's here in the hospital, he's on his way – I promise.'

It was only when she started to panic that she realised her voice had turned into a shout, into a screech, into a wild wailing. Calling for him. 'Where is Roo?'

The people in pink put a syringe of clear fluid into the end of the tube and pushed and she felt the world up-end and go out.

The room filled with the sun's rays, and although it was weak, it was light, and she followed a petal of rainbow as it slid across the bed, filling the room with the jaunty colours of the sky. She spoke carefully, holding on to her words like flames in the wind, precious and fleeting.

'Roo,' she said. 'I want—' But there was no one in the room, just the shifting rays of sun. She looked at the blanket that covered her and tried to sit up, but her head felt strange and her body too flat to lift. Making more effort than she thought was possible, she turned over onto her side. Her chest made a burn-pull that went deep into her. She looked under her nightgown to see a very big plaster that went from the top of her chest, past her breasts to the top of her tummy. She covered it up with the nightgown and then the blanket. Whoever put the big plaster there would have seen her breasts. She felt cold and wobbly and witnessed in ways she didn't like.

'Roo?' she called, panicking. 'Roo?' There was something wrong with her. Her hand had see-through wires going into it and her head knocked the words back at her with red-black pain in her eyes. 'What happened to me?' she asked.

Then she saw a bump in the bed and lifted the blanket carefully. A soft bunny was there. It was dressed in a black-and-white cow-print smock, its face rubbed down with love.

She knew him. She looked at him all over.

He had a scar on his chest too. Their scars were matching. She held him tight and spoke in a voice that was broken.

She remembered that scars bridge the hurt back up and holding him in her arms, he smiled at her, as if she had been lost to him too.

Magic.

Moo Bunny asked her to tell him what happened. She tried to find her voice, but it was as weak as her body, so she whispered to him instead. Trying to find words to explain all that had gone before. She thought she would be able to do that, for Moo Bunny, but perhaps finding words to describe feelings is far harder than living through them. Because to speak them was to remember, and take words to a place where there were none.

She wove Moo Bunny's ears through her fingers, thinking of the last time she had seen him. She thought of Mama. In one of her letters she'd said, *The key to unlocking the cage was to speak.* Lotte's cage had been forgetting. She would speak, she would unlock the cage. She would be free.

Moo Bunny gently placed a paw on her cheek.

Moo Bunny didn't understand the power of the words. They would take her back. And back was losing Mama all over again; she tried to say so to him.

But Moo Bunny listened carefully and took Lotte back to FlatHouse, to Mama and to all that had happened before.

THEN

The day Papa came to FlatHouse

The door went bang and Roo was gone
        The knife went clatter
        A red river dripped down Mama's arm   Like   the   skin
had gone inside out
    Flim-flam-flop
        Mama knows that knives are sharp
she is cutted   but no one is getting a plaster or a tissue
for the red that leaks out of her
        Papa is so crossed up he doesn't look like Papa any more
        That is NOT my papa that is just a bad mans
        Papa-man goes to the door and locks and bolts it
Mama is on her knees on the floor
Mama picks up the knife again
Mama looks at me
Hide   she says In her soft Mama voice
Papa-man turns all big and bad swollen like fuzz-fruit
I hear her soft Mama voice as Papa-man takes big steps
Hide   she says to me
        My legs are wobbly and my tears want to cry
                                BUT
I hide under mine and Mama's bed
and

I am trying not to do hearing
I must be still as statues
Still as stars
So   the   words that scream and cry and shout and tear at the
house   The words that come from the Papa-man   The words that
break and smash and bleed and fall and cry and sob and stutter and
groan   Those words   don't   get   ME

So I stay still
and I count the slats under the bed of Mama and me
There are 1   2   3   4   5   6   7
8   9   10   11   12   13   14   15   16
        16 is BIG
I keep counting and counting and making the still with my body
But
Everywhere
                Everywhere
                                Everywhere else
the words
run
wild
I am *still* doing still
    Thumb snuggles in
but
    I don't know what do
When the words
go out.

I hear the heavy steps of feet huff huffing
        I make small of myself

422

Tiny Lotte

I hear the water swish and the tap and the flush

I peek out from under the bed

I hear the back door   scratch and the pull pull harder
creak of the back door which is always sticky-tight

I pid-pad-patter to the bedroom door and openly peek

The back door closed

Shut

I see through the glass Roo's bike move to the fence

I see feet climb on the seat where bottoms sit
Not where feet should stand

I see legs go Wheee over the top of the fence

Bye Papa-man

And when FlatHouse is silent I whisper

Mama?

Ma-ma?

I seek out my mama   Maybe she is playing Hide and
Seek   now that the words have gone

Mama?   You can come out now I say

But

Mama is not hiding

Mama is open

The red that is inside is now out   everywhere   is   red
around Mama

I walk around the puddle but Mama is in the middle
In the middle of all the red

I need Nanya I think   I need Roo

Nanya and Roo will be knowing how to get Mama back

The front door is shut   I get a chair

I cannot reach the bolt even on my toe-points

The back door is tight   I pull and pull but my hand
hurts so I stop
    I go back to Mama
        I don't want to step in the sticky-red
But
I want my mama
I try to put the red back in
to tuck Mama into my heartbeat
Wake up I whisper   Please wake up
I love you my mama.

No one is coming
    No one is coming I say to Moo Bunny

Roo's door starts knocking gently   Like the handle is tapping against
the wall
        Roo?
    I get up and go to Roo's room
        No one is there   But the curtains flutter   which is funny
because the window is shut
        I step inside Roo's room and the room seems to sigh
Happy   Full
        Hello Roo's room   I say and I know Roo's room is
smiling at me   It flutters the curtains like feathers   Ruffle
and fluffle and
    Open
            Roo's window is open
        Magic   I say and Moo Bunny and I are impressed
                I stand on Roo's bed and lift the window up high-
er it lifts easily
    I have to go and get Nanya

Thank you   I say to Roo's room   as I put both my feet
out the window

I have to go and get Nanya

But

it is a long way down

Roo's room sighs and FlatHouse gives me a gentle nudge
and I lose grip of Moo Bunny as I fall a tall-way down

Moo Bunny is still in FlatHouse

     But Mama is inside so Moo will be safe

I don't know what to do

Because now I am outside without Moo Bunny or Mama and
I cannot get Roo or Nanya because of the fences and the wall and
I cannot get back in because I felled out of the window

I don't know what to do

Roo's bell on his bike tinkles

                    Brriiiiiiinnng

And I knowed that if I climb on to Roo's bike I can try and
reach the top of the fence

But

I am not allowed to climb Roo's bike

I might get falled off

     The bell tinkles again

     With careful grippy feet   I climb Roo's bike and when my
feet are on the saddle I reach up and grab the top of the fence
Just like Papa-man did

     I look back to FlatHouse and it blinks its one-window eye
at me

     I pull and pull and climb   I pull with my hands
and climb with my finger-points and I am up and up and
then   it's   a   tall

Way

Down

I land in a heap
> But I land
> Outside
> On the lane with all the rubbish bins
> My knees are blood and dirt and gravel and ouch

My chin landed bang too and stings to touch
> My tears are red and hot
> My hands are peeled back red

I need Nanya

I walk on sharp paths
> Everything is hot-hurting

But

I am cold   Crawly under skin cold

I climb the steps
> I bang on the big blue door with its peel-ly paint
> Nanya opens the door
> She looks happy then scared   She must know about

Mama

I open my mouth to tell
> But
> There are no words inside my head
> When Nanya takes me back to FlatHouse the door is open and
> > Mama
> > has
> > gone.

NOW

WEDNESDAY 17ᵀᴴ NOVEMBER 1999

BUSS- UND BETTAG – REPENTANCE DAY

RUNE

Dr Ueli met with him a few times after Lotte had the surgery, where they both tried to find the right path for Lotte, to aid her recovery. Papa hadn't been to the hospital since Rune was released. The only thing they had agreed upon was that Rune should be there as often and for as long as Lotte wanted him, but never if Papa was visiting.

'Hi,' he said anxiously, but happily – seeing Lotte sitting up in bed. The skin on her face was red, raw and thin, but she was sitting up, she was awake.

'Hi,' he said again. Sitting next to her.

'You are here,' she said. 'Roo is here with me – Lotte and Rune. Rune and Lotte.' And she started to cry.

When she kept crying and he found no words would soothe her, he did something he hadn't done for far too long. He pulled her into an awkward hug. It was a mismatched thing, all arms and hands and wonky spaces, as they tried to avoid the wires and tubes that were plugged into her. There was a new consciousness of her body to him, how fragile it now seemed, how much pain she must be enduring, that held him stiffly, terribly afraid that he would hurt her further.

'I'm sorry.'

She gulped and pulled back, wincing.

'Dr Ueli told me what happened. Do *you* understand what happened, why you're here? The surgery?'

Lotte nodded, weaving her blanket through her fingers. Beneath it, Moo Bunny was slumped over. 'My head was broken and my heart needed better plumbing. Dr Ueli fixed it. It is good that you are here,' she said, and tucked her head into his chest again. 'I am needing you to be here always.'

'I'm so sorry, Lotte. I did everything wrong,' he said. 'I should have been there.'

'No, you wouldn't have been there. Pepin said you were busy trying to find Mama. Where is Mama?'

Rune began plucking at the blanket himself and spoke of Nanya, of LightHouse, and how Nanya had sent the notebook to them.

He could see the light dust filtering through the air around them and he knew that naming something made it come into existence. Bone-white, harsh; a drug-rush that left him trembling. He named it for her and for himself.

That terrible-terrible word.

Dead.

He said it. Out loud. It felt like he was delivering a blow.

'Mama is *still* dead?'

He nodded.

'But Papa hurt me and I am not dead. Papa hurt Mama too, so she can't be dead either.'

'People who are dead never come back,' Rune said sadly.

'Mama isn't dead like other people. Mama is magic,' Lotte said in a voice so small he looked up to check it was her speaking and not the Lotte of his imagination.

'She *was*,' he said cautiously. 'But Lotte, it wasn't Papa who hurt Mama, it was Mama herself.'

'Everything I remember is lost; it doesn't matter anyway.' And Lotte looked so fragile, he was worried he had upset her. 'But not Moo Bunny,' she said, and wove her fingers over his ears. 'Moo Bunny is magic – he can bring Mama back.'

He let her comment go, unsure as to what she meant and concerned he'd have to repeat himself. Lotte started to mutter under her breath; her skin was clammy and she was grinding her teeth.

With some difficulty, Rune moved Lotte so she was lying down, and then passed Moo Bunny, who had fallen on the floor, back to her. She grabbed him in a tight embrace. Rune was scared, but he knew that only words would help. He had no choice but to accommodate the past and permit the pain of it to find a way to make it legible.

Living. Alive. Present.

THEN

FRIDAY 10TH NOVEMBER 1989

The house was gone from view. Everything he recognised was gone. Sick splatters shrank into his top. His throat was on fire, but still he ran through the crowds, the music pulsing from a long, long line of parked cars.

When he stopped he caught his breath, walked slowly, then saw the look on Mama's face in his mind and ran again.

'Run,' she had screamed. 'Run!' But to where and to whom? Comrade Ackermann was the only one who might help him, but school was closed and he had asked everyone during the day, but Comrade Ackermann wasn't there.

There was no one else, and he had run too far to find his way back. Jeans and denim jackets, cigarettes and bottles, loud music and people talking, laughing and singing. He heard sirens in the background. He was hearing celebrations about the fall of 'our Wall'. No one cared that his world had fallen with it.

He was shivering cold, sweat-wet and with every step he was trying to get away from what had happened and with each step he wanted to go back. He walked through an industrial estate. He walked through a park full of empty glass bottles and cigarette ends. He walked past kids on the swings, too old to fit on the seats. Rune ignored their jibes and jeers and kept walking.

He went past houses and houses and houses, past more and more people; everyone was outside and he was desperately looking for home.

But maybe home was gone.

Finally, he found a police station at the end of a street of shut-up shops and spoke to a police officer, who talked a lot. He asked questions, which Rune responded to politely but briefly. He asked to go home, said there was a problem at home and gave the address. After a bit of a delay while the officer found a working car to take him, they wound down streets he didn't recognise. Leaving much of the noise, the party, the people behind him.

When the car stopped, he was at LightHouse.

'Here?' the officer asked.

Rune unbuckled his seat belt and pulled on the handle. It wouldn't open. He tried again. 'One minute,' the officer said and got out, walked around the car and opened the door. As they walked up the steps the officer put his hand over Rune's, and he knew that Nanya would know what to do. He paused before knocking on the door, his body stiff. He knew that because of him Nanya had been arrested, that she'd gone to prison. She'd been gone for days. It was his fault and the guilt made him look down at the ground as the door opened. He hoped she would forgive him one day. He hoped she would still help him.

The milk bottles were stacked two-high in the corner. The tricycle was still missing its third wheel. Nothing had changed and yet everything had.

He didn't recognise the mama who answered. He asked for Nanya. She looked at him carefully and then at the officer, who showed her his police badge.

'Nanya's not here,' she said. 'She went with the little girl and then the . . .' She looked at the officer again.

'If you're the police, you've come to the wrong address. Nanya called them to go to the flat on Winzer. But that was an hour ago – you're not very quick, are you?' she asked the officer. Rune had stopped listening. He heard *little girl* and *Winzer*. He let his hand drop out of the officer's and ran down the street, around the corner and back home, bumping into a group of people holding placards and talking about travelling to an *SED rally* at Lustgarten park.

His thoughts blazed. His feet were numb.

He didn't see Nanya and Lotte as he rounded the corner. The front door was open. Rune didn't see the police officers, nor the ambulance, nor the paramedics. He ran into the house at full speed. And there on the carpet lay an enormous pool of black-red blood.

He saw the fresh grey sky as he was dragged out with hands under his armpits. He saw Nanya and was plopped in a boneless heap next to her, and finally he saw Lotte.

Nanya picked him up and lifted him on her lap too. They shared her tiny lap, he and Lotte. It wasn't very comfortable. Nanya checked him all over.

'Are you okay?' she asked. 'Where were you?'

He slid off her lap and, sitting next to her, looked at Lotte.

She was holding Nanya too tightly, her thumb in her mouth. She was covered in blood, she had bashed-up knees, chin, hands. Her hair was stuck to her face on one side and a raggedy mess on the other.

Her feet were dirt-black.

He couldn't look at her for long.

She had stayed.

He had left.

It was all his fault.

'I should have come back for you,' he garbled to Lotte. 'Reached out and pulled you with me. Taken you too. I should have taken you when Mama yelled at me to run. But why? Why did she yell at me to run? Maybe she didn't say run, maybe she was calling me? Yelling. Rune. Rune. Rune . . .' And he sobbed until he aged himself, spine bending, shoulder hunching, face wrinkled, weathering. He cried himself old.

Outside the flat, people were everywhere, poking and prodding at him and at Lotte, asking questions he couldn't answer. He just stared hopelessly at the open door. Waiting. Waiting for Mama to walk out, to pick them up. To say it would all be okay.

Nanya's answers poured down her face. Everyone had questions for her too, mainly about Lotte, although he also heard his name. They wrote everything down in their notebooks.

Nanya held tightly on to his hand. He couldn't move if he wanted to. He watched the police cars drive off.

They didn't put the sirens on.

When he awoke, he was lying on a hospital bed, a blanket wrapped around his legs. He sat up, looking for Lotte, and found her wrapped in a blanket also, but sitting crossed-legged by his feet. She was awake and looking at him.

'Are you okay?' he asked.

She nodded.

'What's happening?'

She took her thumb out of her mouth and pointed. At least she looked more like Lotte, thumb in her mouth, and her eyes recognised him; she was engaging with him with her eyes and he moved closer to hug her tight.

'They do not need to be examined,' Papa was saying. 'I will take them home and they will see their own doctor.'

'They'll need a lot of help to manage this, going forward, Herr Schäffer,' a doctor was saying. Her ponytail was long and black and almost reached the end of her white coat. It swished as she talked and reminded Rune of a horse-tail swishing flies away from its bottom.

It was decided.

Papa signed papers and gave details to everyone who asked for them.

'Your mother is dead,' Papa said as they left the hospital.

They were going home. Another useless word. *Home*. Like *Sorry* and *Dead*. He was collecting useless words. Love; another.

He held Lotte's hand in the car on the way home. She was sucking her thumb and fell asleep before they got to the border. The border control people didn't even check Papa's passport; they just let them through. Passing streets like car parks of Trabants snaking through the borders and hundreds of people shouting, 'The Wall has to go!', and hammering at it with everything from a huge sledgehammer to the end of a shoe. Rune watched, disinterested, as they passed.

Everything had changed.

NOW

WEDNESDAY 17TH NOVEMBER 1999

BUSS- UND BETTAG – REPENTANCE DAY

LOTTE

'I'm here to change you,' the nurse in pink clothes said to Lotte, holding in her hands a big nappy and a bowl of soapy water.

'No,' Lotte said.

'Come on, be a big girl now and help me.'

'No. I am inde-pend-ent,' Lotte spat and turned away.

'Independent? Look, let's do this quickly so you don't make a mess of your clothes and sheets. There's a good girl.'

Lotte felt a hand on her shoulder. 'No.'

After a long silence, the nurse said, 'I'll be back in a bit then.'

Lotte spent the next few hours trying hard to squeeze her bladder tight shut. When Sabine arrived, she could have cried.

'Please help me?' Lotte asked straight away.

'Of course.'

'I need a wee-wee. I want to go to the toilet.'

It took Sabine and Lotte almost five minutes just to navigate the tubes and wires to get off the bed. Lotte's feet felt numb and she stumbled. Sabine caught her.

'We'll do this slowly,' Sabine said as Lotte leaned heavily into her.

'Or quickly,' Lotte said, shuffling her feet towards the adjoining door with the toilet. 'I need a wee-wee quickly.'

Sabine held her firmly with one arm and wheeled all the machines that were attached to Lotte as they made a slow-quick-slow journey to the toilet.

As Lotte sat on the toilet and let out the first gush of urine, she cried, 'You are my best-best friend, Sabine. Oh, my best-best friend. Sabine. Thank you. ThankyouThankyou.' Her head hurt and she placed her hands over her cheeks to hold her head up as she tinkled. 'I want to be inde-pen-dent, I do so much. Papa is telling people I am not clever or kind or understanding. No one is listening to me, Sabine.'

Sabine passed Lotte a wad of toilet roll. 'I am listening to you. Rune and Pepin listen to you, Lotte. You have some of the most important things to say.'

'I do?'

'I think so,' Sabine said. 'Done?'

Lotte nodded.

'Let's try and get you back to bed without tangling you into a knot.'

Lotte laughed. 'A Lotte-knot.'

Later, Pepin came into her room with a little girl.

'You're Clio?' Lotte said, looking at a small version of Sabine. 'Oh, I am so happy to be meeting you.'

'You are brave,' Clio said, and her face flushed red as she hid slightly behind Sabine.

'So are you. Little Clio. Little owl.' And she felt tears fall down her cheeks again when she saw the happy in Sabine's face. Clio jumped into her mother's lap.

Behind Pepin followed a nurse with a tray carrying Lotte's lunch of *Schnitzel* and *Pommes frites*. Lotte gazed at them hungrily.

She must eat. Everyone said so. They kept telling her to eat. They watched her refuse.

Constantly.

She did not eat. Because to eat would be to get better and to get better would mean to go away. To a special school.

When Papa last visited, he said that when Lotte was better she would go to the special school in Hamburg. The doctors would talk about this special school in Hamburg and their plan to discharge her to the special school in Hamburg and not one person listened when she said she would not go to the special school in Hamburg. She wanted inde-pen-dence but everyone was making her –pendent on them.

Roo said that wouldn't happen, but the doctors listened to Papa instead.

Clever people were very silly.

She was alone and lost in her head. Knowing that the salty, fluffy *Pommes frites* would stay on her plate helped her remember salt on her lips and Mama's hand in hers after they had been to a big park with a Ferris wheel that they hadn't been allowed to ride. Mama had helped her eat her *Pommes* and then kissed Lotte with salty lips.

Remembering Mama was better than eating ever could be.

'Where is Roo?' Lotte asked.

'At the police station,' Sabine said. 'Follow-up questions.'

'Why?'

'Because he was charged with hurting you.'

'But Roo didn't hurt me,' Lotte said, sitting up.

'We know,' said Pepin, her voice tired and raw. 'It's not as simple as it being true. Your papa happens to have a great deal of power.'

445

'The truth doesn't matter too much to a person like your father,' Sabine said.

'But that's wrong.'

'We know,' Sabine said and held her hand.

Papa was bad. Yet Papa was still her papa, and her thoughts confused themselves.

'I need to tell the police what Papa did-do to me,' she said, making little Clio, who was eating Lotte's *Pommes frites*, jump in alarm. 'I need to tell the truth so Roo will be saved.'

She looked at their sad and worried faces.

'They won't believe me, will they?'

'They should,' Pepin said.

'But they won't,' Lotte added. 'Is it because of my Down's syndrome?'

'I think it's because you love Roo as much as you do,' Sabine said sadly.

'But we gave statements to the police and Rune is no longer in a prison cell so they must have listened to us,' Pepin added. 'At least for now.'

'But Papa hurt me. I want to help Roo too.'

'The police will think you are trying to protect Rune,' Sabine said.

'I am. Protecting him from Papa and from all the untruths and all the hurts Papa did-do. What did Mama's letter say?' she asked, searching her foggy head for the phrase she wanted, the words that were Mama's that were to her and only her. 'Love isn't just something you feel – it's something you do,' she said.

RUNE

He knocked on the door and held himself carefully, unwilling to reveal too much of himself in his posture, his presence, on *Buß- und Bettag*, the Day of Repentance.

Repentance. Remorse. Resolve.

Joann held a nervous smile on her face as she opened the door, but when she saw it was him, both her smile and her hands dropped.

'Is *he* here?' he asked her.

She stepped back, allowing him in. Rune turned. Papa was at his shoulder, slightly taller than him, wider than him, but not by much. Rune stood to his full height; they met eye to eye. Papa waited for Rune to speak.

'I came for our things,' Rune said slowly, softening the edges of his words. Speaking to slow his heart.

Joann jumped and swiftly moved past them. 'I have everything here, all her things – we packed them all up for her,' she said, passing Rune a heavy bag. 'So she could at least have her own clothes in hospital and then they'll move her on to the facility in Hamburg.'

'What?'

Joann bumbled, aware that she had told Rune something he hadn't known.

'Lotte isn't going anywhere,' he said.

'Yes, she is.' Papa's voice made him jump and he hated that he had done so. A flush crept up his neck, but he refused to look down.

'No,' he said. 'She's my responsibility now.'

'You don't make the decisions, Rune, I do.'

'Not for me and not for Lotte. Not any more,' he said calmly.

'They won't let her live with you, after all that you've done. You can't even be responsible for yourself.'

'I did nothing to Lotte. I would never ever hurt her. It's over. You can do what you like, but Lotte and I will always be together.' He stared into his father's face, a face that Rune shared. 'Even you can't change that. Not now.'

'What do you mean?'

'The notebook you destroyed. It's no longer destroyed. The Stasi had a file on Mama too.' He had spent the time away from the hospital in the large LightHouse kitchen with Pepin, Sabine and Nanya, finding sense in the pages of Mama's files that had been recovered before the fire. 'Everyone will know what you did to Mama, and to me and now to Lotte.'

'Careful, Rune.'

'She wrote it all down, all the abuse.' He spat the words out. For the first time in his life, he felt safe. He had Nanya and the puzzle women, and because of them he could keep Lotte safe too. It must have been what Mama felt when she took them there. The thought was bitter-sweet.

Rune turned to the door, carrying Lotte's bag on his shoulder; there was nothing in his own room that he wanted to keep. Before he left, he turned back to Papa, who had followed him into the hallway.

'You failed,' he said to him. Deliberately. Watching his eyes as they held his gaze. Unflinching. 'You failed,' he repeated. 'You won't get away with hurting Lotte. Or Mama. You're weak,' Rune said.

Papa said nothing, arms crossed, tucked into his armpits; he was casual, cocky, just waiting for Rune to finish.

Rune turned to Joann. He looked at her carefully before he spoke. 'This *man* killed Mama,' he said. 'He ruined her. Destroyed her. He took away everything she had, and still that wasn't enough. He killed her,' Rune said. If he hadn't come for them, if Papa hadn't hurt him, threatened always to hurt him and take him and Lotte away, then he had no doubt Mama would be alive. Papa might not have held the knife that killed her, but he had allowed her death. Just by being there and by doing everything he had done leading up to that moment too.

Joann drew a sharp breath and stepped away from Papa; a small step physically, but Rune was glad to see it was a step internally too.

'Run away,' he said. 'Fast.' He didn't like her, but he didn't want her to get hurt either.

Papa spluttered.

'He forgot something,' Rune continued, speaking to Joann. 'Something that means Mama will never be gone from my life or from Lotte's.' He turned to Papa, squared his shoulders, and for the first time in his life he felt bigger, stronger. He was no longer afraid. His voice quivered and tears fell; he didn't catch them. He stood tall and spoke his truth. 'I remember her, and because of that' – he turned to face Papa once more – 'you failed.'

In the letter tucked into Moo Bunny, he heard Mama in his head, not just through the words on the page. He remembered it all. Both blessing and curse. And in her words, and in his memories, she would survive.

'She will outlive *you*,' he spat, wiping his tears on his sleeve and moving to the door. 'You failed in every way. You did not silence me, you did not silence Lotte. Mama wrote words that lasted, she made children that witnessed, she had friends who remember. She existed so far above you, you couldn't even see her.' He took a breath, but it wobbled; he wanted to hit Papa with his voice. It was loud and he made it louder. Shouting, controlled, lifting his voice so that maybe, wherever Mama was, she could hear him.

He was standing up to Papa, for them all.

Papa opened his mouth to speak, but Rune closed it with his own words.

'You killed her once,' and quietly he added, 'and we will not let you kill her again. You are no longer in charge of Lotte. She is my responsibility now and she will be independent, just as she wants to be. You come near her again . . .' He wasn't sure where he was going with the sentence, so he left it alone.

'Don't openly threaten me, boy—' Papa said, his voice low, soft and even. 'You try and take me down—' And he lowered his voice so that it growled, stepping forward into Rune's space. 'If anything happens to me you'll never know the truth about your mother.'

'What?'

'You heard me,' he said. 'If I go down, you'll never see her again.'

Rune looked at him, unflinching. Papa laughed. Papa was laughing at him.

It was bait; a trap.

Rune turned and walked straight out of the door and marched down the street. It was a game, it wasn't true, he was just playing him, manipulating, but still sobs rang out of his chest. He had never felt so broken and yet so free.

Papa's last words struck hard. 'You'll never see her again.' He would never see his sister again – this was what Papa was threatening. Wasn't it?

But was it also possible that Papa meant Mama? Perhaps Papa knew what had happened to her after *that* day? Or perhaps Papa knew where her grave was; that there was a possibility, finally, for Rune to say goodbye.

THEN

SUNDAY 26TH NOVEMBER 1989

TOTENSONNTAG – SUNDAY OF THE DEAD

Eyes squeezed shut, he listened to the soft sounds of the night – wanting to sleep, but not wanting to dream. He lay alone, lost, as mists of bruised darkness rolled before his eyelids.

He heard her push open the door and pad her way to the bed. She lifted the blanket as he moved closer to the wall where the sheets were cool, leaving his body-warmed place for her. Her toes were warm and she smelled cottony and crumpled.

'Roo?'

He made a non-committal noise in the base of his throat. And knowing she was there, with her small body curled into his back, the storm behind his eyelids became restful.

'Is the sky velvet?' she asked, and he heard the suction pop of her thumb being released from her mouth. The noise made him smile. 'Is that why the stars stick?' and, 'Can you forget to be missing?'

He waited for another question to saturate the night air and bring it alive, in quivers of thoughts and questions that made no sense.

'Did Mama have a face?' Lotte asked.

'What do you mean? Of course she did.' The wall was blank and a coldness seemed to seep from it into the bed.

'Do we have a picture of Mama?' she asked. 'I think I am forgetting to miss her.'

He took a deep breath. There were no pictures of Mama, there was nothing of Mama; when they came back home with Papa it was as though the house had been erased of her entirely. No clothes, no pictures, no soaps or shampoos. She had vanished.

'You don't need a picture to remember Mama, and' – he thought about his words before he spoke, allowing them time to arrange themselves – 'you won't find what you want in a picture.'

'But,' and Lotte started to cry, 'I . . . I . . . don't want to forget . . .'

The smallness of her pain hurt him in a way that made him panic. He was drifting in a daze, unfeeling. He thought of Mama and tried, he really tried, to bring Mama back, just for a second: for Lotte. Tucking his pain away in places he dared not go.

'Don't cry. Here.' And he placed her tiny hand on his chest. 'What do you feel?'

'Tick-tick-boom,' she said with a laugh that sliced the darkness open. 'Your heart is beating fast.'

'Yours?' he asked, and she placed her hand on her own chest.

'My heart is skipping too,' and she laughed.

'Mama lives here in your heart, so you'll never forget her.'

'But how? Heart just goes beat-beat-boom, it doesn't look like Mama.'

'Your heart *is* Mama,' he said, and swallowed. It was important he got this right. He tried to remember how Mama had said it to him . . . once, so long ago.

'We both grew inside Mama's tummy and she grew our hearts with her heart. So, Mama lives in you . . . and in me. In our hearts. She's inside us all the time and because the heart always beats, Mama will always be with us.'

Lotte was quiet for a long time. Her hand slid onto his chest and back to hers. The pause made him think he had got it wrong, that he had failed. Again. And in failing, he felt dough-heavy.

'She is very clever to make us,' Lotte said.

'She was.' The past tense tore from his lips, making his mouth feel raw. It was followed by a sob, deep and loud, uncontained.

'Shhh,' Lotte said, and rested her head on his chest. 'I'm listening to Mama.'

He stifled the sob with his fist, biting down on his fingers until it eased. Allowing Lotte to listen. She relaxed into the hug and his body followed. He also listened for the beat of his heart, a hollowed boom.

'Roo?' Lotte asked sleepily. 'Will you leave me too?'

'No,' he said, not allowing the question to hang for a moment in the air. 'No, Lotte. I will never leave you.'

NOW

SUNDAY 21ST NOVEMBER 1999

TOTENSONNTAG — DAY OF THE DEAD

RUNE

Nanya had come back from the corner shop that morning waving a newspaper, grinning widely.

'You want to see what they say?' she asked, opening the pages. Pepin, whose hands were in soapy water washing dishes, and Sabine, who was reading the piles of pages that belonged to Mama's file, both stopped their work and came to stand behind Nanya.

The headline shouted *KORRUPTION* over a picture of Papa's face. *The current president of the federal police is under investigation into claims of corruption that span over two decades. These claims have come to light after a fire was started within the Stasi archives in Nuremberg. President Schäffer did not comment, but the department of federal police have suspended him, pending their investigation.*

It felt good. It wasn't justice for Mama's death; he might never know what happened to her. Nor was it justice for Lotte's *accident*, but justice wasn't just a conviction, it was keeping Lotte safe. Papa couldn't come close to them any more. Rune hoped Papa was in the same cell he had been in.

Safe.

Although Papa's words niggled at the back of his mind: *If I go down, you'll never see her again.*

Papa's last words had fed on his hope like worms, multiplying and multiplying into a maggoty mass that seemed to cover every surface of his body – a second squirming skin.

He knew Papa's games, his threats and his lies, and he had made his peace with it. He knew it couldn't be true, wasn't true, because if Mama were alive, she would have come back for them, she would have found them. He tried so, so hard to convince himself of this, yet every evening after leaving the hospital he would be desperate to read Mama's file, to know if Pepin or Sabine had found anything more in the time he'd been gone.

They were all going back to Zirndorf that evening, taking Mama's file with them. There was nothing in it that he didn't already know; he needed to return it to the archives or he feared he would never be able to look up from it, desperate to find something within its pages that he might have missed.

He would be sad to see the women leave. Sabine had driven back on Saturday with Clio and returned much later without her; they had spent all night drinking vodka and talking.

Nanya had spent a lot of time with Sabine over the following days and he understood that Nanya felt the same way about their leaving. He had found such peace with them; they all ate together and worked together and laughed. He'd never felt safer and their impending departure would leave a void.

They were coming back for Lotte's birthday the following week, they reassured him. Clio too. And if they found anything in the meantime, they would let him know. But he had to accept that sometimes stories don't have a neat ending. There was no way of knowing what had happened to Mama's body, or why it was taken. The page he had read in the offices might just as well have concerned some other person: mis-reported, mis-reconstructed, mis-filed. Anything. He had to try and move on; there was a lot to sort out for Lotte and that needed his full attention.

He was waiting for Lotte on the roof of the hospital. He fumbled for a pre-rolled cigarette to smoke before she arrived. Lighting it, he felt a physical pain – not located anywhere specific, but nonetheless a shattering, fracturing pain that burned all over his skin.

Holding the cigarette between his lips, he took out an oxy from his pocket. There weren't many left.

'Just one,' he thought to himself. 'Just one to get through this.' He couldn't control the shaking of his hands. He placed the tablet on his tongue but didn't swallow it. It stayed there, while he fought with himself to swallow or to spit.

'Swallow or spit?' he asked aloud on the terrace as the wind rattled around him.

He spat and watched the oxy plummet. Over the terrace and down onto the street below.

'Roo?' asked a voice behind him. Lotte, holding on to Dr Ueli's arm, joined him. He hadn't seen Lotte awake for two days. She'd spent one of them being questioned by police, the second sleeping off the ordeal.

'Do you think Dr Ueli thinks we will jump?' Lotte asked, looking over the edge as Dr Ueli left them alone.

'I don't think he'd allow us up here if he thought that,' Rune said. The sky scudded with heavy dark grey clouds and the wind snapped at his skin, bitingly sharp.

'It would be nice, though,' she said, leaning over the side a little, 'to see Mama again.' She was wearing her own clothes – her yellow Doc Martens with glittery laces and her buttercup-yellow coat. She looked healthier in them than in the hospital gown. She was getting better.

They hadn't yet discussed what lay ahead. They had discussed what was behind and what was now, but neither had touched on the forward trajectory of 'next'.

'It wouldn't be nice if she's hopping mad at you for killing yourself,' Rune added, taking a step and touching Lotte's arm.

'But you said *she* killed herself,' Lotte argued.

'That was different. She didn't have a choice. She did it to save us.'

Lotte humphed and looked at him. Maybe Lotte's instinct and Nanya's unease at Mama's death were founded in some truth.

It was Papa's words, again, the power of his threat. What did it mean? What could he know?

'Maybe it's best to stay alive for now,' Lotte said.

She still hadn't eaten anything. She had been drinking. She had been talking. She submitted to glassfuls of special milk feeds, which she sipped through a straw. She refused to go to a special school and until the concept had been completely rejected by Dr Ueli and he had agreed that she could live with Rune and Nanya at LightHouse, Lotte wasn't taking any chances with getting all better. Just in case.

Rune would tell her about the newspaper headlines, but only once they were off the roof. It had been her courage in making a statement that had brought it about. She had changed it all for the better. He owed her everything.

Lotte heard all Mama's thoughts through her words, Mama's love for them both. Papa, in burning Mama's pages, had taken away Rune's own opportunity to read them all, if there were ever to come a point when he might have wanted to. But Lotte had read them – or had them read to her – and in doing so he felt she was closer to Mama than he was.

'Will these be okay?' he asked, showing her the flowers.

'Yellow is the best and only-favourite colour,' Lotte said.

'This bouquet is all the yellows.'

'If Mama thought love was petals, then we can send love to Mama with them. All of them. She was not forgotten,' Lotte said softly. 'Never forgotten. Just lost for a while.'

He had bought the roses from the Wochenmarkt off Karl-August-Platz the day before, on his return from the hospital. He had bought them in preparation for today, the Day of the Dead, and placed them in a vase, convinced they would wilt and die by the morning. Sabine had teased him that by watching the roses so hard they would droop. He didn't mind and they hadn't drooped.

He pulled a single rose from the bouquet and passed it to Lotte. She pressed the bud to her nose; it was a young rose, the youngest of the blooms. Still green at the base, unopened, the tip a brilliant yellow. Sunflower yellow.

'Roo?' she asked, as he passed her another, fuller, open rose, its petals perfect, blossoming, fresh as a spring sky. Daisy yellow.

'Will my heart still be Mama's heart, even though it was broken and Dr Ueli had to fix it?'

He thought carefully about his answer and then plucked out the largest rose, the petals turning over onto themselves, breaking wide open to reveal the innermost layer. Lily yellow.

'Do you remember that in Mama's tummy she made our hearts with hers?' he said. Lotte nodded. 'Well, it wasn't just our hearts, it was our fingers, our toes, our thinking heads. It was even our kindness and our laughter. We are made from Mama – every single bit of us.'

'We are very lucky,' Lotte said.

'She was magic,' he said. He gathered the whisper of petals into his palm and twisted, snagging them away from the stem. Torn. Free. He dropped the stem and looked out over the building to the sunset hidden behind the grey Berlin sky. Barely there. Unnoticeable.

Lotte tucked her small bud of a rose into the crook of her elbow with Moo Bunny and twisted the bloom from another rose.

He looked at her and she looked back at him.

'For Mama,' he said.

'For Mama.'

Silently, Rune lifted his hand to the sky and threw the contents into the air. A flurry of petals flew up, around and then away from them.

Dotting the clouds with tears of gold.

Tears of the rose.

THEN

Tuesday 28th November 1989

LOTTE'S BIRTHDAY

Roo was holding her hand too tight. Her bag was bouncing on her back. She was crying, her words hiccupping out. He was practically dragging her along.

When he got her to the school gate, the playground was empty.

'We're late,' he said.

'Please please please, I don't want to go,' Lotte said.

He looked straight and hard and forward. 'You have to,' he said.

'But I don't want to. I want to go home with you.'

'I'm not going home. I have to go to school, just like you.' But he would have given anything not to.

'You can do this,' he said, and he tried to make it sound like he meant it, but he felt as though his chest had come unzipped.

'But. But. But,' she hiccupped. 'I don't want to be happy six.'

She hadn't opened her presents, stacked high on the table, nor blown out her candles; she hadn't touched her balloons nor eaten her cake.

'I don't want to be happy six,' she started again, and he turned and hugged her, hard.

'I know, Lotte,' he said, his heart hollowed out. He was floundering around, throwing words out of his mouth with no caution; he had nothing else to lose.

'You remember what I said the other night? About Mama making our hearts with hers?' he said.

Lotte nodded and a big fat burp came out of her mouth.

'Eugh,' he smiled, and she laughed.

'Oops.'

'Well, there is something else,' he said. 'Mama made both our hearts with her heart, right?'

And Lotte nodded, putting her hand to her heart.

'And she was very clever. Do you know what she did?' he asked.

Lotte put her thumb in her mouth and her crying stopped. She was listening.

'She made an elastic band, invisible, around my heart and your heart,' he said. 'And elastic bands stretch, so even though we are apart, we will always ping back,' he said, swallowing a lump in his throat.

'Here, let me show you,' he said, taking a risk. For Lotte. For Mama. He took a few steps away. 'Ready?' he asked, and he ran at Lotte, lifting her into a jump. 'Ping.'

'Again!'

'We stretch,' he said, running further away. This time, Lotte ran to him too.

'Ping!'

'Sssttttttreeeeeeeeeeeeeeeeeeeeeeeeeeetch!'

'PING!'

'We can both do this, okay? You go in to school, I'll go to school and I'll pick you up.'

'You will never leave me, because of the elastic band?'

'Never. All I'll do is stretch, and if you wait I'll always ping back to you.' And he smiled.

She placed her hand in his and they walked to her classroom, but she stopped him just as he was about to turn away.

'Maybe,' she said quietly. 'Maybe, only maybe, happy six isn't so bad when you have a Mama heart *and* an elastic band.' She kissed him on the cheek with cold, blue-tinged lips.

'Happy birthday, Lotte,' he said, and she was off into her classroom and he was alone in the hallway.

Wishing, wishing, wishing Mama had an elastic band too.

VI.

I miss the damp smell of fresh cut grass.

The depth of the earth.

The ground under my feet.

A small hand in my own: home.

I miss so much, but I suspect that my memory is fading, that when offered a flower I will not know its name, that I will gaze at colours across a rain-torn sky and not know the name of the enchanting view. I worry and I sink and I wait. Do my children have any memories of me?

I survive for them.

Waiting every day. To know the sound of rain on an umbrella, the feel of sun on my skin. I am waiting to live.

But I am waiting and days go by and still he doesn't come.

I am waiting and waiting and there is no more food and still I am waiting.

He has never left me this long before.

My stomach is alive, its claws dig deep.

I try to pull myself free. I try to bite and scratch and call.

I am waiting, but no one is coming.

I am waiting.

I am—

NOW

SUNDAY 28TH NOVEMBER 1999

ERSTER ADVENTSSONNTAG — THE FIRST

SUNDAY OF ADVENT

LOTTE'S BIRTHDAY

RUNE

He was in the kitchen, sweat pouring from his temples. He had never made a cake before and the one in front of him, cooling on the side, sagged in the middle. He covered it in melted chocolate. He'd bought all the ingredients, followed the recipe, but what was in front of him was limp and saggy and shit. He added paper flowers and colourful jelly sweets. Lots of jelly sweets. But nothing covered up the fact that it wasn't very good.

Nanya tried to be supportive, but it was a joke. His attempt was pathetic.

'You'll have to do,' he said sadly to his creation, and laid it in a cardboard cake box. He placed his gift to Lotte next to it and looked at Nanya. She was wearing a deep purple velvet dress, her hair pulled back; she wrung her hands and her bracelets tinkled.

She was waiting for *them*.

He brushed the flour dust from his trousers.

He heard the knock at the door and smiled. Nanya rushed to it. It had been a week since Pepin and Sabine had left and he had missed them too.

They greeted each other in a mass of excitement and joy. Everyone had made an effort for Lotte. Clio was wearing a pink party dress with matching sequinned shoes. She twirled for him and spoke in her quick, quiet way about her week at her father's. It made him happy to be taken into her confidence.

After a procession of toilet stops and admiration or mirth over his cake, it was time to get to the hospital.

'Come on, Chef, we need to get moving,' Sabine said, still laughing.

He picked up his sunken creation.

'We'll post these on the way?' Nanya asked, holding two envelopes.

One contained a letter to the Berlin Art Institute, asking if they had happened to have made copies of his portfolio, or if not, whether they would be able to write a reference as to the standard of the portfolio. He regretted throwing it away at the top of Teufelsberg but couldn't get it back, so he was asking the Berlin Art Institute for a second chance; now that Papa's empire was falling so publicly, he thought they might change their minds. The second letter was his application to Kunstgut; he was trying again. In every moment he was not at the hospital, he was drawing; mainly he was drawing Mama.

He was starting over.

He had Lotte; if she ever started eating again, she would come and live with them at LightHouse. Dr Ueli was on board now; she just needed to eat again. She needed something to make her want to get better.

'Ready to go?' Nanya called from the door.

'Don't want to keep the birthday girl waiting, do we?' Pepin added.

'The car is full of balloons, so it'll be a bit of a squash,' Sabine apologised as they left LightHouse.

'You can tell Lotte that a balloon squished your cake,' Clio said.

He laughed. 'Let's go.'

LOTTE

There were balloons and a cake and candles and cards and everyone had dressed up for her. They were all shuffling around each other in her little room. She was in bed as they sang *Happy Birthday* to her.

She was sixteen.

Sabine handed her a bundle in yellow wrapping paper. Inside was a knitted hat.

'Do you like it?' she asked. It had yellow and black woollen stripes.

'It's a bumble bee hat!' Lotte said, excited. 'Oh, I love it. Did you make it?'

Sabine nodded. 'Isolde said you like bees.'

'Thank you, oh, thank you.' And Lotte placed the hat on her head. 'I love it and I love you, Sabine.' And Sabine lowered herself so Lotte could hug her.

'Why do you like bees so much?' Clio asked.

Lotte looked at Sabine, who winked. Sabine knew why. She looked at Pepin, who laughed. She knew why too. It made Lotte happy that her friends understood her.

'Because,' Lotte explained, 'they have tiny wings and big fat bodies. They shouldn't be able to fly and yet they do.'

'So?'

'So, sometimes you can be more than what people think you can be.'

'Exactly,' said Sabine and Roo at the same time.

Pepin moved towards the bed.

'Look what your brother made,' she said, and opened the cake box.

'What is it?'

'A chocolate cake,' Roo said. 'Well, it's kind of a chocolate cake. I tried,' he added.

The splodge of goo was covered in chocolate and had sweets all over it. 'Did you open the oven?' she asked.

Roo looked guilty. 'I followed the recipe. Do you want a slice?' he asked.

She shook her head.

'Please eat something,' he begged. And it was a beg.

'I don't want to eat,' she said, and turned away.

Pepin cut slices of the cake and everyone ate a piece. Lotte looked out of the window. Her bed had been moved next to it so she could see the sky.

Roo passed her his gift. It was a yellow tutu.

'For me?' she asked, so happy her cheeks hurt. She stood up slowly and Sabine helped her put it on.

'For you, and' – he pointed to the frame that had fallen out of the wrapping – 'there's a picture of Mama for you too,' he said.

Lotte looked at the drawing of a woman with kind eyes and a warm smile and happy came from the picture; it made Lotte feel warm. Mama was looking back at her; her mama. She touched her fingers to her lips and then touched them to Mama's.

'Thank you,' she said, but she couldn't look away from the picture. Her picture. Her mama. She tucked Moo Bunny into her arm, so he could see her too.

There was a long silence. Everyone was watching her, like they knew something was about to happen.

'Our gift to you, Lotte,' Pepin said, and handed Lotte a big book.

'Mama's words?' Lotte asked, turning the pages to see page after page that she had put back together again, stuck into a book.

'All of them,' Pepin said.

'How?'

'We always make copies.'

'It will be so she is never forgotten,' Lotte said, and Sabine nodded, crying. Pepin passed her a tissue, which she dried her eyes with, and then Sabine looked at Nanya and passed her a tissue from the pack too, then seated herself next to Lotte and looked through the new book that held all of Mama's words.

'Can you read them to me again?'

'Any time,' Sabine smiled, and kissed Lotte on the cheek.

'You did it,' Roo said. 'You did it all. I am so sorry . . .' He trailed off.

'When you are better,' Nanya said, her tears gone and her voice full of hope, 'we will make a memorial for your mama, like a grave, that we can visit any time you like. Maybe take flowers? We could have it in the garden at LightHouse. Maybe there's still life in that old house for us yet.'

Lotte thought about standing in the green-blue air and the wind making music for the daisies to dance to and Mama having a place where she was, and where Lotte could go to her and talk to her, because, by being dead, she had missed so much.

'I miss her,' Lotte said, and realised that in thinking of visiting Mama's grave, Mama was no longer in the 'then' or the 'now' but in the 'forever'.

'I miss her too,' Roo said.

'And me,' said Nanya, taking Lotte's hand in hers; her hands were fresh-mint cool. 'I will tell you everything I can remember about her. She was the most wonderful friend,' Nanya said, and started to cry. 'She was strong, she was brave and she loved—'

'Am I late?' asked Ralf, bounding into the room. He was carrying a file, his face flushed apple-red and sweaty. 'Sorry,' he added, heeding the tears and the hushed silence of the room. Behind him came . . .

'Isolde!' Lotte stumbled out of her bed, to words of caution from Roo and Pepin, and landed herself squarely in Isolde's arms. 'You came for me – you came for my birthday?'

Isolde's skin was clammy and loose.

'What's wrong?' Lotte asked as Isolde tried to get her breath.

Ralf went straight to Pepin and was talking to her in a hurried whisper that sounded like the steam of a train. Pepin gave a small shriek as Sabine joined her. They were all looking in the same file. At the same sheets of paper.

There were gasps and exclamations as all of them gathered around the file, while Roo and Nanya looked on.

'Will you please tell us what that is?' Nanya said, and her stern voice sounded scared.

RUNE

Ralf was about to speak, but checked himself. He passed the file to Pepin, who gave it straight to Isolde.

'It means . . .' Isolde said, moving to sit next to him and Nanya. Lotte joined them on the bed and Sabine moved up.

Isolde chose her words carefully. 'It means that the Stasi officer who was assigned to your mother was HIN X/21. We found his file and these details correspond enough with the information we already have for us to think . . .' She stopped, looked behind her, and Pepin's hand rested gently on her shoulder. 'Enough for all of us to think your mother may not be dead. Or at least,' she added, as Nanya made a gargled, choking sound.

'Or at least she survived that day,' Pepin said directly to Rune.

'What? How?'

Ralf handed him a piece of paper and he read it silently until Lotte nudged him, and then he read it aloud to her.

'Tuesday 21st November 1989

11 am Subject is discharged from hospital.

11.15 am Subject taken in dark blue 1983 BMW Alpina for approximately 25.4 miles.

12.35 pm Subject entered into small industrial building behind Groninger Straße 13357 unit number 124.

4 pm Subject has not been seen leaving.

Report ends.

Officer – HIN X/21

'Does that mean we can find her?' Lotte asked.

'It means we can try,' Pepin said.

And noise filled the room, a buzz of infectious questions, checking the file that Ralf had brought with him.

Rune held Lotte's hand tightly. Her face was stunned and he felt her confusion too. After another round of *'show me, let me see, are you sure?'*, Lotte tugged at his sleeve.

'Maybe we need to go and find Mama,' she said.

He looked at the address. It tugged at his memory; it was a familiar street name.

'That's just around the corner from the police station,' he said eventually. 'And that Alpina, that could be Papa's old car.' He stood, suddenly more alert than he had felt in years. A sharp clarity filled his mind; finally something was slotting into place.

'We need to leave. Now,' he said.

'I'll drive,' Pepin offered.

'We'll follow you,' Ralf said.

'Do you think you're up to it?' he asked Lotte, whose face was pale.

'Does that mean Mama is alive?' she asked, standing and pulling on her Doc Martens. Nanya bent double to try and help her.

'I don't know.' He heard Papa's voice in his head: *You'll never see her again.* 'I think we have to hurry. I think—' But he didn't want to hope, so he left the sentence unfinished as they all stood and spoke at once.

VII.

I do not know how long I have waited.

Waiting.

But there is no one and I am alone. I think only of my children, I keep breathing for them.

But I am lost and I know this is my end.

I hope they are together; I hope they are happy. I have loved them. It is my love for them that has kept me alive.

I know I should close my eyes, I should stop fighting. I should accept my life is over. The irony that I am not dying by his hand, but by his neglect, is not lost on me. Perhaps death has a sense of humour—

But—

Wait—

Footsteps.

Pause.

A scratch in the lock. Then banging. Heavy hard banging; then a crash.

And I crawl into the farthest corner. Away.

Into my dark.

A sharp slice of light enters as the door is opened—

But something is different. The door opens all the way and I see three pairs of feet. Yellow boots with purple glitter laces? I blink, rub my eyes. It's a trick. A trick.

I have died. The sprouting stem of madness has taken hold.

Nothing more.

I see legs and a yellow tutu and I see faces – I see their faces as if from a dream. A raw, joyful pulse of madness. I cling to the image.

'Don't leave me,' I think. 'Don't leave me again.'

Grown older, sadder, paler than in my memories, but standing hand in hand, and an old woman beside them. I know her face. I know her name.

No longer a dream?

Eyes speak before words have a chance. Eyes searching, seeking, checking, believing. Eyes filling, disbelieving, blinking.

'Mama?' they both say: a question. I must look like a shadow. Can their adult eyes recognise me? Am I as real to them as they are to me?

Nanya turns to someone behind her, out of sight. 'Ambulance,' she says.

Ambulance means living.

Rune takes the first step, tentative and then almost at a run. He collapses beside me and holds me.

I hold him with everything I have.

I will never let him go.

Does he know that it was he that made me, that I became for him, through being his mama? My eyes squeeze shut and I listen to the soft sounds of his sobs and the deep booming drum of his heart.

Alive.

Present.

Here. Now. In my arms.

Real.

Safe?

Lotte tugs at his arm and makes space for herself. She touches my face, using her fingers to walk from my forehead, over eyebrows, down closed eyes, across the bridge of my nose and cheeks. I try to keep breathing, to keep living. I know they are here, they are with me. I must keep fighting. I try and hold on to them, but it is Rune who holds me now. Keeping me here.

I feel Lotte's fingers rest on my lips and push their corners, stretching them into a smile. I open my eyes and I see my little girl.

'I pieced you back together,' she said. 'I used the magic you left in my heart.'

NOW

FRIDAY 24TH DECEMBER 1999

HEILIGABEND – CHRISTMAS EVE

RUNE

He and Mama were bathed in firelight, on a blanket at LightHouse on the living room floor. Another blanket was wrapped around Mama's shoulders and he watched her as she watched the dying flames lick and curl. Large chestnuts were roasting on the glowing embers and the smell was powerful and deeply earthy. He found it difficult to believe she was here with him; he kept touching her hand, kept looking at her, kept checking. She was a ghost of the Mama he remembered, emaciated almost beyond recognition, and yet she was next to him.

Alive.

Almost everyone who met Mama and Lotte talked about healing. As he watched Mama stare into the fire, he knew that healing wasn't about closure, it wasn't about turning the page and walking away. Healing was working on feelings as they changed and evolved day-to-day.

They all had plenty of healing ahead, but today – this day, in the present, in the now – Rune was never more grateful to be alive. He could burst with it: this moment, this gift, something he had never ever dreamed would be possible.

Nanya helped them buy Christmas presents for Mama. 'Give her something you would have given her when you were small. Something to help shrink the years you've been apart,' she suggested; and Rune had bought Mama a beautiful notebook, and on the cover had drawn a tiger, in the wilderness, camouflaged by its stunning, sleek, blacker-than-night stripes. A tiger completely free.

The chestnuts slipped from their shiny protections and the charred nuts were comforting, sweet and savoury, rich and earthy, and something else too.

'They taste like magic,' Lotte said, bringing a plate of *Spritzgebäck* to the floor picnic.

As Mama passed him a chestnut, warm to the touch, he felt as if he were nine years old again, watching Mama and five-year-old Lotte laugh. He basked in this illusion, waiting for reality to slide across, but it didn't lift.

Lotte joined Mama under the blanket and Mama lifted a corner to invite him into their safe knitted hug. He joined them, a young boy again, delighting in the loving gaze of his mama and a whole world of possibilities ahead.

She held his hand tightly and her hand was warm and strong around his.

He had found his way home.

Finally.

Human kind
Cannot bear very much reality.
Time past and time future
What might have been and what has been
Point to one end, which is always present.

T.S. Eliot 'Burnt Norton'
The Four Quartets

ACKNOWLEDGMENTS

My deepest gratitude and love goes to my parents, who saw me through to the end – again.

Special recognition to friends who supported, believed and shared the journey with me: Demo Dan, my Evil Twin, Beth Hollington and Clint Badlam.

Thanks also to those I met at Bath Spa University, especially Samantha Harvey (for generosity of both time and expertise), Louise Summers (for finding me in the dark) and Fay Weldon. On many levels this book would not exist without the belief shown in me (and it) at the very beginning.

To Arzu Tahsin, for edits that made me a better writer and for seeing what I am trying to achieve even when I cannot. And everyone at Lake Union for everything they do to continually support me, especially Sammia Hamer and Laura Deacon.

Thanks to Bethan James at EDPR, for offering me kindness and confidence when I feel (perpetually) out of my depth.

Thanks, always, to Juliet Mushens. I keep going and keep rewriting with you by my side; this means I am never completely alone.

Finally, importantly, I also want to thank all the courageous women, the survivors and their children, and those who support women fleeing domestic abuse: You make a difference. You change lives.

ACKNOWLEDGMENTS

ABOUT THE AUTHOR

Anna Ellory has completed her MA in creative writing at Bath Spa University. *The Puzzle Women* is her second novel.